ATRICK'S
GAMBLE

Other Novels by the author set in the world of Arthos:

The Andarian Prophecy

Atrick's Gamble

The Andarian Insurrection

The Imperium Gems

Battle for Gavala

The Arthos Sea Trilogy

The Onyx Crown (coming Spring 2022)

The Black Fire (coming Summer 2022)

The Walrus War (coming Fall 2022)

ATRICK'S

GAMBLE

Book 1 of The Andarian Prophecy

Brian Tenace

Do you like this book? The best way you can show your appreciation is by telling someone else. A review or a suggestion to a friend would be greatly appreciated.

Find an error, or just want to contact the author? Email feedback@arthos.world

Check the Arthos homepage at www.arthos.world for Author insights, custom maps, and other offers and fan art.

Copyright © 2021 Brian Tenace

ISBN: 9798594955639

E-BOOK ASIN: B08T4MTK4T

Printed in the U.S.

To Lynn, for believing in Rianas.
To Mark, for sharing the vision.
To Lauren, who brought magic to the world of Arthos.

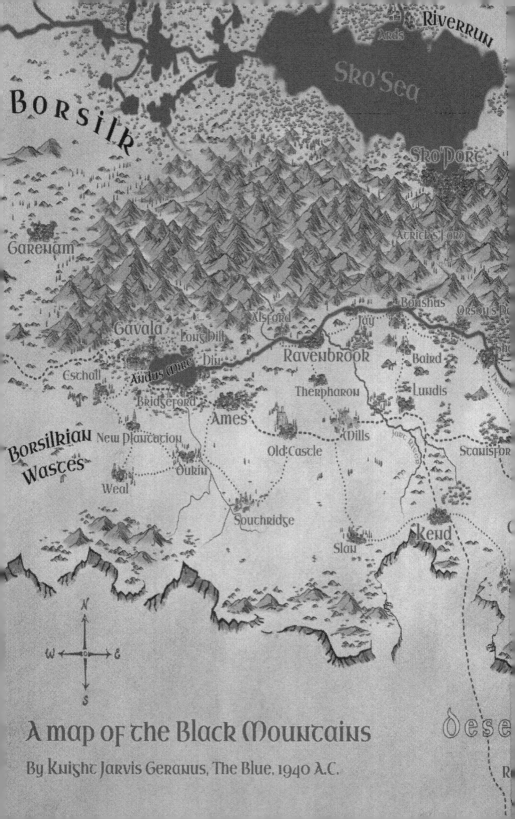

A map of the Black Mountains

By Knight Jarvis Geranus, The Blue, 1940 A.C.

Cidvas

Assyria

Raven's Nest

Gates of Cidvas

argate

Old Weschaishe

Alchspore

Ivy Bridge

Fendrais

Alston

Iuuish

on

Denley

Chumish

Old Assyria

Ters

Geln

ough

OF Roslu

CONTENTS

ACKNOWLEDGMENTS

Arthos is a world of magic that permeates nearly everything, raging like a bacterial infection. While its effects are often small and imperceptible, it is there nonetheless. As our visage is often affected by our own experiences, Rianas seemed the perfect vessel for us to witness the world of Arthos.

The Elves have influenced most of post-Cataclysmic civilization. To that extent, a 12 month calendar with 32 days per month is used. The origins of the 12 month calendar are not completely understood. It does not follow the 20 day lunar cycle. Of note, the lunar cycle is the main reason tendays are used rather than weeks.

Distances are often quoted in standard dimensions throughout because they are familiar to you and me.

PROLOGUE

Merrin looked up at the huge bats as he hastily buckled his pants. Dozens of the flying rodents squawked and flitted among the stalactites toward the higher end of the gaping cavern where the rest of his team was working. He kept his eyes toward the dark ceiling as he dipped his hands in the cold water. None of the creatures seemed interested in him. Merrin was not complaining.

He hated bats. They stole food. They defecated on equipment. In addition, the bigger ones were sometimes brave enough to bite miners. Merrin was not stupid enough to remove his helm or leave his extremities unguarded. Only a surface dweller bothered coming into the Sko'Port mines without studded leather arms and shoulders.

The bats in this newly discovered cavern were the biggest he had ever seen. Some were the size of wolves. In the two days Merrin had been laying rail here, he had seen the giant rodents fly off with two full rucksacks. Master Jorgen had to evacuate a young worker with four bites on his arm. It was dangerous to walk around in the clearing by oneself.

With one hand on his knife, Merrin stayed low. He dipped his canteen into the fast moving water of the underground river. It was time to get back to the rest of the group. Merrin knew he should have asked for a companion before going to relieve himself, but it was between shifts. Almost everyone else was sleeping. Moreover, it was embarrassing that he had to go every hour or two. What a great reward for aging.

The bats kept squawking, but they were louder than before. Merrin put his canteen back on the thick leather belt his wife had bought him for his birthday. He adjusted the belt a little looser and

1

tucked his thick shirt in so it would not catch on one of those wet fungi. Sal said she would need to buy him another belt in six months at the rate his stomach kept growing.

Master Jorgen thought they would need to lay a mile of track. A few volunteers would get to explore the lower end of the cavern tomorrow to determine where to go next. It would be nice to have two shifts off while the surveyors worked. At the end of last shift, one of the other miners said he saw three exits at the lower end of this huge cavern.

A mile of track could take a couple months in the thick underground mushroom forests. Wizard Atrick might call upon Mage Hagat Mund's apprentices. That would speed this work along. Merrin hoped they did not, though. A couple more months laying track would earn him enough to buy the equipment he and Sal needed to start a mine of their own.

He would just have to avoid those infernal bats.

Virgin caverns like this made it easy to delve deeper into the mountain. Most likely, Merrin would lose twenty pounds in the next six months. New caverns meant lots of new track, and Merrin was on the expeditionary team that laid new track. It had taken ten years of apprenticing during his off hours while swinging a pickaxe in the upper sections of the mine.

A skinny white lizard waddled right across Merrin's foot. Just as he was about to kick it away, his attention was directed to the huge glowing mushroom tree to his right. Three more lizards dashed across the path and into the fast moving water. A colorful moth dodged around rocks as it flew into the air. Behind them, something was clambering over the slimy mushrooms that grew near the water.

What happened next may have saved hundreds of lives.

Merrin's surprised move on the slippery ground caused the overweight man to lose his footing on the narrow path to the underground river. His legs skidded across a moldy stone and he landed unceremoniously on his rump behind a short, wide fungus. Before he could curse his luck, however, the little path filled with humanoid lizards three feet tall, brandishing spears. They quickly scampered up the pathway toward the mining camp.

The monsters were still flooding past Merrin's hiding place when he heard shouting from the camp. He took his long knife out of its holster and looked for a way to escape.

A lizard-man almost four feet tall wearing a human-faced mask emerged next. This creature was obviously directing the actions of its more diminutive brothers. It grunted and pointed up the path. Then it easily bounded up behind them with the grace of a cat.

How many of those things were there? Merrin wondered if he could get past them. He took a side path through the overgrown bulbous fungi. Every step sent spores spraying angrily into the air, and his weight was too much for some of the mushrooms to support. His feet sank into the caps as he clambered up toward the camp.

The camp had been resting when the attack began. Merrin saw groups of miners and track-layers swinging pickaxes and hammers wildly as they retreated up toward the mine. There must have been a hundred or more of the lizard-men attacking the group.

There was little time to watch, though. A few miners nearby scrambled to avoid spears as they jumped behind a rail car full of lumber. Merrin used his substantial weight to knock one of the lizard-men down and grabbed another one's spear. He glanced over at the rail car. He was too heavy to jump over it.

A nearby hammer made a better weapon. Merrin swung it over his head double-handed into one of the creature's arms. Then he kicked another one back before it could stab him with its short spear. There were more of them coming. They outnumbered the miners two to one.

Master Raskin Jorgen was organizing miners further up the mine. Merrin swung his hammer over his head again to scare the monsters away and huffed as he turned to his nearby comrades.

"Get to Master Jorgen!" he bellowed.

He was never a fast man, and there was no hope he could follow. Merrin flung a hammer into a lizard-man's head and reached for his knife. A few tried to get past him. He barreled into them. Two more stabbed him in the legs. After that, there was no more running. Fishy breath wafted into his face as the creatures tried to climb over him.

Merrin was a big man. Four of the humanoids pushed and pulled on him, but he flung them into each other. Even as his legs gave out, he punched and bit. Master Jorgen's voice got a little closer. Shouting miners emerged from higher up in the camp to join the head engineer.

Merrin stabbed one of the monsters with his knife. As he withdrew his knife to strike another, a spear struck his arm. His weapon flew from his hand.

The loss of Merrin's knife meant the fat old miner could no longer defend himself from the marauding creatures. As Merrin suffered a final, fatal stab wound, his errant knife set in motion a series of events that changed the future of Arthos.

The blade careened through the air, skipping on a moldy stone before landing blade up in a mushroom cap. Half a second later, the tall lizard-man with the mask stepped on the blade as it led its fellow attackers into the mining camp. Rather than leap over its companions to slay Master Raskin Jorgen, the monster's impaled foot caused it to slip just as the stout master engineer swung his pickaxe at its head.

Two books lay on Atrick's neatly organized desk.

One detailed orders for weapons from Riverrun. Runlarian naval specifications filled the pages. Names of Eastern Runlarian captains topped each ship. Riverrun orders enumerated daggers, arrows, crossbow bolts and spears for delivery through the end of the year. The Riverrunners were exporting tens of thousands of weapons to their Runlarian allies. Hand-drawn rows and columns occupied hundreds of exhaustive pages.

The second book was an Andarian family tree. Messy Elven writing adorned the margins. Galen's own neat print added details to almost every page. A dozen pieces of yellow parchment sewn to the back contained hundreds of names. Many of the names had lines through them. Some had 'dead' written next to them. Others had question marks. The rest listed locations and children.

Galen's thinning brown hair bobbed around on his head as he shook it. "Atrick, how long have we known each other?"

"Almost five years."

"Something is different in the weave," Galen said. "The last healing potion I made only took a third as long."

"Maybe your magic is coming back again," Atrick said.

His own magic seemed stronger, too. Atrick expected as much. Magic ebbed and flowed across Arthos. It was not a constant force. The Elven capital Ede seemed to ooze magic. There were other documented cases of magic 'collecting' around the world.

Galen huffed and set a sheaf of advertisements for mercenaries onto Atrick's tidy desk. He seemed unconvinced. Galen had told Atrick his late Elven wife predicted magic would get stronger around Old Andaria.

It did not mean that the *Prophecy* was beginning, though.

"I'll bring a few apprentices with me into High Mine," Galen said finally.

"I'll be a few days," Atrick said. He opened the second book and looked at the very last page. There were a dozen names written there by Galen. "I'm going to Riverrun. I know a few people in the bay area town of Ards. We will leave when I return."

"You are going to pick up that child," Galen said.

"That 'child' is eighteen. If a way is open through the Black Mountains, I want to bring her. You heard what happened last month."

"She could just be lucky," Galen said. Then he leaned back in the over-stuffed chair. "Atrick, I want to find the 'one' just like you do. But there are a dozen other girls and women who show promise."

"And I've visited half of them," Atrick said. He pointed to the names on that last page. "Two of these girls are still in diapers. Our contacts heard this one is a thousand miles away in the frozen north. That leaves these three. The girl in Ards is closest. I'll take a chance with her."

"What if you're wrong?"

"We will have to hope I'm not," Atrick said.

1. ATRICK

Rianas always knew she had a gift.

When she was three, her father, Lazron, noticed her talking to the neighbor's dog in the yard. That was nothing unusual for a small child, except that, soon after, the dog started bringing her gifts – acorns, chicken bones and the like – little things that seemed to suit the desires of a toddler.

In the beginning, Lazron found it funny. Rianas' ability was a novelty he could show off to the neighbors.

When she was four, she showed her father the holes in the fence. A few days later, the raccoons stopped breaking in to steal chickens. Then she started making sage suggestions about how to get the hens to lay more eggs.

Rianas became popular with the neighbors after that. Her father learned quickly to take her advice when it came to animal husbandry. Her quirky suggestions always seemed to work. The neighboring farmers loved it when he brought her to visit. There always seemed to be something she could do to make their farms more efficient.

When she turned five, she helped tame a wild Gawdichian stallion. She suggested the new owner introduce the stallion to a mare from across the river. Within a few days of introducing the two horses, the stallion was an excellent riding horse. It even knelt to let Rianas up whenever she asked for a ride.

It was then that her father stopped fearing Rianas' exposure to even the wildest of farm animals. Lazron proudly watched Rianas selflessly make suggestions across the entire bay, from how to feed the neighbors' cats to what type of hay the fussy Runlarian cattle preferred. Ards livestock were the most productive in Riverrun.

When she turned eight, it became clear her ability to communicate was not solely limited to animals. She had picked up reading early. She even inexplicably seemed to be able to read and write in Runlarian and ancient Southern when Lazron brought such texts home from council meetings. He used Rianas' help to draft letters for Gawdichian caravans and settle land disputes around Ards between Runlarian natives and the Andarian settlers.

Rianas simply loved to read or translate foreign texts. She never really had an explanation for why or how she could do so. The other translators applauded her ability. A Borsilkian trader hired her every time he came into Ards.

Lazron encouraged her to go explore and seek new challenges around the village. "We Tanth's like to make friends," he would say.

She was already famous in the region by the time she turned eighteen. People would come to Lazron to request his daughter's skills. The Riverrun council sent visitors from the Forgotten West, Borsilk or the Dwarven Kingdoms to Ards just to speak to her of their travels and tribulations.

Rianas loved hearing the stories from the far off west. Visitors spoke about huge beasts stalking untamed forests. There were trees a mile high and cities built deep into mountains. The world of Arthos seemed vast and incredible.

Rianas' favorite stories, however, came from closer to home. The massive city-state of Sko'Port seemed like the center of the world. The city was just a few days to the south by boat. There were fantastic stories of boulder-crushing giants, huge avenues lined by stone buildings, and a wondrous city that stretched from the southern coast of the Sko'Sea up a mile into the Black Mountains. She loved hearing how Borsilkian engineers had designed boulder-rolling roadways to send minerals from the mines at the top of the city down to the sea. She wished she could watch them as they captured the energy of ship-sized boulders rolling down the mountain.

There were plenty of books about Sko'Port in the Riverrun library a few days to the north. Rianas read everything she could find. Sko'Port architecture was beautiful. The city traded with almost every nation in the Northern Realms. Almost everything that came through Ards originated in that huge city.

A few days after her eighteenth birthday, Lazron sent Rianas to Mr. Jones' general store at the docks.

Mr. Jones was an old Andarian who loved to talk. His little warehouse near the main loading platforms on the east side of the bay carried all sorts of odd items. There were chairs, lamps, pieces of thin wire and clothes. Tucked in every corner were pottery, wrought iron tools and pieces of scrap. He traded or bought goods from Sko'Port barges, Gawdichian supply wagons and Runlarian merchants. It was a fun place to visit. Mr. Jones had something new every time Rianas walked through the door.

"Your father ordered this last year," Mr. Jones said. He picked up a small crate and put it on the only empty table in his tight store. Rianas looked over the opening as he pulled a thin parcel wrapped in cloth from between a box of Borsilkian dried cheese and a purplish bottle of wine. He handed the heavy parcel to her with a smile on his face.

Rianas pulled the twine apart and took the cloth away. Inside was a thick, leather bound book titled *The Andarian Wheat Mill of Garlian*.

"It's beautiful," she said. "Where did you find it?"

"The press in Sko'Port," Mr. Jones said. "They owed me a favor after I sent them copies of a few lectures the Riverrun College gave me last year."

Rianas could hardly wait to start reading the book. Last year, her history professor had suffered a fire in his home. He had lamented the loss of his personal collection of Andarian texts. Although most of the books were truly irreplaceable, *The Andarian Wheat Mill of Garlian* had been printed in Sko'Port. There were a few hundred copies circulating. When Rianas had heard her professor talking about the book, she had wanted to read it.

When she was done, she would give the book to her professor. Rianas looked forward to having a conversation with the wizened old man about his life before the Andarian War.

After ordering a new pair of hiking boots from Mr. Jones, Rianas found a bench along the docks. It was a beautiful day. She put the book on her lap and looked around.

The huge wooden cranes creaked as they unloaded half a dozen Sko'Port vessels. Dozens of wagons queued as they waited for goods. A wide, long Riverrun ship puffed smoke at the north side of the docks. Sko'Port cogs could not make the trip up the Anasko River. It flowed too fast.

The Borsilkian technology behind those paddleboats had been instrumental in building Riverrun. They allowed the Andarian settlers to build their small nation. Borsilkian technology and proximity to Sko'Port coal meant Riverrun ships could take huge loads all the way to Western Runlar.

Before Riverrun's founding, only Gawdich and Cidvag had ready access to Sko'Port over the Sko'Sea. The Anasko River had been sparsely populated. Subsistent farmers from Western Runlar and Cidvag had rafted lumber down to Sko'Port a few times a year. Since Riverrun's founding, however, nearly a million people had made homes along the fast moving river. They used the Anasko River to transport Sko'Port's raw materials directly to Western Runlar. From there, the old Runlarian Empire's infrastructure could deliver iron ore and coal across the Northern Realms.

Long lines of oxen pulled heavy barrels across the road to be loaded on the steam ship. Scores of people busily moved freight. The busy docks were always fun to watch.

Suddenly, a crane's load snagged on the side of a huge Gawdichian long boat transporting heavy iron ore. The unyielding crane pulled the entire ship over before the crane operator could stop lifting. Crates full of heavy stone and metal slid to the port side. People shouted and scrambled across the heaving deck as the ship listed and took on water.

"Help!" Rianas yelled to a group of men loading fish onto a cart nearby. She ran toward the leaning crane as three sailors jumped into the water. The men stared at Rianas for a second before dropping their crates and running to the water's edge.

There was no time to think. Rianas simply reacted. She ran over to a team of oxen tied to a waiting carriage. Grabbing a nearby length of chain, she hooked it to a yoke and tossed the other end of the chain to a man nearby. He rushed it over to the dock and threw it onto the sinking ship's deck.

The startled crane operator was still trying to lower the load. Horses and oxen alike spooked. The load came free with a snap of lines, and a few crates flew into the air. People who were running to help dove for cover as heavy blocks of iron clattered across the wooden dock.

"Calm down, guys," Rianas said to the oxen. "Let's go this way." She grabbed the lead ox and started leading him upriver. The animals complied easily, yanking the long chain taught. The other end of the chain slid around the railing of the upended ship before catching on the forecastle deck. Rianas leapt out of the tight chain's path and urged the animals to pull harder.

The entire world seemed to hang in the air for a moment. Rianas yelled at the oxen to pull even as the two slipped on the dock. The crane's load tossed wildly above the heads of men. The chain's hook ripped pieces of the galleon's forecastle deck away as it tore a hole in the upper part of the ship. Masts groaned as their sails dipped into the river.

The oxen team managed to hold its ground. After a few precarious seconds, the iron chain started moving. The yoke groaned and Rianas walked alongside the team of oxen as she urged them across the road into a nearby field. She did not even look back until after she heard the huge splash behind her.

A hundred men raced around the docks recovering what they could. A dozen people were in the cold Anasko River. The barge was upright again. Rianas stroked the animals and spoke soothing words as she unhitched the bent hook from the yoke. Those oxen had never pulled so hard. There were broken planks on the decking where some of the animals had actually splintered the heavy Gawdichian lumber.

A few people thanked Rianas for her quick thinking. The man who had hooked the other end of the chain to the ship shook her hand. Aside from a few scrapes and a sailor with a broken arm, no one was seriously hurt. If not for her actions, the barge might have been lost and half a dozen sailors could have drowned.

A few weeks later, the excitement had died down. It was raining lightly, and Rianas was finally sitting down to read her new book when she heard the little bell ring in the living room. She got up to see the telegraph machine and met her father in the room. He started writing letters on a piece of parchment right away.

"*COUNCIL MESSAGE. Sko'Port wizard wants meeting. END.*" Rianas repeated the message before her father was done writing it down. Lazron got up and grabbed his boots and a thick woolen jacket.

"Can I come?"

"No."

Rianas sensed worry in her father's face. Usually, the council only met once a month. She started to grab her own coat.

"I'm eighteen now," she said. "Can't I start coming to the meetings?"

"The council meetings are for council members," Lazron said. He kissed Rianas on the forehead and grabbed his coat. Then he laughed before he turned to the door. "Why don't you run for a seat next month? You're old enough now, and Ards' council can't deny your value to the town. You're famous after last month's stunt with those oxen."

Rianas' father was usually less dismissive. He had brought her to other meetings. Most of the council seemed to enjoy having her there.

She waited until he walked toward the council house up the road. With a little trepidation, she wrangled on her leather boots, grabbed her work gloves and jacket. She walked out the rusty side door and quietly ran up the lane toward the main road. The rain had subsided an hour ago, but Rianas grabbed a fistful of her shoulder length brown curls and stuffed them behind her hood. Her father was used to his adventurous daughter's muddy boots. However, soaked hair would be harder to explain.

Children were not usually "allowed" in council meetings. Even so, Rianas had attended enough when her father needed her special skills. She was normally an obedient daughter.

There was a wizard from Sko'Port, though!

Last year, a dwarf had paid a visit. He had discussed for hours the laborious details of a Dwarven "super-road" that Rianas had no interest in at the time. The rest of the council members had seemed thrilled at the prospect of having a path to the Dwarven Kingdoms, but Rianas had wanted to know how they would get all the parts the dwarf had kept listing (many of which she and her father had never heard of, despite her voracious reading).

At the end of the visit, however, the dwarf had spoken of his trip around the western edges of the Axarean Empire. She was not sure how much was true, but there had been quite a bit of talk of fighting his way with his compatriots through throngs of orcs on the west coast before rafting up into the great forest until he came to an Elven outpost where he gathered some of the parts they needed for his so-called "super-road".

Of course, as soon as he started talking in stunted Northern, her father had sent her home with a warm squeeze on the shoulder and a "we can take over from here, honey."

Rianas was not usually a difficult child. Her father was kind, funny, and her best friend. He understood her need to read everything she came across. He encouraged her to speak to the barn animals whenever she got the urge. His brow barely wrinkled when she made funny suggestions about how to change the daily routine to better suit one animal or another at the Henley's farm next door. Neither did he force her to answer every question in Riverrun about a slow horse or a cow that had dropped its milk production. Her father had let her decide what was right.

He used gentle words of encouragement when she got frustrated. He never used a forceful hand. That trusting attitude made it more difficult to go against his wishes when he gave her instructions. However, Rianas wanted to see a wizard.

The rain had made the lime roads milky and muddy. She walked along the ditch, hopping across here and there to avoid larger puddles, trying to stay out of sight of the occasional latecomer to the council meeting. Henley rode by on his speckled grey horse, and the two Jones sisters urged their old yellow mare to pull their little cart up the road. As Rianas dove into the overgrown azaleas around the council hall, she saw quite a few horses and carts already there.

Arthur was out front tending to animals as the last three council members hurried in.

Rianas waited until the last adults were inside. Then she dashed across the rear courtyard to the corner where the outdoor kitchen was. Arthur did not see her at first, so she stuck her head out and waved with one finger to her mouth. This brought a smile and a little blush to his fair face. He quietly waved back and finished tying up the Jones' old mare. Then he looked both ways dramatically – the choreographed expression was too exaggerated for someone who thought he might be watched – before coming around the back.

Arthur was eighteen, just like Rianas. He was the child of Thomas and Edith Murry, professors at the College of Ards. Tending horses was *not* his natural talent. In fact, he had been quite bad at it when Rianas met him the first time. She remembered the astonished look on his face when she told him, "I don't think you should tie all the horses to the same post. They will pull it out of the ground if something spooks them."

"Really? I thought horses were friendly!" His overloud reaction alone had startled a few of the poor animals, who immediately pulled the post from the ground.

It had taken Rianas' soothing words and about five minutes of fumbling with knotted reins to sort the mess out and calm the animals down. Rianas might have helped faster if not for her uncontrollable laughing while Arthur dashed about.

She had asked him why he chose horse grooming for a summer job. Arthur had said something dumb like, "It's all I could find. After all, I don't really have any natural talent." In retrospect, that did not seem true. Arthur was good in math, and he had helped her make the hunting knife she kept in her back boot (not that she ever needed to use it) for a birthday present. Arthur was a hard worker, always looking for a way to save a little bit for the traveling he said he wanted to do.

Watching him start to smooth his blonde hair back before realizing his hands were dirty and rubbing them on his cleaning rag, Rianas reflected (and not for the first time) that he may have chosen horses just to get closer to the council meetings. That was, after all, where all the exciting events in town seemed to start. Arthur talked to everyone who came out of the building.

He had caught her sneaking up to listen before, too. He could not have seen her from the stables. Rianas was too careful.

In the beginning, he simply watched her with a smirk. More often now, he joined her. Usually, he would want to talk about what they heard afterward. They would walk down to the marsh behind the council building to watch the minnows and frogs play in the faster-moving parts of the water while discussing what they thought.

"What caused them to call a meeting tonight, Ri'?" asked Arthur in a whisper as he folded his dirty rag into a hip pouch and looked over her shoulder toward the kitchen they always listened through. "My parents got the call around noon and sent me down here. When I got here, there was a middle-aged man with two bodyguards already talking to Earl Chapson about something in hushed tones."

"I don't know, but my father got a council message that said a Sko'Port wizard wants a meeting this afternoon. He is not usually so quiet after a telegraph arrives. I had to know what was so important."

"Do you think there'll be a wizard taking apprentices in the College of Ards?" Arthur asked. He did not have the innate talent that some people had, but it did not stop him from talking about magic all the time. "Maybe wizard stones were found in the Sko'Port mines? That would be so great; they could sell them to Riverrun and we could use them to make magical items!"

Arthur's enthusiasm was unabated. "Maybe there is a new vein of copper or the Sko'Port Wizards' Guild has discovered a new way to smelt Adamantium. That would be worth a visit to the college."

"Will you be quiet so we can listen?" Rianas whispered very quietly into his ear, slipping her boots off so she could creep into the kitchen on her stocking-feet. Arthur followed suit, slipping off his leather boots and holding the half-door open for her. Then he gently pulled the door closed so it would not scrape the tiles on the back patio and followed her in.

The two snuck up the cook's stairs into the attic storage. Even for late fall, the warmth of the fire pit in the center of the council hall heated up the open storage area nicely. Rianas moved deftly along joists to avoid squeaky planks, and the two of them found their usual place above the rear of the room, where they could peek down through the unfinished slats onto the council table.

The council table for Ards was not a work of art, but still showed the care the community gave to its self-governance. Only about two feet deep, it consisted of flat tables just large enough to sit a person, pushed together and lashed with leather straps into a rectangle large enough for about twenty council members. Around the edges of the room were rough-hewn wood seats three rows deep. Arthur had proudly announced there were two hundred seats one evening. The table had two breaks in it, and a small platform with a podium sat in the center for guest speakers. All the surfaces were carefully polished and varnished, and a few pieces of opaque glass hung behind the table on the rear of the room where notices and figures could be written and erased easily. Normally, the building was used for serving dinners to locals, but the council tables themselves were always reserved for council members. Each had a stone nameplate nailed to his chair back. The thick, decorative ropes pulled around the table marked the members' walking room.

Currently, the table itself was full, but the observation seats were completely empty, save two young men in black full-length robes sitting impatiently in the front. Each had a long sword strapped to his back. Arthur pointed at the thin leather armor under one of the man's robes.

"Sko'Port Wizard's Guards," he whispered. "I bet those swords are enchanted."

Rianas nodded and looked at the center podium. A middle-aged man with a close-cut black beard and greying hair was hanging a map up on an easel. The rest of the council was quieting down, and finally Rianas heard one of the council members ask for quiet by lightly tapping his ink blotter on the table.

"Good evening, I'd like to call this special session to order," the heavily accented and booming voice of Renauld Flambeau carried through the hall. "This is Atrick Silversmith, head mage for the High Mine in Sko'Port. He arrived this afternoon on the *Lark* and requested an emergency meeting as soon as he disembarked."

"Yes," Atrick stood at the podium impatiently, and he almost interrupted Renauld's introduction. "Yes. Thank you, Mr. Flambeau. I do not believe I have made the trip up here since I was an apprentice. I apologize, I do not know your faces, but the events of the past week warranted my trip. I hope you will listen carefully and think on the future before responding." He started walking around the room with his easel as he spoke.

Rianas could not see the images on the map very well. He showed the council members something on the top left. "This is the High Mine of Sko'Port," Atrick said. "It is the most productive mine Sko'Port has opened in the past 100 years. I received the post of wizard for the mine a few years ago when they broke into the second cavern. It has nearly 100 miles of tunnels. This mine alone produces enough iron to supply all of Cidvag's needs, and it has a boulder-slide capable of moving ten-ton boulders all the way to the chipping houses outside the docks. It is the jewel of Sko'Port, both literally and figuratively, and the mine employs nearly 20,000 people directly. Quite frankly, it is probably the most valuable mine in the Northern Realms."

The council members did not say much. While Sko'Port was nearly three days away even using a *Riverrunner*, Ards sat at the mouth of the Anasko River. The small city saw ships from Sko'Port almost every day. Their craft pushed Sko'Port barges up the river, and most of the wealth of Ards came from processing minerals from the mountain city or shipping foodstuffs on the return trip. While the details of each mine were not common knowledge, everyone there knew at least what Atrick had said thus far.

"Eight days ago," Atrick said, "an entire expeditionary team disappeared. Two days after that, the track-layers at the end of the mine stopped delivering reports, and nearly two miles of track-lighting went dark. There was no mine collapse according to my resident apprentices, and our foreman sent a rescue crew in to ascertain the damage. Only one returned, badly injured. He claimed there were nogs in the mine."

His statement had the group talking over each other.

Renauld was the first to speak above the din, his Assyrian accent clearly discernible over the rest of the council members. "I thought the last nogs were driven out of the Black Mountains twenty years ago. Are you saying there was a clan just above Sko'Port this whole time?" A few other council members also conveyed their incredulity.

Atrick seemed to have had this conversation before. He waited for a few of the others to question the commitment of Sko'Port to the eradication of the Nog menace. He lowered his head a bit as if to accept responsibility for this problem. "Here is where that claim breaks down. I live at the entrance to the High Mine. There are chained gates, guarded warehouses, and even daily security checks along the first two miles of the mine. Without many magical safeguards, it is always possible for an occasional violation, but there are *thousands* of miners going through the first two miles every week. Even if a few miners were somehow compromised, I don't see how a force this large could get through to the deepest part of the mine undetected. Not to mention they would have to travel through Sko'Port just to get to the mine.

"I think," now Atrick paused, placing his map easel back at the podium. He was a good speaker, obviously making eye contact and using his intonation at the right times. The council was giving him their undivided attention. Rianas wondered quietly if he had cast a spell. "I think our world is about to change again."

Atrick continued, "Lazron, you recall my apprentice years. I came here to research Axarean incursions into Cidvag and Assyria." Rianas saw her father giving Atrick a knowing nod. "That was nearly twenty-five years ago. The incursions after the Andarian War were minor. There were small groups that came through the more dangerous footpaths that connect North and South through the Black Mountains. Assyrian towns were attacked a few times. Caravans throughout southern Cidvag, Assyria, and even the land routes into Sko'Port were ambushed for years. Cidvag and Assyria settled the problem by putting bounties on the heads of Southerners."

Rianas recalled a similar history lesson from school. The bounty used after the Andarian war was a violent way to establish peace, but it was highly effective in both Cidvag and Assyria. The Assyrians had very little government. Their method was to allow the poaching of Southerners throughout their lands by Cidvagian headhunters and mercenaries. Within a few years after the Battle of the Gates of Cidvag, the Nog incursions had all but ended.

"However, in the city of Sko'Port, they took a more pragmatic approach. Sko'Port has an Axarean consulate and allows Southerners to trade and work in Sko'Port's lower quarter. There are a few orcs running wagons, some Southerner blacksmiths, and even a few lower lords who swear open fealty to the Empire. Sko'Port has maintained a neutral stance because of the wealth these Southerners brought to the city-state after the Andarian Gate ended. Many Southerners living in the Northern Realms fled there to avoid persecution.

"Sko'Port's Lord Cerric has maintained for decades that not every Southerner is from Axarea. The relative peace in Sko'Port since the Andarian War supported his claims.

"Of course, I agree with your council that the Axarean Empire's tendrils reach to every corner of Arthos. There have been spies, outright assassins, and political operatives captured throughout the region. However, their power here lies in deceit and influence, not direct conflict. I fear that something much worse is happening in the High Mine.

"I fear," Atrick said, "that the Axarean Empire has somehow found or created a way *through* the Black Mountains, right into Sko'Port. Moreover, with the considerable size of their consulate in Sko'Port, I fear Lord Cerric may have lost perspective on the Empire's machinations. In essence, I think the lost miners are the harbingers of an invasion."

Rianas' father spoke, this time over a few of his less-tactful council members. "Atrick, it seems like an invasion through one of the Sko'Port mines is a little far-flung. You would need an army of miners, and it would be almost impossible to connect two tunnels across the Black Mountain range, would it not?"

Atrick shook his head, a look of disbelief at what he was going to say coming across his face. "That would seem true, but the High Mine has grown successful precisely because it is so easy to traverse.

About 40 years ago, the previous Head Wizard of the High Mine, Hasand Therian, oversaw a breakthrough into an underground cavern created by a river that runs through the mountain. The miners have followed that river ever since.

"When I took over as Head Wizard for the mine two years ago, I discussed this at length with Lord Cerric. You see, the river that Mage Therian discovered does not come out on the north side of the mountain range anywhere that we know of. He understood the risk and agreed to start building a guardhouse around the entrance to the High Mine."

Atrick gestured emphatically. "Imagine a force taking over part of the mine, though. From inside, it could take months or even years to secure those tunnels again."

It was Mr. Adams' turn to speak. He cursed, then said, "So you fools have been cutting a straight path to Old Andaria for almost forty years while the survivors of that war provide you with food, supplies, and even mining gear?"

A chorus of agreement joined him. Atrick looked visibly pained at the attack.

"Nearly two centuries ago, when Sko'Port first surpassed four million residents, there was a major mine collapse in one of the lower mines, and hundreds of miners were trapped. A few mages banded together with a rescue crew and managed to save many of those trapped by using magic they had developed in conjunction with the rescuers. Sko'Port's mines have hired wizards to help at every mine with more than five miles of tunnels since then, by decree.

"But we do not *run* the mines," Atrick said. "Instead, you might say we are on retainer. The mines pay us well for helping – we offer spells for levitation, air, healing, and manipulation of basic metals – and we sit at the table during planning meetings. Few of us make the decisions of how to proceed through the mines, though. There are exceptions, of course, but I am unfortunately not one of them. Nor was my predecessor. We advise, and sometimes our advice is not taken."

Lazron spoke again. "Why come here?" he asked. "Why not simply go in with the Sko'Port militia? We have very few soldiers in

Riverrun; this place is surrounded by friendly allies."

Atrick leaned against the podium and withdrew a sheaf of folded papers. Rianas could see the familiar accounting ledgers the dockworkers often brought when making deliveries. "I confess I have been tracking some of the Ards shipments for a few years. I know the forge at Mr. Locks' warehouses near the dam produces parts for crossbows and daggers. I also know he sends most of them to Eastern Runlar. The great ships use them in the Eastern Ocean.

"I also am aware a shipment will be ready to send out in a few weeks. I asked to speak with your council because I want to divert that shipment to Sko'Port. A few hundred crossbows, a few hundred fine quality daggers, and some new spears made with quality Gawdichian oak could be enough to convince the Upper Ward Guard captain to send his men into the mine. I don't really have that amount of time to wait. As we speak, the High Mine is hiring mercenaries and has sent recruiters into Cidvag to bring back as many men as they can."

Daniel Locks, the owner of the Ards Bay Forge, was out of sight, but Rianas imagined she could see his earrings swaying on his huge head while he shook it back and forth. "I can't just reassign carga' like tho't, ya' know. Me' word is me' honor, und tho't's 1,300 Runlarian Eagles' worth of weapons. They'se impossible to replace right 'way, und the cap'n of the *Sea-Guard* would eat me' alive."

Atrick nodded. "I know. I have an account to draw from and am sure we can compensate you accordingly, Mr. Locks. I think this may be a request even the Runlarians would appreciate."

Renauld stood up and quieted the group down. A few were talking openly of the chance of an invasion, but a couple others were laughing off the matter as a Sko'Port problem. It was clear the meeting was becoming disorganized. "Let's see what there is for us to make decisions on here, gentlemen," Renauld said. "I believe we have the authority to confiscate Mr. Locks' shipment."

Immediately, there was fist pounding and shouting from Daniel and the other businessmen in the room about requisitioning people's livelihoods. Renauld stood his ground, waiting a moment for them to quit shouting before he continued. His hands were up in a placating manner.

"This statute hasn't been used since the formation of Riverrun. When they settled here, the founders intended us to use this only in times of severe need. Daniel, how long will it be before your shipment is ready to load?"

"Five days," came the terse reply.

Rianas' father spoke more calmly from where he was sitting. "Maybe we can make this work. The *Sea-Guard* was not completed last we spoke with the Eastern Runlarians. If we send word to him directly, the captain may be willing to wait three months while Daniel has his forge churn out another set of weapons. It would not hurt to ask. Besides, I believe he will be in Riverrun tomorrow to inspect the dried fruits and travel biscuits he is purchasing from Gawdich. If a few of us leave tomorrow, we might convince him it is in his interest to give us some more time."

Daniel said something equal parts rude and affirming. Despite his angry reply, Rianas smiled. She liked the large man. He often got angry about requests. While he sounded angry, the other council members knew he would deliver well beyond his promises. His forge business had grown large because he knew what he could do – and that was a lot, with the river providing power and Sko'Port providing quality iron, copper and coal.

Lazron had told Rianas when she was much younger that if anything ever went wrong while she was on the opposite side of the river, she was to seek out Mr. Locks. Even now, her father was flashing him a smile in recognition, and a few of the other council members were chuckling at his reply.

Atrick, who did not know the group as well, seemed much more at ease. "I cannot come with you," he said. "I must return to Sko'Port on the next Riverrun boat. My guards brought two hundred Gold Eagles as a deposit for any help the council can deliver. I have already given the payment to Mr. Flambeau. I implore you all to take me seriously."

Some brief exchanges between the council members followed, and Atrick gathered his papers and walked off to join his bodyguards. Rianas and Arthur looked at each other with wide eyes. However, when Rianas saw her father gather his things and walk over to Atrick, she decided to head back to the house quickly. She wanted to beat her father home.

Out behind the building she put her boots back on. Arthur touched her shoulder after closing the rear kitchen door. "That was pretty wild," he whispered, an uncontrollable smile fleeting across his face as it often did when something exciting was happening, good or bad. "Do you think there are really nogs pouring through a cave to attack Sko'Port?"

"I don't know. Have you read much about them? It sounds like they aren't very bright, and their mining skills aren't considered very organized. The whole thing seems strange to me." Rianas had read some about nogs. They were easily manipulated, but they would often attack other humanoids to steal whatever they liked. According to one book she had read by a Sullarian adventurer, there were millions of them living further west in the Black Mountains. Somehow, they had been brought into the Axarean Empire along with their larger Rannog and Orcan cousins. She had seen a stuffed statue of a rannog at a traveling circus when she was younger, but she only knew nogs from drawings in school.

"Maybe they are being used by an Axarean commander." Arthur enjoyed reading about Axarea, and loved to talk about strategies the Empire had used to defeat other armies. He was walking briskly with her now to the edge of the ditch. He watched her cross under the azaleas and waved. "I'll be back in the morning if you want to talk."

"Sure," she waved bye and slipped as stealthily as she could back toward the house. Her head was full of questions about nogs, how big the mine really was, and whether there might really be a battle in Sko'Port.

2. THE LARK

Andaria.

What power does their stolen homeland hold over the million residents of Riverrun? Why does that lost Nation provoke such a visceral response from Cidvagians and Sko'Portians alike? What hopes could motivate mercenaries to put their lives at risk against such horrible odds?

Andaria was lost to the armies of an emotionless, indifferent menace from the southern reaches of the Great Continent. Theirs was merely the most recent among many nations lost. In the last five centuries, the Axarean Empire has swallowed dozens of nations and kingdoms. Andaria was perhaps the largest. However, its people were powerless to stop the army of Southerners that invaded its fertile plains south of the great natural divide of the Black Mountains. There were no castles, walls, or fortresses to slow the Axarean army down when they attacked. There was only the Desert of Roglu – and the Andarians themselves.

From: "An Incomplete History of Arthos"
Grandmaster Ar'Ishan's lecture on Axarean aggression
1943 A.C.

Rianas got back before her father. The house was darkening quickly with the sunset, and the temperature was dropping now that the clouds had started to part. She quickly struck the flint through the stove starter, dropped a few cut carrots, onions, peppers, and eggs onto two skillets. Then she added a little olive oil. She was glad she did not get home later, or the whole dining room would have been cold.

Just as the eggs were finishing, she heard the kitchen door open and her father sniff loudly the way he always did when she cooked.

"That smells wonderful, Ray! Would you mind throwing a little extra on for our guests?"

"I guess," she said. "We have enough for about eight people, though, Dad."

Turning around, Rianas saw two young men in black robes walking through the door. Each one started around an opposite side of the room before settling in the center. Atrick stood patiently at the threshold with an amused yet friendly smile on his face the entire time.

"You haven't seen these two eat, miss." Atrick's gaze flicked to the taller of the guards, whose head bowed slightly, before stepping into the room. The wizard carefully wiped his spotless leather shoes at the threshold. "I once saw Berryl eat an entire turkey, and I'm not sure Teran has ever said 'no' to a meal." He chuckled and reached his left hand out to pat the taller man (Teran, apparently) gently on the shoulder.

Atrick wore a ring on each finger. They offset the black tattooing that ran from his palm out between his fingers like the legs of a spider. She had read about the cost of practicing magic. Some of the great wizards of Sullaria were said to have broken bones or even burned off parts of their hands practicing spells that were beyond their skill level. Wizards that were more powerful often enchanted rings or trinkets to help focus their energies when casting. She bet his left hand alone wore a thousand Gold Eagles' worth of enchantment or more. Those rings were not adornments –Atrick wore each jewel for its magical properties.

Rianas stood at the counter with a large spoon moving the food around, leaning around to see her guests. Her father squeezed her shoulder in passing to the rear of the house. He quickly introduced Atrick, Berryl and Teran as their guests for dinner.

"Something has come up, Rianas. I must attend an important meeting tomorrow. I'll be riding with Renauld, and we probably won't be back for four or five days. I'm going to grab some things before Renauld gets here. Can you please help these gentlemen get a solid meal? They will sleep in the guest house tonight." He did not wait for her reply, just turned and rushed off to pack his bags.

Atrick pulled back one of the bar stools quietly and stood there with a polite smile, as if waiting for Rianas' permission to sit. She told the three to sit as she pulled the skillet off the stove and grabbed a basket of sweet tomato rolls from the pantry. "There are plates in the cabinet here, glasses there, and silverware here. Help yourselves. I always make extra so we can feed Mrs. Potts down the street if she doesn't have the strength to cook."

Berryl smiled warmly as he placed a large portion on his plate. Atrick waited until Rianas had served herself, looking at her quizzically the entire time. When she sat down with them at the table, he looked toward the rear of the house, then back to her and asked quickly, "Do you think I convinced Mr. Locks to hold his weapons shipment?"

Rianas froze. Her face seemed to catch fire as she debated what to say. How did Atrick know she had watched the council meeting?

Atrick maintained eye contact and broke into an infectious grin as he whispered, "Your secret is safe with me, young lady. I am a High Wizard of Sko'Port. I've caught spies from twelve different kingdoms in my time in those bureaucratic reviews of Sko'Port activities."

Atrick chuckled, "Of course, most of the time the information they were looking for should have been made public, too. I'm frankly glad you attended; after all, I came here looking for you."

Rianas' face felt like it had turned to stone. She had no idea how to react, or if this wizard was playing some strange game with her. Finally, she opened her mouth, and something like "Uhh" came out.

Atrick said, "Thank you so much for the hot meal, Rianas," loud enough for her father to hear in the next room. "The Riverrun boats serve only dried meats and fruits with some deplorably-selected, watered-down Assyrian ale."

Then the wizard winked at her.

Rianas did not know what to do. She thought about speaking again, but the prospect of displaying her intelligence with another inevitable "Uhh" did not appeal to her. She quickly finished the tea she had poured and used that as an excuse to stand and walk over to the cupboard to get another glass.

Her back was to Atrick when he said, *"I am serious, Rianas. I have heard of your translation skills, and I could use them if I capture nogs in that mine."*

Rianas finally found her words. "Sir, I don't speak Nogese, or whatever language nogs speak. Why on earth would you – what?"

Atrick's fork had dropped to his plate. He had stopped chewing. Now, the wizard's face froze. It was almost as if some mystical creature were playing with people's faces tonight, she thought.

Atrick spoke again. *"What is two and two?"*

"Four."

That was when she noticed his mouth was closed.

"Yes, Rianas, you have a natural ability I have never seen in a linguist. There have been others born with some degree of natural telepathy. But yours occurs so easily. Most telepaths require years of training to read another's projections so easily! Amazing!" He was whispering so quietly, mouth full of his last bite. Yet, now she understood everything he was saying clearly. It was as if he had written his words on a piece of paper in front of her to read at will.

Rianas had never done that before. She was about to start asking questions when she heard a knock at the door.

Her father walked briskly back into the room carrying one rucksack full of papers and another overflowing with clothes. "Rianas, Mr. and Mrs. Potts will be checking in on you for the next few days, so just let them know if you need anything. Here is some money in case something happens. Be safe. I apologize for leaving so quickly, but it is very important I get going now. We may be able to save lives." Her father, normally more astute, did not even seem to notice her lack of badgering questions. Instead, he opened the door and gave a bag to Renauld as they both jogged out to his carriage.

Suddenly, Rianas was sitting at the table again. She was alone with the wizard and his guards. "I cannot leave home without Father's permission. He would never allow me to travel to Sko'Port, spelunk twenty miles or more, and participate in open warfare with nogs!"

She attempted to scoff, but her nerves only let her laugh awkwardly.

Atrick suddenly had a pouch in his hands. Rianas was sure he had not had it a second before, but she was distracted when he spilled the contents on the table. One hundred Gold Eagles was more than many people earned in a year in Ards. Despite her amazement, though, Rianas did not flinch. "I've never left Riverrun," she said weakly. It did not sound like a good excuse, even to her, after she had said it.

"I know it is rude to offer money like that. I am not trying to buy your help, Rianas. You could use this money for buying supplies. Please consider helping me. Also, consider this: your skill brings you attention from across the Northern Realms. There are most likely recruiters looking to bring you on board from Sullaria, and there are possibly others from one of the Runlars. I need a translator and telepath to help translate for the foreign mercenaries I will have to hire. Plus, think of all the things you would get to see."

Rianas was dreaming of her upcoming adventure. How amazing would it be to see the great boulder-slides of Sko'Port and tour the Miner's Highway. Sko'Port was one of the most populous cities in the world. She could eat the famous lizard stew that people passing through Ards from Sko'Port always bragged about buying from street vendors in the Lower Ward. She would be wandering through the fabled underground caverns, where they might meet Nog warriors. Truthfully, Rianas could not think of something she wanted to do more. School was out for the fall, and she had two months while the other students tended farms. Unlike Arthur, she had stayed home and devoted her time to reading for the summer break. There was very little keeping her in Ards.

Except her father.

Her father would go crazy if she asked him for permission to go with a wizard to explore a mine in Sko'Port.

Atrick lifted both hands as if to acquiesce to her unspoken protestations. Nevertheless, he left the coins on the kitchen counter. He then set down a piece of parchment that seemed to appear out of thin air, just like the coins. It was a map of the High Mine. Beautiful decorations, cursive notes and multi-colored sketches broke down the mine's multiple levels.

Rianas could not help but reach out her hands and smooth the folded parchment on the table. This brought smiles to the eyes of the three men. "Take the map for your collection," Atrick whispered, "I understand you are an avid reader of Sko'Port lore."

"Look, Rianas, I don't want to force anyone onto my expedition. It will be dangerous, and I need men and women who will commit for the greater good of protecting the entire Northern Realms. I just ask you think it over. I leave two hours after sunrise tomorrow on the Lark." Rianas watched Atrick's motionless lips as he spoke to her, amazed at the new skill she seemed to have acquired. "And if you come with us, I promise to help you harness more of this gift you have been given."

With an inclined head, Atrick excused himself to bed. Teran stayed to help clean the dishes, refusing to allow Rianas to do them; then he let himself out politely.

Rianas stared at the door and out the window as the last made made his way to the guesthouse.

What had just happened? Did she really read the wizard's mind? Could she learn how to do more?

She did not want to leave her father without talking to him, and she feared all the things that could happen should she simply leave. However, she did want to see Sko'Port, ride across the Sko'Sea on a *Riverrunner*, and see the peaks of the Black Mountains. In addition, the huge Sko'Port library had thousands of texts from before the Great Andarian War.

Her mind was made up, it seemed. She wanted to find a middle path, one that would keep her safe. However, in her heart she already knew what she would do.

Rianas went to her room and packed some clothes, her binoculars, the knife from Arthur, and a book about Sko'Port. Looking around her room, she also picked up a thick leather tool belt, removing the tools and thinking it would make a great holder for whatever she needed to carry. After considering a few other small items and packing a few days' worth of hard fruits and biscuits in her bag of camping gear, she laid down.

There was no sleep that night. Rianas vacillated between guilt and excitement, then got up an hour or two after midnight. She wrote a short letter to her father, telling him she would be gone a few weeks with Atrick to help with translation services. With hands shaking from excitement, she washed and got ready before finally deciding to go down early to the docks.

The way to the docks went past the council building, through the local town center to the main part of Ards. Around ten thousand people lived in Ards, with most of those working on the west side of the river in Mr. Locks' forge or on one of the five Riverrun craft. A few people, like her father, managed the communications links between Ards and the main city of Riverrun. Some worked in the smaller craft shops that had grown up in the past few years with the help of the Borsilkian engineer who had taken residence in town. Rianas stepped into the brisk morning air with her two bags, which she placed on either side of the cart on her bicycle, then maneuvered up onto the road.

Going past the council building, she saw Arthur standing outside with a bucket of dirty rags. He waved and walked up to the road when she stopped. "Where are you going so early? Is something wrong?"

Rianas got off the bike shaking her head, and then she said, "Well, not really. You wouldn't believe what happened last night." She took a few minutes to fill him in. When she told him she had read Atrick's thoughts, Arthur smiled goofily, but he let her finish before speaking. Usually he interrupted her halfway through a conversation with questions or expostulations.

"You've been doing that for a while now, I'd say. You always seem to know what I'm thinking. Are you really going to go to Sko'Port? That's so dangerous!" He looked like he wanted to say more. The grin disappeared as he looked into her eyes and saw Rianas' resolve. "Do you know when you will be back? How long will it be before they enter the mines?"

"A few days after we get there, I think. Atrick seemed to think I would be helping him set up contracts with mercenaries." She fidgeted with the strap of the tool belt she was wearing. She had decided to wear it a while and see if she needed to make any adjustments. The coin pouch and map tucked easily into a bladder on the belt. Arthur heard the faint jingle and his eyebrows lifted comically.

"What do you think you will buy?" Then, digging in his shoe sleeve, he withdrew the cord-cutting knife he used with the horses. It was about twelve inches long, and Rianas remembered when he made it from a piece of scrap metal he had purchased with two month's pay last year. He had worked it in the shop at school for a month, finally affixing the oak handle to it with four steel rivets he had begged the Borsilkian for at his little shop. "Why don't you put this on your belt? Maybe you can use it better than that little hunting knife we made. I haven't needed it for a few months, and my parents say I shouldn't be playing with daggers after they found me training with Mr. Potts."

Rianas knew better than to argue with Arthur, he would just find another way to give it to her anyway. She realized she had probably taken this route hoping to see him on the way. "Thank you, Arthur. I will be careful not to get any stains on it." This brought another strange look on his face. This time he gave her a sideways glance.

"That wizard posted a hiring notice on the council door. They are offering 25 Gold Eagles to anyone who wants to come along. You know, he doesn't really sell it. The poster says there will be food and some basic gear provided, but that they expect some close quarters fighting. Why would he say that if he wanted people to join his expedition? It seems to me like he will frighten away lots of volunteers. The money is great."

Rianas shook her head. "I don't know. He seems to be a very open man." She was starting to get a little nervous about what she was doing again.

"Is there anyone from Ards coming? Are you sure you can trust this wizard?" Arthur had broken eye contact and was staring at his feet. He looked like he wanted to say something else.

"No, I don't think so." Rianas knew her father had invited Atrick into their house. That alone was unusual, and it spoke of how much he trusted the man. "As far as Atrick's character, I am not completely sure I understand his thoughts. But Arthur, I think I have to do this. The more I think, the more I realize it is what I have wanted to do for years."

Arthur nodded. "Okay." Then he looked up from his feet with a more determined look. His serious eyes met hers and he put his hands on his legs to stand up. "I've got some things to do here. Watch your back, and don't be afraid to do whatever you think is right." He saw she thought he was angry and shook his head. "Rianas, this sounds like a great adventure. I wish I could come along."

Rianas had not thought about that. It would be great to have Arthur along to keep her company and share some of the sights. "Why don't you? You would make more money in Sko'Port than in an entire summer working with these horses."

Arthur smiled. Then the smile turned into a wide-faced grin, and he shook his hands at his sides a little in excitement. "Yeah! Look, maybe I can just run back to the house and tell my parents I am going on a trip. I'll figure out a way to get there. Don't go sightseeing without me!" He did not even look where he was going. The gangly young man just started running backward toward the other road until he tripped over the wash bucket. Muddy water spilled across his whole front and he landed face first in a pile of mucked-out hay.

Rianas could not help laughing as she helped him up. "Be quick, maybe you can make the *Lark* before it leaves. I am so excited, too. This will be a real adventure!"

Arthur waved as he ran off.

Rianas got on her bike and finished the trip to the docks. Of course she was hours early, but she had wanted to get there early and buy some gear for the trip since she did not feel prepared in the slightest. There was a leather shop next to the docks, and Mr. Donaldson was usually tinkering in the back at an early hour, so she stepped in.

The smell of leather permeated the small shop, and Mr. Donaldson looked up from his sewing wheel, squinting through the magnifying glass he wore to do his work. A large dog came around the chair and whined happily when it saw her. She knelt down to eye level with it and gave it a gentle rub under the ears.

"Good morning, Rianas. You are here early this morning. Is there something special you're looking for?" The small man was all fingers and arms, and he unfolded himself from the sewing table to walk over to Rianas. Mr. Donaldson had lost his wife two years ago, and Rianas had helped him adopt Hector (the dog) from the Potts', giving suggestions and helping him train the animal. Now it fetched supplies, alerted him when people entered the store, and even carried pieces of leather for him without putting teeth marks in them. Rianas loved Hector and she was glad the dog had such a loving owner.

"I need something I can use to carry my rucksacks while I'm hiking." She lifted the two bags to show Mr. Donaldson.

His bushy eyebrows bounced around a bit, and he turned toward the back of the shop where he had some pre-made bags. Rooting around in the corner, he brought up a contraption of leather straps. "I made this for a young man who was heading east to do some adventuring, but he ended up sticking around here." Mr. Donaldson brought it over, fiddling with the knotted straps for a few seconds, and then said, "Here, I'll show you how it works."

It took half an hour for Rianas to understand the various loops and buckles, but Mr. Donaldson patiently suited her up twice and watched her do it herself the third time. She had to admit the weight distributed nicely. Bouncing around the shop, all her gear seemed to stay snug, and nothing poked or chafed her back or shoulders. The stained black wool strap-guards even gave some style to the harnessing. Rianas paid and looked out to see the sun was starting to rise.

Shortly, she arrived at the dock where the *Lark* was moored. The *Lark's* crew was busy loading heavy crates with a set of pulleys suspended from the loading platform overhead. There were barrels of apples, oranges, olives, and all manner of fresh fruit loaded into crates. Others were sealed and likely contained juices or oils. Toward the stern, the paddle wheels were idly turning in the water, just fast enough to keep the vessel pressed against the upriver side of the dock. Rianas watched the puffs of smoke gently rise from the boiler room for a few moments. There were over a dozen people obviously from Sko'Port pointing and talking about the paddle wheels in amazement. A young Runlarian man next to the water was putting his hand out to feel the power of the wheel turn his arm slowly, and a woman with him kept pulling him back.

The technological achievements of the Riverrun community were far beyond those of its neighbors. After the founding of Riverrun following the Andarian War fifty years ago, the largely Andarian exile community had decided to depend less upon magic, mostly because none of the new residents had magical skill. Riverrun's college had spent a large grant from the Borsilkians to research ways to harness the Anasko River.

Some of the grant helped the college hire dozens of the best Borsilkian researchers. The diminutive Borsilkian engineers were happy to try some projects they had dreamt of but were never able to try in their more arid homeland.

Borsilkians were universally incapable of creating their own magic. For nearly two hundred years, they had been creating experimental technology to wage their never-ending battle against Axarea in the Badlands. Despite the Borsilkian technological advancements, the Northern Realms saw little use for most of their inventions. Magic could usually do the work more easily.

The Northern Realms did not respect Borsilkian technology. Borsilkians seldom travelled outside their hills in the central region of the Great Continent. Their long Gawdichian border was largely unpopulated and nearly impassable. Borsilkians preferred their centuries-old farmland to thick forests. Gawdichian politics were to blame, too. The royal family enjoyed hunting in those forests, and few settlers dared to enter the western section of the kingdom.

The largely uncivilized lands to the west of the Borsilkian Alliance and the Elven Empire were other nations that sometimes traded with the Borsilkians. The Elven Empire, however, had often scoffed at Borsilkian machinations.

The Borsilkians shared trade and a border with Andaria before the Andarian War. Rianas remembered her physics professor in school referring to this old allegiance as the reason the Borsilkian Alliance granted Riverrun so much help when it first formed.

The Andarian exile experiment of Riverrun was an odd exception to nearly 500 years of Borsilkian separation from the Northern Realms.

A phone system ran along the Anasko River for the length of Riverrun, and the Riverrun boats were perhaps the fastest in Arthos. In addition, the water-powered forges running in Mr. Locks' warehouses produced steel that rivaled the quality of even some magical metals from the Runlars and Sullaria. Rianas had read about the differences between Riverrun and the other Northern Realms. Visitors would come through and marvel at the mechanical works of Riverrun.

However, no other kingdom had devoted funds to similar projects as of yet – at least as far as Rianas knew. The wealth of Riverrun came from its embrace of new technologies. Ards College had the best College of Engineering outside of the Dwarven Kingdoms, but Andarians made up over ninety percent of its students.

Rianas remembered what her science teacher had said. "Why would they? If you could do the same or more with magic, why not just pay the mage or wizard to do the hard work? Sometimes, necessity drives innovation."

Atrick was sitting on a crate marked as tomatoes, eating food from one of the fish vendor stalls. Berryl and Teran stood off to the side, Berryl finishing some sort of breaded meat, while Teran hawkishly examined each person passing by. It looked as if Atrick had bought a few crates of his own to bring back. He sat next to a neat line of the wooden boxes.

Rianas approached nervously, noting one of the crates Atrick had was marked as "MISSILES – CLASS I". That meant arrows for type one long bows. That was most likely a case filled by Mr. Locks. Those would be cast steel tips with fine Gawdichian war-hawk feathers and wood from the Northern forest. She had seen these arrows before. She knew how expensive Mr. Locks' arrows were.

Gawdich had even fought wars with the Elven Empire over the trees that could reach a thousand feet and more. The Elves claimed every one of the Archon trees. As the immortal trees grew, even the Elves found the need to thin their lower branches.

"I've bought what I could while I was here. There is enough dried food to feed

34

three hundred men for two weeks in these crates." Rianas looked up and saw Atrick was talking to her telepathically. It was both exhilarating and somewhat terrifying to have so quickly developed this new skill. She wondered if Atrick could read her mind.

"Good Morning, Rianas," Atrick said. He spoke this time. "I'm so glad you have decided to join us."

"Can you really use bows deep in the mines?" she asked. This brought a huge, meat-covered grin to Berryl's face. Something fell off his lips, and he caught it just in time to put back in his mouth.

"You are an observant young lady." Atrick pointed to the crate she had indicated. "These I will trade to a good friend of mine who is guard captain in the Upper Ward. I hope to convince him to bring a few hundred men into the mine. There are some of Mr. Locks' fine long daggers over there, but that is all I was able to convince him to part with this morning. I am hoping your father is successful in convincing that Runlarian ship captain to accept late delivery of his weapons."

"If you have friends in the guard, why not just ask the guard to clear the mine? Isn't it part of their mission to protect Sko'Port?" Rianas remembered reading the covenants of the Sko'Port guards and Royal Navy. Although both groups were small in comparison to other nations, the Sko'Port city-state's population of over 6 million residents supported a substantial police force capable of maintaining order and projecting power beyond the city's borders. It had marched into Cidvag more than once when brigands or pirates had thought to take advantage of the city-state. The covenants explicitly stated that the guards would defend the mining interests of the city. There was even a specific "Guard Tax" on each mine. In essence, the revenue from the "Guard Tax" on mines in Sko'Port paid the salaries of all the guards and most of the Royal Navy in the city-state.

Berryl chuckled a bit, and then got serious again when he saw the glare from Atrick.

"Young lady," Atrick explained, "you will find that not everything is simple in Sko'Port. For example, did you know that three Sullarian knights have died shadowing guard activities in the Lower Ward in the past twelve months?"

Rianas, who had taken a seat on a barrel of tomatoes, gasped. "No, I didn't know that. Is the city getting dangerous, or do you suspect something is amiss with the guards?" It was amazing how openly she felt she could speak with Atrick. "I apologize for asking, it is just that the only information I have read on Sko'Port comes from dock gossip and official transcripts from our library here."

"Not at all," Atrick said. "I encourage you to speak your mind. It is, after all, the way to enlightenment. In answer to your question, however, the news has not made its way far because the telling has become dangerous. Sullaria does not check the status of its knights often, so they may not discover missing emissaries for a year or more. I suspect these deaths have resulted from their company rather than their missions, if you catch my meaning."

Atrick glanced left and right, then leaned closer to Rianas, looked her in the eyes, and telepathically spoke to her, "*My suspicions are well-founded. I believe there are dozens of infiltrators in the lower guard, and I have been working for months to help the Upper Ward Guard surreptitiously eliminate their own infiltrators. Do not trust any Lower Ward guardsmen you meet when we arrive – your life may depend on it.*"

Rianas' eyes widened and she again wondered what she was doing. Berryl spoke into what he perceived as a protracted silence, "I was in the Lower Ward Guard for five years before I joined Atrick, Rianas. I would be careful who amongst them you trust."

Atrick laughed at Berryl's unknown repetition. Berryl rocked back a bit on his heels in surprise.

Rianas relaxed a bit, but wondered, "Who would infiltrate the Sko'Port guards? What good would it do?"

Berryl still thought she was talking to him. "Our suspicion is that there are people at the top who have been compromised somehow. There have been mounting deaths in the lower mines from 'accidents,' and dozens of wizards have either left the city or chosen to retire early in the last few years."

Atrick nodded his head, the mirth disappearing. He spoke in a low voice this time, "I've lost some of my most capable colleagues since taking this position in the High Mine. I suspect my predecessor, Hasand Therian, was pushed out early because of this. Two cave-ins happened in the same stretch of mine he was inspecting. A cart came loose one evening and ran him over, nearly killing him. Pirates, of all things, attacked him during his last visit to Gawdich to secure wood for support pillars. When he retired, he selected me because I am young and because he knew I had been working with the guards."

"Do you think Sko'Port is really that corrupt?" Rianas asked.

"Yes. And no." Atrick equivocated. He looked out on the dock. "But for now, it appears the *Lark* is ready to load our gear. Berryl, help the workers out. Teran, let's load our personal items into the quarters." With that, Atrick picked up a small, gold-trimmed yellow sack the length of his upper arm. Teran grabbed two large bags and slung them onto a wagon he had apparently borrowed from the dockworkers. He politely took Rianas' bags as well, remarking about the utility of her harnessing kit as he lifted the gear into the wagon and walked toward the passenger loading area of the *Lark*.

"This is a fine bit of leather work here," Teran said. "I used something similar when I marched for the Assyrian army. It's good to see you know how to pack your gear. Have you done a lot of hiking?" It was the most Teran had said in the few hours Rianas had known the trio.

"Yes, I've travelled the Anasko River up to Western Runlar's border a few times with my father to help him settle trade questions for ranchers. I like working with the horses and cattle. Of course, we usually ride horses. My father likes to camp, though, so we make the trip on foot a couple times a year."

Teran nodded and pushed the cart up the walkway to the passenger entrance. He took out a couple papers with the *Lark's* seal and showed them to the man at the foot of the gangplank. The man waved them in, looking curiously at Rianas as she walked behind Teran. Atrick came last, staring over the gangplank into the river water. So close to the Sko'Sea, the river was full of silt that had traveled hundreds of miles from Gawdich or Western Runlar.

Rianas, however, was busy looking around the *Lark*. This was the largest of the Riverrun ships. It was nearly two hundred feet in length, and the ribs were each carved from a single solid length of Gawdichian lumber.

She had seen the blueprints for the ship in the Riverrun library. Because of its size, it paddled between the Runlarian border and Sko'Port most of the year. During the dry season in the fall, the *Lark* ran this shorter route, dropping its cargo right in Ards instead of paddling upriver to the main city of Riverrun. Ards had expanded the docks to accommodate this larger craft.

Each shipment brought hundreds of tons of raw ore, iron, copper, and coal. The ship was open in the center. Its broad hull was deep enough for pallets of barrels to be stacked atop one another. Some were stacked so high they barely cleared the deck. A thin rope railing warded off falls, and the walkway was barely wide enough for three men to walk abreast.

The land-based loaders swung pallets aboard using cranes, while crewmembers down below directed them with shouts and hand signals. They strapped each stacked set of barrels or pallets in a long row, then they cross-strapped them with built-in netting. The crew loaded parchments in wooden lock-boxes at the end of each row to identify the products and their respective merchants. The pallets filled the *Lark's* belly quickly, and the crew was already working on Atrick's goods as Rianas leaned against the rope to look down.

Toward the stern, where Teran and Atrick were walking, were the passenger quarters. The *Lark* only had about two dozen small rooms – it had been built primarily for transporting goods to and from Sko'Port – and there were a dozen narrow benches set up in front of the passenger quarters for eating and entertaining during the voyage.

Unlike the Runlarian naval vessels Rianas had seen in the library or occasionally voyaging down to Sko'Port through the Anasko River, the crew of the *Lark* was only about twenty people. Most of the *Lark's* crew spent their time managing the coal fire. No sails flew above her decks. The *Lark* was unlike any other ships in Arthos.

Atrick turned to Rianas as she joined them, gave her an orange-painted piece of wood with a key attached by a piece of leather, and said, "Here is a key to your quarters for the trip. I apologize for the accommodations. They designed the *Lark* for cargo, not passengers. Fortunately, the trip is only two days. I have some meditation to do, but Berryl and Teran will be on deck most of the voyage." Atrick nodded politely and brought his small bag with him into one of the small rooms.

Rianas decided to inspect her quarters and drop off her travel pack. Teran removed her bag and handed it to her, then walked toward his own room to unload the other bags.

The living quarters were small. There was space for a plank bed with a small pillow, a thin sheet, and a blanket. The ceiling was so short she had to crouch. Rianas placed her things down, sat on the corner of the bed, and took out the dagger Arthur had given her. She wondered if he would be true to his word and come along. She positioned her gear on the harness she had purchased, and found a comfortable place to hang the dagger along her right thigh. Satisfied, she unpacked a little and went out the thin wooden door to wait on the deck.

As she came down, Arthur was coming across the plank with two other young men and Berryl. Berryl was instructing them on their accommodations while handing out more colored keys. Arthur waved at Rianas before walking off with Berryl.

The ship was already fully loaded, and the crew was scampering around the cargo hold checking straps. A few other passengers came up the passenger entrance, followed by the attendant.

Dockworkers pushed the *Lark* into the river, where it floated aimlessly for a moment while two workers stoked the boiler. Then, with a rush of smoke from the stack in the rear, the huge paddle wheels began to turn and the ship slowly floated into the center of the waterway before straightening course and picking up speed. For all the times Rianas had seen the *Riverrunners* taking off, she had never been on board one for a voyage. She stood at the railing and watched as the water started to move quickly under the ship.

Berryl returned with Teran a few moments later, and Rianas joined them on a bench, still watching the buildings of Ards move by with increasing speed. Berryl told a story about working in the Sko'Port Lower Ward and how he had chased a giant rat through the sewers and out to the Sko'Sea, before the rat had jumped onto a fishing vessel, where it decided to turn and fight him. Teran shook his head as Berryl described a battle across multiple fishing ships, short sword in one hand and buckler in front of him, warding off the rat's teeth as he tried to stab it. The story ended with Berryl finally swinging from the sail of one ship onto another and landing on the giant rat's back. Teran and Rianas laughed as he reenacted the battle through to when he rode it straight into a wall, waking up with a dead rat between his legs that had drowned in a hold full of fish while his arm had gotten wedged in a doorway, trapping them both.

Arthur came out a little while later with the other two men, looking a little pale. "Does the boat rock like this all the time?" he asked. Teran gave him a piece of soft wood to chew on.

Berryl made introductions. The other two men joining were Samuel and John. He went over each man's skills and gave them some exercises to do on the deck. Arthur seemed to be the most fit of the three Riverrun volunteers. He was skinny, but his long arms and time tending the horses had helped him build strength and dexterity.

The day went quickly, with Berryl and Teran providing instructions on how to carry weapons and fight underground, and discussing what nogs looked like.

When the new recruits seemed tired, Teran suggested they break for lunch. Everyone sat at the benches and ate a fish soup the captain had ordered for the passengers.

Rianas picked idly at the catfish in the broth with her spoon, wondering if she should get something more appetizing from her room. Arthur, whose seasickness had subsided with the wood Teran had given him, looked freshly pale after the first bite. One of the recruits, Samuel, practiced loading and firing a small hand crossbow into a target across the cargo hold while Teran spoke about his days in the Assyrian army fighting nogs on the east coast.

Assyria was a kingdom of small villages, with a few cities on the coast. The kingdom was mostly rocky, following the eastern edge of the Black Mountains from Cidvag all the way to the coast, where the mountains broke into millions of sharp crags as if a giant had taken a hammer to the tops of the mountains as they spilled into the ocean. Raven's Nest was one of the larger cities on the coast, built along two broken spires of stone. Teran described the city's rope bridges and buildings carved into the faces of the two spires. An ancient castle sat atop the higher peak, with rope elevators and steep stone steps leading up.

A few years back, nogs hiding in the foothills had started attacking caravans traveling to Raven's Nest along the highway that led into the town. Teran was part of the unit tasked with stopping the raids. A few hundred soldiers marched through the lowlands for a week before they found the first evidence of the Nog raiders.

Nogs are not very smart, Teran explained, but they usually have a warlord leading their raiding parties. Since their kind typically live underground, their eyesight is poor in bright environments. Teran's search party stumbled across an encampment of the raiders shortly after noon on the seventh day. They were surprised to see nearly one hundred tents scattered in a large clearing. The nogs had only posted a couple of sentries, so his party reported to the main force. They decided to surround the camp and capture as many as they could.

Knowing their advantage would wane with the daylight, the commander ordered his men to begin the assault within moments of arrival. Teran remembered charging through the underbrush into a camp of unsuspecting raiders. At first, the attack went exceptionally well. Many of the surprised raiders at the outsides of the camp simply gave up because they could not get to their weapons. As the Assyrians made their way into the camp, however, the warlord sounded his horn and bounded out with a great axe and a contingent of elite fighters. Teran, busy tying up a group of captured nogs, was surprised when the warlord picked up more men from the central tents as he raged right toward where he and his squad were tying up prisoners.

He dropped the prisoners, picked up his shield, and lifted his long sword just in time for the nogs to attack. Teran explained that since nogs are so small, they often attack individuals in pairs. While they are not strong enough (or tall enough) to wield long weapons, some will use spears. Most, however, will stick with daggers or rarely a short sword. Teran fought the bandits with his back to four other companions while the battle for the rest of the camp raged around him.

"The Warlord saw that we were in the way of his escape route," Teran said. "When the Warlord blew his horn, it motivated half the remaining force to rally around him. You see, nogs are generally not very brave, but they will follow their pack leaders viciously.

"My companions and I faced him. He was perhaps a head shorter than me, but his scaly skin and arms were much larger. He attacked one of my companions and left himself open. So, I stabbed him from his left side. That is when one of his underlings gave me this." Teran lifted the right side of his robe to show a long scar along his right thigh.

"As soon as we had defeated the Warlord, however, the fight seemed to weaken in the bandits. Some continued to fight," Teran said, "but only to escape. A few dozen got past us into the forest, but the rest were either captured or killed."

Teran and Berryl both spoke for an hour about their battle experiences while the men in the group listened. After finishing their meals, Berryl put the group back to exercises, and offered to show Rianas how to use her dagger.

It was after sunset before Berryl let the group rest for the evening. Arthur sat down wearily next to Rianas, a goofy grin on his face. Rianas grabbed some of the vegetable stew that the ship's cook offered to the group. She marveled how far they had traveled that day. A small fishing boat was off to the port side, but otherwise the water slipping quickly by was the only thing to see. There was no shore within sight in any direction. The paddle wheels turned with the ever-present sound of wood planks slapping together, and the yellow moon began to rise in the east, illuminating the water with an eerie glow. The temperature had started to drop, but the breeze from the water carried the heat from the day with it.

Arthur practiced a few dagger thrusts he had learned from Berryl. "My parents think I'm going on a trip to work in the mines for the rest of the summer. I don't think my mother understood the whole 'nogs might be down there' statement. I probably should have explained it better." He smiled and put the dagger in his side pocket.

Rianas chuckled, but then she turned serious as they walked toward the edge of the ship to look over. "Atrick seemed to think there are infiltrators in the Sko'Port guard. I've only spoken with the man for an hour or so, but I get the impression he is expecting a major conflict. Berryl and Teran don't even seem to question the fact that fighting will occur." She told Arthur what Atrick and Berryl had said about the lower guard in Sko'Port.

Arthur nodded as they looked into the greyish water. The moon was illuminating pieces of seaweed that had drifted to the surface. There was a bright stripe in the direction of Sko'Port. Aside from the light, she could not make out anything from so far away.

"The position of High Mine head wizard isn't ceremonial," Arthur reflected. "He was selected for his skills by the Sko'Port wizard's council. When I told my parents I was going with Atrick, they both apparently remembered him. My father said he was a good man who would keep me safe in the mines. I honestly think that was what convinced him to let me come."

Rianas and Arthur talked for a while, and then they went off to their little beds. Rianas slept soundly despite the uncomfortable quarters. She was too tired to worry about much more than washing out her mouth and pouring the wastewater over the rail into the water.

The next morning, the new companions shared stories of their previous experiences. Samuel and John had both been farmhands in the bay area of Riverrun who saw an opportunity to make some extra money. Samuel had hunting experience with a hand crossbow, but John had little experience beyond harvesting fruits and grains. Neither had any children, so it was easy for them to simply move on and follow the gold.

After breakfast, Berryl and Teran brought out a few daggers and sheaths for the other four. That made two daggers Rianas had. She wondered why she needed so many weapons, to which Teran opened his robe and showed his assortment of knives, daggers, and sword-sheath.

"I always keep at least four daggers on me when danger is near. Two on the legs, one on the belt, and one in the breast pocket," he explained. "A sword is too large to carry in tight spaces, but if I can, I do. Berryl likes to sling a hand bow like Samuel, but if you are in a protracted battle, you will run out of ammunition. Plus, the Black Mountains do not produce very high quality lumber, so you have to buy your ammunition from Gawdich or Cidvag."

Berryl unslung his crossbow seemingly from nowhere, which surprised Samuel and Arthur. Then he brought out his ammunition pouch from behind his belt and showed he had about forty bolts. His ammunition was fine iron. Some sort of glass-like material tipped the bolts. Berryl explained he had purchased them from a wizard in Sko'Port. "They are enchanted to fly true. Each one cost me five Gold Eagles. Altogether, they represent nearly half a year's salary. A rule I learned a long time ago, though, is that you can only die once. I have fired them a few times in combat, but I usually am able to retrieve them."

Samuel demanded a show. Berryl was more than willing to load a few shots in and take aim at the target across the cargo hold. He fired four in a row to within an inch of the bull's eye. For one hundred feet, Berryl's shots with such a small crossbow were amazing. Samuel clapped excitedly after each shot.

3. THE WEAVE

Andaria had not fought a war in centuries when the attack came. Its Southern cousins, the Roglun Kingdom, had been nomadic. Their Borsilkian neighbors to the West traded metals and machinery in exchange for Andarian foodstuffs. Cidvag to the North happily collected taxes on trade through the mountain, and the Old Assyrian Empire had peacefully traded from the Eastern Sea. Andarians did not know what war was.

Hawkish historians often blame the leadership of Andaria for misleading the people about the danger of Axarea. The Axarean Empire consumed the Old Assyrian Empire all the way to the Black Mountains. The Roglun Kingdom waged war on the Axareans for decades from their traveling wagon cities before finally succumbing. The Borsilkians had fought with the Axareans forever, it seemed. In retrospect, the Andarians should have seen their fate.

From: "An Incomplete History of Arthos"
Grandmaster Ar'Ishan's lecture on Axarean aggression
1943 A.C.

After lunch, Atrick came down from his quarters. He spoke with Berryl and Teran for a few moments. Then he came over to where Rianas was practicing maneuvers Teran had shown her with two daggers at once.

"I'm glad to see everyone is taking weapon training seriously," he said. "I have no doubt we are going to be in combat."

Rianas put the daggers into the pockets she had rigged in her outfit. "If nogs have invaded the mine, then how did they get there in the first place?"

Atrick smiled his friendly smile again. "I believe Sko'Port is waging a quiet war with Axarean operatives as we speak. The Axarean consulate in the Lower Ward is a den of suspicious characters. I think they are gathering intelligence on the city and somehow sending word across the Black Mountains."

"Why wouldn't the nogs just invade across however those spies got here, then?" Rianas asked.

"The way over the Black Mountains would be treacherous. Some Sullarian knights have made the trip across a few of the passes. The passes that have been found can only be traversed single file, and there are giants and even wild dragons that live across the peaks. The dragons are primitive and wild, and the stone giants do not take well to trespassers. The best time to cross over those passes is in the winter, when the giants are not as active and the dragons are hibernating. That high in the mountains, the winter can be bitter and deadly, even this far south. I doubt many would have the strength to make the trip, and nogs don't tolerate the cold.

"When we get back to the Upper Ward, your language skills should be able to help me identify any would-be saboteurs in the rescue party I'm putting together. If the Upper Ward Guard is as safe as I believe it is, I'm hoping this mission into the mine goes well. I'm not sure how long it takes communication to get across the Black Mountains. Messages would have to go by wing or by skilled mountaineer. I assume we have at least another two weeks before news of the breach reaches whoever directed these nogs, unless the nogs themselves are providing reports. I suspect we have a few weeks before their leaders learn of the nogs' breakthrough to this side of the mountain. If Axarea is truly behind the Nog invasion of the mine, there will be enough nogs there to shut the mine down for months once they find out they have broken through."

"How would I help you identify saboteurs?" Rianas asked.

Atrick winked at her. "There is an enchantment I learned a few years ago from a Sullarian wizard who has helped Blue Knights build trade networks for decades. He showed me how to enchant a chair I have in my home. You answer some easy questions. Then, you answer questions about your intentions. If you lie while sitting in the chair, it can detect it, and one of the legs will glow faintly.

Unfortunately, it requires you to speak with the interviewee in his native language. You will ask the questions of each interviewee before he is allowed to join the party."

"Why not just ask them in Northern?"

"It is not every mercenary's first language. Some will hail from Eastern Runlar, some from the far northern reaches of Arthos, and some come from the western edge. Cidvag has a reputation for hiring all sorts. There are even some mercenaries that cross the Black Mountains from Axarea."

"How does the chair work? Does it have some sort of thermometer, or a heartbeat monitor?" Rianas was thinking of the tiny Borsilkian doctor who visited Ards once a year and offered remedies, fitted glasses, and helped deliver babies. The tinker had used a metal funnel to listen to people breathe and count heartbeats, and Rianas had read that people's heartbeats changed when they lied or got excited. It seemed difficult to use equipment like that, though.

Atrick shook his head and chuckled. "Rianas, the world outside of Riverrun is full of magic. Your abilities to speak and read minds are powerful magic. I am not one of the Great Wizards of Sullaria, but my skills with light, transposition, and fire allow me to do things the Borsilkians cannot do. The enchantment in the chair uses basic concepts surrounding mental states and calibrates itself to each person who sits in the chair. The chair can, however, work much better than a horn or a thermometer strapped to your head could."

Rianas considered. She had read about enchantments, but Borsilkian technology formed the foundation of Riverrun. The small nation of exiles from Old Andaria had possessed no magical powers when they founded Riverrun. As a result, everything had been built with mechanical self-sufficiency in mind.

She had seen enchanted lamps that stayed lit for hours without any oil or wax in the school. The dockworkers occasionally used healing potions on men who were injured on the docks. Rianas had never seen one used, though. Her father had always stressed that the people of Riverrun owed their well-being to trusting in the engineering works of the Borsilkian Alliance.

"If magic is better than mechanical ingenuity, why are the *Riverrun* craft the fastest, largest ships in the Sko'Sea?" Rianas asked.

Atrick's infectious smile returned and he nodded. "You make a great point. The problem is not that magic cannot create faster ships. Rather, magical power is concentrated among humans. I am one of a few thousand wizards in Sko'Port. You could add another ten thousand or so apprentices, perhaps, out of nearly six million residents. Most of the apprentices have only slight ability, and many will never actively perform Shortcasting."

Seeing her confusion at the term, Atrick expanded. "Shortcasting is the act of casting a spell quickly, or at will. This is versus the more technical casting where you weave the magic slowly over time. Normal spellcasting should be a result of quiet study. It can take hours or even days of meditation. Shortcasting is much faster. It controls the mindful organization of the weave of magic from within us as it swirls. I can do this, for example."

Atrick lifted his left arm and extended his forefinger. The ring there, a smoky pearl the size of a small coin inlaid in a piece of what looked like steel, turned jet black. Rianas marveled at the stunt.

Then the actual magic appeared a few feet away where he was pointing. A translucent white cloud seemed to coalesce from the moisture in the air, glowing as if lightning had flashed and been frozen in time. Even in the full afternoon sun, the head-sized cloud lit up the water and caused Rianas to lift her arm to shade the light.

Arthur exclaimed from the stern, "Wow! Look at that, it's like a giant lightning bug just appeared out of nowhere!" The other men on the deck stopped practicing to look at the ball of light.

Atrick stood calmly now, his smile gone and a look of concentration on his face. He moved his arm, and the lightning ball floated around according to his gesture. "This is a light spell I learned when I was an apprentice. It is one of the first spells a wizard learns. I enchanted a ring to help me cast this spell with very little effort. The ring took months to make, but the 'Shortcasting' of the *Light* spell only took a second. If I stop concentrating, the light will fade very slowly. Without the ring, it would wink out as soon as I stopped weaving it together."

He closed his hand, and the light slowly began to fade as he talked.

"Imagine trying to run a ship with enchantment. There are definitely Sullarian wizards and even some in Sko'Port and elsewhere who *could* do that. But they use their skills for more profitable ventures. And each wizard is skilled in areas he has studied. Certain stones, plants and even animals can increase our power, but it takes time and work. I meditate at least an hour a day to keep my ability sharp."

The books Rianas had read on magic were superficial, written by scholars more interested in the results of the magic than its origins. Atrick's words fascinated her. "Where does the magic come from? Is it something that grows within you, or do you just grasp it from the world around you?"

"Think of magic as a symbiotic creature that grows within you and inside of other creatures and objects. If it is properly nourished, it gets stronger. If it is merely used, it is consumed. Inside most human wizards, magic will grow with repeated use. If we magnify the strength of what we cast with other magical items, we can tap the power more vigorously or consistently. The magic within a wizard is something of a chaotic power. It waits to be weaved together into a spell."

Atrick put both hands out, as if measuring two sides of a scale. "Apprentices weave slowly, as if shaping clay, but a true wizard shapes the magic with gestures, words, and thoughts very quickly. I have learned to cast that light spell with very little effort because it is something I use all the time. Battle mages learn to cast magic that can wield the elements in dangerous ways quickly, and healing mages have learned to weave together healing spells with alacrity. My predecessor, Hasand Therian, could weave spells that increased miners' strength for hours at a time – an interesting twist from other mine wizards who used their magic more directly to rend veins of stone from the walls of the mine."

"Wow." Rianas watched the ball of light shrink to about the size of a fist, slowly losing its brilliance. "You said my ability to speak many languages was magical. Will I be able to weave magic? How long would it take to make a ball of light like that?"

Atrick leaned against the railing and looked overboard, considering. "It would probably take a few weeks. Your ability is unlike anything I have seen in an untrained magic-wielder, so I don't know. You have used your telepathic abilities before without knowing it, I suspect. Normally, it could take a few months to learn enough control to manipulate light. It takes longer to manipulate objects themselves. The light spell takes very little from the surrounding world, but other magic requires us to rearrange the physical world itself.

"If you wanted to cast a spell that was beyond your ability sooner, however, you could use a scroll." Atrick pulled back his robe and produced the sack he had carried with him onto the ship. The gold trim gleamed brighter in the presence of the fading light of the spell Atrick had cast. He pulled the rope that sealed it shut on the top loosely, and then he opened the sack as far as it would go. It was just enough to stick in a large open hand. He touched the gold trim and muttered a few words under his breath. The inside of the sack instantly lit up.

Atrick reached his hand in, a look of concentration on his face. He looked into the sack and said, "Ah, over here," whispered another few words, and then started withdrawing his hand. To Rianas' amazement, he pulled out a scroll nearly as long as the sack. He held it carefully under his right arm as he cinched the sack closed, muttered a few words under his breath, and tucked the sack back under his shirt.

"How did that fit in there? What did you just do?" Rianas asked, agog at the scroll that could not have possibly fit in the small sack while his arm was also in it. "What was that light?"

"Slow down, Rianas. Magic is something I use all the time. The sack is a special spell I devised after speaking with a traveler from the Dwarven Kingdoms about two years ago. It uses magical portals that allow me to connect two parts of the world together. I have a small portal enchanted upon a metal ring in my house, and another in the metal ring on top of the sack. When I open the portal from the sack, I can reach into my storage room. It is really quite helpful for times when I have to pack quickly or if I forget something at home."

Rianas felt as if the whole world was flipping upside down. Nothing she had ever read talked about magic like this. "You can reach across hundreds of miles? You could transport anything you could dream of!"

"Not really. The farthest I have been able to go and open this portal up is only about 100 miles. It takes quite a bit of my power to pull the path together, so I can only keep it open for a minute or so at a time. But think of it more like this: I am transporting only exactly what I need." Atrick saw Rianas staring at the sack. He pulled it out to show to her.

"The gold trim is actually Elvenite, a rare mineral that is often extracted from the bones of magical creatures. The trim for these two rings came from a dragon skeleton found in Gawdich. There was enough left over for me to write about a dozen scrolls. And that is what I planned to show you." Atrick closed up the belt in a 'that is all' manner and took the scroll gently from under his arm.

Rianas immediately saw that the writing on the scroll was different. It glowed with the same gold as the Elvenite on the sack, and the words – more like symbols that wanted to burn into the mind – seemed to shimmer and shift along the page.

Atrick left the scroll rolled up, showing her the words on the outside. Rianas easily read them, "Fire, ice, and air."

Another chuckle from Atrick made Rianas look up at him. "Of course you would be able to read Elven. I'm not sure why I am surprised. The words, are 'ignia, glacia, caelia' in Elven. Much more poetic, I would say. The Elves are the ones who invented what we call 'scrolling.' They have used their ancient magical language to lace the very words of the pages with magic. This particular scroll is a basic power weave used to manipulate some combination of fire, ice, and air. A little thought and some understanding of the weave of magic would allow you to create a ball of fire, perhaps a snowstorm, or a huge gust of wind. I have used this basic power weave many times to cast a spell more powerful than my ability. The words in the scroll, when read, will magnify your power many times.

"The Elven tongue itself is imbued with magic. Speaking the words as written organizes the weave of your magic. Basic scrolls like this are written vaguely enough that you can still weave your own spell from them, but structured enough that you need little skill to do so."

"Could I read some of it?" Rianas wondered aloud.

"You already have," Atrick said. "The title of the scroll is part of the magic. I won't open the scroll up, because each reading removes some of the magic from the page. A skilled wizard can use a scroll like this hundreds or even thousands of times before using up the last of the Elvenite. Someone with my skill level would be lucky to get a hundred readings. You might find yourself so taken by the surge of power you feel that you weave it all into a single spell, thus wasting much of the scroll's potential." Even while saying this, Atrick handed the scroll to Rianas.

Misunderstanding, Rianas drew back slightly. "I couldn't waste your magic like that, Atrick. I imagine Elvenite is terribly expensive."

"I am giving this scroll to you, young lady, not asking you to cast it now. I have others. Consider it a loan you can repay me when you have learned how to use it." Atrick had that friendly smile on his face again, but his eyes spoke of his utter seriousness. "I have trained a few apprentices since becoming a wizard, but I am confident you will one day outshine all of them combined. Do not squander what you have; search for ways you can help the world."

Rianas gently touched the words on the scroll, the gravity of such a gift not lost on even her inexperienced self.

"For now, let's concentrate on your mind-reading skills. Can you give me your hands?" Atrick casually reached out his right hand.

Rianas put the scroll in her side pocket, where she would not be able to easily lose it or sit on it, then placed both hands in Atrick's. Almost immediately, she could feel a jolt run through her, as though she were being connected with Atrick by a link of electricity. Atrick jumped slightly himself. His eyebrows shot up.

Suddenly, she was in a long, narrow hallway. Books filled shelves in the long room that continued in parallel rows from either side of her. A doorway was dozens of feet ahead. Along the shelves every few feet or so were small baubles of light, suspended close to the ceiling. A thick carpet lined the pathway, with a rainbow-like pattern that seemed to be constantly changing.

Atrick was there, too. Rianas knew this without actually seeing him. She looked toward where her body would be and saw nothing. She felt as if she had become an apparition. When Atrick "spoke", it was as if his words were coming from within her mind.

"This is my study in Sko'Port." His words were concrete, tangible. She knew what he was saying without actually hearing it. *"This hall contains thousands of books collected by myself and my family. Some are hundreds of years old. I have read many of them. Find one on the shelf and see if you can read the title."*

Rianas felt herself move as she looked in one direction. She was immediately drawn to a copy of *The Andarian Wheat Mill of Garlian*. Suddenly, it was as if she had read the book in another life. She intrinsically knew the story of the last days of the wheat mill before the Axarean invasion. She felt the panic at the hands of the writer as he described a great fire and the plague of Axarean soldiers riding through Garlian, burning and killing. She knew the feeling of guilt the writer had at surviving the onslaught, and the fear that poured from the pages as he described his harrowing climb through the Black Mountains in the middle of summer, narrowly escaping an angry giant and finding a dragon egg, then rushing down the other side of the mountain to escape various perils. It was as if Rianas had read the entire book just by wanting to identify it.

Suddenly, Rianas was standing by Atrick again on the deck. Or rather, Rianas was standing while Atrick collapsed into a heap at her feet. Rianas grabbed his arm to support him. She leaned him against the railing.

Berryl was at his side only seconds later. He pulled Atrick over to one of the benches, speaking gently into his ward's ear. Teran had aimed his crossbow at Rianas, and she suddenly felt the situation was about to deteriorate further.

"Wait, he fell over when he touched me," Rianas said, her voice quavering. "Somehow he must have transferred knowledge to me, and he passed out."

Rianas saw Atrick slowly coming awake in Berryl's arms. He weakly said something to Berryl, who nodded at Teran.

The immediate danger passed, Rianas looked at Atrick's pale skin. "Are you okay?" she asked.

Atrick's impossibly infectious grin was already returning. Weakly, he lifted his left hand and said, "Remind me not to do that again. I feel like I just got hit in the head with a sack of flour."

"What happened?" asked Arthur, coming up with the other trainees. "Ri', are you alright?"

Rianas nodded her head, feeling the way she always did when she finished a book – slightly introspective and a little disappointed that the read was complete. "I think you showed me a book you had read once. *The Andarian Wheat Mill of Garlian* was quite an adventure, discussing a summer climb through the Black Mountains to escape the Axarean assault on Andaria. I guess I don't need to read my copy now."

With Berryl still mostly supporting him, Atrick nodded weakly. "It is partly my fault. I intended for you to read my mind, not just my thoughts. I opened myself to you. When you reached out, you found an entire novel and took all of it at once. That was quite the sensation, as if you forced me to remember reading a book that I read when I was probably your age. Fascinating!"

Arthur looked at Rianas now. "You stole a book from a wizard's head?" He stood back a little, and then started laughing the way he tended to when something was exciting and made him nervous at the same time. "That's great. Can you read minds, now?"

Rianas was not sure what she could do anymore. Only a day ago she had discovered she could hear the telepathic words of a wizard. Now she had literally shared an old memory with the mage against his will. Before she could answer, Teran walked up on the other trainees and motioned them back toward where they were training.

Berryl asked Atrick what he needed, and he said, "Just a little rest and I'll be fine."

Rianas sat next to Atrick. "I'm sorry," she said. "I didn't intend to hurt you."

"Quite all right. Your latent ability is simply more than I expected. I will need to meditate a little before trying that again, but I think you will be able to use contact telepathy at will with a little training."

Atrick sat up, laughed weakly, and then put his left hand on Rianas' shoulder. "*Heed my advice and keep your ability hidden as much as possible.*

Your raw power will be sought by others." She felt the words course into her.

"Yes", she thought, wondering if he could read her thoughts as well. Atrick smiled and nodded, then suggested they practice telepathically speaking from increasing distances.

For hours, Rianas and Atrick had conversations, mostly about the book she had 'stolen' from Atrick's mind. It was tangible, easy for conversation, and allowed her to focus on the thin tendrils of thought that came from Atrick's mind to hers. Rianas quickly discovered her limit of projection to be only a few feet, but the limit of her telepathic detection was nearly twenty paces.

The two walked slowly around the ship, varying distances while Atrick strove to help Rianas 'see' the weave of the telepathy. He explained how he was practicing telepath, while her skill was a passive skill. He could only keep up a continuous range of telepathy focused on her, but hers grew and shrank as her concentration level changed.

Just before the crew served dinner, Atrick took hold of her hands again. He showed her the feeling of the weave of magic he had cast, this time carefully guiding her to take just the knowledge she needed. Rianas moved slowly, and together they 'sat' in the wizard's study reflecting on the way the weave seemed to hide behind the curtain of sight, almost like a mote of colors just outside her line of vision.

When Atrick released Rianas' hands, he looked drained and tired. He patted her on the shoulder and asked her to practice controlling the weave. "But not tonight. Eat, rest, and be ready for tomorrow. We will land in Sko'Port, and I don't want to take any chances traveling through the Lower Ward."

Rianas ate with the other trainees and spoke with Arthur about the day quietly as they finished their soup. Arthur's eyebrows rose. He asked her to read his mind.

She told him, "No, I don't think you could win a sparring bout with Berryl."

Arthur's mouth opened. "You really can read minds. That's amazing. Think about all the things you could do. And Atrick thinks you could learn magic, too. I better stick close to you, because it sounds like you will be a famous wizard someday."

Rianas laughed. Arthur talked about funny spells she could cast on the various people in Ards. After eating, they all went to bed.

4. SKO'PORT

Rianas slept for a few hours. Well before dawn, she woke up thinking about magic. Knowing how to recognize it now, she felt like it had always been there. It felt like there must be more of the power there now than a few weeks ago.

Rianas tried to grab a tendril of magic. It seemed like there were colorful tendrils floating freely in all directions, but they were just out of sight. For a few moments she struggled, envisioning control as Atrick had shown her. Slowly, a tendril grew tight, and then it started moving toward her line of sight. Just as she thought she had harnessed it, the tendril broke, and both pieces floated off around her head.

She tried, repeatedly, until the first light of day peeked through the flimsy wood door. Each time, the tendril seemed to slip away as she was wrestling it into shape.

Exhausted from the effort of controlling her magic, Rianas came back to the present. That was when she noticed the commotion outside her small door.

As she walked out onto the deck, Rianas felt a strangely cool breeze. She looked over the railing to see half a dozen fishing boats in the distance. A brownish fog hung about five feet off the water. The *Lark's* paddlewheel sloshed more laboriously through the water than the night before, and she could hear crewmembers shouting from the bow.

Suddenly, the ship lurched to a nearly complete stop as the paddlewheel sluggishly changed directions. The wooden paddles creaked loudly. A few seconds later, Rianas could hear wood shearing at the front of the ship. As she looked over the railing, she saw planks of lumber all over in the water. Berryl came into sight on the starboard side, hauling one of the crew members back aboard with a rope he had apparently cut from the safety line that prevented people from falling into the cargo hold. Teran bounded past her from the captain's deck, crossbow in hand. The Assyrian bodyguard ran to the port side and scanned the water along the ship's edge.

Rianas started toward the seating area, buckling on the harness. She could not see anything in the brown fog beyond a few feet. As she came beside Teran, she saw Arthur unstrapping a dagger and looking about, confused. Behind him, Atrick was walking out of his room calmly, with his hands by his side.

"What is going on?" Atrick asked, looking up, then over at Teran.

Teran kept his eyes down, scanning the edge. "A fishing ship just rammed the *Lark*! No one was onboard."

Berryl had pulled the crewmember onboard, and he was examining the water on the starboard side. The rest of the crew was shouting amongst each other as they worked their way toward the stern, looking into the water. Atrick peered into the cargo hold, looking at the water in the bottom and pointing.

"It looks like whoever commandeered that vessel managed to poke a hole in the hull. Rianas, come with me," Atrick said. With more dexterity than Rianas thought possible for a middle-aged man, he jumped over the rope onto a lower stack of barrels in the cargo hold, then used the netting to climb the rest of the way down.

Rianas followed, a little slower. There were already six inches of water on the starboard side. She could feel an obvious list in that direction and she could see the water pooling up. Her hiking boots splashed in the water as she worked her way between barrels toward the bow, a few feet behind Atrick. After a few moments of treading water, she saw the hole. A steel beam was wedged between two slats of the ship, pushing aside the hull and protruding into the ship nearly an arm's length. Water rushed around the sides of the beam in a torrent that could knock a man over.

Atrick looked back at Rianas. "We must act quickly. I will push the beam out so we can start moving again. Keep me from being knocked over into the water. I need to concentrate and I must be close."

Without thinking, Rianas took a bracing stance behind Atrick. Almost immediately, he raised his arms up and uttered a few words in Elven. He pushed at the air in the direction of the beam. The beam, easily weighing more than a draft horse, slid backward slowly until it broke free of the ship, disappearing behind a curtain of even faster-flowing water.

Struggling to keep herself braced against the onslaught of the Sko'Sea, realizing how cold the water had become, Rianas watched as Atrick started another spell. The flow of water turned ice cold. Despite the cold, she could feel heat radiating from his chest as Atrick pushed the flow back.

Three crewmembers had come down. Seeing their chance, they pulled several heavy repair planks along the floor into place and set to work nailing them in immediately. A fourth man appeared a moment later, carrying a small bucket of tar, which he started spreading about on the new planks. As they started sealing up the man-sized hole, Rianas released her grip on Atrick. He was gesturing and mumbling under his breath as he stared at the groaning sheet of ice where water had been pouring in seconds before.

Atrick maintained his spell while the workers hammered in hundreds of nails. Rianas could barely believe only ten minutes had passed.

Some water came in, but two of the crewmembers immediately took to the bilge pump while the other two started adding a few more pieces of repair lumber. Atrick smiled wearily and released his spell. He started toward the deck, motioning Rianas to follow him.

Up on deck, the brown fog had started to lift. The cause of the fog sat about half a mile away off the stern, where dozens of fishing boats seemed to have been nestled together and set afire. Most had already started to capsize, and they had spread out over a half-mile or more. Looking off the port, Rianas could see three other burning ships slowly sinking into the water, as if they had sailed that way while on fire.

"Someone hijacked those ships in an effort to take down the

Lark," Berryl said, pointing across the port. "My guess is they knew we were coming and waited out there. Then they sent as many ships as they could in our direction. They had to know it would not work. Those ships are so much smaller; they could barely damage the *Lark.*"

Atrick nodded thoughtfully. "I think it was a delaying tactic. If they managed to stop us out here for a day, it could make a pretty big difference. With such a small crew, the *Lark* would be the perfect target. Even without the current cargo, the ship would be worth hijacking. Imagine the power of a pirate ship this size that could outrun the Sko'Port navy."

The ship's captain was on the deck now. "There were three ships we passed just before entering the fog. As soon as we entered, they started following us. They are only a quarter mile behind us now. You seem to have been right to suggest we maintain speed through the fog, Teran. Thank you." The paddlewheels had already started spinning again.

The immediate excitement abated nearly an hour later as the sun rose over the mountains that now blocked the sky to the east. The ships that had been following broke off when two ships from the Sko'Port navy sailed warily past the *Lark.* Rianas watched the much smaller, heavily armed craft, marveling at the ballistae sitting on turntables at the front and rear of each vessel. The captain spoke quickly to the captain of the second ship before having the *Lark* steam onward.

With the sun, the city of Sko'Port began to take shape in the distance. Still many miles away, there were ships everywhere now. Most were small fishing ships, but some were larger sailing ships off to trade with Gawdich in the west or Cidvag in the east. Rianas spied another Riverrun ship in the distance. It was easy to spot with its telltale trail of black smoke and lack of sails.

The city took Rianas' breath away. It stretched along the coast for miles in either direction. Even from this distance, she could see the broad avenues, hundreds of yards long, stretching straight through the city every mile or so. Towers in the central part of the city seemed to be miles tall because of the way the city crawled up the mountains.

Arthur walked up beside her, sweating from working the bilge pump. "It's amazing a city so huge is so close to Riverrun, yet so few of our people ever go to see it. My parents never took me, and no one in school has ever been. I hope we have some time to walk around when we get there. I'd like to try some of that famous fried meat on a stick the dockworkers always talk about."

Rianas laughed lightly. "There are so many buildings. The main library there is dozens of times larger than the central Riverrun library. It has texts from long before the Andarian war. There is even a section in Elven that the wizards use for research."

Arthur jabbed her lightly with his elbow. "Yeah, and meat on a stick."

Before lunch, the *Lark* was pulling into a maze of docks protruding half a mile from the shore. Rianas could see hundreds of vessels, some with ten and twelve masts, while the vast majority had only one or two. Dock attendants helped guide the *Lark* into the end of the dock next to a large yacht. Men and women all along the docks came running up pushing handcarts, and a set of six giant horses pulling a long wagon with over a dozen wheels rolled up.

The head dockworker, a huge man covered in yellow tassels that seemed to accentuate his weight, barreled aboard with three small, dark-skinned men carrying folders full of parchment. After a few moments speaking with the captain, he instructed the workers on what to take where. Then, he exchanged some papers for a sack of what Rianas could only assume was Gold Eagles, and left quickly for the next location. In no time, there were dozens of men lifting heavy barrels into place. Workers wheeled around a massive crane on a turntable in the center of this section of dock. Within minutes, it was lifting pallets out one by one.

Atrick motioned Arthur and Rianas over to the rest of the group. John and Samuel were likewise staring at the fast-moving army of loaders and workers, but Atrick brought everyone in focus by giving instructions. The trainees could take their time getting up to his manor at the High Mine, but this evening the first interviews would start.

While Berryl and Teran discussed a few landmarks they thought Rianas, Arthur, Samuel and John would want to see, Rianas read Atrick's telepathic admonishment.

"Be careful out here," he said. *"Don't trust the lower guard, and stay to the main roads. Feel free to explore, but keep the other trainees out of trouble. I will see you this evening, Rianas. We will be working for hours to question new recruits, so do not run around all day."*

Atrick's manor was in the height of the city. From here, that was nearly three miles, much of it up the steep, sloping streets that zigzagged up the mountains. There were thousands of stairs to traverse on the way up. At the end of each long stretch of road before the turn, there would be a five to ten story drop. Up against the brick wall, there were rope elevators for heavy equipment and those in a hurry.

Atrick explained briefly how to use the system to travel up the mountain faster. He gave some directions for finding his manor. Then he climbed aboard the front of the horse train. It had been loaded with his personal goods from the *Lark's* cargo hold, and he seemed eager to be on his way.

As Atrick rode off down the dock, Arthur elbowed John in the side. He pointed excitedly down the dock at a row of vendors. Rianas laughed and joined the other three as they strolled up the dock, noting dozens of vendors with small carts offering a wide range of culinary treats. There were vendors selling everything from Gawdichian sweet breads to Sullarian dried cherries. Every other stall had skewers with foot-long tails of what each vendor called "mine lizards." They were seasoned and blackened, then cut into pieces and stabbed with skewers of wood for serving.

It took five minutes of rushing stall to stall for Arthur to attain a handful of different "meat on a stick", as he was calling it. He tasted each one, then offered a bite to the rest of the party, extolling the "sweet flavor", "spicy heat", or "tangy aftertaste" of each as he tasted it.

John bought some Sullarian cherries, while Samuel joined Arthur sampling the local delicacy. Rianas' surroundings impressed her so much that she merely took a few flavorful bites of the lizard tail as

Arthur offered them.

The vendors on the dock occupied a narrow center aisle, but as the four got closer to the land, the aisles on either side grew more packed with thousands of pedestrians and hand-carts wheeling goods to and from the docked ships. The smell of fish was everywhere down here, mixed with garbage. There were street lamps hung between stalls along the center of the dock every couple hundred feet, bright even in the daylight with a magical glow. Every few moments, another set of horse-drawn carts would barrel down the aisle-way, with a man or woman up front yelling at the slower pedestrians who got in their way.

Everywhere she looked, there was something to steal her attention. Sko'Port was not only huge; the city itself seemed to be moving everywhere she glanced.

As they got to land and navigated an ad hoc intersection to cross the street, Rianas could see the dockside warehouses. Nearly a dozen grey-skinned giants twice the height of a man lifted entire barrels with their muscular upper arms onto storage shelves. Oxen taller than Arthur plodded down the roadway, carrying huge loads of cotton, wood, and foodstuffs directly on their backs in wide, netted bags. Others used carts and horses. A dwarf counted ingots of iron and copper lined up on the ground. He occasionally scratched at an ingot with a tool in his hands before resuming his count. There were thousands of people on this main artery of Sko'Port, moving goods further up the mountain or bringing them down to waiting ships.

Four men in black uniforms buttoned up the front, carrying crossbows over their shoulders and swords at their waists, were coming down the street from the west. Rianas immediately saw the seal of Sko'Port on the decorative capes they wore, even from the distance. The throng of people parted around them, giving a wide berth as they marched single file down the road and turned onto the dock Rianas and the others had just left.

Arthur, licking his lips and depositing the bones from one of the lizard tails into a nearby trash bin, looked back at the soldiers. "Those men have the insignia of the Sko'Port guard. I like the uniforms. Do you think they came to escort Atrick back to his manor? He seems pretty important around here."

Rianas considered. "I don't know. But they don't look very friendly. Maybe we should head up the hill a way. We could visit the library, or watch one of the boulder-slides. Also, there is a bazaar about a mile up that way." Rianas pointed at a huge sign painted onto the side of the warehouses they were walking between.

The sign read *"Wizard's Corner Bazaar: Trinkets, Clothes, and Enchantments from Around the Continent"*. It was written in Gawdichian, with Northern in small words underneath. The wall-sized painting pictured swirling stars, glowing clothing, and a pickaxe with a lightning bolt blowing apart a boulder.

John, spitting out a cherry pit, said it sounded like a fun sightseeing detour on their way up the mountain. Samuel said he would like to find an enchanted light to bring on the expedition. To that, everyone agreed.

They started climbing the gently sloping, curved road around the dockside warehouses onto one of the main twisting arteries of the city. Stone buildings with shops on the first floor lined the brick-laid street. Sewer grates dotted the side of the street, and the buildings were dizzyingly tall on the uphill side. Some towered like cliffs above them, with front walls supported by beams built into the side of the mountain. On the other side, doors opened into upper levels of warehouses or onto rooftop stores or shops. The slope of the road was even and easy to traverse, but where it turned to the right to go uphill a quarter mile ahead, the slope was visibly steeper.

This road was just as busy as the first. Large workhorses and people pushing handcarts stayed in the center lanes, while pedestrians walked briskly on the sides of the wide street. For midday, the weather was cool, and some families gathered at outdoor eating areas or looked through windows at clothing stores.

With the bazaar in mind, the four Riverrunners walked briskly, trying to stay out of the way of the press of people. As they got to the turn, the road opened up. A short line of horse carts and well-dressed older men were waiting at a cargo elevator, where a dozen large men in bright purple, loose fitting uniforms took turns working pulleys to move a huge lift up the steep ridge.

The pulleys noisily lashed about each time the elevators started moving. As one elevator reached the top, another platform gently landed near where the first had taken off. Rianas could see people getting off up above, one hundred feet higher.

John spit out another cherry pit and exclaimed, "That is the way to travel. You could see the water for miles from up there, I'd bet." He walked up to talk with the clerk and hire them a ride.

Arthur threw away the last bones from his meal and gestured inconspicuously down the hill where they had started and looked at Rianas, his eyebrows raised as if to say, "Look."

Suddenly, it was as if she knew what he was thinking. "*The guards from before just came around those warehouses we walked between. They're talking to vendors. I think they're looking for us.*" It was as clear as day. Just thinking about what he was thinking had taken his thoughts for her.

Rianas stared a little, which made Arthur start to open his mouth, but she cut him off with a finger to her lips. "I see them, too. I think they are following us."

Samuel, standing on her other side staring at the lift, looked over questioningly. Arthur gestured, this time with just his eyes, and said what he had been thinking. Samuel looked over Arthur's shoulders and shrugged. "Maybe someone wants to meet us. Shall we wait?"

"I don't think so," Rianas said quietly, pretending not to watch the four men as they made their way through the crowd in their general direction. One of the men broke off and spoke briefly with a tailor they had passed. The tailor gestured vaguely in the direction of the elevators. All three of them made up their minds when the guard looked in their general direction, then pointed and broke into a slow jog, pushing a pedestrian to the ground as he started up the hill.

"Maybe we should take the turn here and walk up the hill?" said Samuel. He looked visibly worried as he unconsciously stepped back. "I don't think I want them catching up with us. What did we do wrong?"

John came back with four copper tokens. "That was easy. We are on the next elevator. I guess pedestrian traffic is a lot lighter than those carts so they let us on with the guys pushing all those boots in the cart. What is going on?"

Arthur showed John the four guards loping quickly up the street now. They were closing the distance fast, only a few minutes away. With all the foot traffic on the street, the guards had not spotted them yet. Even so, Rianas pulled Arthur and Samuel to the other side of the cart full of boots. "Atrick said we shouldn't trust the lower guards in Sko'Port. He thinks there are dangerous agents in their ranks. I say we should get to the Upper Ward as quickly as we can."

Just as she was speaking, she saw the lead guard draw his weapon from his cloak, pointing it at a man on the street corner. The man waved in their direction. Now the other guards drew their weapons as well. They pushed an elderly man walking down the street to the side roughly and broke into a trot. Now they forced a horse-drawn cart to drive out of their way and trotted into the main part of the street.

The elevator operator motioned the next group on. The four got on quickly, hiding inconspicuously behind the cart, and waited for the elevator to start moving. With a lurch, the pulleys began pulling them almost vertically up the ledge, just as the guards were closing the couple hundred feet to the elevator.

About halfway up, the first guard reached the elevator operator.

The operator spoke calmly with the guard. Suddenly, he put his arm up to shield against a blow from the pommel of the guard's sword. Rianas could not hear the conversation, but the rest of the people in the line scattered, trying to get out of the way. Suddenly, the workers stopped operating the elevator, and the moving platform came to a halt. A few of the men picked up chairs and stones as weapons, and the largest one shouted at the guards, "I think you've come far enough. There is no call for violence here today, Randor."

Randor – the head guard – snarled at him, "If you allowed those foreigners through here, I will find out about it, Groble. I would hate for something awful to happen to your son on his way back from the mines next week."

The large elevator operator took a few steps forward, a dagger in his hands. The other operators fanned out around him, makeshift weapons raised up. For a moment, it looked like the guards might attack them. Two of the guards shifted their crossbows into their arms menacingly. The fourth guard had his sword in front of him. Randor stared a few seconds before looking up at the elevator where Rianas hid. Then he lowered his weapon slightly and motioned to the others, before turning and jogging up the steep walkway that led up the hill. The other guards holstered their weapons and followed after him.

Rianas stared after the guards, wondering why these soldiers would be after them. Samuel, who had casually drawn his hand crossbow to his side, slid it back in his holster. John let his hand fall off the dagger at his waist. It appeared they had just avoided being caught. It would be another quarter mile before the guards could get to the top of this ledge.

After helping up their ticket-operator, the elevator operators worked the pulleys again, sending the elevator to the top of the ledge.

The four shaken Riverrunners rushed off, avoiding the questioning gaze of the man pushing the boot cart.

Samuel pointed to an alleyway. "Let's get off the main streets. Maybe we can avoid those guards altogether."

The others agreed. They walked quickly into a side street and turned down another alleyway. After walking generally southward toward the higher side of the mountains for about ten minutes, they slowed down a little. There were very few people out on these side streets. An occasional fig tree or spot of grass on landings to homes told Rianas they were in a residential part of the city, but for the most part, stone buildings surrounded them on either side. On the northern sides of these alleys, there were steps or even steep walls to the next street down. Arthur stopped at one of the landings for a minute to adjust his pack. While he was adjusting it, Samuel peered down at the lower street.

Suddenly, he pulled away from the wall. "It looks like the guards split up. One of them is heading to the next landing."

"This is our chance to see what they want," said Arthur. "Rianas, stand in that doorway there. Samuel and I will meet him. John, hide behind that wall across the street."

John dashed off and Rianas slid into the stone doorway, while Samuel and Arthur took up casual poses in the middle of the street. Arthur pretended to be adjusting his pack, and Samuel stood over him.

A few moments later, the guard approached them.

Rianas could not see very well from her position. The guard had his sword out as he trotted up. "Stop where you are. Put your daggers and bows on the ground."

Arthur feigned astonishment. "What have we done?" he asked, putting his dagger gently on the ground. Samuel pulled his crossbow out in a non-threatening manner, placing it in front of him as well.

"Where are the other two?" The guard gave no explanation as he kicked the weapons away with his feet. The entire time, he kept his sword between himself and Arthur. Samuel edged slightly off to the side, keeping his hands out to either side of his body. Arthur stood slowly.

"They went back down the elevator to get lunch," Arthur lied easily. "Is something wrong? We are here visiting our friend up in the mines."

"You came with Atrick. Don't try lying to me, young man. We don't need that wizard recruiting mercenaries." Rianas felt the hairs on her neck stand up as she watched the man. "Maybe if I kill every one of you little shits, Randor will pay me handsomely. Atrick will pay for pushing us out of the Upper Ward."

The guard pressed forward, clearly intending to stab Arthur in the stomach. As he lunged, Samuel kicked out with his leg, pushing the man off balance. Arthur leapt back, drawing his second dagger from his leg strap. Rianas immediately jumped from around the stone entryway, drawing the dagger Arthur had given her. John stepped out as well.

The guard saw he was surrounded, but pressed the attack. He raised his sword again, pressing toward Samuel with a guttural cry. Samuel jumped to the side, causing the guard to turn his back to Arthur. With amazing speed, Arthur moved forward and grabbed the guard's sword arm. John punched him in the side of the head, and Rianas grabbed his other arm before he could reach his short sword.

A few moments of tense wrestling ensued. The four Riverrunners disarmed the guard and avoided punches from his spiked gloves as best as they could. Rianas pulled the guard's arm behind his body while Samuel pushed his head onto the brick road of the alleyway. Arthur finally removed the guard's last dagger and crossbow while John held a dagger to the guard's back and told him to lay still.

"You fools! Randor will find you and kill you." The guard was shouting. Amazingly, no one had come out of the surrounding buildings.

Arthur started tugging on the guard's cloak, removing it completely. He took one of the guard's leather straps, pulled it around the man's mouth and strapped it on the other side of his neck.

Now he gagged loudly, struggling against the four even more as Arthur continued taking the man's clothes off. Briefly, he was laying on the bricks in no more than undergarments. John nodded when Arthur held the cloak up to show it was his size. The Ards farmer put it on over his other clothes. He slid his pack down to the ground.

Rianas did not know what Arthur's plan was, but she quickly tied the guard's arms together behind his back with his belt. Then, she used the lace from a boot to tie his legs together. It would not last long, but the bindings might buy them enough time to get further up the hill to someplace safer. When she finished, she saw John belting the man's long sword and short sword to his waist.

Arthur looked at Rianas and said, "I think we need to get to the Upper Ward as quickly as we can."

The adrenaline was running through her veins, and she nodded.

"Why take his uniform?" she asked as they dragged the still-struggling guard into a doorway. Together, they tied him up more securely to a metal handrail with rope from John's pack.

"It may draw unwanted attention, but perhaps it will slow the other three down since they will need to take care of this one." He motioned to the guard who was now completely restrained.

Rianas nodded. The four dashed into the side streets again, trying to put as much distance between them and the guard as they could without breaking into a run.

Within a few minutes, they came up a walkway and saw the main thoroughfare again. This time, it led into the bazaar they had seen advertised earlier. Thousands of men and women in colorful outfits shopped amongst the one and two-story stalls on what was a huge, flat, if somewhat sloped, fairground. Most of the stalls looked permanent here. Handcarts selling meats, foods, and small trinkets lined the outside edges of the street.

John took the guard uniform off and threw it into a basement doorway. The four Riverrunners quickly dashed across the street behind a lumbering cart pulled by oxen, trying to draw as little attention as possible.

A vendor looked up and threw his hands in the air as they got to the other side, offering a "fine assortment of Runlarian dancing shoes." Rianas smiled and pretended to shop for a moment before following the other three further into the bazaar.

Within moments, the mood between the four got less tense.

The crowd was dressed in all manner of working, casual, and fine clothing. It was apparent that their appearance would not draw any attention. Just to be safe, John and Samuel bought overcoats. Rianas found a pair of leather trousers she thought would work for hiking. They all looked completely different after visiting a couple clothing shops.

"I can't believe we did that," John said as Rianas and Arthur came back from scouting the next alley of the bazaar. "That guard wanted to kill you. He didn't even wait for an explanation of why we were here."

Rianas briefly and quietly told the others what Atrick had said about the lower guards being compromised. Samuel cursed under his breath, but John no longer seemed surprised. Then Arthur chuckled and pointed to a larger building two blocks away. Dozens of small metal poles with lamps hanging down fronted the store.

"It looks like we found what brought us here in the first place," he said. "We might as well get what we came for before we head out."

Arthur started loping toward the building, shaking his head as he went.

Inside the building, there was a very small person twisting copper wires around a decorative street lamp. Two young men sat at a large table in the center of the room, with a well-dressed woman in front of them discussing the shape of a lamp she was ordering. The room was smoky, and a whole wall of oil lanterns flickered as they entered.

The tiny person looked up, and Rianas saw it was not a human but an elderly elf. Her legs barely supported her despite her tiny frame, and she grabbed a crutch to help her way over to them. In a beautifully fragile voice, she asked, "Have you come to see my lights?"

Arthur said they were going hiking in one of the mines and asked what the elf might have. The little elf smiled and told them to follow her. She hobbled carefully between lamps to the rear of the store. There were rows of shelves full of white stones with bone, wood, and decorative handles. Little velvet curtains obscured the contents of two shelves. Inside one of the curtains, a single stone hung from a cord, brightly illuminating the shelves with a rich white light.

"These are my famous hand lamps. The sleeves are shaped so you can carry them to light your way without getting blinded." The elf leaned against a post and picked one of the stones up by a handle, pushing the handle and stone together until the stone began to glow brightly. "There is a piece of enchanted dragon bone on the end of each handle. If you push them together, you can release the light. The enchantment lasts for five to six months, depending on how long you use it each day. To preserve the light, you pull the handle away from the stone." She demonstrated by pulling on the stone to release it. She showed the leather straps made for holding the lights in the on and off position, then said she was selling them for four Gold Eagles apiece.

"That is really expensive," said Arthur, looking into his coin pouch. Samuel walked to another part of the store to buy an oil lantern and John shook his head before following. Rianas, however, was intrigued. She quietly found a comfortable hand lamp and paid for it before stowing it away and joining the others. Arthur's eyes went up when he saw Rianas pay, but he said nothing to the others.

After shopping for a few minutes, each of them found something they thought would work. Rianas bought a small cooking lamp and some oil as well. The four of them left the shop happily, but Rianas did not participate in John's conversation about the expensive enchanted lights.

The four Riverrunners walked casually up another street of the bazaar, purchasing things they thought were useful for their trip. After another hour of shopping, they stole across the upper avenue, took another elevator up, and walked into the Upper Ward.

There was not much immediately different in the architecture between the Upper and Lower Wards of Sko'Port. Casual observers would not have noticed the change. However, the streets were narrower, the crowds were smaller, and the buildings started to take on more architecturally challenging aesthetics.

A wizard's shop adorned with gold-colored stones sat across the street. Horse drawn carts drove by more frequently now. Wizard's apprentices strolled along the avenue, too. They were easy to spot with their colorful velvet capes. The apprentices carried books, scrolls, and various small items. Even the Riverrunners sensed the palpable difference among the pedestrian traffic.

The cacophony of the huge boulder-slide nearly a mile away interrupted Rianas' examination of the avenue. She could just make out the man-sized boulders sliding down a chute as the huge boulder-slide directed them down to the Sko'Sea. Samuel pointed to a building along the boulder-slide, about a quarter mile up the hill. That would be the entrance to the High Mine. Just to the east of that was Atrick's manor.

The four walked more easily on the streets now.

As the sun started to duck around the buildings to the west, they came to a walled complex with apple and plum trees barely visible on the other side. Brick siding topped with iron spikes lined the wall. A thin strip of grass in front brightened it up. An entry gate with guards standing on either side was in the middle of the wall. The symbol for the High Mine — two triangles within a bright golden circle — adorned the center of the ten-foot tall gate.

Rianas introduced herself to one of the guards, who looked at a roster before opening a side gate for the four to enter.

Atrick's manor was a red brick building large enough to house ten families. The yard was short, but full of winding pathways leading to trees of various shapes and sizes. Two pecans framed the main doorway.

The view to the west drew Rianas' attention, however. The right side of the yard sloped quickly down, affording a full view of a giant hole in the ground in the staging yard beyond. The mine entrance yawned nearly a hundred feet in diameter. Miners had carved the opening at a forty-five degree angle to the earth. Huge iron carts slid along tracks to carry various stones toward warehouses further down the mountain. All the grass and trees had been removed further down. Dozens of workers maneuvered the great iron carts between the warehouses, using oxen in some places.

From the road, very little sound had carried up. Here, however, the mine opening's bowl shape magnified the sound. As they walked toward the edge, Rianas could hear men yell instructions while others tallied their carts on huge chalkboards. With the sun getting lower in the sky, a crew of miners was walking the perimeter to set up lamps for the evening.

Above the mine, two dozen soldiers stood guard in a small stone building, huge crossbows on iron pivots pointed lazily in the air, but the soldiers stood at complete attention. In a clearing beyond them, further up the hill, an encampment was taking shape, with a few soldiers taking inventory and organizing the growing tent city. Some men were setting up dozens of small tents and others were lighting campfires.

Samuel pointed out Berryl in the tent city, and the three men excused themselves to report what had happened that day. Rianas said she had to speak with Atrick, and went back toward the manor.

Apparently, Teran had been watching from a window. As soon as Rianas walked up to the manor, he opened the massive oak front door. "Atrick is waiting for you upstairs. I will bring you." Teran did not speak another word as he turned inside.

The inside of the manor was full of bright yellow and blue patterned tiles, with a mixture of porcelain and wood paneling lining the walls. Thick wooden furniture adorned the entry room, while wall hangings covered most of the open spaces. There were tapestries of Sko'Port, colorful renditions of the mine, and paintings of people whose faces were universally older but otherwise showed no visible relation to Atrick.

Teran motioned Rianas up a narrow stone staircase to the second floor. A hall to the right full of books made her do a double take. She realized she had been there before in Atrick's mind. It brought the reality of the last two days into focus as she walked toward the door at the end.

Teran opened the door, letting the light from the sun into the hallway. Atrick was behind a large desk in the corner, staring out in the direction of the mine. An out-of-place utilitarian chair sat in the middle of the room. Large lamps lit each corner of the room.

Atrick looked over and smiled at Rianas. *"How was your trip?"* he asked clearly. Rianas read the telepathic projection with ease now.

Teran nodded and turned to leave. Atrick stopped him and said, "Bring up the recruits when you are ready. We will take three or four at a time until an hour after the dinner call."

Rianas talked for a few minutes about their experience in the Lower Ward. Atrick listened seriously. He laughed, however, when he heard they had stolen the guard's uniform. "I suspect this Lieutenant Randor has come after me before. This is serious, however. Corrupt guards working in daylight, threatening elevator operators and moving around the city with no check to their abuse of power implies a truly weakened lower guard. Fortunately, the others who I have recruited would be simply replying to flyers. I am so sorry your first experience in this beautiful city was tainted in that way."

"I have read Arthur's mind now, twice." Rianas took a footstool near Atrick to sit down, removing her boots to rub her feet.

"You will likely continue to develop new skills without much control over how they manifest – or even when – for some time," Atrick said, nodding. "I remember a young apprentice who began setting small fires against his will when he turned twenty. The poor man kept lighting scrolls and books afire when he would be agitated or run into problems with his studies. It took him a year before he could master it. He is one of the best pyromancers in Assyria today, from what I hear.

"Magic feeds off of our bodies, you see. It is a symbiotic relationship, obviously. Most humans find their magic manifesting itself as they mature into adults. As we age, it is like a muscle that develops. It strengthens with use. If you feed magic, it grows. If it is meditated upon, its finesse can be improved."

Rianas wondered what other skills she might find next, but as she started to speak, Teran opened the door and ushered in a middle-aged woman and two young men in mine uniforms. "These are the first three, sir. I will be right outside."

Atrick chuckled. "Teran is a very devoted man, but his people skills are not that great. Please, each of you take a seat outside. I have just a few questions to ask you and then we will let you get back to camp so you can prepare for tomorrow. Ma'am, I'll speak with you first, if you would sit in the chair over here."

The two men went back into the hallway. Atrick looked at Rianas as he grabbed a piece of rope she had not seen tied loosely around the chair. "*This rope will heat up if it senses a lie. I need you to ask a few questions. They are written on this paper right here.*"

The woman sat uncomfortably in the plain chair. She was slightly nervous, but her eyes were steely. "My husband hasn't come home from the High Mine in eight days. I plan to follow you into that cave whether you want me to or not."

Atrick stared and nodded. "I am so sorry you have had to wait for the rest of this group to gather. Please, send in the next man."

Rianas had only just picked up the page. "I didn't ask the questions," she said.

Atrick shook his head as the woman left. "She was telling the truth. I will need help with the ones who don't speak Northern. I hope we find her husband."

The next man came in. Rianas asked four questions. "What is your most comfortable language? Can you see the cave out there? Where did you hear about this expedition? Are you here to help us?"

"Northern, yes. A poster, yes." She heard those answers over and over. A few dozen Cidvagian mercenaries spoke Runlarian, Assyrian, or Gawdichian dialects. A few more had heard by word of mouth in a tavern about the expedition. Some young miners knew first hand that miners were missing. Rianas asked the same questions for hours.

Three similar looking men came towards the end. Each man had tattoos across his face and arms, and their native language was one she had never heard before. Rianas easily spoke with them, wondering about the strangely guttural words and their heavy use of sharp sounds. Atrick was impressed with them.

"Those were westerners," he said. "I rarely see them in Sko'Port. They have to travel across the Borsilkian Alliance or through the Elven Empire, then across the southern border of Gawdich to get here. The tribes and small nations in the far west train great warriors. They're a little hard to get along with, though."

For another hour they questioned people. Atrick sent two men and one woman away, asking Teran to inform the guard captain when he did. Rianas saw nothing unusual about any of them.

The sun was truly setting behind the Black Mountains now. The temperature had dropped a few degrees, and Atrick pointed to a fireplace in the corner. He spoke a few words and motioned with a finger. Rianas watched in amazement as a few pieces of tinder lit up and started to burn evenly.

Teran came in. "That is all of them, Atrick. The cooks have finished dinner if you'd like some sent up."

Atrick offered some to Rianas as well, then walked over to the fireplace, gesturing her to follow. "Are you still up for this adventure?"

She nodded.

"There are not enough people out there. We've only attracted about three hundred men and women. Most of them are only amateur adventurers, probably brought here by the money more than anything else. Only about a third of them are trained."

Atrick sighed, "We are going to put them into harm's way." The mage stoked the flames with a poker before turning to her. His face seemed that of a wizened old man with the flickering shadows dancing across his wrinkles. Streaks of Atrick's hair gleamed almost white in the light, and lines of worry stretched from his eyes down to his chin.

"There is a text," he said. Suddenly a book was in his hand, as if he had been holding it there the entire day. It was a small book, just a few dozen pages, with a wooden cover blackened with carbon as if from a fire. It fit almost completely in his hand. He flicked it open with his left hand and gently manipulated through a few pages.

"Do you know much of Riverrun's history, Rianas?"

She recounted what she knew. A textbook description of Riverrun said the nation had formed when the refugees from the Axarean war with Andaria fled through the Gates of Cidvag. The survivors negotiated with the Runlarians and Gawdichians to establish their new homeland. The fertile Anasko River had been abandoned by Cidvagian farmers after a year of awful flooding. The Cidvagians agreed to cede the territory, and it became the new nation of Riverrun. The Borsilkian Alliance had provided enough funds and workers to open the Ards port and help build the University.

"Yes", Atrick said, waving his hand dismissively, "but there is more than that. Everything you recounted happened nearly 45 years ago, when I was a very young boy. I still remember the thousands of ships setting off to ferry Andarian survivors from Cidvag to what is now Riverrun – most of them against their will. That tiny hamlet grew in size to a nation within a few months. Probably a million men, women, children, and everything they could carry settled along the lower Anasko River. Cidvag refused to take any but the strongest warriors from the refugees. Assyria closed its borders to refugees completely. The Runlarians took in traders and tradesmen, but they politely 'relocated' the rest back to Riverrun a few months after it was created. It was a terrible couple of years. The Sullarians eventually traded millions of Gold Eagles' worth of supplies to various groups to help set the new nation on a path toward prosperity.

"This is the *Andarian Prophecy*," Atrick continued. "It was written five years after the fall of Andaria. The prophet Harbinas wrote the *Andarian Prophecy* just as those refugees started to settle in Riverrun. Here is a copy I attained a few years ago." Atrick handed her the book opened to the passage he had found. "Please, read it aloud."

Rianas looked at the old paper. The Elven words gleamed like gold on the page where a scribe had painstakingly copied symbols he probably could not even read. For Rianas, however, the text jumped out at her clear as day. *"Chased on sea, chased on land, she gathers her army and fights through the mountain. She brings the voice back to her people."*

Atrick chuckled. "I had read it as 'fights the mountain.' Your translation is ironic considering where we are going." He chuckled to himself as he thought about her words. Then he said, "I think Harbinas is speaking of you."

Rianas laughed a little uncomfortably. "Surely not. I wasn't even born, and you said yourself this book was written forty five years ago."

Atrick shook his head and turned the page back. "Perhaps I should have had you read the beginning of the section."

"Speaking tongues; in their minds; a new leader of Andaria is born at home and far away," Rianas read. "That is pretty vague. I don't know that I would pay much heed to prophecy. My father always says prophets are what we call people who guess about the future so much and so vaguely they eventually get it right."

Atrick smiled. "I've heard that many times. Harbinas has been writing these short books of prophecy for over five hundred years, though. This one only has a few pages about a war to retake Andaria, presumably from the Axareans. It is worth considering, Rianas. I used the prophecies in this book pertaining to Sko'Port to my advantage when I started helping the Upper Ward clear out their ranks of unsavory elements a couple years ago.

"What I truly fear, however, is that the prophecy comes to pass as it is. It predicted a disease would fall on the protectors of Sko'Port, and that disease could tear apart the city from within. It also predicts a great war is coming that could reshape the entire Great Continent."

Atrick sighed and looked out the window. "Of course, it doesn't take a Prophet to predict war with Axarea; in the past fifty years they have won ground against the western wilds, the Borsilkian Alliance, and even the Dwarven Kingdoms. A foothold north of the Black Mountains would give them the ability to bring war to the entire Northern Realms."

Rianas sat back. Teran brought in two huge plates of food,

covered with vegetables, a fish stew, and Gawdichian sweet tarts. She and Atrick ate silently for a few moments, then she said, "Will the Upper Ward send its guards into the mine to reinforce it, or must you use mercenaries?"

Atrick nodded. "Eventually they will. Maddox Oren is the Captain of the Upper Ward Guard. He agreed with my request when I spoke with him this afternoon. Unfortunately, I must provide evidence there is some sort of coordinated attack, first. Lord Cerric has said he needs the guards patrolling the streets as long as they can. I think he fears ceding some control to the lower guards if he sends a small army of Upper Ward guards into the mountain. That is why I used my own funds to purchase those weapons in Riverrun. I assume your father will find a way to direct that shipment here.

"If the Riverrunners can get weapons to the Upper Ward as I requested," Atrick said, "I should be able to convince Guard Captain Maddox Oren to send half a legion into the mine. Better armaments would make his men less vulnerable to 'mysterious disappearances' in the city, and he could remove some men from the streets for a few weeks if that was what it took."

He discussed logistics for the trip into the mine for the rest of the meal. Atrick did not want to wait much longer, so he would lead the mercenaries in early the next morning. They would go straight to the end of the mine where the exploratory party had gone missing. Atrick felt confident they could get to where the miners went missing in about two days.

Rianas enjoyed the fruit juice and fresh vegetables Atrick's cook had served with the meal. She stuffed the hard sweet bread into a pocket for the trip the next day at Atrick's urging. Despite her fear, Rianas felt a strange excitement about entering the mine. Atrick's laugh was infectious, and she found herself smiling by the time she was mopping up the last of her dinner.

Teran and Berryl joined them as Rianas finished her meal. Berryl made light of how some mercenaries had prepared for cave diving, while Atrick instructed them to provide daggers to whoever needed them. Teran silently finished his own meal. When he was done, he informed Atrick that the suspicious mercenaries had been apprehended.

One of the men Atrick identified had been carrying poison-tipped darts in his travel bag from Assyria. When the lieutenant started asking questions, the Assyrian had tried to stab one of the other guards to escape. The guards killed the assassin in the resulting scuffle. There was a folded parchment identifying Atrick in his bag, along with the poison.

Atrick took it in stride, thanking Teran for the help. Then he asked Teran to show Rianas to the guest quarters. "Tomorrow," he said, "we will leave an hour after sunrise. I will speak to the volunteers before we enter the tunnel. Once we get underway, the two of us can meditate some more together."

Rianas followed Teran to a guest room. Like the other rooms of this house, the walls were covered in tapestries depicting different parts of Sko'Port. Rianas looked into a mirror on the wall and yanked on her curly hair. It was knotted from the events of the past few days. She washed her face and hair in the basin, combed her hair out, and wrapped it up so it would not get in the way. The day had been long. Within seconds of lying on the oversized, plush bed, she was asleep.

5. THE HIGH MINE

The entrance to the High Mine was well traversed. Nearly five thousand workers walked through the entrance at every staggered shift change. Even more remained underground for days at a time.

Throughout the day huge rail cars would run down the main track. Noisy iron brakes slowed trains of twenty cars or more. The warehouses brimmed with thousands of tons of raw stone, separated by material type. Coal, iron, salts, copper, and even gold came out. Warehouse guards and headmasters organized and accounted for the materials.

Men occasionally tumbled large slabs of granite into the great boulder-slide, sending them down a miles-long track to a holding pit near the water. The energy of the fall was used to work forges along the route, and construction workers plucked the otherwise unused stones out of the pits below for their projects.

When the sun rose in the east the next morning, the three hundred mercenaries seemed meaningless in comparison to the true army of miners passing through the worn granite steps of the entrance. Iron helms, pickaxes, ropes, food, heavy iron boots, and thick leather clothes to stay warm, along with satchels of water and hand lanterns made the men and women entering the mine sound like an army of Sullarian knights in full plate marching into the earth. There were songs, shouts, and chants coming from different crews as they stoked their courage for the work ahead.

Rianas followed Atrick to a huge placard inlaid on the ground above the entrance. The two brass triangles inside a golden circle symbolized the High Mine. It acted as a natural speaking platform for the assortment of men and women gathered in front of him. Even so, he had brought a copper horn to project his voice above the sounds below.

Three men in fitted tunics and finely cut pants joined Atrick, speaking with him a few moments before nodding and walking off. Berryl told her those were the owners of the mine. They would be providing some transport and guides along the path.

Atrick raised his arms for quiet. After a few moments, the group of volunteers and mercenaries calmed down enough for him to speak.

"Good morning volunteers," he said. "Today we will embark on a journey through the Black Mountains. We have given each of you long daggers and metal helms, a small oil lamp and enough oil to keep your lights on for four days. You also will receive a fifty-foot section of rope and a pack with about five days' supply of food. The rest of your gear is up to you.

"I expect," Atrick continued, "that we will meet some resistance at the end of the cave. There is a possibility there has been a cave-in, but our reports point to nogs in the mine. Such an adversary will carry primitive weapons, but they will likely outnumber a group our size. Treat any miners we meet with respect and help our apprentices heal them, if possible. I will lead the expedition myself, with Berryl and Teran as my commanders. Six apprentices are joining us further down the mine. They will be equipped with healing potions and more equipment. They will be in charge of healing services.

"The trip will be about two days to where our miners disappeared. The first section of the mine is traditionally managed and operational. There is a lot of traffic here. Stay to the left walls and follow the light above my head. By later today, we will be deep enough to spread out. I hope to camp in Cavern Number Four this evening."

With that brief description, Atrick left the organization of the rest of the group to Teran and Berryl, who separated the mercenary group into teams of four and five. Teran put Rianas with Arthur, a woman, and an older man.

Rianas walked over to the others and saw that the woman was the first person she had interviewed the day before. Her name was Sal, and she had huge arms and a homely face, but she also seemed very familiar with the mine. Sal gave a firm handshake to the other three while saying that if her husband were in the mine, she would be sure to find him.

The man was Elias. He introduced himself, and then asked Rianas why such a beautiful young woman would be taking up adventuring. Rianas smiled politely and said Atrick had struck her as the sort of man who could keep an expedition like this together long enough to do what it came for.

This apparently was the right answer for Elias. He nodded and said, "I've followed men with less resolve. Sometimes it means nothing, but other times it is the difference between success and failure to have a leader who truly believes something must be done."

The march into the High Mine was unlike anything Rianas had ever experienced before.

No one clapped, waved, or sung as they marched single file along with the hundreds of other workers entering the mine. They simply walked in, keeping a few feet between each other and arms out to the side for balance as they climbed down the huge granite steps.

Within moments, though, the lightning blue of enchanted lanterns hanging from the fifty-foot high ceiling of the main entrance replaced the sunlight. The echo of thousands of voices mixed with the occasional "good luck" from passing miners. The huge crowds of miners lasted maybe half a mile.

Then the turning, ever-descending granite walkway took them around a bend, and the sound diminished. A hush came over the group. They continued passing hundreds of miners going into side tunnels, but the weight of the mountain started to take its toll.

The party marched without much talking for nearly three hours. Each side tunnel carried sounds of picks, shovels and rolling cargo cars. Sweaty miners pushed a few of the huge cars past them, laden with various stones. Women or smaller men pushed the empty cars on the other track. With so much traffic, these darker inner passages demanded the attention of the rescue party. A rail car could easily run them off the track.

Rianas used this time to meditate the way she had learned from Atrick. She pulled on the weaves of magic, tried to direct them where she wanted them to go. She felt like she had more control, but still could not hold the threads long enough to weave a spell. The weave was a force she *knew* was there, but she could not see it. She was blindly reaching around, trying to manipulate the threads that she would need for a spell.

Rianas wondered what she would do when she finally reached the goal. As they descended deeper into the mine, it seemed like there were shadows everywhere down here. She thought how great it would be if she could cast a light spell to light her way.

Atrick had shown her the weaves of a few simple spells. The first three simple spells he had shown her were *light, spark, and lift.* The *spark* pulled heat from the surroundings and created a small flame. The *lift* spell picked up small, lightweight objects. The simplistic names had amused her. Atrick had explained they all had Elven names as well. When written with enchanted ink on a page, those words acted as the conduits for spells.

Just as Rianas' legs were starting to get tired and her stomach was growling, they turned into a small side tunnel. Atrick directed the group to take a short lunch break.

Atrick made his way through the group, talking briefly with his apprentices, Berryl, Teran, and a few other mercenaries who seemed to be well armed. Eventually, he made his way to where Rianas and her small team were resting. The ball of light floating over his head completely washed away the darkness of the cave. He joked with the four for a few moments, produced an apple from his pocket, and moved to the next group. His chuckle helped liven up the entire rescue party, and soon the voices of the mercenary volunteers were echoing across the mine.

Elias adjusted a short sword he held on his waist and asked Rianas if she had ever fought nogs before.

"No," she said, a bit sheepishly.

"They seem harmless because of their size," Elias said, "but the little monsters are capable of killing. I've seen groups of them attack people. Nogs are not good at fighting, and they aren't especially smart, but they usually work in groups. We humans could learn better how to fight as groups if we watched the way they swarm their enemies. They are attuned to the needs of their leaders. I suspect that is why the Axareans use them so often in combat."

Arthur asked where the nogs came from. "I've never seen a nog before, except in books. If they don't get along with humans and Axarea has a lot of humans, how do they survive?"

"Nogs are at home in low hills. They are opportunistic hunters, but generally don't require very large ranges. When I used to run with the Borsilkian army, we would see units of the nogs led by their larger cousins, Rannogs. The Rannogs are really just giant Nogs. Much like ants with queens, their groups will only produce a few of these Rannog leaders. The Axareans didn't send humans to fight the Borsilkian Alliance very often. When they did, their units would basically act as officers or leaders for the nogs."

"So you think the Axareans basically give nogs lands they are trying to take over?" Arthur asked.

"No, I think somehow the Axareans have usurped the natural leadership structure of nogs to their own advantage. The rannogs are better armed. They are being bred somewhere deep within the Empire, trained for battle, and sent to lead Nog hordes."

Elias checked the string of his crossbow while he said, "The nogs themselves had a huge empire that Axarea took over long ago in the southern reaches of the Great Continent. The Sullarians say the nogs spilled out of the Stathros Gorge after the Cataclysm. Apparently they are provided food and weapons from other parts of the Axarean Empire, along with all the other tools to exact their hatred on the other nations of the world."

"Wow," Sal said, taking a swig from her water bladder. "So nogs are just pawns sent to invade and destroy everything in their path?"

"Essentially," Elias said. "And they usually fail. However, when deployed as part of an Axarean army, they can wreak havoc on their enemy and force the local populous to gather into cities or forts. When the Southerners finally invade with their heavy infantry, they can focus on strategic assets. It is impossible to fight a guerilla war against a force that kills everything."

Elias flipped the leather button off one of the daggers in his tunic and took it out. The nearly eighteen-inch blade was dull, almost black in the half-light of the lanterns. An inscription in Elven was on the hilt, which he held out to Rianas to read. "The elves have been fighting nogs throughout their history. Their weapon smiths have produced thousands of these."

"It says 'flames for dark times'," Rianas read, admiring the beautiful gold lettering. "It is a very beautiful dagger."

"This is a flame dagger. It glows red hot when held in the presence of nogs. That is very useful for piercing leather and soft armor. I have defended myself many times with this dagger." Elias gently put the dagger back after showing it to the others.

"How did you know what it says?" Sal asked. "Do you speak Elvish, too?"

Arthur piped up, "She can read pretty much anything. It's a special talent she was born with."

"Magical?" Elias asked. "That is why you were interviewing all the mercenaries last night, isn't it?"

"Yes, I can read some other languages, and speak a few, as well. It isn't something I have much control over, though," Rianas said carefully. She did not want to talk too much about the skill she did not really have any control over.

Arthur noticed her discomfort and changed the subject. "Do you think there are really nogs in the tunnel ahead? I mean, do you think that Axarea is really trying to shut down the mine by sending nogs in to take over? It seems like it would take lots of effort and years of planning just to make something like that possible. Plus, if nogs are not very good at strategy, couldn't they easily be driven out of the mine?"

Elias smiled crookedly. An old scar above his right lip made it look almost like a snarl. "That is one reason I jumped at the opportunity to come down here. When nogs fought the Borsilkians, they did so to test the Borsilkian defenses. Sometimes, nogs attacked to weaken points the Axarean Empire already knew were weak. The nogs themselves are something of a creeping battering ram that doesn't think much as it advances. This type of battle would seem to make little sense. There are easily ten thousand soldiers available to Sko'Port. A few thousand could rid a cave of entire legions of nogs with minimal casualties."

Sal shook her head. "It would take weeks, or even months to clear this mine if it was occupied. There are hundreds of side mines miles long. Large equipment is everywhere. It would be easy to hide. A few times, other mines further down the Black Mountains have had bandits or outlaws hide inside them for years without being caught. The darkness down here is an enemy of its own for humans. Especially the deeper you go."

Elias nodded his head in agreement. "True, it is hard to think of how dark it can be down in these mines when you are surrounded by a wizard's light. Nogs have an advantage over us in the dark. They have huge eyes that let them see well at night." He motioned toward the ceiling. Even this deep, lanterns hung above. They were spaced farther apart than at the beginning of the mine, but their light pierced the darkness.

Arthur looked up, too, fingering his lantern. Rianas took out the hand lamp she had bought in the bazaar and showed it to the group, pressing the stone onto the handle to make it shine. The light was bright as day for twenty feet in every direction. A few people in other groups looked over.

"Wow!" said Arthur. "Where did you get the money for that? It cost more than I could make in a month working horses."

"It seemed like an investment I would not regret," Rianas said, deflecting the question. "Hopefully it will help us if we get attacked." She took the helm from her head and played with the leather lamp-holder, strapping the light to the top of her head. Without the glare in her eyes, it was almost like looking around in the early evening in the mine. Hard stone and hard packed dirt all around seemed to glisten.

"That will definitely help," said Elias. "The nogs are so accustomed to darkness that their eyes do not work well in the daytime. Fighting them in the daylight is always a great way to give yourself an advantage. They cannot fight well because they will be stumbling around half-blinded. Remember that if we get attacked."

Atrick had gotten up, and the rest of the group was starting to move out to the main hall again. Shortly, the entire rescue party was back on its feet, walking single file down the mine.

In a couple hours, the mine highway opened up into a cavernous hall.

Storage crates filled with various types of food lined the rough-cut walls. A few small food vendors had actually opened up shop in the open area. The size of a city block, there were hundreds of miners getting meals and sharpening tools. The hall here was spacious, and the floor was relatively flat. Several wooden bridges spanned over a wide, shallow creek that oozed out of the walls on one side. Mine cars queued up in lines on the tracks. Workers loaded and organized them against the walls before sending them on their way. Multiple pathways left the cavern, but the widening creek led straight into an even larger cavern.

As they entered the Arena – as Sal called it – Arthur pointed at a huge mushroom growing out of the side of a wall. It glowed faintly.

More glowing mushrooms were up ahead. As the rescue party proceeded into the larger cavern, they began to see a forest-like setting. Bulbous fungi, some covered in algae themselves, towered as tall as a horse. Cut into the forest was a large pathway for the mine cars to travel. There was no traffic coming out of this tunnel, though. Instead, a few dozen miners with crossbows slung in front of them were looking in that direction.

Atrick walked up to them and spoke a few words, then motioned the group to stop. "This is Cavern Number Four," said Sal to the other three, just before Atrick did.

"Look," Arthur whispered to Rianas. He pointed to seven men wearing robes. "More mages."

Atrick walked over to the seven mages. He grasped a man whose hair was light brown and traded some personal words before turning to the rest of the group.

"We will rest here for the evening. Please get as much rest as you can. After this, I am not sure what lies ahead," Atrick said to the group.

"Those are mage apprentices," Sal corrected Arthur as she unslung her pack. "Wizards wear brighter colors. Brown is reserved for apprentices. It looks like they brought healing potions with them."

Atrick was still talking to the apprentice with the light hair as he rummaged through two heavy crates full of glass jars. He pulled out the jars as he spoke. When both of them looked in her direction, Rianas realized she was staring and turned away.

Arthur helped Rianas take her rucksack off, and she began setting up the small sleeping bag on top of the soft, almost loamy soil between two glowing mushrooms. She saw a few other people cutting off parts of the mushroom to use for light and did the same. When it was compressed, the thick, wood-like pulp of the undersides of these giant mushrooms glowed brighter. Sal informed them that the miners would use small pieces to keep their workplaces lit for hours by adding a little of the nutrient-rich water from the stream in a small glass bottle.

Placing a flask she was carrying with her in the water, Sal grabbed some of the pulp of the mushroom near her, stuffed it into the flask like a cork until the water would not spill out, and held it up. A pale orange light bright enough to read by emanated from the inside of the flask.

"This," Sal said, "will stay bright enough to help guide your way for a day or two. Take a few pieces and keep them dry and padded. Don't let them get crushed. It is a great light source. Don't try to eat them, though," she smiled tightly when she said that.

Arthur collected a couple pounds of small pieces he had broken away from the bottoms of the stalks. He put them into a jar that he had been carrying full of dried berries. He placed the berries on his leather mat and offered them to the group.

Rianas only had a little space in her sack, but she gently packed a few pieces away, just in case. Elias had already fallen asleep. Arthur stepped over to his sleeping bag, a few feet from Rianas.

"Are you scared?" he asked. "*I am. I'm terrified that we will be overrun by Nog hordes tonight.*"

Rianas nodded in agreement to Arthur's thoughts. "I hope we find the missing miners tomorrow," she said.

Sal looked over. "My husband Merrin was supposed to be working copper down there. A few months ago, they discovered a vein full of copper and a crew started opening it up. The tracks end about three miles after this cavern, and a crew was down with them helping to lay more track. We are many miles below the mountain, now. I wouldn't be surprised to find some sort of magical beast this deep."

Arthur's eyes got wider. "You mean monsters live down here?"

"There are the cave lizards. Some of them can get as big as a dog. There are so many in the lower mines that miners hunt them and sell them to vendors for meat. You didn't think those things were raised on a farm, did you?"

Arthur picked up the salted lizard tail he had tied to one of his belt buckles, his eyes raised. Then he looked around, as if expecting one to jump out at them.

Sal pointed about fifty feet away where, sure enough, a lizard was eyeing them from atop a mushroom cap. It was maybe two feet long, with sharp claws on the front. If she had not pointed, Rianas was not sure she would have seen it. Its scales took the color of the iridescent mushroom cap almost completely. The only parts that were easy to discern were its eyes. They were like huge black holes sticking out of its head. They reflected the light from another group's lantern. "They aren't very dangerous. The bats eat them. The flying rodents are the real danger in here. That's why I keep a crossbow on me any time I enter a mine. The bigger bats have been known to attack miners who disturb their nests. Usually killing one or two will get them to back down."

Arthur was looking up into the top of the cavern now. He pointed, "Are those bats?"

"Yes," said Sal. "Don't worry; they are harmless with a group this size."

Nevertheless, Rianas and Arthur both covered their heads up with the helms they had been provided.

The evening (at least Rianas thought of it as evening when Atrick let his light fade away and only the lanterns of a dozen miners on watch illuminated most of the group) was beautiful in this section of cavern. The lizards made short, high-pitched calls, an occasional bat would flutter over the water, and the water in the stream dashed steadily across outcroppings of rock. The mushroom cap Rianas was lying under provided enough light for her to read the map she had brought. It ended shortly after this cavern. Rianas took out a piece of paper and some ink she had brought by accident from her school bag and decided to draw the place.

Every few minutes, the movement of a lizard across a mushroom would sprinkle mushroom spores onto the ground in a rainbow of tiny lights. The water itself seemed to glow from the spores, and tiny sightless fish nibbled at the surface of the small creek. The serenity caught her by surprise. As the sounds of the blacksmiths and food stalls disappeared for the 'evening', Rianas found herself lulled into a peaceful sleep.

The next morning, the rescue party packed up quickly. The armed miners and mage apprentices guarding this section of tunnel were coming with them.

Rianas wondered – a mix of suspicion and curiosity – when she saw the light-haired apprentice staring at her. Soon, though, they were busy preparing to move, and she had to focus on packing her gear.

Atrick instructed a few dozen people to grab foodstuffs and extra gear from the shops. Berryl set to work organizing the group for its search. Each group of four would stay within hand's reach, and each team would be no more than twenty yards from the next team. Rianas' group was two teams away from the right side of the cavern. The team on either side had the tattooed westerners mixed with a few Gawdichians and a Cidvagian lifelong mercenary. Rianas relayed Berryl's instructions on how they would report issues or findings to the westerners. They merely politely nodded without asking questions.

Shortly, the entire group picked its way deeper into the mine. Rianas found herself staring into the darkness, the hand lamp she had bought strapped securely to her helm providing just enough light to make out the faces of the group on either side of them. The westerners had taken their shortened spears out and used them as walking sticks. Sal had her crossbow loaded and held it aimed down at her side. Arthur released the leather buttons on the two daggers he held at his waist. Rianas asked him what he thought he would do with four daggers and a knife, and he joked he would use his feet and hands together.

Rianas laughed at that. Sal shook her head, and Elias eyed Arthur peculiarly. Elias had perhaps a dozen weapons, from a sharpened pick to a small single-hand crossbow. His thick leather armor housed multiple daggers, some sort of stick with a spiked ball hanging from it, and a short sword. Rianas had even spied two concealed daggers on the inside of his leather shield. He walked with the shield across his left arm, adjusting it up and down from time to time. The other arm he kept free, but his crossbow was also now loaded as it swung easily from a strap across his chest.

After an hour of walking, there was one final fork in the mine to the right. Atrick sent a third of the group down the side tunnel with Berryl and Teran in the lead while the rest of the group took a short break. Nearly two hours later, they returned to report it was completely empty save for some mining equipment.

Arthur jumped a few times as they proceeded. He claimed he had seen something moving up ahead. Sal lifted her crossbow occasionally, as if a target had appeared. The entire group was jittery.

After marching like this for another two hours, Atrick had the group stop. The mineshaft was now only thirty paces wide, so most of the group was a few people deep. The creek had grown, with water seeming to come out of the walls in some locations. The tracks down the center kept to the right of the creek, crossing over it occasionally, but the miners had obviously tried to keep the track dry. The railing here looked barely used.

Skittering sounds echoed from ahead. The darkness of the mine made every sound seem dire.

There were no lanterns lit this deep in the mine. Chains hammered into the ceiling were empty, or broken jars barely lit the hall. When Atrick walked along the group, his spell seemed to take a blanket of darkness off the people with whom he spoke. Rianas was glad for her headlamp. Without it, she surely would have felt the weight of the mountain. Sounds echoed for hundreds of yards in some places. They were muffled in others.

Sal pointed out mushrooms growing by the creek. "Those mushrooms look to be pretty old. Perhaps the cavern opens up again ahead."

Rianas snacked on a hard fruity biscuit and added some water to a dry soup mix she had brought. Before she was even finished eating, Atrick was rounding up the group again. She snacked idly with one hand as they moved ahead. The entire party was tense.

Rianas' feet were getting tired from navigating across the tracks when the way ahead became brighter. As they rounded a bend, Atrick waved the group to a temporary stop and grabbed Teran and Berryl. Berryl walked in their direction, instructing everyone quietly that they would proceed around the next bend in complete silence.

Arthur leaned down toward Rianas. *"That is almost impossible with all the gear these people are carrying."*

Rianas looked up and nodded, then adjusted a few of the buckles on her harness to make them as quiet as she thought she could. Atrick dimmed his *Light*, and the group proceeded quietly around the bend.

After a few moments, the track ended. There were pieces of lumber and metal laid neatly to the side, as well as a few buckets and long iron rail anchors. A few hundred yards beyond that, the light was brighter. Rianas stifled a gasp when she saw how the mine opened up into a massive cavern.

The water here flowed nearly twenty feet across, and its sound masked most of the sounds of the group. Unlike the man-sized mushrooms from the previous cavern, these were obviously much larger. From a quarter mile away, she could see the mushroom spores hanging. They were like apples hanging from trees.

Rianas felt Arthur next to her shift, and then she watched him take a dagger out of its sheath. Wordlessly, she did the same.

As the group closed the distance, the tension rose. There was obvious evidence of people in the entrance to this cavern. Dozens of dragged and overturned mine cars formed a circle in a makeshift clearing. Knocked over mushroom caps the size of horses and small houses lined the clearing. Miners had pushed them up against the spaces between the mine cars or piled them atop each other.

What had Rianas' attention, however, was the smell. Even from this distance, the smell of death hung in the air.

Sal sniffled audibly. Rianas reached her free hand over to grasp Sal's shoulder gently, unable to see her face clearly in the faded light. Sal touched the hand and stopped sniffling.

6. RESCUE

On the far southwestern coast of the Great Continent, the Dwarves fought bravely. Millions of Axarean soldiers had been slain or buried under the onslaught of the Dwarven Empire five hundred years before. The Dwarves had sent armies deep into their overrun mines and slaughtered all sorts of monsters harnessed by the Axarean Empire. They had freed many of their people.

Five hundred years of conflict had fractured the Dwarven Empire, however. Now, the great underground city-states had to band together to ward off the relentless incursions of Orcan armies, southern armies, and every manner of monstrous beast. Without a single Dwarven Empire to organize counter-offensives, the various Dwarven Kingdoms had been unable to mount serious counter-offensives against Axarea.

From: "An Incomplete History of Arthos"
Grandmaster Ar'Ishan's lecture on Axarean aggression
1943 A.C.

The light from the forest of mushroom "trees" was enough to make it seem like the huge cavern was in perpetual daylight. The cavern itself was beautiful. The creek turned into a river here, with small streams and creeks feeding it all the way down the opening. Rianas could see miles of open cavern from here, nearly half a mile wide. Sounds from inside the "jungle" made it seem like a true forest.

Dozens of bats soared a hundred feet overhead, and protesting frogs leapt away from the boots of the marching mercenaries.

Rianas' focus returned to the clearing. A shout came from the pile of carts, and a weak cheer rose in response. The heads of multiple miners poked over the makeshift barriers. Atrick rushed forward, stepping over the small corpses of what must have been nogs.

Rianas looked at one of the creatures. She wondered at its lizard-like face, its sparse clothing, and its stone-tipped spear that was only about three feet long. The monster was about three feet tall itself, with muscular, naked legs and arms and large eyes.

The miners inside the barricade were speaking with Atrick. Sal rushed ahead. Rianas and the others followed, still alert to the imminent danger. As Rianas got closer, she could hear one of the survivors talking.

"Every time we tried to move, there would be a couple hundred of them around us. We have no real weapons except for our picks and some spears we took from the first attackers. Nearly a hundred have perished, and most of the rest are injured. There are many stab wounds. Those monsters are too short to cross this barrier easily, but with so many wounded we couldn't escape. You can hear them in the forest."

That was when Rianas noticed an unnatural sound coming from within the noisy forest. It sounded like chanting—rhythmic, short words followed by some sort of drum. Arthur gestured to the right of the barricade. Then he tilted his head slightly and pointed further down the cavern. *"There are more of them that way. I can hear at least two groups."*

The apprentices climbed over the mining cars to look at the wounded. Several men had horrible wounds, but most were stab wounds around the torso, legs and arms. Rianas overheard Elias as he took out some cloth to help tend to the wounded, saying, "Nog spear wounds. Most likely they have some weak poison on them that will slow you down, but it won't kill you so long as you drink lots of water and get some rest for a few days."

Arthur helped Elias look after the wounded. The apprentice mages rushed in to apply their healing magic. Rianas walked over to Atrick and helped him instruct the westerners to set up watch with some of the other men who had brought long-range weapons. As she finished, she heard Sal speaking overly loud to one of the surviving miners.

"What do you mean you left him out there? He came in with you. It is your job to keep your men safe!" She was slightly hysterical, tears welling in her eyes. Rianas started walked over to try to comfort her as the large miner Sal was talking to lowered his head and said something quietly to the heavy-set woman.

Rianas stumbled when she read his mind rather than heard him say, *"Sal, I don't know how to say this any other way. We left him because we couldn't carry him. When the first attack came, we had no time to prepare. Merrin jumped out in front to knock some of the nogs back. The nogs swarmed him, though. By the time we drove them back, he had bled so much he wasn't even breathing. I'm so sorry. He was gone before we were driven away from his body. But he saved five or six of us. No one saw the nogs coming."*

Rianas, still reeling from the projected telepathy, finally got to Sal. She could think of nothing else to do except to wrap her arms around the much larger woman. Sal, about to punch the miner, simply fell to pieces in Rianas' arms. She sobbed loudly, letting all her weight fall onto Rianas. She could not hold the larger woman up. The two ended up half-kneeling on the ground.

Rianas comforted her as well as she could. She agreed with the miner, who was standing uncomfortably above them both, that they would help her find her husband's body so he could be buried. Sal would have none of it. She sobbed into Rianas' shoulder, unresponsive.

After a few moments, she began to regain her composure. The miner whose mind Rianas had read, Gerald Narus, apologized repeatedly to Sal, who spat a few venomous words in response that she did not truly mean. Gerald took the words in stride. He was sympathetic and passionately seemed to wish there was something he could do to make things right.

From where she was on the ground, Rianas saw Atrick's apprentices healing dozens of the injured. They used the small flasks they were carrying, either rubbing the oils on skin or apportioning out small doses into wooden glasses to drink. As the injured imbibed the healing potions, their wounds seemed to disappear.

When Sal released her, it was to go speak with Atrick about retrieving her husband's body. According to Gerald, it was about one hundred yards into the mushroom forest, just this side of the river. Rianas followed, watching with amazement the dozens of miners walking around. Many of those men had been immobilized with stab wounds through their abdomens and lower extremities just minutes before.

Atrick was taking an inventory of injured and dead. His eyes were wet when he looked toward Sal. Without even asking, he knew the fate of her husband. The emotional mage reached out to her with a hand as she approached. "About thirty of those lost are buried here, Sal. We can bring your husband here to be buried with these other brave men, or we can have him brought out with the survivors to be buried wherever you see fit."

Sal calmed under Atrick's touch. Still sniffling, she nodded and thanked him. She seemed small and fragile, suddenly. Rianas touched her back as well, wishing there was something she could do. Atrick looked over at her, the unshed tears sitting brightly in his sunken eyes.

"These people have suffered mightily because I did not predict this. Rianas, I must make this right for them."

Rianas nodded and asked if she could go with the group that was retrieving the bodies. Atrick asked her to stay and help him organize the upcoming counter-offensive.

Sal went with Teran, who walked up with a few dozen miners and mercenaries who had volunteered to collect the lost miners. Atrick stepped around one of his apprentices to Berryl. He was speaking with a short, muscular bearded man holding a pickaxe like a walking stick.

"Hello, Raskin," said Atrick, shaking the burly man's hairy hand.

Raskin nodded. "I'm glad to finally see you, Atrick. We weren't sure how much longer we could hold out. They test our strength daily. A few of them took to slinging stones. Any time we went for water, they sent a dozen attackers. If they had better weapons, we wouldn't have been able to survive this long. I pulled the wagons together out of sheer luck about an hour after the first attack. Looking back, we should have just backed out of the cavern."

Atrick shook his head and took a seat on a broken barrel. "You probably saved countless lives by staying. The nogs have been so focused on you they haven't established a presence further up the mine. With no soldiers further up, they could have trapped hundreds more."

Raskin ran a greasy arm through his disheveled, long black hair, pulling it back behind his head. His dark brown outfit was covered in bloodstains, and he had bandages around his left foot, right leg and both hands. The helm hanging from his belt was so dented it did not look like it would fit his head anymore.

"What are we going to do next, Atrick? Those nogs don't live in this cavern. I killed one of their leaders during the first attack, and he was wearing this." Raskin fished in a small bag sitting next to his gear and took out an odd wooden mask, carved to be smooth on the outside, painted in the likeness of a human with a mustache and high cheekbones. Gold-colored paint and pieces of black stone lined the insides of the mask. "It's wood, and doesn't appear to be very old. We also found dried corn in one of their satchels. There is obviously no place they could get wood or corn so deep under the mountain. They came from somewhere else."

Atrick was lost in thought as he stared at the mask. "This is an Axarean war mask. I've seen renderings of them before in the Sko'Port library." He turned to Rianas. "Can you read this inscription in the mask?"

Rianas looked inside at the inscription etched into the golden paint. As Raskin turned it in the light, she could barely make out the words. She had not seen the language before. It looked almost Elvish in its lettering. Somehow, the words were darker in tone and meaning, though. It was as if the writer had removed the soft edges from the message. "Serving the True One," she read. "It isn't Elvish, but it is definitely close. This is a language I have never read before."

Atrick nodded, considering. "It's Axarean. The Southerners almost all speak it. It was adopted by the Axarean Empire a few hundred years ago to help unify the Empire, from what I understand. It is very close to Elven, but I cannot read it. Very few texts exist outside of the Empire written in that language. This mask would have been provided to an elite soldier or commander, someone trusted by the emperor himself to fulfill a task. This portends calamitous events.

"There is another mask I once saw in the library of the Lower Ward in Sko'Port on loan from Cidvag. It was captured toward the end of the Andarian War from an Axarean battlefield commander who had waded headlong into the Cidvagian King's guard. He took down a dozen men before Charles the White took him down. Brigands ambushed the Sullarian knight in his tent a few nights later. That war mask would have been lost if not for the fact that the knight had sent the mask to the wizards of Sko'Port for study the night before. Charles the White died of poison a few days later. The Cidvagian king did not leave his keep again, after that. He died a few years later of a suspicious fall from one of his keep's towers."

Rianas had read about 'cursed masks of Axarea'. There were a few of them held in the Northern Kingdoms, but the 'curse' had always seemed a consequence of the capture more than of some magical curse. At least, that was the way the writings in the Riverrun library had cast the results. She said as much.

Raskin, who had visibly edged away from the mask when Atrick started talking about it, seemed to relax a bit when Atrick nodded and smiled gently.

"Yes," Atrick said. "It would appear that the Empire puts a lot of effort into getting them back. However, rumors and fears of curses persist, and those fears can be as dangerous - if believed - as if they are true. The Sko'Port wizards who have studied the masks say there is a dark magic surrounding them. The High Wizards of Sullaria have simply destroyed the ones they have ever come across. They say the magic is too dangerous. Their knights typically destroy these masks when they are found. I believe the one in Cidvag is the only one still in existence outside of Axarea."

Raskin's fear was palpable. For such a large man, his shiver seemed out of place. "Then why did those monsters not kill me already? I have no doubt we are outnumbered."

Atrick was looking at the front of the mask. Rianas felt more than saw him using a small tendril of magic to probe it. He did not seem to be listening to Raskin anymore. When the seconds drew into an awkward minute, she reached over and lightly pushed Atrick's hand off the mask to get his attention back.

Atrick's cloudy eyes went up, and he seemed to come back to the present. "What an intriguing mask. I need to study it more. There is definitely some magic within it. A magnifying force. I would bet it lends strength, stamina, and even greater agility to its wearer. Raskin Jorgen, you were very lucky to defeat that leader."

Raskin took his turn to laugh uncomfortably. "That is an understatement."

Rianas saw Atrick starting to lean back into the mask. "Atrick, wouldn't this mask be the perfect evidence to get Lord Cerric to send more men into the mine? What if we sent it back and requested reinforcements from the city guard? We could probably get them in a few days. If the nogs are truly all here in this cavern, it would be easier to fight them back if we had help, right?"

Atrick nodded. He finally released the mask into the sack where Raskin had stored it. Then, mustering his resolve, he nodded again.

"That is a great idea," he said. "We will send a few men back to request reinforcements. The Wizard's Council will want to see the mask, too. If nothing else, we should be able to use it to convince the Upper Ward guards to send in the constabulary.

"Berryl. Put together a dozen of the fastest men here. Raskin, put this satchel in a locked box and have them bring it back to the entrance of the mine. The key goes with you, Berryl. Give it directly to Guard Captain Oren, and tell him we will need as many soldiers as he can muster." As he spoke, Atrick's gaze never left the sack that held the mask.

Berryl took the satchel and started off toward a pair of long-legged Gawdichians Rianas recalled interviewing. Atrick lifted the hand he had used to hold the mask, gently rubbing his fingers together. "A dangerous mask, indeed."

Atrick pushed the barrel he had been sitting on away. He looked down at the dirt. He drew a small knife from a pocket and started drawing in the dirty cavern floor. "If the nogs haven't attacked, there must be a reason. We can assume their force isn't strong enough to ensure easy victory against this many men defending a reasonably good position like this. If that is so, we should be able to rout them with our force. Raskin, would any of the miners care to join us?"

A huge smile broke across Raskin's bearded mouth. "Of course, Atrick. Dozens of these men would love to bring the attack to those little monsters. I'd personally lead the charge."

"Good. Now, how many entrances are there to this cavern, do you know?" Atrick drew an oval with a line in from one side, a circle to symbolize their location in front of that entrance.

"There are three entrances further down the cavern. The one on the left and right go uphill from what I've seen, while the main river continues to flow downhill from the one in the center. It is almost completely across from here." Raskin gestured out across the mushroom forest. "I would guess that is where the nogs came from, but we were mostly working at this entrance to the forest when we were attacked."

Atrick agreed, but said, "We need to be sure. It is possible they have sent word of their engagement to whoever sent them in here. That means time is our enemy. They obviously haven't gotten reinforcements yet, or they would have attacked your men. If we attack now, we should have the advantage."

"It looks like you brought a few hundred men with you," Raskin said, looking at the brimming barricade. "If you sent about a hundred men right to that lowest cave as fast as they could get there, you might stop them from reporting your reinforcements. Then you could drive them that way with the remaining mercenaries."

"That is an excellent idea. We will split into two main groups. The search group will fan out to flush the nogs back. This is a huge cavern, so it could take a few hours even with this many men, but we would be sure to get most of the resistance. Maybe we could even capture some of the nogs to find out why they are here."

Raskin shook his head, scoffing, "I doubt you have anyone who speaks their language. Nogs don't speak Northern, you know."

"If you could bring some to me, I think I might be able to understand them," Rianas interjected. Atrick nodded and introduced her to Raskin.

"This is my newest apprentice, Raskin," Atrick said with a grin.

"Rianas has surprised even me with her ability to understand foreign languages. She reads Axarean, speaks Kabaran, Elven, even Dwarvish."

Raskin's bushy eyebrows rose. Then, in his native Dwarven tongue he said, "No one ever bothers to learn Dwarven this far from my homeland."

"It is more a magical ability than something I have had to work hard for," Rianas answered sheepishly.

Raskin chuckled deeply. "Amazing. Perhaps we can interrogate a few of those little monsters, after all." Rianas noticed he had been speaking Dwarvish and was embarrassed that she did not even notice the easy translation she had done. Atrick chuckled.

Raskin excused himself to go recruit as many of his miners as he could. Rianas asked Atrick if Raskin was truly a dwarf. "Not exactly," he said. "Raskin is what you might call a Claw Mountain 'dwarf'. It has been a hundred years since the Dwarven Kingdoms have traded freely with the Northern Realms. The Orcs of the Axarean Empire cut off the direct land route when it started attacking the west coast of the continent.

"Dwarves have never been good sailors," Atrick continued. "However, humans live on the western coast of Arthos, too. Many live on the Claw Mountains. They man ships, trade for goods Dwarves aren't interested in, and generally do what the Dwarves can't or won't. Some of them even have children with Dwarves. Raskin is one such child. Northern Realms humans are taller, and they often consider his people Dwarves. All the Claw Mountain humans I've met have looked like Raskin – short and broad-chested."

Two of Atrick's mage apprentices went with Raskin, and he started rallying the remaining miners.

Atrick had Rianas translate for him to various mercenaries as he divided them into two groups. Teran and the volunteers finished returning the dead miners' bodies to the camp, so Rianas helped Atrick's apprentices split up the rescue party.

Atrick ordered teams of four organized again. The wizard instructed each group to spread out within sight of the next. He would go down the center with the bulk of the force. The nogs would not be able to hide from the armed search party.

Arthur made his way over to Rianas and said, "We are going to be fighting those things, aren't we?"

Rianas nodded.

She felt funny. Each time she used her ability, it seemed easier than the last. In Riverrun, her father used her translation skills a few dozen times each year. With Atrick, she found herself conversing with people in rare languages all the time. It left a strange sensation in her head, almost as if a feather had tickled her through her curly hair.

7. NOGS

Every miner who could walk volunteered to help rout the nogs.

Reinforced by about fifty heavily armed mercenaries, Raskin and two wizards' apprentices climbed over the barricade and quickly marched toward the exit of the river on the far side of the cavern. Atrick's mercenaries slid a few carts out of the way on the high end of the barricade, and the remaining mercenaries fanned out across the cavern.

Rianas, Sal, Arthur and Elias all had daggers at the ready. Rianas was very nervous – she had never had to fight before. Elias calmly scanned left to right as they walked, and Sal had a determined look on her face. Each time they stepped around a mushroom tree, Sal clenched her teeth and studied the shadows. The drumbeat sounds of the nogs seemed to be everywhere in the trees ahead of them, reflecting off rocks and hardened mushroom caps in a way that projected the sound evenly throughout the cavern.

The nearest group started out just a few yards away, but as they went deeper into the forest, the cavern widened and the rescue party separated. Rianas nervously scanned ahead, but she found herself watching her footing almost as much. The ground was soft and even muddy in spots. Several times, Arthur's arm shot out to grab a mushroom stalk for support, and twice Rianas stumbled into him over a greasy tangle of rotten undergrowth.

Crickets and moths flew away from the noisy humans. A lizard longer than Rianas' arm skittered from under a toadstool, attempting to bite Sal. She kicked at the creature with her boot and it fled into a hole created by two fallen stones. The creatures in this cavern seemed to have no experience with their human invaders.

By the time they had explored a quarter mile into the cavern, the drums stopped. There was shouting on the other side of the cavern, followed by a relayed command to proceed again. Arthur's eyes were wide, and Rianas suspected hers were as well. Despite the cool air, she was sweating under her leather armor.

A few moments later, a scurrying group of the multi-colored lizards came at them from the left, and Elias let out a shout of "There!" just before a dozen short, fast nogs burst from around a particularly thick mushroom tree.

Time seemed to slow for Rianas. She felt that she had forever to reflect on the twelve nogs. Half carried stone daggers, and the rest carried short wooden spears tipped with sharpened stones. Their heads were mostly bald, except for a few horse-like hairs. That let her see the greenish-yellow skin, with its scaly, almost slimy appearance. However, what drew her attention were their faces. Their mouths curled into monstrous snarls. Large lidded eyes took up a third of their faces. They burst into the open clumsily, running with slightly bowed-legs as if they were better suited for squatting than running. A few of them held their weapons up to shield their faces from the luminous hand lamp Rianas had mounted on her helm. The others had their eyes partially closed, squinting.

Almost immediately, the one on the left flew back with a crossbow bolt in its torso, sending it writhing in agony to the ground. Elias dropped his crossbow and drew his short sword. Sal used her own crossbow to hit another nog before it could close the distance with them.

Rianas had just enough time to think ironically how nice it would be to have twelve crossbows before the rest of the monsters were upon them. She saw Arthur lurch forward and grapple the spear from the first nog at her right side. She raised her left leg and kicked one near its neck, sending it sprawling backward. Fighting nogs in this way was akin to fighting crazed young children with deadly weapons. They did not seem particularly dangerous until they attacked you.

Another two almost immediately took its place.

Rianas spun away from a spear aimed at her gut and felt a tear forming along the lower leg of her leather pants. She stabbed out blindly with her dagger in her right hand. She felt, then heard, bone crunching as the dagger Arthur had given her made contact with the small nog's arm. It dropped its spear long enough to let Rianas bat another nog back with her left arm.

The dagger was stuck in the nog's arm, so Rianas simply let it go and fumbled for the other dagger in her belt.

The first nog was getting up, and Rianas felt rising panic as she saw Sal fall in her peripheral vision, letting out a blood-curdling scream. She could hear movement in the trees ahead. More nogs would be there any minute. Her hand finally felt the dagger come free of her belt, and she pulled it in front of her just as the first nog jumped at her head. The danger they were in was becoming clearer. Rianas could feel her heart in her throat.

The nog never got to Rianas. The three-foot tall creature crumpled against Rianas' arm as she pressed the dagger into its chest. Rianas felt its cold blood run down her hand, but had little time to consider what she had done as the second nog – the one holding the spear and ignoring her dagger in its arm – tried to stab her again. Its off hand was on the spear now.

Rianas let the second dagger go and pushed the first nog in the direction of the third. Its dying body pinned the third nog to the ground. Somehow, she managed to dodge the spear.

Mostly.

She kicked the creature in the face, noticing the blood streaming down her leg as she did so. Deep in her mind, a sarcastic voice was telling her she would have a hard time mending *that* rip in her leather pants.

The third nog scurried on its hands and feet backward to avoid another kick.

Elias was suddenly standing a few feet in front of her, behind the nog. Unflinching, he stabbed the creature and wiped his blade across its chest in a single motion. The macabre scene was quiet for a moment as Arthur stood up, wiping a dagger from each hand on the scaly back of one of the dead nogs. Sal was on the ground. She had a long dagger in her right hand and an empty crossbow in her left.

She dropped the weapons and began wrapping her thick legs with her overcoat to cover the stab wounds across her thighs.

Four of the nogs were running back toward the mushroom tree. Elias calmly loaded his crossbow. He did not turn back to the group as he spoke. "Is everyone okay? They will be back with reinforcements in a minute. It sounds like they are trying to find a way through the gauntlet."

Indeed, the sounds of fighting echoed to their left and right. Rianas lifted one dead nog off another dead nog to retrieve her two daggers, which she held in each hand, now. Sal finished binding her wounds and reloaded her crossbow wordlessly. Arthur pulled one of his own daggers from the nogs and put it back in his leg sheath. He had a long cut on his left thigh that looked painful.

As Rianas stood back up, the second group of nogs approached. Now there were ten more, but one was larger than the others. He was only a foot or so shorter than Rianas. They approached slower this time, one of them dodging the crossbow shot from Sal, who cursed loudly and started to reload, then gave up and tossed the crossbow behind her to lift up a spear from one of the dead nogs. She hurled it at one just as it was closing the distance.

Elias swung his sword in front of him, slicing across the shoulder of one of the nogs and putting himself in the path of the taller beast. Rianas had enough time to admire his form before another attacker forced her to kick a spear away.

Rianas heard Arthur grunt to her right, and a flying nog knocked the second nog attacking her over before it could stab at her with its long, primitive dagger. Arthur smiled at Rianas for a split second before swinging toward another attacker.

Rianas stabbed at the two nogs in front of her, pulling her head back to avoid the short spear. She spun just enough to catch the middle of the spear with her shoulder harness instead of the tip. The one with the dagger tried to get up, but she stepped hard on its foot and lunged forward, stabbing it and landing on top with enough force to push its dagger away.

So close to the nog with the spear, Rianas could smell fish on its breath and see pieces of meat in it sharp teeth. She pulled away and grabbed at the spear, but the nog was faster. It hit her in the stomach with the hardened end, with enough force to knock the wind out of her. Off balance from stabbing the first, Rianas decided to roll away onto the ground.

Arthur was there again. He stepped over Rianas and swatted the nog's spear away. Rianas had a moment to catch her breath, and used the daggers still in both hands to ward off another nog.

Elias, meanwhile, had felled three more nogs. He turned around and plunged his sword into the spear-wielding nog's back. He left his sword there and pivoted toward Sal, pulling his flame-dagger out. It lit up the entire underside of the brown tree canopy briefly before slicing across the back of the nog attacking Sal. Sal stabbed the beast when it turned its attention away from her. The second wave had been defeated.

Rianas could barely breathe, and the wound on her leg was throbbing painfully. Elias was unscathed, but Sal and Arthur both had large cuts on their legs. Arthur had another wound on his left arm, which hung limp at his side. Elias pulled his short sword out of the nog's body and sheathed it while he grabbed some loose cloth from the waist of one of the dead creatures. He quickly tied the cloth around Arthur's arm to slow the bleeding.

"Rianas, reload my bow," Elias commanded, motioning to where it was lying on the ground with a nod. Rianas gladly complied as she shook off the shock from the battle. Her hands fumbled clumsily as she worked the clasp.

Sal had already reloaded her crossbow and was standing up again. "I don't know if we will get lucky like that a third time." She was clearly winded. As soon as she stood up straight, she bent double again and vomited.

"It's the poison," Elias said, finishing with Arthur and slapping him gently on the uninjured arm as if to say 'good job'. "Remember, it isn't deadly. Try to drink some water before they come back."

Arthur was moving slowly, too, and his eyes seemed glazed over. Rianas felt a bit sick to her stomach, but the pain in her leg was enough to distract her. The out-of-tune sound of a poorly constructed horn about a hundred yards away was enough to bring her back to full attention. She looked around for some place they could better defend. Elias motioned back about ten feet against a large stone. She grabbed two of the short Nog spears and helped Arthur back up against the stone. The mushroom trees grew close enough here that the nogs would only be able to attack them five or six at a time. Maybe it would buy time for help to come.

Sal crawled atop the stone last, looking ready to vomit on Rianas, but her crossbow was ready when the third wave of nogs broke from the tree line.

Sal and Elias' crossbows immediately took down two nogs, but Rianas' heart sank when the nogs kept coming out of the trees. Probably two dozen crossed the clearing beneath the canopy. In seconds, the only thing she could do was kick and stab to push the onslaught back, Elias to her left and Arthur to her right, with Sal firing from behind.

Just when she was thinking this might be the end and pushing a spear away weakly with her dagger hilt, the air above turned hot. A huge ball of fire sailed slowly across from Rianas' right side, dripping hot ash on the nogs. The entire Nog war party panicked. Rianas stabbed a distracted nog in the chest. Arthur struck another nog, and Rianas kicked its spear away. Elias let out a war cry and used his shield as a ram to push two nogs back, stabbing one with his short sword and violently stepping on a third nog that he had pushed to the ground.

Atrick climbed over a short mushroom cap, directing the wave of fire to rake across the nogs a second time, while a dozen other mercenaries charged in to join the fight.

Within a few moments, the battle was over. A few nogs had run down the hill toward the lower cavern entrance, but the rest were dead. Atrick's fireball had burned many of them. Atrick stepped over the small corpses to Rianas' group, yelling for one of his apprentices to bring healing potions.

The tall, pale apprentice approached, opening his cloak to take out a clear glass wine bottle. He uncorked the bottle and poured thick brown liquid on rags before using them to bandage each of the wounded. For Sal, he gave a small brass thimble full of the liquid before bandaging up the rest of her wounds. "Take it easy for a while; the wounds will heal faster if you don't stress them. The poison should be taken away by my potion."

Atrick introduced the apprentice to them as Galen, and congratulated the four on pushing back the nogs. "I am so sorry it took us this long to get here! There were other nogs that attacked our flank from the opposite side of the cavern just before you were attacked."

Rianas, sitting on the large stone while Galen wrapped her leg, winced. "We were almost lost. A few more minutes fending that last wave off and they would have killed us all."

Elias shook his head. "I had plenty of fight left in me, young lady. And you fought well. We could have held them back for another few minutes."

Arthur laughed. "Yeah, I was about to start stabbing them with my second set of daggers!" That even got Sal to laugh weakly.

Atrick shook his head, and Rianas easily read his thoughts. *"Rianas, I am sorry."*

Galen stared at Rianas for an uncomfortable moment after applying the bandage. His fingers brushed her calf when he tightened the cloth. Atrick's telepathic words faded as Galen's thoughts filled her head.

"Twice born away from home comes another truth speaker."

Rianas jerked away from Galen's hand. Galen inclined his head and looked over to Atrick.

Arthur asked, "Is there some sort of anti-venom you have heard about for the poison the nogs are using?"

Rianas wanted to know what was going on.

Elias interrupted her thoughts as he cleaned and sheathed his sword. "Oakroot the night before battle seemed to work for the Borsilkian soldiers I fought with. They would make a soup from it. I wouldn't suggest it though. The stuff always gave me horrible gas."

Atrick said he knew of some magical poison remedies that provided protection and pointed to one of his rings, a small emerald on a steel ring. "This ring I purchased from a Sullarian trader provides resistance to all sort of poisons." He seemed to recall a previous purchase. Shaking his head with a grimace, he continued, "My experience is there are five times as many rings that claim to do such a thing as actually do."

Arthur asked how one would know a fake from a true magical ring. Atrick took his off and held it in his palm, then fed a small tendril of magic into the ring, which caused the Elven inscription inside the band to glow.

"Usually, a small amount of magic can bring the Elven script into focus, and you can read a short description of the enchanter's spell. This one says '*Victus Potionem Sanguine*'."

Atrick chuckled a little. "It helps to know the enchanter, or to purchase such a trinket from a reputable guild. I've tested this one a few times. I've found this particular ring handy especially when eating in the Lower Ward."

The apprentice Galen laughed, as well. He had stayed busy applying healing salves to the three injured adventurers. Now, he carefully packed away the remainder of his potion and gear and stood up. "I am done, Atrick. We've used up almost a third of what I brought with me. It will take me months to recreate that many potions again."

Atrick gave Galen a knowing, almost apologetic nod. "I know, Galen," he said. "We will use the rest of what you and the others brought by the time this expedition is done, I fear. We have not finished here. Hopefully the remaining nogs surrender peacefully." Atrick stood, directing men to fan out and finish the trip down to the bottom of the cavern. "We will station fifty men at each of the other entrances, in case some of the nogs retreated into those tunnels. Let's get moving."

She wanted to know why Galen was thinking about the *Andarian Prophecy* Atrick had showed her. How did he know Atrick, and why did he seem different from the other apprentices? He was as old as her father. His blue eyes and fair hair suggested Sullarian ancestry. His steely gaze kept darting in her direction, too.

The healing salve on her leg made Rianas feel much better physically. She looked at the bloodstain. Suddenly, she felt sick about killing the nogs. Her hands were shaking, and her teeth chattered with the unwanted excitement.

Arthur stood over one of the nogs, then leaned over and closed its lids. Elias saw this as he was belting his crossbow back onto his side and walked over.

"Son, it won't get easier. These creatures have no love for humans. Don't regret what you have done in defense, or it will eat at your soul." He gently began pulling the Nog bodies out of the way and into a line. "The bats and lizards will take care of the corpses in a few days. Let nature reclaim these abominations."

Atrick led the group further down the mushroom forest. A few times, fighting broke out toward the creek, but Rianas did not see any more nogs until they had gotten close to the bottom of the cavern. There was a small, abandoned camp. Some primitive fire pits still burned. These creatures had been cooking fish caught from the underground river.

Just two tents were standing. The mushroom forest had been hacked away to create a space where all the garbage created by two hundred nogs was strewn. Fish bones, lizard bones, and even bat wings littered the ground. Combined with the smell of feces and urine, the small camp smelled so bad they knew they were upon it before they got there.

A few dozen mercenaries - among them the westerners - held about twenty nogs tied up in the center of the clearing. Occasionally, one of the nogs would move too much, garnering an impolite shove from their captors back into the clearing.

Atrick asked Rianas to come with her. Together, the two walked behind one of the tents and sat on a stone in front of a captured nog. This one had just enough hair to pull into a tassel over his scalp. The thick spindly hairs stood straight up in the tassel, making the nog seem taller.

"Let's find out what they can tell us," Atrick said. "Can you get him to talk?"

Rianas did not know where to start. She had never spoken Nog before, and did not even know what it sounded like. She stared at the creature, wondering how to make it speak, before saying, "Hello, my name is Rianas. You attacked these miners. When we came, you attacked us, too. I'd like to know why." She spoke in her native Northern, not expecting any response.

The nog looked at her from the dirty floor, the huge eyes blinking without comprehension. Its lips curled into a snarl and a low sound like a dog growl came out of its throat.

Rianas swallowed, trying to maintain her composure. Atrick sat patiently to the side, as if he had no doubt Rianas would be able to discuss the vagaries of Runlarian politics with the monster. Rianas tried again in Kabaran, Elven, Dwarven, and even Assyrian. Nothing happened.

Atrick sat patiently. Rianas tried not to become frustrated. She stared at the creature, thinking about what she might try next.

"Perhaps this one is mute," he said finally. A small smile played briefly across his face when Rianas looked – a little more like glared – at Atrick.

"Hold on, let me think," Rianas said. A challenge was a challenge, after all. She thought about the last week and all the new things she had seen.

A thought came to her, and she reached her hand out to the nog's head. It pulled back, but with its arms tied behind its back there was very little it could do to avoid her touch. Rianas pressed her hand to the creature's sweaty, greasy forehead.

Rianas asked the question again, maintaining her palm against the creature's forehead. The nog struggled violently, trying to twist away. Atrick held its arms to keep it steady.

Then the tent disappeared, and Rianas was floating in a field of wheat. A black storm was to the left, with rolling lightning playing violently across half the sky. On the other side, there was a man with a black mustache. He had close-cropped dark hair and a staff darker than night. One arm reached toward her. The man was, in Rianas' understanding of the nog's world, the one portrayed in the mask she had seen a few hours before. His face was friendly, like a father figure, and he was gesturing as if he would lead her away from the storm. Just past him was a makeshift mine entrance. As Rianas looked at the mine entrance, she could see 'fellow' nogs racing in, flooding through to the other side.

The dream world disappeared, and Atrick was stepping back. The nog had gone limp, its eyes open in terror as it took one shuddering breath. Rianas withdrew her hand from its head, and it fell forward. The nog had passed out. The stress of having its memories stripped from its head must have been too much to handle.

Rianas shuddered. She wondered if she had always had this ability. Could she control it? She felt fine, as if she had simply opened a door and walked out of the dream world into reality again. The nog, on the other hand, was breathing very heavily.

Atrick looked at her, his eyebrows raised. His face seemed to say, "I thought you would figure it out."

"There were no words," Rianas said. "Just a field with storm clouds on one side and a man that was the inspiration of that mask you got from Raskin Jorgen on the other side. He was beckoning me to come with him into a mine. This one, I guess."

Atrick pondered, idly pushing the unconscious nog into a more comfortable position so it would not choke against its bindings. "The mask is obviously some sort of power-projection device for whoever that character is. Perhaps it is an Axarean general, or some sort of royalty within the empire. Either way, this verifies that someone who controls these nogs led them to this cave."

Atrick had a few more nogs brought over, one at a time. Each time, Rianas repeated the procedure. Each time, the exact same scene played out.

"It is almost as if someone painted that scene into the nogs' minds," she said. "There is no variation."

"That's interesting," Atrick said. "Perhaps that is what was done. Perhaps they have all somehow been brainwashed into following orders." Atrick got up. "This may work to our advantage. If these creatures were single-mindedly trying to take over the mine, they might not have informed whoever is on the other side that they are having trouble."

Rianas got up, too. "Then now would be our chance to break through." She could feel the adrenaline from earlier surging back up within her.

"Hold on, let's think through options," Atrick cautioned, as one of the mercenaries led the last nog out of the interrogation area. "There could be an entire army waiting to come through on the other side. If we had help from the Sko'Port guard, we might be able to push them back. The guards could help us build defenses on the other side."

Rianas shook her head. "Atrick, this is our chance to see the other side of the Black Mountains. Very few outside of Axarea who are alive today have seen it, right? There would be Andarian lowlands on the other side of the mountains, according to my history classes. Axarea took Andaria years before my parents were born. Andaria is where my ancestors were born. It calls to me. Can we pass up a chance to break through to the other side?"

"The path would be difficult." Atrick warned, but then he shrugged and said, "Waiting, however, could give the Axareans time to mount another incursion."

"Don't think I am a zealot looking for battle," Rianas said. "I know there could be danger ahead. The Axareans could drive us back. But if we can reach the exit on the other side, we might establish an outpost. This cavern would be a huge benefit for mining operations, too. And look at it from Sko'Port's perspective: an outpost on the other side of the Black Mountains could drive down the amount of mountain crossings by Axarean spies and infiltrators."

Rianas thought for a second.

"You might also open up a new trade route," she said, appealing to Atrick's business sense.

Rianas felt inspired. Something about the visions in the nogs' subconscious had connected with her curiosity. Why was there nothing written about life in present day Axarean-occupied Andaria? What good could come from Axarean invaders shutting down a mine that led right into the largest city in the Northern Realms?

A gnawing tug inside her made Rianas want to see the other side of the mountain. She felt, beyond her selfish thoughts of self-preservation, an overriding need to push back at an empire she was growing to see as a corrupting influence on the Northern Realms. She might not be anything spectacular by herself, but Atrick had been willing to risk his life for a greater good in coming this far. How could she step away from whatever was on the other end of this cavern now?

"I would follow you, Atrick," she said, somewhat surprised at her own words. She shivered, but the words felt right even as she said them. Growing more certain, she asked, "Do you think you could convince the rest of these volunteers?"

"We must," he answered. A smile started to spread across his face. "Of course, you're right. We will take these volunteers to the exit, secure it, and see what there is on the other side! Come with me. Let's get the rest of the group together, search those last two tunnels, and go."

When they arrived at the left-most tunnel, Atrick asked Galen, Rianas' group, and about fifty others to guard it. While Atrick took Teran and about sixty other mercenaries to the other auxiliary entrance, they pulled a few stones together to make a small barricade and rest for about an hour. Samuel and John were also there, each wearing a few bandages around their arms from combat earlier in the day.

Samuel was busy sharpening his retrieved crossbow bolts, while John had taken a few of the Nog weapons and was making himself a longer spear. He waved at Rianas and Arthur, and the four spoke like old war friends for a few minutes while they reviewed the day's events. Rianas told them what she had learned from the nogs and asked what they thought about fighting through the mine.

"Would you follow Atrick to Old Andaria? For me, there is no question. It would almost be a privilege to return to our ancient homeland," Rianas said nervously.

Arthur nodded. "It could be risky, but those monsters had nothing but hatred in their eyes for us. If you think it is a good idea, Rianas, I would follow. Besides, someone has to keep you safe." he laughed, and then fell off the mushroom cap he was sitting on when Rianas shoved him.

Samuel considered, but agreed. "We came to help save people. This is a fine group of men and women here. They have worked together very well so far."

John nodded. "Arthur is right. If the three of you would follow

Atrick, I would too. Besides, Rianas makes a good point about seeing our homeland of Andaria. We owe it to our people in Riverrun to at least see it."

8. SIGNET

In the middle of the Great Continent, the Borsilkian Alliance aided the small city-states on their western border against imperial incursions. In five centuries of conflict with the Empire, they had succeeded in creating a no-man's land between the Borsilkian Alliance and Axarea to their south. Their ferocity and single-minded attention to victory over the Axareans was perhaps the biggest setback the Axarean Empire had ever faced. However, the Borsilkian Alliance could not fight the entire Axarean army alone, and in the fifty years since the fall of Andaria, they had lost a key trading partner. With it, the Borsilkians had also lost another buffer between them and Axarea.

From: "An Incomplete History of Arthos"
Grandmaster Ar'Ishan's lecture on Axarean aggression
1943 A.C.

An hour of rest was not much time, but Galen was walking around the makeshift camp soon enough, gathering the group up to march into the side cave. He avoided Rianas' gaze when he first arrived, but his eyes met hers when he said he would be coming with them to search one of the side caverns.

Unlike the main caverns they had been in, this section of the cave was smaller. In parts, it was only a dozen feet across. Rianas walked along a wall toward the front, Samuel behind her with his crossbow at the ready. Galen marched down the center, and the hand lamp Rianas had brought lit up a few dozen yards ahead of them all.

Stalactites and stalagmites along the edges of the cave made it seem as if someone had crunched a much larger tunnel down like an accordion. It was difficult to walk. Fallen stones the size of carriages rested across the uneven floor. All around, water seeped slowly from the walls until it ran into a small stream in the center of the cave that ran lazily back toward the main cavern. The party slipped their way up the corridor. After a few minutes, the treacherous path had slowed them to a near crawl as they struggled to prevent injuries.

Fortunately, the cave ended abruptly as they came around a bend. Rianas' light illuminated an overflowing pool of bluish-white water. The cave wall completely submerged a few dozen yards beyond the small pool.

Galen shrugged. "No nogs could have hidden down here. We can go back, I guess."

However, Rianas was staring into the pond, watching the hand-sized fish and wondering how deep the water was. Her light shone deep down into the pond, and she thought she saw another light further down. "Look there," she said, pointing.

Arthur looked. "Something big is swimming down there." He took a dagger out of his belt. Samuel aimed his crossbow, and Galen watched curiously.

For about fifteen minutes, they watched as the light drifted slowly up to the surface. It seemed humanoid, and everyone was tense as it broke through the water.

A skinny, shirtless humanoid no more than five feet tall came to the surface. The creature flung a small net full of crabs onto the ground in front of Rianas. There were thick goggles around its face and a huge cured lizard hide with a small metal tube wrapped around its waist and inserted into its mouth. The creature spit the metal tube out of its mouth as it removed the thick goggles. Its oversized head bobbed a bit, as if the comparatively small neck could barely hold it up out of the water.

Rianas watched the long fingers gently package the metal tube into a side pocket. The creature looked old and wrinkled, but its fingers worked the tube deftly into the pocket.

Despite the dozens of humans confronting him, the strange creature appeared calm.

"Hello," said Rianas awkwardly. She felt a need to break the silence.

The creature looked straight at her and smiled. "Hello," it said back in its own language. The rest of the group heard something along the lines of "Gir'un." The language he spoke was different from the others Rianas had heard. Its origins seemed vaguely Dwarven, but the consonants rolled more lightly off its tongue, almost like Elven.

The creature kept speaking. "My name is Signet. This is my pond. I take it you have cleared those nasty nogs away from the main cavern?"

When Signet started speaking, Rianas felt the tension start to ease in the cave, despite the fact that only she knew what he was saying. The creature was obviously not threatening them. Samuel lowered his crossbow, Arthur pocketed his dagger, and the men behind her followed suit.

Galen, unable to understand the creature, edged closer to Rianas. "What is it saying?" he asked. Rianas told him.

"Uh, what are you doing here?" Rianas asked.

"I am a gnome. And this," Signet motioned toward the sack of crabs, "is what I've been forced to eat while those disgusting nogs have been running around destroying the cave for the last few months."

"Oh." Rianas did not even know where to begin. Signet had a small dagger at his waist and some stones tied to his legs. He knelt down to remove the ballast from his old grey pants while he stood ankle deep in the water. He handed the stone weights to her as he untied them. Rianas took them, dumbfounded and not sure how to react.

"Did you meet any more of my people?" Signet asked. He stepped out of the water. There was quite a bit of shuffling as Samuel, Berryl, and a few others stepped back to give the gnome space.

"No."

"Hmm." Suddenly, the gnome stopped and turned in surprise to Rianas. He looked her up and down before saying, "Your Gnomish is excellent. Have you been to Garenam to study?"

Rianas had no idea what the gnome was talking about. "Who is Garenam?" she asked.

Then her history lessons came to mind. The Borsilkian Alliance was largely composed of this peculiar sub-species of humanoids. Gnomes were really what the rest of the Northern Realms called Halflings, but these particular Borsilkians had a reputation for their insulated culture even among their own kind. The Garenam province was in the western parts of the Black Mountains, and the so-called Gnomes who called it home had focused on the sciences to the exclusion of almost all else. "Oh, Garenam is the city you are from, right?"

"Yes." Signet's voice was raspy, and Rianas noticed how old and wrinkled his skin was. In the light of her hand lamp, his grey skin was nearly translucent. Veins on his bare chest stood out, winding beneath his wiry, sparse chest hair. He walked over to the cave wall, a few yards above the pond, and ran his hand along the wall.

"I haven't left this cave in seven years, though. Axarea is unsafe for our kind."

At first Rianas couldn't tell what he was doing, but then Signet pulled a non-descript stone, and a small stone door easily slid open, revealing a tight but tidy room a couple yards across. Signet dropped the glowing mushrooms he had used for light into a metal lantern as he walked into the tiny space and started fiddling with a scrap-metal and stone stove. He put a clay pot full of water on top to boil and turned back around.

"I can't offer all of you tea, but I hope you don't mind me serving myself. All that swimming wears me out." Signet had a mushroom cap that he pulled out to use as a soft stool. He sat down with a deep sigh, looking out on the group.

Galen was still standing next to Rianas. "What is he saying?"

Rianas told Galen what she had learned about Signet. Then, turning back to Signet, she asked, "You have been living deep in this cave for seven years?"

Signet nodded, looking more serious now. "That isn't the worst of it. The Gnomes built Garenam deep into the hills, so our people have grown accustomed to working with the stone. The part that has made it hard is the lack of younger settlers. You see, we Gnomes are not strong fighters. I am a decent swimmer, but I can hardly run.

The rest of us are old, as well. Axareans have horses, hunting animals, and nogs. When the Axareans cut us off from Garenam, the younger members of our group helped us escape by luring our pursuers into a trap. Their goal was to slow the soldiers down for a week or so. They must have succeeded, because we managed to avoid detection for months after that. But it cost us the bravest, youngest members of our group." He shook his head.

"How horrible," Rianas said. "You must have thought you would be stuck in this cavern for the rest of your lives, never able to get back to your homeland."

"Yes, it has been hard. A few of our group even struck out on their own about three years ago. I decided to stay here with a handful of the rest when we found the mushroom cavern out there. It was a rich and beautiful place, where we could safely build homes to live out our days. We were going to introduce ourselves to those miners when they broke their way into this cavern, but just a couple weeks later the nogs arrived."

Signet sighed and stirred the tea in his cup. "Those monsters destroy everything in their path. I've been hiding here, hoping they would move along when they didn't find anything else to kill."

Rianas turned to Galen and told him some of what she had learned. "I know we will be moving on soon. Would you mind if I stay? I want to speak some more with Signet. Arthur, Samuel and John could stay with me. I want to find out what he knows about Andaria. I will catch up in a few hours."

Galen nodded. His face said he had a thousand questions for Rianas. She thought about asking him what he wanted, but he said, "If you feel comfortable with this gnome, I will let you stay behind. Atrick may be angry with me if he doesn't see you return. Please don't be terribly long. I understand we will be following the river as soon as the other side cave has been cleared."

"I won't be long," Rianas said. She nodded at Galen as he turned the rest of the group around.

Signet watched as the mercenaries stumbled off, going slowly to prevent falls, then he pointed along the wall. "There is a path right there that I have kept clean. You can follow it when you leave. I poured ground mushroom spores onto the ground along the edge of the wall."

Rianas could make out the path clearly, now that Signet had shown it to her. However, she wanted to know more from the gnome. "Can you tell me more about the Axareans?"

Signet took four more clay cups from above the tiny stove and offered the tea he was brewing to the four of them. He dragged his mushroom stool out near the pond where the other three were standing, and sat down. "Axarea has been at war with Borsilk for centuries. They began attacking the state of Garenam over a hundred years ago. The main city of Garenam is where most of the Gnomes have fled to, now. We have provided materials and experiments for the Borsilkian armies to use, and that has slowed the Axarean attacks.

"Axarean armies are endless, though," Signet said as he sipped his tea. "Their plans are made for centuries of war, not years or months. Nogs, Southerners, even monsters have been sent in to our lands. The Borsilkian armies are better armed, but every defeat, no matter how small, brings the Axareans closer to victory. Garenam cannot be easily attacked, and our cannons have been enough to keep the Axareans miles away from the city, but they keep probing the surrounding hills for ways to cut us off completely from the rest of the Borsilkian Alliance. Our city sent out scouts to find rare minerals and wood. "

Signet sighed. "It still seems like only a few days ago I was there last. I remember the grain elevators, cannons, underground fountains, thousands of experiments running on river water, thermal energy, and coal. It was a wonderful place to work on your inventions. There were tens of thousands of engineers at work in the deeper parts of the city. Those engineers were always building something to make life easier for the residents of Garenam. That is where I designed this."

Signet pulled the strap off his shoulder that was holding the leather lizard pouch to his body. He pulled it around and set it on his lap, unfolding the small metal hose. "It is an underwater breathing bladder I designed."

Rianas looked at it, amazed. "That is how you were able to swim underwater for so long, isn't it?"

"Yes." Signet's ancient face lit up with pride. He pulled open a small flap on the top and unscrewed an earthenware lid covered in some sort of oily resin. As the top came off, the breathing bladder deflated, making a hissing sound. "You see, air goes in here. I use this part here to push it into my lungs when I need to breathe." He pushed on a spring-loaded part where the lizard's tail would have been. As he gently released it, the metal hose hissed loudly.

Arthur, not understanding what they were saying, asked if that was how Signet had swum underwater. Rianas explained the contraption to the other three.

Arthur could barely contain his excitement. He ran his fingers over the lizard skin. He pushed the hose around and pulled on it, examining Signet's expert workmanship. As Rianas kept talking, Arthur showed the others how the contraption worked. The excitement in his voice was evident even though Rianas was not really listening to him.

"Well, we came from Sko'Port," Rianas said. "Atrick is the head wizard of the High Mine. He brought this group with him to clear out the mine of nogs. Unfortunately, it seems Axarea sent the nogs here. We are going to see if we can secure the southern entrance. You and the nogs both confirm that there is a pathway straight through the mountain, now."

"Interesting." Signet put one of his long fingers to his temple, pushing the loose skin on his forehead around with the digit. "Perhaps I can secure safe passage for my people to get to Sko'Port? If we can get to Sko'Port, we might be able to return to Garenam." Signet sighed, and his body seemed to shrink. "It has been so many years. I never thought I would see my homeland again. I should tell my people what we have witnessed since we were separated."

"I should think you could," said Rianas. "You would need to go soon, though. There is a chance our rescue party will fail. If we do, an army of nogs might be on their way into the caves."

Even as Rianas was saying it, she wondered if Atrick had been right. Maybe he should be more cautious. The others could not understand her Gnomish, but she feared she might have convinced the rest of the Riverrunners to put their lives at risk again. Her gaze lingered on Arthur's boyish grin long enough for Signet to smile.

"Perhaps I should find the others and we should leave while we can." Signet stood, still barely taller than Rianas when she was sitting. He looked into the small room he had made into his exile home and pulled out a tunic to place over his grey, wrinkled torso. "I'll be glad to stop eating cave crabs for a while. Tell me, does the sun still burn the ground in the summers? Does the rain still fall from the sky?"

Rianas helped the old gnome gather some things together, all along asking about what he had witnessed on his trip to this cave. Signet described the southern side of the Black Mountains as full of fallen stones and small creeks. He had not ventured off of the mountains in fear of being found by Axarean forces, but he described the terrain south of the mountains as flat grassland, with a wide river meandering a few miles from the foot of the mountains as it made its way west. Hundreds of small streams like this one fed it.

Rianas told Signet about Riverrun. She suggested he try to get there first. With Riverrun's Borsilkian College, Signet might be able to find another Halfling professor there who could help him make his way home. He agreed.

As he finished packing, Signet picked up the breathing bladder. "This is too heavy to take with me. Would you take it, Ms. Rianas? Consider it a thank-you gift for clearing those nogs from the cavern. If not for your group, I might have died here, hundreds of miles from my homeland."

Rianas was overwhelmed. "I couldn't possibly take this from you, Signet. Why not bring it with you and sell it to a vendor in Sko'Port?"

"I couldn't carry it through these caves that far. I am an old gnome, and the things I've packed here will be too heavy as it is."

Rianas hefted the bladder. It weighed about ten pounds. "At least let me give you ten Gold Eagles. It will give you enough money to buy passage for yourself and a few others across the Sko'Sea, perhaps. If not, it will be enough to help you start off from Sko'Port."

John whistled when he saw the coins. Arthur asked what Rianas thought she was doing. "I am helping these people get back to their homes," she answered.

Signet graciously accepted the coins. He patted Rianas on the shoulder. "May you always find your way, young lady." With that, he hefted his small bag.

Rianas and the others followed Signet out along his less treacherous trail. Arthur offered to carry the underwater breathing bladder, and John commented he thought Rianas had paid too much for the contraption.

In common, she reminded them all they were in this tunnel to help people. "I have no need for that money if we can't secure the exit. If we do, we will be heroes. Riverrun will be able to find out what happened to Andaria."

Arthur laughed as they made their way back to the others. "Rianas," he joked, feigning a Runlarian salute, "you will make a great commander one day."

9. DESCENT

Axarea never sent its emissaries to Andaria. There were no impossible demands, no offer for alliance, nor request of fealty. For over two hundred years, Axarea's border with Andaria steadily grew. Very little trade occurred between the Axarean Empire and Andaria, but neither was there conflict.

Many scholars think that should have been the real indicator of Axarean intent.

The Axarean Empire never gave the Andarians a warning. Half the nation was lost within the first week. Only the brave or lucky escaped through the Gates of Cidvag, and the Andarian warriors who did take up arms knew from the beginning that their land was lost.

Those brave few could only buy time. They bought time for the Cidvagian army to advance into northern Andaria and evacuate families while they fought a long retreat toward the gate. They bought time for Sullaria to send a legion of knights and some of its best wizards to the Gates of Cidvag. They bought time for Sko'Port to use its own small garrisons and stone smiths to fortify the Gates. They bought time for Western Runlar's acting lord to ride with his royal army right to the field in front of the Gates.

However, time was not something with which the Axareans ever seemed concerned. The Axarean Empire did not operate in months or years. Instead, the Empire moved, planned and attacked in ways that were more insidious. It did not matter if a battle was lost, only that the war was won. There were countless Nog, Orc, and Southern volunteers, it seemed.

From: "An Incomplete History of Arthos"
Grandmaster Ar'Ishan's lecture on Axarean aggression
1943 A.C.

When Rianas and the other Riverrunners came to the bright

mushroom cavern, Signet bade them farewell. Rianas wished him luck after instructing him on a few useful phrases in Northern he could use to help his people get out of the High Mine. He joked that the younger Gnomes all knew Northern. "I never had time to learn, though. It seems like a bad excuse after spending seven years sitting in a cave, doesn't it?"

Gnomish humor was a little beyond Rianas, but she smiled anyway.

The four Riverrunners watched the gnome hobble around a few mushrooms until he was out of sight.

They set out for the lower cave entrance. It was easy to find. They followed the sound of the stream. In a few moments, they saw the entirety of the mercenary group gathered along the stream as it led into the lower cave. Galen found them first. He walked right up to Rianas and told her that Atrick's other party had found no nogs in the other entrance.

Rianas could see Atrick speaking with some of the miners who had helped them. Galen said Elias and a few other veterans were helping to convince the others that it was the right path to fight their way through the caves.

"Atrick is the best thing that ever happened to the High Mine," Galen said to Rianas as they walked toward the gathered mercenaries. "His passion to do the right thing inspires these men and women."

As they got closer, they could hear Atrick's voice. "The injured and any who don't want to come with us can stay behind. We hope to have reinforcements from Sko'Port's guards in a few days if Berryl is able to convince them of the Axarean threat. In the meanwhile, you will be the first line of defense against an Axarean invasion. If you come with us, you can be the first expedition to break through into the Black Mountains since the end of the Andarian War fifty years ago."

Sal was in the front of the group Atrick was addressing.

"I'll come with you," she said. "Those Nog monsters attacked us without provocation. My husband is gone. It doesn't matter who is on the other side of the mountain, I intend to make them pay for what they have done."

Some of the other miners cheered her resolve. A few dozen of the mercenaries did not seem so sure. One man – Jalek, a Cidvagian mercenary Rianas remembered interviewing – asked, "We have already risked our lives once. How do we know this isn't just a trap? This expedition we were hired for was only to clear the mine."

Atrick responded, "Jalek, your grandparents fought the Axareans off at the Cidvagian Gates, did they not?"

Jalek nodded, his massive arms folded across his chest.

"If we are successful in establishing a base on the other side of the mountains," Atrick said, "you will be a hero in Cidvag. The allied army that has stood guard at the Gates for fifty years would be thrilled to know another front has opened to distract Axarea from them. Sko'Port has the manpower to garrison an outpost, so Cidvag and Sko'Port would be able to coordinate together in defending against any future attacks."

Jalek was unconvinced. He had become the de facto leader of a few dozen Cidvagian mercenaries. Rianas remembered most of those faces. Those men behind him had been more interested in the large purses Atrick had offered. "I don't care about heroism. Heroism buys nothing for the dead. We should stop here and wait until the reinforcements arrive. If they arrive and still need help, they can hire us on to go further."

A few of the mercenaries grouped around him agreed loudly. Rianas could sense the group's position against going further hardening. A quick glance around told her if those skilled soldiers left the expedition it would only be about two thirds of the original size – maybe two hundred mercenaries, along with a few dozen miners.

If the Cidvagian mercenaries refused to come, the battle for the mine exit might be lost before it started. Many of the mercenaries thinking of giving up were more heavily armed; some even had chain link armor and swords. Most of the rest of the expedition had brought short weapons in preparation for combat in the mine.

Atrick shook his head. "You make a good point, Jalek. I understand you signed on only to clear the mine. I am asking for something more. We see an Axarean-sanctioned leader was leading the nogs. It is only a matter of time before they decide to send a search party in to find out why none of their explorers has reported. I am sure you would rather take them by surprise than risk battle with Axarean elite soldiers in this huge cavern. If we stay, we must defend this huge entrance." Atrick motioned toward the lower exit.

Indeed, the lower exit was wide. It was wider than a major road, only covered in stony outcroppings. Huge mushrooms protruded at strange angles well into the exit. A few places looked easy to defend. Standing next to her, Arthur whispered as much and gestured.

Jalek was unconvinced, too. "We could go a few hundred yards," he said, "or until the cave gets narrower. This cave hasn't been widened like the mine we were in before. It would be easy to find a section that was only fifty feet across."

Galen came to Atrick's defense as he joined the others. "Jalek, I have fought the Axareans before. A Baron or some other type of lord usually directs an advanced unit such as this. They would have an entourage of servants, and enough gold to support their endeavors and purchase supplies from the locals. If we pushed them back and captured their leader, you would find great riches!"

The thought of riches seemed to break the unity of the men behind Jalek. A few seemed excited at the prospect of looting an Axarean lord's treasure chest. Jalek scowled at Galen, seeing his newfound leadership role starting to dissolve.

"I've never heard of such a thing," Jalek spat.

Galen nodded, lowering his voice a bit as he got closer. "We've probably dealt a pretty severe blow to their unit, too. If we had the benefit of surprise, we might be able to capture a lord and ransom him back to the Empire for even more."

Jalek's eyes moved, but his mouth did not. He was silent for a moment while the cacophony of mercenaries arguing about how they would split their treasure grew.

Finally, Jalek turned to the others who had positioned themselves behind him. "We will follow Atrick's foolhardy advance through the cave. When we get to the outside, we will claim whatever treasure there is, and we will return to Cidvag as heroes!"

More cheers went up through the group. The dissenters grew

quiet. Jalek walked back amongst his 'men' to start developing strategies. Teran and Rianas walked over to Atrick, who was speaking quietly with Elias and two other older veterans whose names Rianas could not remember. One was shaking his head, and Elias had a serious look upon his face. Atrick motioned Teran, Galen and the others to come with him.

"We need to leave right away," Atrick said, looking over his shoulder at Jalek. "Thank you, Galen. You never cease to amaze me, old friend."

Galen put his hands in his robes. "It has always been an axiom of the world that people will believe what they want to believe."

Teran grinned. "That small lie will be excusable if it helps us secure this entire section of the cave."

Arthur could not help interjecting, "You made up that story of rich lords leading Axarean units, didn't you, Galen?"

Elias, Galen, and Atrick all said yes at once. Despite the serious nature of the discussion, it made Rianas laugh.

"What are those men going to do when they see it isn't true?" asked John. "They may just run away, right?"

Atrick nodded. "Galen may have bought us some time. I doubt we will have a strong enough force to take the exit when we get there without them, however. I hope Berryl is able to convince Captain Oren of the upper guards to send men in. If they do not, we will surely be overwhelmed shortly after we breach the entrance to the cave. I sincerely doubt the Axareans sent just a few hundred nogs to capture this mine."

Atrick looked over to Rianas.

"Rianas," the wizard said, "these are the men you should trust most in combat. Elias you have fought with before. Harold and Sunduin are also war veterans. They have fought in Eastern Runlar against the Axareans. Harold, Sunduin, please bring your groups up with me while we march down. I hope strong leadership will help us take the exit when we arrive."

Atrick took each of the older men by the shoulders and introduced them to Rianas, having them shake her hands. Rianas thought it was a bit strange. "Rianas, you are with Elias, so keep close to him if something goes wrong."

Elias nodded. "Atrick, I will fight the Axareans until my last breath if that is what it takes."

Rianas thought she saw Galen nodding emphatically beside Atrick.

After a few moments of Atrick instructing his apprentices, the group began its descent into the cave. Jalek's men were slow to follow, but they caught up before the light of the cavern dissipated completely.

This cave was raw, barely traversable by humanoid feet. Marks from Nog pickaxes were everywhere. Jagged scrapes marred the walls and ceiling. Instead of hauling the stones out, the nogs had dumped them into the deeper parts of the stream. The cold water was twenty feet or more across now. Water ran haphazardly around the cave, splashing into walls and around huge boulders that had been knocked from the ceiling. In most places, the water was no more than a foot deep. Rianas could see how the nogs had created walking paths for themselves a few feet wide, but the small army of volunteers had to move two or three abreast through this cave now. Some braver miners would hop along to get ahead, but for the most part the going was slow for so many men at once.

In a few hours, they had traveled only one or two miles. The group spread out beyond bowshot as the passage grew more difficult. Atrick suggested they rest for three hours before starting up again, but he was visibly agitated when Teran suggested they rest for five hours and try to get some sleep.

"No, Teran. We have seen no other evidence of invaders in this cave. My preference is to get out of here as soon as we can. The nogs will have the advantage if they catch us on this icy river. They are smaller and could navigate these slippery surfaces better than we could. We might bottleneck them, but I doubt our rearguard would hold. It could turn into a disorganized rout."

Teran nodded. Rianas, her bright hand lamp illuminating the stony brook below, sat down and took her boots off. Her feet were sore from navigating the hard stones for hours and she was tired, but adrenaline still coursed through her veins. A few men here and there tried to nap on the hard stone, but most simply sat in reflection.

Arthur had his cooking lamp out and proceeded to heat up some water for a tea.

Sal sniffled beside her. When she checked her bandage, Sal exclaimed and took it off. Rianas stared when the burly woman showed her healed legs to the rest of the group.

"Wow", said Arthur, "I've never seen a healing potion at work before. It's like you didn't even have an injury!"

The rest of them checked their injuries and saw the same. Rianas could not believe that just a few hours had been enough to sew her skin back together.

Arthur leaned toward Rianas. "I think I know why Atrick had those two men shake your hand," he said. He looked proud of himself in his own goofy way.

"Why?" asked Rianas, smiling at the absurdity.

"Because your touch helps you sense people's thoughts. I bet he talked to them about it. In a fight, knowing what someone forty feet away says or thinks might give you an edge." Arthur smiled at his genius.

Rianas let the smile drop from her face as she considered. "Perhaps. I don't think I have that kind of control over my ability, though, Arthur."

However, that did not stop her thinking about it. Rianas lay down uncomfortably on her sleeping mat and said she was going to sleep.

Instead, she closed her eyes and reached toward the tendrils of magic that seemed to be everywhere, just out of sight. Rianas focused her thoughts. She practiced controlling the weave of magic. She lay there for hours. She carefully constructed weaves for a light spell. The weave never seemed to coalesce. The strands always fell apart at the last moment.

A little while before Atrick would be starting the trek up again, Rianas felt more than heard Atrick's words.

"*Rianas,*" Atrick said, "*we've only a mile to go. Let Elias and your companions know, please. Can you come see me?*"

Rianas sat upright, looking around. Atrick was staring into the abyss of the descending cave from a nearby boulder. "*Okay,*" she thought, wondering if he would 'hear' her.

Atrick looked in her direction and nodded. Rianas packed her bag quickly, leaving the heavy gear behind to go see Atrick. Arthur, nodding off in a sitting position, made a soft snoring sound as she stepped past him. Elias inclined his head as she walked by.

Atrick had a piece of parchment and a small ink pen spread out upon a particularly flat piece of stone that he had dried meticulously somehow. Rianas wondered aloud, thinking how heavy the spray of water was that hung in the air.

"I used a little heat from a fire spell, just enough to heat this stone. I weaved a small amount of magic around it to keep it dry," Atrick explained.

Rianas felt the stone and marveled at the idea. "How did you come up with a spell like that? It seems so delicate."

Atrick smiled. "Sometimes just a little magic is all we need to use, Rianas. You are trying very hard to harness the weave, but you need to learn to 'ride' the magic, not just try to harness it. I find often if I simply meditate upon my needs I can find a path to my goal."

Rianas did not understand. "The weave seems to be everywhere around me, but I can't see it. How can I follow a path I can't see?"

"You already cast magic all the time, Rianas. How do you think you were able to see what those nogs were seeing?"

Atrick lifted the sheet of parchment. He had scribbled Jalek's name on top, and beneath it was a sort of tree, with names of other mercenaries, most of them Cidvagian, in some sort of organizational chart. "In the meanwhile, I think I have a request you can help me with, Rianas. Jalek's been working his way into a leadership position amongst a sizeable group of professional mercenaries here. Some are men and women he has worked with before, and others he has convinced he is the man to follow.

"I don't think he has ill intentions toward any of us," Atrick continued. "To the contrary, despite his words a few hours ago I believe he truly wants to help. He just needs an excuse to rally his men around him. Galen's lie about gold will be apparent when we fight the next group of nogs. We need a way to keep Jalek's trust. Galen has put together a list of men he is treating as his aides. This should help us maintain order if something happens to Jalek, or if I am wrong about his intentions. In the meanwhile, I'd like you to stay close to Jalek if battle ensues."

Atrick had other calculations around the margin. There were numbers written, crossed out, and inserted all along the margins of the page. "I've taken inventory of our weapons. We can probably fight a few more hours before the healing potions start to run out." Atrick opened his robe enough to pull out a long, heavy glass bottle, with a small brass serving glass wedged into the leather carrying case. "I would like you to carry this potion. It has enough healing potion inside to heal perhaps ten men, so long as you carefully portion it out. Keep it someplace you can get to it easily, but watch that it does not get stolen."

Rianas tucked it in her side belt, listening carefully to Atrick's quick instructions on how to use the precious liquid. She was to give a small glassful to an injured person right away, then wrap the injury in a piece of cloth doused in the liquid. She could ignore cuts. It was important to treat stab wounds and critical injuries, however, as soon as possible. Rianas thanked Atrick and asked why he was entrusting her with the potion.

"The magical scroll and this potion should help keep you safe," Atrick said. "I wish I had sought you out in Riverrun a year ago. We could have developed your abilities more. Nevertheless, I want to give you some tools for what is coming next. You should practice casting a spell with this scroll. It will most likely be something small you choose to direct, but the feeling of the magic being weaved for you may help you understand the art of weaving magic yourself. Reading scrolls helps some casters learn to understand their own magic. Others it does not help at all. Either way, having the scroll will help you cast magic when we come to the surface.

"Also," Atrick looked back toward the group spread amongst the stones. "If Jalek's men see you casting magic against the nogs, you may convince them to continue fighting."

"I don't understand," Rianas said, looking back at the soft glow of hundreds of small lamps. "Most of the people here are better fighters than I am. Your apprentices have a grasp of spells. Even Arthur is faster and stronger than I am. Why do you think I am so important?

Maybe I can read people's minds. And apparently, I can knock some of those nogs out when I do. It doesn't seem like an ability that will change the world. In fighting those nogs, I felt like I could barely hold my own, much less help someone else out."

Atrick shook his head, and the prophecy book he had shown her before once more seemed to pop into his hand from nowhere. "You don't put much faith in prophecy – that's fine. I, however, have studied dozens of prophecies written by the Elves. They always come true in one way or another. You should be more cognizant of the way people look up to you, Rianas. Arthur, John, Samuel, Sal, even Elias – they all speak highly of you. As soon as you mentioned going further into the caves, I would bet they all agreed. Do not dismiss the power of suggestion you hold. I suspect some of it is because you are so confident, and some may be because you are a woman doing what so few choose to do. Do not take such power for granted."

Rianas had never thought twice about being a woman amongst these adventurers. The excitement of hiking through the mines, the fear of the Nog attack, and the beauty of the great caverns they had found had been more interesting to her. She had always loved hiking and running through the farms of Riverrun, so she was more muscular than most girls at school were. Her presence in this group seemed natural to her.

Atrick telling her she had influence over others was strange. In school, she had friends, but most of the time she was more interested in the lessons professors had to share. Her friends had all liked to do the same things as she did, so it was not as if she was influencing anyone. Arthur had followed her because he wanted to explore. John and Samuel had made the decision to come based on their respect for Atrick, not her. Rianas kept her thoughts to herself, but she suspected Atrick was seeing something that was not actually there.

Atrick, his wise eyes piercing into Rianas, seemed to know she was not convinced. "You aren't sure of yourself yet, Rianas. That is okay. Many great leaders go about their business for years before realizing their true calling. Don't be so fast to dismiss your abilities, though, young lady. Something," and with this, he reached with his ringed index finger and tapped her on the forehead gently before repeating himself, "something inside of you is trying to make its way out. You must catch hold of it when the time comes, and direct it in your favor."

Atrick folded his parchment. Almost as soon as he placed the paper into his pocket, Rianas felt the light mist of water blow gently against her face again. "Now, let's cast something from that scroll. I want to see what you are able to do."

Rianas pulled the scroll from the leg pocket of her harness, where she had put it to safeguard against the water. She gently unrolled the scroll, looking at the bright, almost glowing lettering in Elven. Atrick muttered some words about how to control the weave, but they were meaningless to her. As soon as she saw the words on the page, Rianas felt a surge of energy well up all around her.

Rianas felt the words on the page without actually understanding them. It seemed as if the actual letters began dissolving as soon as she read them. They were symbols of her intent, tied inextricably to the weave. This was unlike the magic she had tried casting before. The words themselves seemed to contain the weave. Rianas felt the tendrils of magic move back and forth.

The words she pulled from her scroll molded her thoughts into physical form. A strange prickling sensation of heat and cold crept along the fingertips of her right hand, and she was aware of a rustling of wind that had not been there an instant before. In the background, Atrick was saying something. Rianas' body seemed incapable of deciphering anything beyond the magical page. Distant sounds filled her ears. Her eyes could not move from the glowing Elven letters. The power of the scroll transfixed her.

As she read the last word, she felt the world shift. Feeling the intention of the scroll and directing it with her need, Rianas unconsciously lifted her right arm and pointed down the cave about forty feet. Suddenly, a burst of light sprang into being. This light was unlike Atrick's lightning ball. Instead, this light seemed unbound, directional, full of pent up energy. With a mere thought and a flick of her wrist, the ball of energy uncoiled like a rope of fire.

Fiery lightning streaked deep into the cave.

The string of light brightened both sides of the cave as it sailed down and away. Stalactites and stalagmites reflected the bright blue, sparkling in the spray of the water. Here and there, white bugs zipped to the side to avoid the foreign light. Half a dozen bats took flight, squealing in protest as *she* chased them downhill.

Rianas felt a strange connection with the rope of light. As it streaked further away, she could sense the walls around it, the reflections from the water. She was the conductor, turning left and right to avoid walls and ground alike as she sped like a galloping horse along the center of the cave. She heard the gasps of the other members of the expedition behind her, and knew Atrick was still speaking to her, but they were muffled.

She did not care. There was nothing else in the world that could touch her at this moment. She was the ball of lightning. She struck out, blasting over stones, waterfalls, little blind crabs and fish. There were giant bats in a small side cave she zipped past, a few of them singed by her blazing hair.

She sliced around a corner – now a thousand yards away from the encampment and her corporeal self – nearly slamming into a wall. There was a light in the distance, as if from day. She longed to approach it, but there was suddenly a tether pulling her back. The 'rope' of lightning could not extend any farther.

She could not extend any farther. There was a limit to her omniscience. The sudden end to the stretch brought *her* careening around like a whip, and *she* crashed headlong into the river.

Just like that, the sensation of the weave was gone. Rianas was standing there, her arm slowly falling to her waist and looking out on the fading light of the fiery lightning rope she had just seconds before controlled like an extension of herself. The cave was lit up for a quarter mile before it twisted out of sight, and Rianas remembered every bend in the fading rope of light as if she had traveled it herself.

Around the corner, a flash was fading.

"—ver seen anything like that before! Rianas, are you okay?" Atrick was standing slightly to her right and behind her, his right arm holding the scroll where it had fallen from Rianas' hands.

He started to say something that Rianas could not hear. The howling sound of thunder down the cavern from where the lightning had struck the water drowned out all other sounds.

The entire expedition was awake, and many were on their feet. The thunder faded quickly, and the rope light was almost gone, still hanging like the after-image of lightning in the air. Atrick quickly folded the scroll up and handed it back to Rianas.

"Do you still think you have no talent for magic, Rianas?" Atrick asked breathlessly. "That is an interesting use of fire, light, and wind. I never would have been able to weave something so complex without a scroll. Hmm, I'm not sure I could weave a spell like that without a day of meditation."

"I *saw* the light at the end of the cave, Atrick," Rianas said, looking at her hand and wondering how she was unharmed. It felt as if she had placed it in a fire and doused it in snow, but it was fine. "I couldn't control the weave, but I felt like I was inside of it. I could describe the bends, the stones, everything I flew past. It was like being an eagle, but having a string tied to my tail. When I reached my limit, all my momentum sent me crashing into a wall."

"Your sympathetic powers seem to complement your control of the weave. This is fascinating, Rianas," Atrick said.

Galen lightly jumped over a jagged rock to reach Atrick's observation point. "Was that you, Atrick?" He asked, pointing down the cave. "I don't think we'll be sneaking up on anyone now."

"There was nothing within sight of the light. I would have seen or felt it," Rianas answered.

Galen looked suspiciously over at Rianas. "You cast that?"

"Yes. I wanted to know what was ahead, and I wanted to cast a light spell. I guess when I read the scroll my desires were mixed together somehow. I really don't seem to have any control over my magic."

Atrick laughed at this. "Rianas, you accomplished what I had to send four men to do while everyone was resting." Then he became serious. "You are right, though, Galen. Send word back that we are leaving now. We must move quickly and be prepared for combat. Whoever is at the end of the cave entrance will wonder what that sound was. Hopefully they will assume it was a cave-in and send a small party to assess the damage."

Rianas fingered the scroll as she put it away.

Atrick said, "Be careful opening that up. The words on the page are full of magic. Reading them releases the magic into your body."

"You could have explained THAT better before," Rianas said as she sealed the scroll. The possibilities of casting another spell danced in her head. Outside, she could have explored an entire mountainside in just minutes. She started to walk back to where Arthur and the others were putting on their gear.

Atrick was commanding the other apprentices and Teran to get the expedition moving behind him as Rianas jumped across a stone. Before she reached Arthur, the mage started walking briskly down the cave.

Arthur lifted Rianas' rucksack, already packed with her sleeping gear, and helped strap it onto her as the others filled their bags quickly. "Did you see that lightning ball race down the cave?" he asked.

"Yes. It is the first spell I have cast. Atrick gave me a magical scroll. I guess I don't really know how to control it."

Arthur's jaw dropped. "You did that?"

Rianas tightened the sack to her harness and turned the rest of her body to face him. Arthur let go of the sack and pulled his mouth back closed. "I believe you, Rianas. I just can't believe everything that has happened in the last week."

Rianas agreed. Everything seemed to be happening so fast. It seemed like years ago that they had been spying on secret council meetings and laughing at current Riverrun events. Now, they were out in the world, miles beneath the ground and chasing down Axarean invaders as if it had always been their job.

There was no time to think, though. Atrick was disappearing down the cave already. The rest of the camp had picked up to follow him as quickly as they could. Teran was motioning a group across the path the nogs had cut in the stone four abreast. Rianas and the others had to walk quickly to keep up.

In about thirty minutes, they passed the spot where Rianas'

"lightning rope" had crashed into the floor of the cave. Black scars zigged out of the river. There were marred stones for twenty feet in every direction. It was as if a ball of lava had flung itself into the water. There were melted spots of stone and the smell of burned metal hung lightly in the air.

What got the real attention of the group, however, was the light down below. About half a mile beyond, Rianas could see the obvious light of day hitting rocks. Atrick and the frontrunners of the group had pulled off to a side of the cave behind some large boulders. Teran directed each group as it jumped down a small waterfall to take a short break behind the boulders that littered this area. The expedition stayed out of the line of sight of the cave entrance.

Half a dozen men took up positions with crossbows along the high point of the short waterfall. There was very little talking now. People leaned close to whisper. Some of the men who had come around the tunnel's bend first were telling others they had seen nogs working their way up the cave.

This natural bottleneck in the river created a small pond big enough to hide the three hundred men and women. The water from a small waterfall cascaded through a series of rocky falls here. Small streams bumped back and forth down the last few hundred yards to where the cave turned one last time. The end of the cave was not visible from their hiding place, but it was obvious there was only one turn left.

It was dark here with almost all the lanterns extinguished.

There was only the ever-present sound of the water making its way to the bottom of the mountain. The last men in Jalek's group quietly descended and hid behind the giant boulder where Rianas and Arthur's group was. Rianas found herself only a few yards away from the burly man.

"I heard that you are the one who cast that spell earlier," he said by way of introduction. Jalek's hard black eyes seemed to disappear in the darkness. His helm had been dented severely somehow, presumably in the combat with the nogs, and it sat askew on his large head. His muscular arms were bare, and he wore a piece of black painted plate armor on his chest.

Looking up at the huge man nearly half a head taller than even Arthur was, Rianas felt like she was looking at a black hole with arms and legs. Everything he wore was painted black, so that despite all the steel he wore, he seemed to blend in with the cave in the darkness. "We will keep you safe while you cast your magic. I don't intend to die on the other side of the world."

Rianas looked up at the hulking man, unable to read his expression in the darkness. "I will do my best," she said. "Andaria lies just outside this cave. Samuel, Arthur, John and I will be the first of our people to return there in over fifty years. We won't let this chance go to waste."

Jalek seemed to stare, and his helm inclined slightly as if he were making a gesture. Then he turned around and softly commanded one of the men behind him to get the rest of his crew ready for battle. "We take the fight back to Andaria today, men. Ready yourselves to write history!"

Atrick signaled the group to move forward, but now he was doing more than walking fast. He broke into a sort of skip, moving quickly across the stones. Teran and a group of sure-footed mercenaries took off behind him. Elias tapped Rianas on her shoulder before lightly brushing by her. Within a minute, the entire expedition was moving as quickly as it could across the treacherous stones.

10. BACK TO THE LIGHT

The Empire enslaved those who did not join, and the Emperor's power over the southern reaches of the Great Continent was completed.

Few from the Northern Realms have ever traveled through Axarea. Fewer still ever manage to return. Most of the information gathered on this state comes from places on its periphery – almost all of them nations at war with Axarea. Precious little information comes north from the Empire.

Along the eastern coastline of the Great Continent, the splintered seafaring nation of Eastern Runlar fought naval battles against the Empire. They had taken back numerous small Assyrian islands in the past century. No nation in the Northern Realms fought harder. But with the constant stand-offs between the various Runlars, the naval strength of Eastern Runlar had been redirected further north in the past two decades.

From: "An Incomplete History of Arthos"
Grandmaster Ar'Ishan's lecture on Axarean aggression
1943 A.C.

A person who spends days underground comes to appreciate the sky, the light, and the space of the world above in a new way. Nothing inspires camaraderie in a group, an army, or a people like a common harrowing experience. The feeling of exaltation as the light of day seemed to grow in front of them lightened the mood of the entire expedition.

Within two hundred yards, the now noisy group could smell the fresh air of the outside world stretching into the cave. It felt to Rianas like they were returning to the world of the living.

The first sign of resistance came a moment later. The men in front of the group dashed past Atrick, daggers gleaming under his ball of light as it brightened the cave around him. The charging mercenaries took nogs carrying picks and shovels by surprise. Many of the lizard-like creatures surrendered almost immediately. Those that fought back died quickly against the onslaught. When Rianas caught up to the front of the group, she found herself tying a captured nogs to a stone with its surviving companions.

Atrick was now talking loudly enough for most of the party to hear. He commanded those with bows to get in the second line and those with swords and daggers to take the front. "We must take whatever high ground we can – and quickly. There will only be a short window of surprise. Do not let these monsters drive us back, or we will be fighting a messy retreat for miles. We have the advantage while the sun is still out. Nogs have horrible vision in the sun. Use it!"

Jalek's hand was under Rianas' left arm. "Stay behind me." Then louder, as if to his audience, "Let's see what you can do, sorceress."

Arthur had his twin daggers drawn. He looked out of place amongst Jalek, Elias, and the other Cidvagian mercenaries Jalek had around him. They were all huge and muscular, while Arthur seemed like a bundle of thin sticks in comparison. He made eye contact with Rianas. *"Are you okay?"* he projected.

Rianas nodded and smiled. She wondered how reassuring it was.

Atrick took one last look over the captured nogs and seemed satisfied. Raising his arm into the air he declared, "Now!" and actually started running toward the end of the cave.

The Nog excavators had beaten flat these last steps. The creatures had removed or pushed most of the larger boulders out of the way. The small army charged out fifteen across, some on either side of the creek.

The light of a fading day washed over Rianas as she kept pace behind Jalek. Arthur ran just ahead and to her right. Small stones crunched under her feet. As they breached the opening, Rianas could see the broken pieces of the original cave. Where a waterfall had once been, a wide pool of shallow water now trickled down the mountain through thousands of stones. Water splashed around boulders simply flung downhill, making a wide, wet entrance. There were a few bent bushes struggling to grow in the breaks of the stony mountain beyond, but no trees in sight. A path full of pebbles and rubble wound up to a flat encampment far above them. The river passed beneath that higher ledge and continued its path down the remainder of the mountain.

There was a small camp of Nog miners on the flattened outcropping of stone above the cave entrance. A few nogs were looking out, pointing down at them as Atrick's mercenaries breached the daylight. The nogs shaded their faces from the light as they looked down. Most looked on in disbelief, and a few ran off at the sight.

A cry of alarm went up among the Nog camp even as Atrick was shouting from the very front of the expedition, "We must take the camp!"

One hand in front of him, Atrick dashed faster than a man his age should be able to run toward the steep path and up to the flat camp. Teran was there, and two apprentices flanked them. A dozen other mercenaries who had brought long swords ran at full speed just a step behind them.

From such a long distance, crossbows would be ineffective. Rianas felt the scroll in her pocket as she stumbled across the last few large boulders into daylight. The crush of warriors behind her pushed forward relentlessly into the clear opening. With some effort not to fall on her face, she withdrew the scroll.

About fifty mercenaries had started up the embankment toward the Nog camp. Atrick and the lead group were nearly to the top, running five abreast. Rianas thought about what she would do for a second, planted her feet, and looked down at the scroll.

"*Ignis,*" she heard herself say as she tore the word off the page and into the weave. The rush of power from the word was upon her, and she looked up, pointing fifty yards ahead and a hundred feet above her toward the Nog encampment.

Jalek, whose followers seemed to have stopped just outside the cave, gasped. Rianas just barely heard a few curses before her consciousness seemed to move into the giant ball of roiling fire she had created in the sky.

Rianas once again felt the disembodied power of the weave as she took control of the great fireball. A moment of trepidation quickly passed as the weave itself seemed to take her original intention from her. The ball/Rianas began to spread into a fiery bright cloud a dozen yards wide. The air itself seemed to feed the flames, which licked and stretched forward, until – like a soaring hawk – it dove forward onto the Nog encampment.

Rianas was there. *She* was the fiery hawk, watching pointing hands and terrified Nog faces as they dove for cover. Some chose to jump down the embankment, others simply cowered on the ground. Rianas flew low over the camp. Her many hands reached for tents, wooden weapons, the heads of those too brave or slow to get out of the way. Her hundreds of fingers brushed over the ground. They touched the backs of running nogs. She coated everything beneath *her* in flames. She seemed to touch a hundred things at once, leaving behind pieces of her burning *self*.

After passing through half the length of the encampment, she felt her control slipping. She quickly swept around to maintain the distance with her corporeal self this time. *She* came back a dozen yards to the left of her first path. In seconds, the flames were dying away. *She* condensed to keep the fire raging a little longer, searching for a place to end her path.

A few dozen yards away, there was a huge tent. Rianas swept around. She strained to keep the ball of fire lit as *she* screamed forward into the tent.

Just as before, the experience was over. Rianas was staring at the scroll. An explosion rocked the Nog camp above them where her fireball had made its final fiery mark on the world. Nogs were screaming and running about, trying to escape the fire that had destroyed half the camp.

Now she thought she understood the power of the enchanted lettering enough to observe the scroll without immediately casting a spell. The word "*Ignis*" was slightly faded on the page. Reading the word had brought it into the physical world. The other words still shone brightly. However, each casting would take more of the magical ink from the page, until the entire scroll was a blank page.

With her return to her body, she began to hear the din of combat. Jalek was yelling something to his men and running toward the hill now. Arthur was standing a few feet to her left, shouldering the bigger men around him to keep them from hitting Rianas as they went by. The thrumming of a drum was starting up somewhere in the Nog camp.

Elias was suddenly in front of her. "We need to go. Good job, Rianas, I think you convinced Jalek's men we are going to be on the winning side of this battle."

Above her in the camp, flames reached toward the sky where the huge fireball had blown through like a tornado. Dozens of nogs had jumped to their deaths. Even from this distance, she could hear the death cries of many who had been caught in the fireball's path.

The camp was huge, though. Rianas reflected on what she had "seen". There were perhaps two hundred tents. If each held four or five nogs, the mercenary army would be outnumbered by three or four to one. Moreover, the benefit of surprise would be gone in a moment when the camp had a chance to get their weapons and organize a counterattack.

Atrick had reached the summit. His hands above his head, a wall of force projected in front of him, sending nogs skidding across the ground to the edge of the camp and off the steep cliff. He screamed a battle cry that was incomprehensible from so far away with all the other sounds.

Elias took that as his cue. There were still nearly a hundred men milling around, waiting for a chance to get up the steep path only five or six abreast. Elias signaled Rianas and ran forward behind the next men. Arthur and Rianas joined him.

Samuel, John, and Sal joined Elias at the foot of the path. They ran up, slowing down behind the rest of the advancing group. The sound of fighting above them drowned out everything else. Elias lifted a tall mercenary off his feet in front of him when he stumbled. Rianas' feet slid backward a few times on the loose stones of the steep climb, but Arthur shot out a hand for her each time.

As they approached the top of the path where the Nog camp was, the pathway leveled out and spread out a bit. Climbing over the last hump, Rianas watched Galen use his own scroll to cast some sort of shockwave across a group of approaching nogs. Atrick and Teran stood side by side.

Teran swung his long sword at approaching nogs. Atrick lifted his arms again, sending Nog weapons off in errant directions. Rianas could see the nogs beginning to surround them as the mage and his bodyguard pushed far ahead of the rest of the group. If not for their daring tactic, however, the battle would already be lost. Atrick's brave advance created space for the other mercenaries to reach the ledge.

Most of the Nog encampment carried daggers, picks or short spears this time. Some of the larger nogs held shields or wore thin pieces of leather across their chests. However, most were unarmored. The nogs had been taken by surprise – at least enough that the mercenaries had been able to gain a foothold in the camp before their first real resistance. Rianas' fire attack had sewn chaos in the middle of the camp. Dozens of tents were in flames.

There was a score of mercenaries and miners lying motionless already. The nogs had lost far more, though. Atrick's initial attack had thrown fire pits, weapons, and tents on their sides, clearing nearly fifty feet in front of him. The men with the longer swords had broken into groups of two and three, pushing over tents and driving back the nogs that were prepared for battle. The monsters were now attacking the advancing mercenaries from the front and the right, though. A few dozen nogs were using slings to throw stones down from a small ledge. A cohesive attack from the center of the camp led by a particularly large nog in chain armor was advancing menacingly toward Atrick.

Elias pointed toward the ledge. "Let's take that ledge. If we take the high ground, those Nog slings won't be able to do as much damage."

Some of the other men around Elias followed. Rianas drew out her dagger as they jumped up a few stones onto the little rock outcropping, dodging a few rocks slung at her on the way.

Elias took the first nog down with his crossbow, followed by two others from Samuel and a third bowman behind Rianas. Arthur, to the right of Elias, charged forward into three nogs holding slings still in their arms, stabbing away. Rianas held her position and supported Arthur when he seemed about to fall backward from one of the monster's punches.

The nogs quickly dropped their now-useless slings and started to pick up daggers and spears. The ledge was narrow, so Rianas kicked at one, sending it over the ledge headfirst. A second nog avoided Arthur and picked up its dagger just in time to deflect Rianas' dagger.

Rianas panicked, sidestepped, and slid down the stone ledge nearly two feet before Sam grabbed her by the arm and hoisted her back up. He smiled briefly at her, and then grunted as he took the full force of the nog's dagger in his right side. He did not let go of Rianas, but slammed his crossbow into the creature's face, breaking his crossbow's handhold with the blow. Sal screamed and stabbed the nog as it staggered back.

Sal seemed to have lost control. She stabbed the nog a second time before pushing past Arthur, who was still tangling with another nog. She swung her dagger to attack a third. Sal screamed incoherently, slicing as she moved forward past Elias into the main group of sling-throwing nogs. Elias called to her as he sliced at another nog that had gotten too close to him.

Rianas spared a few seconds to look at Sam's wound. He waved her off. He was clearly in pain, but thought he could manage for the time. Rianas grabbed his hand and said, "Thank you!" before getting a good grip on her dagger and rushing forward to join Sal and Elias.

Arthur to her right, Sal to her left, Rianas rushed forward toward the ten or so nogs that were flinging rocks. She barely dodged one stone aimed at her head, but two more hit her in the shins with such force she cried out and almost fell. Sal took a stone to the helmet with such ferocity that it almost knocked her over.

Elias, his shield up, rushed into the group. Suddenly, the elder mercenary seemed to have three swords in his hands. He spun in a circle, stabbing two nogs and slashing at two more. Two fell to the ground clutching their wounds. Arthur used his two daggers to attack a nog that had dropped its sling too slow, felling it quickly.

Behind the first few nogs, Rianas saw another with a leather vest and a short sword. It pushed three of the others forward, and then flanked the right side of Elias. Sal, too busy swinging her daggers wildly at two nogs in front of her, did not have time to react to the spear from one of the newcomers. Rianas plunged her dagger into the nog's chest a second after the spear went into Sal's abdomen.

With a bloodcurdling scream, Sal lunged forward on top of another nog. Rianas found herself facing the armored nog and sidestepped its first sword thrust. Elias and Arthur were on either side of her, and Sal fell on top of a nog attacking her. Rianas felt like retching at the sight of all the blood and the idea that Sal might die. Arthur brought her back to reality when he slammed an elbow into another nog jumping at her over Sal's back with a pick in its hands.

The armored nog swung wide the second time – or so Rianas thought. Then, its sword hit the bottom edge of Elias' shield. The blow dislodged Elias' shield from his grip. With two other nogs still attacking him, he flung his shield to the side and drew his elven dagger. The dagger glowed white-hot. The super-heated steel slipped easily through the leather breastplate of the armored nog. Elias kicked away another nog, sending it over the edge of the small ledge.

Rianas stabbed a nog before it could swipe Elias' leg with a spear. She grabbed the dropped spear and used it as a club against another beast as it tried to stab the barely moving Sal in the head. Arthur plunged his dagger into his adversary's shoulder blades just in time to save Rianas from a dagger in her own side.

The battle raged all around. Rianas could see balls of light out of her peripheral vision floating through the advancing throngs of nogs below. The apprentices used their powers to push weapons out of the way at the last moment, and Atrick seemed to have cast a fireball of his own. The fire was pulsating. It seemed to roll in a straight line through an advancing group of armored nogs.

Rianas thought briefly about trying to cast another spell, but she knew she did not have enough control over the weaves to keep from hurting her allies. Instead, she took her dagger from where it was wedged in the nog she had just slain. She jumped over Sal's slumped body to take on the next group of nogs running for them.

Arthur used his size advantage to throw a spear-wielding nog back into the advancing group. The resulting chaos saved Rianas from at least one of the three spears aimed at her. She turned to the side to avoid another, but the third slammed into her right leg when she lifted it to shield her body. The blow knocked Rianas off balance onto her back. She felt the tearing leather of her pants, followed by a white-hot pain in her leg.

The fall knocked the wind out of her. Her helm was all that stopped her from cracking her skull on the stony ground when she landed. Time seemed to stand still. Rianas stared to her left, where Sal was gasping for air. She seemed to have an eternity to wonder if Sal was about to die and she with her. The world was full of pain. It radiated up from her right thigh.

From her vantage point, Elias seemed to be overwhelmed by four Nog attackers at once.

There were no more reinforcements coming up into the camp. Every mercenary and miner had reached the top. It did not seem to be enough to force the nogs back. There was no third wave of soldiers behind her. The rest of the men who had come up the small ledge had raced into a mass of partially clothed nogs. Rianas could see a tangle of swords, shields, spears and daggers. Two more nogs were coming for her. The one that had stabbed her was letting go of its spear. She could not be sure, but it looked like it was smiling at her.

Rianas had dropped the spear in the fall, and her dagger in her left hand was pinned under her body. She reached for the nog with her bare hand, not sure what she would do. As soon as she made contact, however, a plan formed in her head.

Rianas jumped to a familiar plain, with clouds to the south − the ubiquitous Nog brainwashing she had witnessed in the cave. This time, however, Rianas wondered what else might have caused the nog to have such hatred for humans. She "pulled" at the nog, trying to tease an answer from its subconscious.

Then Rianas was back on the battlefield again. Only a few seconds had passed. The nog was slumping over, passing out from her invasion of its mind. Rianas sucked in a breath of air herself as she pushed the comatose creature off her, grabbing a small dagger out of the slumping nog's hand that it had been about to use on her. She wrestled the dagger up just in time to block another incoming blow from a nog to her left.

Still prone on the ground, Rianas stabbed at the nog as it jumped on top of her. They tangled as she flipped herself around, bringing her uninjured leg up. Her rucksack kept her from harm when the nog's stab pushed its dagger between her rib and a strap. Rianas quickly took advantage of the trapped weapon by shifting her weight to the left again. The motion pinned the dagger harmlessly against her side and gave Rianas a chance to stab the monster in its own side.

Arthur was there, kicking the dying nog off Rianas. He flung one of his daggers at the second advancing nog, uncannily hitting it square in the chest. Rianas had only a moment to wonder at Arthur's luck as he hoisted her up. *"Fight back to back with me. Try to put your weight on your good leg."*

Rianas said aloud, "Alright," and lifted her last dagger from its holster as she leaned back toward him. Elias swiped again with his flaming dagger. The motion swept two nogs at once down the short cliff. He was suddenly free. He spared a glance at Sal, still breathing laboriously on the ground.

Nearly two dozen nogs remained on the ledge, but the tide had turned here. Now Jalek was leading a dozen heavily armored men up behind the monsters from the opposite side of the outcropping.

The sun had begun to fall below the western horizon, and dark shadows were crawling across the battlefield from behind the mercenary army quickly now. The burning camp backlit Atrick's group as they charged forward. They pushed the Nog soldiers back relentlessly.

With Jalek's soldiers in front of them, Elias and Arthur got on either side of Rianas and they took a dozen steps into the rear guard of the nogs.

A brief battle ensued on the narrow ledge. This time, panicked nogs tried to defend themselves as mercenaries overwhelmed them from both sides. Elias stabbed three more nogs himself. Rianas tried to ignore the pain in her leg as she distracted two other nogs with her weak dagger thrusts long enough for Arthur to take them down. The battle for the small ledge was won.

Rianas quickly hobbled over to Sal, removing the healing potion and the rags Atrick had provided her. Arthur saw what she was doing and came over. He flipped Sal onto her back with a grunt.

Sal's stomach was still moving laboriously as Rianas gently took the spear out of her gut. Immediately, Rianas poured a small amount of the potion onto the wound and covered it with a rag covered in the liquid. "Drink this." She gave the little glass to Sal, who weakly took some into her mouth.

There were other injured up here, but Rianas spared a moment to watch Arthur remove the spear from her own leg. She screamed in pain. Then, she applied a similar rag to her leg. She wrapped the cloth around the wound. Her leg immediately felt better. The pain receded to a more manageable level before she finished wrapping her wound.

Jalek approached. "Are you okay, sorceress?" he asked. The dark haired man adjusted his blood-covered black shield. Jalek used his sword to break loose two spears that were sticking out of the front. "This would be a good time to cast more of your magic."

Rianas looked over at the injured. Arthur, still kneeling over her, projected, *"The man may be ignoring the injured, but he's right. If you have the energy, now would be a good time to cast another spell. We might turn the battle down there in our favor. Perhaps you can convince Jalek to bring his men down there when you cast?"*

Rianas considered as she looked up. She lifted Atrick's magical scroll out again. "I'm not sure what I can do, Jalek. If your men will make a charge, I will send something out in front of you to clear the path the best I can."

Jalek's black gaze lingered a moment on Rianas' injured leg before he turned and scanned the battlefield where Atrick and a few dozen mercenaries were pushing deeper into the never-ending throng of nogs that nearly surrounded them. Atrick and the other apprentice mages looked tired as they used waves of force to sweep weapons dangerously out of the nog's hands. "Do what you can. If you can break those nogs up around Atrick, I think we can drive the rest of these creatures off the ledge."

Rianas nodded. Jalek did not wait. He simply turned around and raised his sword above his head. "To me! Drive these monsters off the cliff!"

Arthur helped Rianas up yet again as she considered what to do. Atrick had his arm in the air, and his ball of light was brighter than before, almost like a small sun across the battlefield. Many of the nogs raised their arms to block the light, allowing Atrick's group to advance again. Jalek and his armored mercenaries charged headlong down the opposite side of the ledge. A few of the other men from the ledge followed directly towards the hundred or so nogs that had armed themselves around the rear of their camp while the battle had been raging.

Rianas waited until Jalek's men had gotten a few dozen yards away. Then, she lifted the scroll up, "*Glacia, caelia!*" she called. Her words ripped the written magical weave out of the page again.

The weave formed a thundercloud of frozen, roiling air where she gestured with her left hand. Once again, Rianas became the magic, directing it as if it were her own body. The cloud, nearly devoid of ice in the dry evening air, contained a huge potential of wind and cold air, which she gently dropped down like a huge blanket upon the now charging group of heavily armed nogs. Instead of hitting them from the front, she "landed" in the center.

The freezing cyclone lifted nogs in confusion up into the air, tumbling them over each other. Dozens went sprawling for cover. The ripping winds threw fifteen or twenty of the unlucky monsters from the center of the group into the air like toys.

As the cold air blew outward from the center like an exploding snowball, those who managed to avoid the wind were hit by freezing air so cold that it robbed some of the ability to breathe. A few others, covered in frostbitten exposed skin, screamed and ran. The spell sent the nogs into complete disarray.

Rianas tried to keep the blizzard going as long as she could, but as she sensed Jalek and his men getting nearer, she released control of the weave, jumping back into her body again.

155

Arthur and Elias watched the scene unfold with Rianas. Atrick had used another spell of his own to drive the last group of attackers back, and now the small mercenary army was advancing quickly on the remainder of the Nog encampment. They picked off stragglers and captured injured nogs that had lost their weapons. Jalek's men had broken the otherwise substantial gathering of nogs Rianas had hit with the blizzard, and sandwiched the remaining fighters between themselves and a group led by Teran. The battle turned into a rout, and the few surviving nogs fell over themselves to surrender.

Rianas groaned and turned toward the injured mercenaries who remained on the ledge. There were perhaps a hundred men and women on the ground between her ledge and the tents where Atrick stood. Two apprentices had already started providing healing potions down below, so Rianas was determined to help as many as she could up here.

Elias excused himself and took three other young men with minor injuries down below. They helped round up the remaining nogs, some of whom were trapped behind the smoldering wall of fire, unable to escape. Arthur, meanwhile, gently held his arm out for support as Rianas hobbled over to the injured.

Darkness was almost fully upon the ledge now. Rianas brought out her hand lamp and fastened the strap around her helm to help guide the way. Arthur ran ahead to bring the injured into one place as Rianas cared for chest and stomach wounds that would have been deadly if not for the healing powers of Atrick's potion. She wrapped bandages around arms, legs, and torsos.

One man had grabbed a dagger with his hand to stop a nog from slitting his throat. Rianas tried her best to wrap his index finger, which seemed nearly detached from his hand, as she wrapped his hand up. The man's throat wound stopped bleeding shortly after he swallowed some of the potion, and although he could not speak, he smiled weakly.

A portly older miner with no armor had perhaps ten stab wounds, yet somehow managed to walk over to the other wounded, carrying his companion who had a spear lodged in his shoulder where it had struck bone. A stone had knocked out the speared man. Rianas marveled at both miners' fortitude as she tended their wounds, and Arthur helped a hobbling woman remove the spear from her companion's shoulder.

As soon as the woman removed the spear, the comatose man moaned. Rianas turned away from the miner to douse the hole in his shoulder where the spear had been. Then she shoved one of her last rags inside it to help heal the gaping hole.

"Hanus jumped in front of one of those monsters before it speared me in the back. Please do what you can to help him. He is a brave man. He has two children in Sko'Port," the big miner said. He had lost so much blood he could barely hold up his head.

Rianas poured more of the potion down Hanus' throat and listened to his steadying breathing. Then she turned back to the portly miner. "You've got wounds all over. You need to sit and rest; I don't have much of this healing potion left." She poured the last of it onto some loose cotton that had been the man's shirt, and used it to spread around the liquid on his many wounds. As she was doing so on his now bare chest, she noticed dozens of other scars across his body and face.

"I've been stabbed before. The secret is…moving through…the pain." He winced as Rianas moved his left arm to shove the last bit of rag into a six-inch gash he had been holding closed with his elbow on his side.

Rianas watched the wounds close. She did not have enough to treat all his wounds, but the man seemed to have stabilized. "What is your name?"

"I am Tziporo," he said. "I've fought these monsters now for nearly three weeks, ever since the first attack when they tried to take the cavern. Thank you for the healing potion."

Rianas nodded and told Tziporo to try to get some rest. The remaining injured had less life-threatening injuries, so she helped those who could still walk care for as many as she could. The work lasted for hours. Her leg screamed with every step, but it slowly improved with the miraculous healing power of the potion. Arthur finally grabbed her arm as the moon rose above the mountains and the night sky filled with shining stars.

"I think you should take a break," he said.

Atrick's light still flickered over the camp. He was directing the uninjured and barely injured in the ash-covered remains of the Nog camp below. Arthur suggested they go see him, and Rianas agreed. They scrambled carefully down the ledge, walked past a group of men gathering spears and daggers from fallen nogs, and climbed over a small pile of stones that were being pushed down the pathway that led up to this large ledge.

"What are they doing?" asked Rianas. She stopped briefly to watch an apprentice weave enough force to lift a boulder that had to weigh two hundred pounds and move it slowly toward a growing pile of rocks.

Arthur thought for a second before he continued toward Atrick. "I think Atrick is directing people to fortify the entrance to the cavern." Then a smile came across his face. "We did it, Ri'. We made it to Old Andaria!"

11. LORD CERRIC

As the moon rose over the Nog mining camp, a couple hundred Cidvagian mercenaries, Sko'Port miners, and Assyrian ex-soldiers were working together to establish a foothold in one of the newest prizes of the Axarean Empire – Old Andaria.

Atrick, haggard and barely able to stand, was politely instructing two miners on how to construct a wall across the creek at the foot of the cave's entrance. His arms barely moved as he gestured, and he swayed lightly from side to side.

Teran stood nearby, cleaning his weapon absentmindedly while watching for Atrick's inevitable stumble. He had already attempted to make the wizard rest a few times to no avail. Each time Teran suggested Atrick sit down, he was waved away impatiently with a "This must be done," or "I'll rest later."

Rianas and Arthur made their way around a huge broken cooking pot and a few knocked over tents to get to Atrick. He looked over at them, not truly seeing them for a moment. Arthur offered to help him sit down on a nearby stone while Rianas set the emptied healing potion bottle on a makeshift table that was set up in front of him.

"I see you two fared okay this afternoon. My heart is lifted to see you in good health," Atrick said. His words were slurring. Teran set his weapon down and gave Atrick a drink from his water flask. "I won't be much use soon. That much weaving of magic is very taxing on the body. How do you feel, Rianas?"

Rianas showed her healing wounds to Teran. Atrick nodded as if he had seen. His eyes drifted closed while she recounted her use of the scroll he had given her. "I wish I could have done more, Atrick. It looks like there were many lives lost tonight. I couldn't control the magic enough to keep the spells going."

Atrick shook his head, taking out a small root from inside his robes and sticking it in his mouth. His eyes opened up a bit more as he chewed it, and he looked over to Rianas. "You did very well today. I don't think I could have done any better myself. Besides, your ability to – ah, sympathize – with your magic gives you control most veteran casters never gain. I only wish your casting had been in a more peaceful setting, I would have liked to study it more closely.

"For now, though, I need to ask a favor of you, Rianas and Arthur. Rianas, I need you to go back through the cave as quickly as you can. If Berryl has succeeded in convincing Maddox Oren and Lord Cerric of the need to send a garrison into the tunnels based on that mask Raskin managed to luck into, he may have already brought reinforcements into the tunnels. If not, I need you to convince them to come."

Atrick paused. He looked around at the quickly organizing mass of people caring for the wounded and setting up camp. Jalek was a couple hundred yards away, directing a watch to be set up on the high ground. Raskin Jorgen, the leader of the mining expedition, was organizing a group of uninjured miners to clear a section of the plateau of stones and debris from the battle. Harold and Sunduin were directing others to collect weapons and manage the Nog captives.

"Go back for Berryl. One way or another, Captain Maddox and Lord Cerric must be convinced to send a garrison out here. We may have a day or two before we are attacked. Do you see that – village or tent city, I'm not sure which – down there?" Atrick pointed down the creek, almost to the foot of the mountain. There were campfires along either side of the creek. In the moonlight, Rianas could barely make out the black dots of hundreds of additional tents. They were perhaps two miles away, but there was no way they had not heard or seen the battle that just ended.

Rianas wondered aloud who could be in that tent city.

"A Nog army – of that, I have no doubt. There was no evidence of human activity in this mine. Perhaps the Axareans sent a Nog army because they would be best suited for working underground. It will take them some time to arm themselves and make their way up the mountain. We will have the high ground to our advantage."

Arthur cursed lightly under his breath. "There could be a few thousand nogs in that tent city," he said. "If Sko'Port doesn't send reinforcements, they will overwhelm this place."

"Yes," Atrick said, "and I have expended myself today. No doubt the other Apprentices have, as well. We have little magical ability left among us until we get a chance to rest. That is why Teran, Harold, Sunduin, Jalek and Elias will be organizing the defenses tonight and through the day tomorrow. Hopefully, we mages can rest enough to be of some help by the time the first attack begins. If help does not arrive in about three days, though, I fear we will be lost."

Rianas gave the magical scroll back to Atrick, insisting he would have more use for it in the next few days. He stole a look at the faded lettering and nodded. Then he took a ring off his right hand and gave it to Rianas. "This ring will give you more stamina for the trip you are about to make. Wear it or hold it in your hand if it won't stay on your fingers. I will need it back," he chuckled, as if remembering some old story he wasn't going to share, "but it may make the difference in you getting help in time, so please use its power."

Rianas nodded and slipped the ring loosely onto her middle finger. She felt more invigorated just wearing the ring, as if some magical hands were helping to prop her up.

Atrick looked even more tired than before. Turning to Arthur, the wizard said, "Protect your charge with your life, Arthur. Bring her right to the leaders of whatever group you run into along the way. She can do the rest."

Rianas said, "I doubt I can convince miners or anyone else to join us, Atrick. I will try, but if they have decided not to come to the end of the cavern, there won't be much we can do. We won't waste too much time. I will come back to let you know, so we can retreat if help isn't coming. We won't fail you."

Atrick smiled his infectious smile again. His eyes closed as he spoke, "Thank you, Rianas. Now, go. I need to rest as much as I can, and you unfortunately have quite a bit of hiking ahead of you."

Two hours later, Rianas and Arthur were still jumping across boulders. They followed the old Nog path up into the mountain to the great cavern. Rianas paused after going up a small waterfall. "Don't you ever get tired, Arthur?"

Arthur, breathless but still upright, nodded and chuckled. "Whenever I get tired, I just think how I don't want to fall asleep in a dark cavern full of man-eating bats, dragon-like lizards, and sightless insects that would probably just as well make my face their new home, all miles away from another person."

Rianas laughed. Ahead, she could make out the light from the huge cavern of glowing mushrooms. A few bats flitted about overhead, as if testing the humor in Arthur's statement. She gestured to the light and Arthur nodded. "We'll be there in about thirty minutes if we keep this pace up. Are you okay to keep going?"

Arthur nodded and joked, "I'd be faster if I didn't have to keep hauling you over stones." The funny part was he had needed help twice when he had slipped. Rianas and Arthur took turns jumping up and giving each other a hand to the higher stones. They had both scraped their legs despite their thick leather leggings. Rianas had cuts on her hands from the sharper stones, and Arthur had a gash along his left arm where he had missed a jump and tumbled toward the water before Rianas had hauled him up by his rucksack.

They were going too fast. Rianas knew it, and Arthur knew it, but neither one of them wanted to slow down. They had talked briefly before entering the mine, while they were checking their gear and eating a quick bite of dried meat and cheese.

Rianas had wondered how long they could move, since the cave was steep in places. Arthur had suggested they could take a rest in the huge cavern if the mine garrison had sent men in to secure it and pick up the wounded miners. They had both agreed they could send word ahead of them if they got there. It was getting more difficult to navigate the small Nog path without slipping. Neither Arthur nor Rianas knew how long they had been awake.

The last half mile was hard. Each step up made Rianas' healing leg scream in pain, and she used a hand on her knee a couple times to make the steps easier. Arthur helped her take a few shortcuts by leaping or climbing up stones, his long legs able to find footholds she could not reach. However, his arms were tired. Rianas could tell that by the way he wrenched his entire body around just to give her a leg up.

Finally, they stumbled into the first group of man-sized mushrooms. A couple lizards, one of them almost four feet long, scattered as Rianas took a brief second to catch her breath on a toadstool. Arthur drank from his flask and adjusted his lightened pack.

"Why did you bring all your gear, Ri'?" he asked between sips of water before putting his hands on his knees and doubling over in exhaustion. "You must be carrying thirty pounds' worth of canvas, leather, food and tools."

Rianas was sheepish. "Sorry, Arthur. I thought I should bring everything in case I needed something. What if we got lost in these caverns and needed food, or a little rope could help climb up fallen rock. I guess I just couldn't bring myself to leave anything behind."

Arthur nodded, and his grin returned. "You could always use that swim bladder and try to catch some fish for us!"

"Yeah, I guess I could have left that. I'd hate to lose something so unique, though." Rianas fished out some dried fruit Teran had given them and gave some to Arthur. "How do you think Signet is faring?"

Between bites, Arthur looked around. "The gnome? He seemed to know his way around a cave pretty well. Still, for his age it may take him a while to get to Sko'Port. We may pass his people on the way."

"I don't think those gnomes will be found unless they want to be." Rianas swallowed the last of a dried biscuit and looked back the way they had come. "I think we may have broken a record for cave-climbing."

Arthur nodded, chewing quickly and straightening up as Rianas got back on her feet. From here, the huge fungi made it easier to traverse. There was light, and the mushrooms and dirt on the cavern floor were softer under Rianas' boots. Arthur pointed out a path by the creek that would take them up faster.

It took perhaps twenty minutes to get to the upper entrance of the cavern.

As they approached the site where the miners had rolled the carts into a protective barrier, they saw two men with crossbows sitting atop an oak-sized mushroom plant. They called out to Rianas and Arthur before yelling behind them. Two dozen miners with chainmail, well-worn iron helms, long swords and shields were waiting for Arthur and Rianas by the time the two made the clearing. Another twenty or thirty men lounged in various states of readiness atop overturned carts. Some acted as lookouts from the taller mushroom caps, each with a bow and full quiver, or a crossbow. These soldiers were preparing to protect the cavern against incursions. There were scores of other men without armor or weapons behind them, working on the railway ties.

In fact, in the time since Atrick's expedition had left, they had managed to lay a few hundred yards of track, if not more. There were maybe a thousand men all the way back into the darkness of the tunnel. Rianas heard the clanging of hammers and saw teams of miners moving sand, stone and iron tracks with wheelbarrows. Half a dozen mages were lending their magical help to move the larger boulders and pieces of track, or to seal metal onto stone by melding the materials.

The leader of the guards approached, a look of concern apparent beneath his well-worn helm. "Hello, I'm Sergeant Thorgeir." Two other men rushed forward at his gesture to help Rianas and Arthur sit on a makeshift bench. One helped Rianas out of her pack, and the other took Arthur's pack and placed it safely to the side. Thorgeir, meanwhile, looked back into the mushroom forest, as if expecting more visitors.

"Where is Atrick's expedition?" The sergeant seemed worried. He kept his arms clasped behind him, but his twitching eyebrow belied his confidence. His gaze settled on the bloody rags that had been Rianas' leggings, and he slowly looked up her body. Rianas felt uncomfortable under Thorgeir's piercing gaze. "Neither of you seem to have sustained any serious injuries. What happened to you?"

Arthur spoke first. "We followed the river to where it exited the mountain. It comes out in Old Andaria. There is a Nog army just a few miles down the mountain preparing to invade. Atrick sent us back to get help."

The soldier taking Rianas' harness off gasped just loudly enough for Rianas to hear. Sergeant Thorgeir bravely kept his cool, staring into Rianas' eyes. "That is all, privates. Resume your watch." The sergeant waved the two soldiers off, and then he motioned for the rest of his team with another wave of his arm. Rianas noticed the long, thin flask tied to the arm. It must have been filled with mushroom powder, because it glowed dimly, producing enough light that the other soldiers easily saw his arm motions.

The rest of the foot soldiers broke up into groups of three and briskly went into the thicker parts of the mushroom forest once more. Thorgeir waited until they had gotten on their way before sitting down on a barrel a few feet in front of the two weary travelers.

"I was hoping for better news." His gaze softened. He brought his arms in front of him and rubbed a gloved hand over his clean-shaven face. "Atrick's guard – Berryl – came through nearly two days ago, but he only spoke with me long enough to send me down here with every mine guard I could muster. I brought every able-bodied man I could to help fortify this cavern and get the railway assembled so we could bring in supplies. Why does Atrick not retreat? I could easily defend this cavern against a force thrice our size. We have the advantage of height, good lookout locations, water, and easy resupply."

It was because of Rianas. She was the one who convinced Atrick to advance. Rianas felt panic welling up at the thought that she had helped convince so many men and women to go into harm's way. Was Atrick camped on the other side of the Black Mountains because she wanted to see Andaria? Was he only there because *she* wanted to see the other side of the world?

Rianas opened her mouth to speak, but Arthur seemed to read her mind. "Atrick wants to send a message to the Axareans. He intends to claim the entire cavern for Sko'Port."

Thorgeir shook his head, clearly believing Atrick's actions to be those of a lunatic. "I have a little less than one hundred guards here. I can secure your passage back to Sko'Port on one of the enchanted carts, but I don't think you will convince anyone there of this folly. I

just hope Atrick is able to retreat when he realizes his mistake. He is a good man, and one of the more capable wizards I've ever met."

"What is an enchanted cart?" Rianas asked.

Thorgeir pointed back toward the upper entrance, where the ringing of steel continued as they spoke. "The apprentices have enchanted a few dozen of these carts to follow the rails back to the entrance – uphill or downhill. I've used them before to transport injured men, and the miners use them routinely to transport supplies and heavier ores. You would have to share the cart with a half-load of stone, but you would be back to the entrance in a couple hours. It would also give you a chance to rest a little."

Rianas, despite her fatigue, was beside herself at the thought of riding in one of the huge cars. "It travels purely based on magical enchantment? That is the most wondrous magic I've ever heard of!"

Thorgeir was a man obviously accustomed to the magic of the High Mine. He smiled condescendingly. "Young lady, how do you think Sko'Port became the biggest city in the Northern Realms?"

Thorgeir seemed eager to rid himself of Arthur and Rianas. He instructed a worker to get them back to the entrance and then walked back toward his growing fortifications without even wishing them well.

The cargo car was three-quarters full of some bright colored ore. Rianas was thankful she had all her gear, because she and Arthur were able to spread out her sleeping gear and all their other belongings beneath them to soften the ride. Even so, the rear wall of the car only partially supported her back. The jagged edges of stones poked them both uncomfortably from beneath their equipment.

A short hairy man with a chalkboard marked up a chart and stuck it to the front of the car. He gave a few instructions on how to stop and start the cart if needed, then flipped down the brake. With a lurch, the cart accelerated to about the pace of a fast jog right up the hill and into the upper reaches of the mine.

The slight breeze on their faces was cool, and Rianas fell asleep within a few moments despite the screeching of the wheels across the iron tracks and the excitement of riding a magically driven rail car at breakneck pace through the mine.

Rianas woke a couple hours later to the sounds of miners all around them. Arthur had fallen asleep with his long arms wrapped around his legs and his head resting atop them. The permanent lighting fixtures of the last mile of the mine lit up the hundreds of helmets of the miners going about their business sorting stones near the entrance.

Coming out of the mine was almost magical on this side of the mountain. Huge iron-wrapped stone columns and concrete pillars stretched far above their heads. From above, the polished floors reflected magically lit fixtures hung on long chains. It was darker outside than inside still. However, even at this early hour the entrance was a hive of activity.

Rianas nudged Arthur, who groggily looked around. They gathered their things to disembark as the cart came to a rest in a long line of other carts. A spectacled attendant with two large sacks of parchments and a portable desk slung over his shoulder was walking down the line of carts, putting colored flags on each car as he passed. When he read their chalkboard manifest, his eyes went up to see the two Riverrunners getting out of the cart.

"Uh," the older man said.

Rianas tightened the straps of her harness, settling the sleeping gear back into place. "We came from the end of the mine where they are expanding the track. We need to see the Upper Ward Guard captain as soon as possible. Is there some way we can get a horse and cart to take us to him?"

The man was obviously not used to having conversations with mine cart passengers. He blinked a few times and then pointed toward a squat horse stall just outside of the mine entrance. "There are horses in the stall for hire, usually."

As Rianas started to walk off, the man seemed to get his wits about him. "Was there fighting in the mine?" he asked. "I heard there were nogs down there and they were sealing a section off."

Rianas turned and stopped. "We took back the cavern and drove the nogs all the way back to Axarea. Now we're looking for some help from the guards to defeat the Nog army for good. Last night, we broke through to Old Andaria, and the wizard Atrick intends to build an outpost on the other side of the mountains."

The old man's jaw dropped. "Really? Are you saying that this mine goes all the way through to the other side of the Black Mountains? Is there a Nog army getting ready to attack Sko'Port?"

"Yes." Rianas thought it was close enough to the truth. "And it is Sko'Port's chance to strike before lasting damage can be done. If we take the other side of the mountain, we will establish a springboard to strike back at the Empire." A little aggrandizement seemed in order. Rianas turned and beckoned Arthur to follow her, walking as confidently as she could toward the stables. After the sergeant's response to Arthur, Rianas felt she and Arthur would need to come up with a plan for convincing the guard captain to send men in.

Arthur spoke to her fears as they left the mine entrance and stepped into the early morning air, walking across the open yard and dodging between occasional slow-moving mining carts being directed to the various furnaces down the mountain. "We should probably practice what we are going to say when we find Captain Oren. We can't just walk in and say 'let's get going'."

Rianas nodded. "I wish I knew where Berryl has gotten to. That mask Raskin Jorgen captured from the initial war party seemed to be the key piece of evidence indicating that Axarea orchestrated the Nog raid. No one will believe I interrogated all those nogs. It doesn't matter that I saw into their minds."

Arthur looked over the workhorses at the stable as they approached and pointed out a pair he thought would be best. Rianas got out her coin pouch and the two of them haggled with a tired young man in colorful clothes for a minute. Finally, the man agreed to hire out the two horses and a three-man cart he had in the corner of one of the stalls. Another young man in a similar outfit, this one no more than seventeen, came out to set up the equipment. The hostler introduced his young employee as Ronald.

"Ronald knows upper Sko'Port," the first attendant said. "He can take you wherever you need to be. Those horses are the best I have here. I'll need them back by tonight."

Arthur asked what time it was as Rianas stowed their gear into the small trunk space of the cart. The sky was cloudy and dark. Ronald said it was about two hours to dawn, pointing toward a huge clock constructed above one of the storage warehouses uphill from them.

Arthur looked for a moment. "Rianas, why not try Atrick's mansion first? Berryl could be there, and it is early enough we could change into some cleaner clothes. If he is there, we can make the trip to Captain Oren's headquarters just as the sun comes up."

Rianas looked down at her torn leggings. Her leather pants were scratched and ripped in over a dozen places. Evidence of the near misses from Nog daggers and slipping on the wet rocks at the lower end of the cavern had turned her hiking clothes into tatters. There was dried Nog blood in smears all over her clothes. Mud, coal, and blood splatters covered her bare arms. It was a small wonder the horse keeper had haggled with them; they looked like beggars. She agreed they should try to clean up, and they instructed Ronald to wait with the carriage in front of Atrick's manor until they were ready to leave.

In the pre-morning darkness of the street lamps, Rianas and Arthur approached the manor gate. The same guard from before recognized Rianas and immediately asked if she was okay as he exited the guard shack. After a few moments spent updating the guard on Atrick's plans, he let the two travelers through. He even suggested they use the guest quarters to freshen up. "I'm sure Atrick would not mind."

Rianas thanked the man and asked if he had seen Berryl.

"He has come and gone a few times. First, he rode straight to Captain Oren's estate on the eastern outlook. Then, he brought that crate he had with him to show the mages at Lord Cerric's manor. He hasn't returned since then."

Inside, Rianas barely paid heed to the beautiful walls this time. Instead, she and Arthur filled two small basins of hot water and borrowed towels from Atrick's doting, grandmotherly head of the kitchen staff, Hanna. She brought some clothes from Atrick's wardrobe for Arthur, and offered some fine white Gawdichian pants and an over shirt of questionable origin to Rianas. Within an hour, they had washed and dressed.

Coming out of her dressing room, Rianas chuckled at Arthur in his finery. The shirt opened down past his chest, and the pants were an opulent loose silk that hugged his skinny legs. He had left his boots on, and was buckling his belt around his waist complete with its knife holsters. Arthur looked like a young Runlarian pirate from a book she had once read.

"What, your highness?" Arthur quipped, twirling his oversized shirt for effect.

Rianas cinched her belt around the fabric of her own dress-like shirt and laughed. Hanna had told her she was beautiful while she brushed stones out of her soft curls. She had even tried to get Rianas to wear a necklace and a headpiece that had somehow ended up on the dressing table. Rianas finally agreed to borrow the simple hemp necklace Hanna offered, mostly because Hanna said the huge brownish-green amethyst hanging from it matched her eyes.

"Let's go to Lord Cerric's keep, first," Arthur said. "If Berryl is still there, we can catch up and hopefully help convince Lord Cerric to send a legion into the mine."

Rianas agreed. The two thanked Hanna multiple times for her hospitality as they extracted themselves from her worried hugs and headed out the door.

Ronald was waiting at the manor entrance when they came out. The gate guard wished them luck as Arthur and Rianas stepped into the carriage. Ronald said they would get to Lord Cerric's palace a little before sunrise.

Lord Cerric was not a king, but Sko'Port's population was larger than the entirety of the kingdoms of either Assyria or Cidvag. There were individuals who called themselves kings ruling over other northern city-states in the far north. Sko'Port, however, had traditionally called its leader a lord. The Sko'Port royal family traced its lineage to the founders of the city nearly two thousand years before. They did not claim to be god-like royalty, as some rulers would have their subjects treat them. Instead, the royal family came from miners who had the vision to see the economic and strategic importance of the deep-water port at the very foot of the richest known mountain range in Arthos.

The Sko'Port High Council had chosen Lord Cerric to be the

leader of Sko'Port for the next thirty years. The High Council's city judges, selected for lifetime terms by the lord, claimed the power to select their next leader from the hundreds of royal members every thirty years (sooner if the previous lord died). The system was imperfect, but largely effective at ensuring each new lord was deemed the most capable and respected by the previous lord's ruling elite.

The High Council had chosen Lord Cerric for his shrewd understanding of the world surrounding Sko'Port. He had doubled shipments to the Runlars and increased overall exports by nearly fifty percent. Miles long caravans of horses left westbound along the land route to the Borsilkian Alliance from the western Gawdichian ports of Sko'Sea. They brought a wealth of copper and coal to Borsilk. Cidvagian militias bought entire carts full of weapons and castings.

Sko'Port was richer now than ever before in its history.

Lord Cerric had cultivated direct relationships with the Northern Realms. With the growth of Riverrun on the northern side of the Sko'Sea, he had taken the opportunity to lift exports of raw materials with Riverrun craft to transport heavier metals directly to the Western Runlarians.

The wealth of Sko'Port was easy to see as Ronald led the carriage along the lane to the royal keep. Pear trees ripe with fruit lined the street for nearly a mile, with well-tended flowering shrubs under each break in the cobblestone road. The shops along this stretch of the Upper Ward had beautiful window dressings. There were clothes from all reaches of the Great Continent, elven fabrics, leathers, and magical items on display. Men in immaculate robes walked the lane despite the early hour, and carriages and wagons were everywhere.

The lamps above lit the way. As their carriage approached the palace, the cobblestones turned to an almost mirror-like marble. A few dozen workers in rope-cinched robes swept the road as Ronald led the carriage into the main entranceway.

Black granite traced in golden filigree supported the lower levels of the palace. Stained windows lined the upper levels, which were high enough to overlook the rest of the city. The rear section seemed to climb a hundred yards up the mountain. Rianas had the impression the building could house a thousand people. Each level was set back from the previous. Long white marble patios lined with beautiful shrubberies topped each level. The palace was the grandest building Rianas had ever seen.

The mountain peeked out from behind the palace, almost seeming to grow out of the building itself. A huge cut from the rock wall created the cavity from which the palace grew.

The palace grounds were short. They began with a small, shallow moat of bluish water surrounding the building. The moat gave way to flowers, followed by thick shrubs. The palace grounds finally climbed into a mass of trees planted so close together that there was surely no space for more than two men abreast to walk between them. There was one exception in the main gate, where the iron palisades that encircled the crystalline moat climbed into a gilded reflection of the palace behind it, leaping up forty feet into the air.

The palace gates were open, but four guards stood on either side. They wore white chain armor that flowed down to their waists, with plates of purple painted steel stitched into the chests and abdomens. Each had a black cloak running down his back. What truly drew the eye were their pikes and longswords. Immaculately shaped weapons sported dragons carved into the handles and golden studs along the hilts. Embedded ruby red stones glittered in the steel. The guards gleamed even in the near darkness of a cloudy sunrise.

On the way to the palace, Arthur and Rianas talked about how they could get an audience with Lord Cerric. Arthur insisted Rianas should do the talking. He said she was very convincing when she wanted to be. Rianas thought Arthur was faster, but she finally agreed when Arthur reminded her Atrick had put his faith in her specifically. Rianas folded down the uncomfortable collar of the long shirt Hanna had given her and stepped as regally as she thought she could out of the carriage.

Ronald looked nervous. Rianas smiled – reassuringly, she hoped – at him and approached the guards.

"I am Rianas of Riverrun, come to speak with Lord Cerric about the nogs in the High Mine. The High Mine wizard Atrick sent us to request an audience with utmost urgency." Rianas tried to look as serious as she could. She put her 'in-charge' face on.

One of the guards stepped forward after consulting with a skinny man dressed in a black tunic and pants carrying a board and papers. "Go ahead, Rianas of Riverrun. The carriage must stay outside. O-Gan will take you to the meeting."

Rianas covered her surprise the best she could. Ronald said he would park in the stables and meet them when they came out. She and Arthur followed the skinny man through the massive gate.

Masterfully maintained interior gardens greeted them. Birdbaths and statues lined the walkway, and lamps brightened the entire garden. Early fall in Sko'Port had turned some of the leaves different shades of yellow and orange. Here and there, beautiful maples were displaying bright red leaves.

O-Gan did not speak to Rianas or Arthur. He simply walked briskly along a small side path to a nondescript side door to the palace. He rapped three times and whispered something through a hole in the heavy door. A moment later, he pulled the heavy iron door open when a guard sitting on the other side unlocked it.

Inside there was a cold, black stone walkway lined with similar oaken doors. Every few yards, candles provided light from hand-carved recesses in the wall. O-Gan proceeded quickly down the hall. The hall was wide enough to walk five abreast easily. Arthur and Rianas stayed behind O-Gan, though. The lord's aide briskly kept up his pace. He passed five doors, then turned to a stairwell and started climbing the granite steps.

They walked this way through similar hallways and stairs, passing by butlers, servers and other wait staff. There were even occasional nobles dressed in finery. Finally, they turned down a carpeted hall. From here, they passed through a few very tall arched doors. Finally, they walked out onto a verandah overlooking the palace gardens from six floors up. Rianas was sure she could never get out of this building without some sort of map.

To the left, a painted iron railing was wrought into floral designs. Beyond the railing was a view of the entire terraced city. The cloudy morning sky obscured everything beyond a mile in any direction. Even so, Sko'Port radiated away from the palace toward the Sko'Sea. Stone tops of buildings strained to block the view but failed. Many of the closest buildings sported rooftop gardens. The great avenue to the west clearly marched all the way down to the sea. Rianas could imagine seeing all the way to Riverrun on a clear day from this vantage point.

Arthur was the first to see Rianas' father. Rianas was so busy looking out across the painted iron railing at the city beneath them that she did not think to look at the casual seating area to their right. Lazron bolted up and ran over to her before she had even turned around.

"Rianas!" Her father breathlessly grabbed her in a huge hug. Then he pulled back to inspect her. His eyes appraised her new clothes. Rianas felt embarrassed and overdressed in the fancy dress.

"How and why are you here?" he asked.

Rianas was taken by surprise. "I could ask the same of you, Dad."

Berryl walked over from the seating area. He had a piece of chicken in his hand and a flask of some dark liquid in the other. He nodded at Rianas. "I told your father why you came along, but I don't think he really believed me."

Another man, older and white-haired, walking with a thick white staff topped by a golden eagle, slowly came over. As he approached, O-Gan bowed his head all the way to the richly carpeted floor. "Your Lordship Cerric, here I have Rianas of Riverrun and Arthur of Riverrun. They are also here at the behest of the wizard Atrick."

Lord Cerric nodded. "I see that, O-Gan. It seems Atrick wants my attention today." He let his eyes bore into Rianas' for a second before his lips curled into a grin. "I hope you haven't terrified the young lady too much."

O-Gan laughed at some inside joke. Then he bowed again before walking briskly back into the hallway.

Rianas did not know how to act around a lord. Riverrun had no such royalty, and royal etiquette was not part of her education. She started to bow, then thought to curtsy, and ended up looking quite foolish. Fortunately, Lord Cerric did not seem to be very interested in etiquette. He turned around before she even bent her legs.

"Come, girl, sit with the rest of us on the verandah. I am an old man, and sitting suits me well. It sounds like you have some

explaining to do to your father, and some convincing to do with me."
Lord Cerric did not even wait for replies. Instead, the old man
hobbled over to one of the opulent over-stuffed lounge chairs and let
himself fall back into the silken cushions.

A servant from a corner jumped up to move pillows into place for
Lord Cerric. A second servant brought his half-eaten meal out.

To the left of Lord Cerric's seat, the Axarean war mask sat in a
huge copper dish lined with a silk pillow.

Berryl grinned ear to ear and shrugged at Arthur. Rianas' father
gave her another large hug. Then he walked her over to the seating
area with her, whispering, "Do you realize you could have gotten hurt
or worse out here? Nogs!"

Lord Cerric cleared his throat. He was not a man used to waiting
on others. He pointed to Rianas' father and said, "So, Lazron, you
said you delivered an entire shipment of fine blades and arrows to
Captain Maddox Oren this morning. It would appear your ship
broke a record for time to cross the Sko'Sea, as well."

Rianas' father assented, "The *Promise* is the fastest ship Riverrun
has. It does not carry as much cargo as the *Lark*, but I was able to
catch the ship up near the Runlarian border on its way back south.

"Maddox," Lazron continued, "says he can have the new
armaments apportioned to the Upper Ward Guard in two or three
days. I assured Mr. Locks that the Runlarians are happy to take
delivery of their weapons in three months. Mr. Locks thinks he can
ramp up production to send another twenty thousand crossbow bolts
and five hundred crossbows to Sko'Port at just his cost with labor
before winter starts. He only asks you not tell any of our other
allies."

Lord Cerric nodded. His face was non-committal. He turned to
his servants. "Leave us." Then, looking toward a set of shrubs on the
other side of the verandah, he rapped his staff on a nearby copper
pot as loudly as he could. "You, too, Rodrick. I am safe with this
Riverrun crowd."

A tall, lithesome, dark-skinned man armed with two long swords
and clothed in a dark green tunic and pants stepped silently around a
corner. Tattoos covered his face. The rest of his skin was wrapped

in fine fabric. He wore dark black gloves studded with chain along the top. A small arm-sized buckler rested comfortably on each forearm. Thick, braided hair fell to his shoulders, and as he bowed, the beads at the ends of his braids clinked together around his ears. Rodrick exited through a door on the other side of the verandah, but not before locking his deep black eyes for a moment with Rianas'. His eyes dared her to try something.

Lord Cerric looked around the verandah casually. Although imperceptible to the others, Rianas could see the hunted look in his eyes. This man feared spies.

Rianas thought about what she had learned about her ability over the last few days. If Lord Cerric were truly unable to have a conversation in private, his palace might be a very dangerous place. If she could talk to him telepathically, he might be more willing or able to help. Rianas reached, the way she had learned to communicate telepathically with Atrick. She tried to formulate words in her mind to project.

"Lord Cerric, this is Rianas. Atrick asked me to come with him because I am a natural telepath. I see you think this place is not safe to talk, but if you project toward me, perhaps I can help?" Rianas projected her thoughts as clearly as she could. She had not tried communicating directly on her own with someone else before.

Lord Cerric's eyes shot up, and he looked around. *"Truly? You are a mind reader?"*

"Yes."

"Amazing." Cerric maintained his flat gaze, but looked over to Rianas. "Come over here, young lady, and play a game of checkers with me. I am quite fond of checkers."

Rianas took the queue from Lord Cerric. She projected toward Arthur, *"Keep the conversation light. I will speak with Cerric telepathically."* She got up and walked over to sit on a nearby chair. She had to fold her legs underneath her and lean forward to set up a board that had been on a small nearby table. Apparently, this was one of Lord Cerric's pleasures.

Arthur took a couple steps toward Lord Cerric and motioned around the verandah. "Is all the stone in Sko'Port so beautiful?"

Lord Cerric smiled graciously and started talking about the granite colors common in this part of the Black Mountains. Lazron and Berryl seemed dumbfounded that the Lord of Sko'Port would want to talk about something so inane, but neither said anything.

Lord Cerric did not look at her. *"Berryl showed me this mask last night. The Cidvagians had another one that the Wizard's Guild says bears a similar inscription. I cannot keep that information from the spies that lurk here, but I can keep your success in the mines a secret for a little longer. How does Atrick fare?"* Lord Cerric's hand absently reached toward the mask. He stroked a finger down the painted nose almost lovingly before returning his attention to the checkerboard.

"Atrick was right — the river in the High Mine flows through the Black Mountains and comes out on the southern foothills of the Black Mountains. Based on our best guess, we came out in Old Andaria yesterday evening. Atrick led a successful attack to take a high ledge where the Nog miners had a large camp. At least half the mercenaries and miners who were there had injuries of some kind, but Atrick had brought quite a few apprentice mages with him, and they used all the healing potions they had with them. I think most of the people survived the night."

Rianas watched Cerric move a chip idly across the board. She moved one of her own. Lord Cerric shook his head. "My dear, you have already lost this game."

"Maybe we should discuss Riverrun," Lazron said. He leaned forward. "The *Promise* is heading back tomorrow. Does Sko'Port need more Riverrun steel?"

"That is a long way to go," Lord Cerric said. His eyes peered up from his bushy eyebrows at Rianas. "Sko'Port may not be prepared for that.

"I am an old man, Rianas. I remember the Andarian War well. My sister and I were in the capital of Cidvag studying swordsmanship. A particularly well known mercenary worked for Cidvag's king at the time. The royal family wanted us to study with him."

Lazron sighed and leaned back in his chair. "The wizard Atrick led us to believe you may want more weapons."

Lord Cerric turned a steely glare to Lazron. Rianas' father shut his mouth and inclined his head politely. His face betrayed his emotions when Lord Cerric moved another chip on the board.

"When the war broke out, the Axareans flooded across the Andarian plains from the desert to their south. Their cavalry crushed the resistance so fast that dozens of cities fell before Cidvag even knew there was a war. By then, there was a true panic in the Cidvagian capital. The Cidvagian 'King' had a standing army of only a couple hundred soldiers. Most of his army occupied outposts across the northern edge of the Black Mountains. Even then, the Cidvagian Black Mountains were quite a wild and untamed place.

"To make it worse, Cidvag's individual cities are pretty spread out. The kingdom is small, but the foothills of the Black Mountains make travel longer there. And since the individual cities hold most of the power, the king has very little control, save his name recognition.

"My sister and I had only been there a couple weeks. Suddenly, there were thousands of men, women and children coming through the Gates of Cidvag. At the time, it was a highway for commerce with the South. Cidvag guarded it with a few dozen regular soldiers, who charged a small entry tax for all the goods Andarians brought through. With no nearby reinforcements, the soldiers simply chose to let the flood of humanity pass north.

"The king, however, sent word to the surrounding Northern nations for help. Then he drafted every boy and man over twelve in Cidvag. He ordered they be sent to fortify the border, and rode to the makeshift barricade himself. We found ourselves personally involved in the conflict. Even the kitchen staff came with the king. He completely emptied his palace. Soldiers impressed every man and even many of the healthy women in the capital to service, too.

"When we arrived at the Gates a week later, there were already a couple legions of Cidvagians there. The existing legions were disorganized and poorly armed. The better-trained mercenaries amongst them had the forethought to start felling trees to build a wall, though. My sister and I immediately saw an opportunity to fortify the wall with stones from the edges of the pass. The king put us to work organizing the rabble to construct stone fortifications all along the road. If the King had not acted so decisively, the first few legions of Axarean cavalry would have ridden unchecked into the Northern Realms."

Lord Cerric's mind was fast. He moved the pieces on the checkerboard as he 'spoke' to Rianas, muttering a 'ha' or 'you thought you had me' as he countered Rianas' moves. He looked up to her now, though, as if gauging her response. Rianas nodded.

Rianas' father fidgeted in his seat uncomfortably. "I apologize for being rude Lord Cerric, but …"

Lord Cerric cut him off. "Lazron, I appreciate your concern for the guards. I will properly compensate Mr. Locks for his generous offer of munitions for the naval brigade I'm thinking of building. It seems we have a problem with piracy on the Sko'Sea."

Lazron balked, "That is not what the weapons were requested for, Lord…"

Lord Cerric shot Lazron a cautionary look before loudly saying, "The Lower Ward has requested additional munitions, and I intend to help them as best I can." He turned back to Rianas. *"Your father is a good man, Rianas. I fear his life is in severe danger in the Lower Ward, however. It seems you Riverrunners are rather disliked down there these days."*

Rianas stole a glance at her father. Could the Lower Ward really be so dangerous? Why would Lord Cerric tell her something like that? At least her father was here now. She would not let something happen to him.

Rianas almost broke into a smile at her thought. Then Lord Cerric clapped two pieces together and gestured for Rianas to make her move on the board.

Lord Cerric continued his story. Rianas could feel the emotion as he projected it toward her. To Lord Cerric, it must seem as if he was reliving the experience as he described it to her. *"I was there when the Cidvagian 'army' sealed off the Gates. It was messy. Forty thousand conscripts — and quite a few of them women or children — had to block a canyon nearly a mile wide at its narrowest. I was young, but I sent a courier back to Sko'Port to ask the lord at the time to send as many stonemasons and blacksmiths as he could.*

"The king did not have the heart to turn the Andarians back at first.

"Probably two hundred thousand Andarians fled through in the next couple weeks. The Western Runlarian king brought his royal army through the wall of stones after that, and they fought a campaign within Andaria against the Axarean cavalry. Nevertheless, in that time before the Runlarians arrived, I have no doubt hundreds of Axarean agents managed to infiltrate. Cidvag's king perhaps rightfully rejected the requests for asylum from all but a few of the Andarians. The Sko'Port royal family did not offer amnesty, but they brought in

tens of thousands to help work its mines.

"That leads us to today. Atrick is all too aware the Axareans hold quite a sway with Sko'Port's royal bloodline. They offer gold, rubies, and all manner of false promises in exchange for influence in Sko'Port. The Upper Ward Guard has caught hundreds of suspicious men crossing the mountains in the past few years. They have found dead giants and even dragonlings in some of the known passes. We are not just under threat of invasion, you see. We are already being invaded."

Rianas moved twice in a row, not paying attention to the game as the reality of what the ruler of the largest city in the Northern Realms was saying. Lord Cerric corrected her quietly. She thought this might be her chance to make a good argument for sending help to Atrick.

"Atrick knows that, Lord Cerric. It is time for you to bring the fight to Axarea. Old Andaria lies on the other side of the mountain range. If you had a southern base in the mountains connected to the High Mine, you would be able to send men through quickly. You could use that base to slow down the Axarean infiltration of Sko'Port."

Lord Cerric nodded as Rianas moved a chip and looked her in the eyes as he said, "Good idea."

Now, Rianas projected what she and Arthur had spoken about on the carriage ride over. *"Besides Sko'Port's security, you could probably improve your relationship with the Andarian refugees who make up Riverrun. A chance for the Andarians of Riverrun to see their homeland again would make them a useful ally to Sko'Port."*

Lord Cerric reached his wrinkled hand over to cover Rianas' hand as she made her next move. "Slow down, it's my turn." He winked and smiled. *"You are a very convincing young woman, Rianas. I have other things to worry about, however. Atrick has worked diligently to remove as many Axarean agents as he could from the Upper Ward Guard, but there are hundreds of them in the Lower Ward Guard. Not a day goes by without the body of a merchant or bodyguard or lesser noble washing ashore. Captain Waltus Rian of the Lower Ward Guard is a fine soldier, but there has been a huge turnover in the past ten years, and he cannot properly vet that many soldiers himself.*

"If I send the Upper Ward Guard through, they cannot all stay there. I will

have half the upper guard sent in for about a week. Only a few hundred would be able to stay after securing the exit to the mine. Even those could only stay until we found suitable replacements. Do you think that would be enough?"

A smile came across Rianas face. She had not thought Lord Cerric would be so accommodating. She took his purposefully sacrificed chip with her own and said, "I think you just gave that to me, Lord Cerric."

Lord Cerric smiled as well, "There are many ways to win this game, my dear. I think this sacrifice will help me to win in the end. But for now, I fear I have other business to attend to." He took a folder full of folded papers from a long, heavy pouch at his waist. Inside, a short ink pen and a seal dropped out when he poured them haphazardly onto the table. He removed one of the beautifully embroidered pages and wrote some instructions on them for Upper Ward Guard Captain Oren to provide eighteen hundred men to secure the new southern exit to the High Mine, and then leave three hundred men to build fortifications until the beginning of winter.

On a second sheet, he wrote instructions to deliver the new Riverrun weapons directly to Maddox Oren for his personal disbursement as he saw fit. Rianas marveled at the elderly man's beautiful handwriting. The letters swirled and looped across the page in perfect cursive, and the pen left flecks of red every few letters. Lord Cerric placed his royal seal on each page, folded them and handed them both to Berryl.

Berryl seemed a bit surprised. He wiped his hands on his tunic and started to speak, but Lord Cerric just said, "I've decided my course of action. Go tell Maddox the bad news before I decide to have you lot whipped for wasting my time."

Arthur's eyes shot up. Lazron protested. Lord Cerric put a wrinkled hand in the air and pointed to the door.

"Act quickly, Rianas of Riverrun. Speak with Maddox. Tell him his men must enter the caves tonight, under cover of dark. I will send word to shut down the mine in about an hour. If my ruse works, I may be able to capture some of the worst actors who have been betting on the High Mine's closure. Either way, the Axarean consulate will soon know that Lord Cerric of Sko'Port is openly at war with these evil Axarean agents. I fear there will be dark days ahead. The

next time we meet, there will be blood in my beautiful city's streets."

Lord Cerric looked tired as he shook Lazron's hand. "Thank you for your generosity, Lazron. I hope your trip back to Riverrun goes smoothly."

Rianas' father was nearly beside himself. He did not seem to understand why Lord Cerric had brushed aside his offer to help so quickly. Rianas put a hand on her father's arm as she stood to leave, and he calmed considerably. Arthur shook his head almost imperceptibly, his goofy smile returning already. Berryl dutifully placed the folded pages in his jacket pocket. He bowed slightly to Lord Cerric.

Lord Cerric wasted no time calling back the servants. He demanded one servant to show the four travelers back to the exit, and he immediately started requesting different aides. The Lord of Sko'Port had other business to address.

Rianas watched Lord Cerric caress the mask again as they were being led out. It seemed odd that the mask was sitting beside him instead of with the mages.

12. A RIDE THROUGH THE UPPER WARD

Rianas tried to keep the peace as they exited the palace. As soon as they exited the gates, however, she turned to her father.

"You have to come with us, Dad," she said. "It isn't safe in the Lower Ward."

"This is Sko'Port," Lazron said. "Stay to the major avenues and you are always safe. There are more city guards in Sko'Port than soldiers in the Cidvagian army."

Ronald looked surprised that he was going to have so many riders, but he made room up front. Rianas told him all four of them would be traveling together eastward toward Captain Oren's main guardhouse, where Berryl thought they could find the captain. Arthur climbed up front with Ronald, while Berryl tried to stay out of the conversation between Lazron and his daughter.

Arthur leaned back from the front and said they were about an hour from the Upper Ward Guard headquarters.

"Rianas, how could you run away like that?" Lazron asked. "You could have gotten killed."

"I had to," Rianas said. "Atrick showed me I had magical abilities I didn't even know I had. Once he had talked to me telepathically the first time – well, I had to know what else he could teach me. It seemed like the only way to learn more about who I am becoming."

Rianas' head buzzed with projected thoughts almost without her willing it now. Speaking with Lord Cerric for so long seemed to have strengthened her need to speak telepathically with those around her. It had taken physical effort to keep from telepathically answering her father.

"When I came back from the High Council the next day, I couldn't believe you had gone," Lazron said. He looked hard at her and placed his arm around her in a fatherly hug. "You need to come back home." He sobbed, and then regained his composure. "I cannot lose you, Rianas. If your mother were alive, she would have gone crazy just knowing I left you alone with Atrick."

"I'm not a child anymore, Dad. What Atrick is doing is very important. Do you know I stepped foot on the other side of the mountain? I was in Old Andaria. Don't we owe my grandparents at least an attempt at seeing our homeland again?" She closed her eyes. "Something calls to me from the other side of that mountain."

She gestured vaguely southward as she spoke. It seemed every time she spoke of Old Andaria her decision was clearer. She *did* feel the need to go back. It was as if some invisible force was pulling her.

Her father, still hugging her, relented a little. "You can't just run away, Rianas," he said. "We can help Berryl here get Captain Oren his orders. Let the guards fight whatever comes their way. If you must see Andaria, we could go through a few days later, after it is safe. I can even go with you."

Rianas shook her head as she looked at her father. It would not be enough. "You can't go back to Riverrun. When we get to the Guard headquarters, send a messenger to the *Promise*. Tell them to send every weapon Riverrun can make. The Upper Ward Guard will need them."

While Ronald directed them through the crowded, tree-lined streets, Rianas told the others what had happened. Berryl looked down with wide eyes at the writs Lord Cerric had *actually* given him. He laughed heartily when she described the lord's ruse.

As she looked at her father, a pair of horses caught her eyes. She could not be sure, but it seemed to her the same two horses had been following them when they rode to the palace that morning as well. "Do you know those two?" she asked Berryl. She inconspicuously pointed behind him into the growing morning crowd.

Berryl nonchalantly leaned out of the carriage. Lazron glanced back himself, taking his arm from around Rianas. She could feel his legs and arms tense.

"No." Berryl normally was much more talkative. The hair on

Rianas' arms immediately stood up. She leaned forward across Berryl to speak to Arthur.

"Ronald, Arthur – we need to lose those two men on horseback behind us," she said, trying not to sound alarmed.

Berryl was taking off the jacket he had used to speak with Lord Cerric. Underneath, his full array of weapons seemed to have been strapped to his chest. Lazron looked quite alarmed. "Aren't we overreacting a little bit, here?"

The horses took the cart down a side street. The entire carriage shifted to the left. The sudden direction change threw all three of them to the left of the cart as they started down the hill. About a minute later, Arthur said the horses were still following them. "They slowed down a bit. I don't think they know we saw them."

"Why not just slow down and see what they want?" Rianas' father asked.

Lazron looked with alarm at the two daggers Berryl withdrew. His eyes widened when Berryl offered him one. Rianas took out the dagger Arthur had given her.

The carriage bounced unceremoniously over iron drainage pipes. About fifty yards later, Ronald took another sharp turn to the left and slowed. Then, the entire carriage jerked quickly as Ronald directed the horses into a short alleyway.

Arthur leapt out of the front of the carriage, holding the horse blankets. *"We will hide here. Quickly, we must hide behind those storage crates. Ronald will lead them through the city and try to lose them."*

Rianas pulled at her father. She projected into his mind with her touch, *"This way, Dad. Ronald will see if he can lose them. We need to hide behind these crates."*

Lazron blinked at her as she pulled him, his jaw dropping slightly. She had never spoken telepathically with her father before. A hundred questions bubbled to the surface of his mind. Nevertheless, he followed. He jumped down from the carriage to run behind a stack of emptied crates five feet tall that ran along the wall of a restaurant.

Berryl needed no instructions. He had his sword drawn as he jumped nimbly to the ground and dashed to the cover of the crates with Arthur, Rianas and Lazron.

Arthur and Rianas pulled the two horse blankets across the empty crates, creating a small shelter. Ronald nodded, to which Rianas felt his thoughts of *"Good luck!"* just before he hitched the reins and bent over, pushing the two strong horses into a gallop.

The cobblestone had broken away to uneven gravel and larger stones in the alley. Empty crates sat on a small brick pad the restaurant owner had built. There was moldy food in a puddle, and a stench radiating from further down the alley could only be the result of something dead lurking beneath the crates. Rianas spared a glance around as they waited. She spotted a small black cat perched on the top of a bucket, staring at its new companions in a challenging way. Two rats scurried further into the alleyway behind them, obviously disturbed from some 'fresh' rotten food.

Arthur had drawn two daggers from within his coat, and now even her father was fingering the dagger Berryl had offered him nervously. Berryl held his sword loosely pointed downward, clearly preparing for an upward stab.

Rianas peeked carefully around the musky horse blanket as she heard the two horses approaching. Her heart was in her throat as they approached the alleyway. She reached out consciously to find the two riders with her mind. She hoped to ascertain something about their intentions. Her skill was not necessary, though, for the two were talking as they approached at a slow canter.

"—be going? This is a minor street," one was saying. His voice was raspy, as if he had been yelling for hours.

The two horses appeared first. They were mottled grey and white, tall horses obviously bred for riding. The horses slowed to a walk as they approached the alleyway. As the first horse head came into view, it neighed loudly.

There was cursing, and Rianas just made out the closer of the two horses craning its head toward her before bucking just as they came into sight of the alleyway. The other horse sidestepped out of the way, and both came to a halt, nervously pacing sideways on the main road.

The second man struggled for a moment to regain control of his horse. Rianas ducked back behind the cover of the small blanket. She could hear the whips of the riders as they regained control. Finally, the second rider seemed to be satisfied again. "Damn horses are so stupid. They're just scared of a black cat."

"Come on. We will lose sight of them. Remember, we find out where they were going and report to Lieutenant Ronag. If they are being sent to recruit soldiers for the mine, Lieutenant Ronag will want to know." The first one snapped his reins and galloped off. A few seconds later, the cursing second man was galloping off as well.

"What language was that, do you know, Rianas?" He father asked quietly as the hoof beat faded down the street.

Rianas had not even noticed the two speaking Axarean. "They are Axarean spies, I think. One said they needed to find out where we were going and report to someone named Lieutenant Ronag."

Berryl nodded. "Jadil Ronag, most likely. He is an Axarean immigrant and second in command of the Lower Guard. He selects new recruits when Captain Rian is unavailable, which is most of the time. The captain is quite wealthy and spends most of his off-time peddling influence with the other nobles and elite."

Lazron offered Berryl back his dagger, but when Berryl told him to hold onto it for now, he nodded without arguing and slid the dagger into a loop on his waist. "Why would an Axarean be in such a high position among the Lower Guard? And why does he have men following you two around, Rianas?"

Rianas was folding one of the horse blankets and tying it to her rucksack as quickly as her nervous hands could work. It amazed her how quickly her father had accepted what was going on. "We were almost caught by some other crooked lower guards when we got off the *Lark* in the lower parts of Sko'Port. We ambushed one of the guards and took his uniform to buy ourselves enough time to get away."

"Lieutenant Ronag has friends throughout the Sko'Port elite. He has garnered power through gifts and favors. Judges, mages, and members of the royal family owe him debts. He can do no wrong in many people's eyes." Berryl walked to the edge of the alley and poked his head around. "We need to get moving. It is about three miles to Captain Oren's headquarters from here, and I don't think we will find another set of horses for hire."

The four stepped out onto the street and began going back toward the main road. Rianas' father had always been lanky and was used to hiking with her. He kept up with the group easily. Rianas, however, quickly noticed she had much more energy than the others did. Atrick's ring was aiding her, keeping her legs from tiring. She had forgotten about the ring until now, and it was glowing faintly in the burgeoning morning sun as they came out onto the main avenue again. "What if I ran ahead? I think I could get there in about an hour, maybe less. With Atrick's ring, I think I could run the whole way. Maybe Arthur could carry my gear?"

Rianas did not wait to hear anyone's reply. Most of the straps on her harness were already loose from the fast exit of the carriage. She put the writs from Lord Cerric into her belt pocket and eased the rest of the harness onto the ground. "Here is the money pouch, too. Maybe you can hire some horses with this?"

"Hold on, Rianas," her father said. "I just found you. I'm not going to let you run off again in this dangerous city!"

"Dad, we need to get to Captain Oren before the false news about closing the mine gets to him. If not, the ruse may not work. Lord Cerric doesn't have a true standing army. He has to use the guards to protect the city. Atrick needs help, and I intend to make sure it gets to him as soon as possible. Stay with Arthur and Berryl, and I hope to see you in a couple hours." Rianas was already starting down the street, despite the protests from her father.

Berryl bowed his head and wished her luck. He picked up Rianas' harness full of gear and started helping Arthur get it around his arms. Lazron trotted with Rianas for a few dozen yards. "Rianas, please be safe. We will keep up the best we can."

Rianas smiled at her father and grabbed his hand in camaraderie, then took off at a run, waving behind her and projecting, *"For Andaria!"* It seemed appropriate and brought a smile to her face that she did not let them see.

Sko'Port's main avenue in the Upper Ward changed elevation slower than the north/south streets, but it was still hilly. The avenue wound around the taller parts of the Black Mountains, and every few blocks a street or path would cut across. The other streets went up and down the mountain in a north-south direction. To the north, these intersections afforded a view nearly to the water. To the south, the view opened up to the naked peaks of the Black Mountains. The intersections afforded a grand view of the huge city.

Towers ten stories tall clung to the sides of the steep mountain. Some seemed to fly out of the mountain itself. Many of the buildings had small gardens atop them at this height, but the Lower Ward buildings were mostly brown and grey stone when she spied them around the closer buildings. Mages, people going about their day, food vendors, and mineworkers streamed into the street as the sun made its way further into the morning sky. A dark grey smoke seemed to float across the city, trapping the heat from the sun despite the time of year.

Rianas did not think she had ever run so fast for so long. She remembered running downhill from the hills of Riverrun's main farms toward Ards one afternoon. Her friends had decided to have a race, and it seemed like a good idea. She had come in third, but the run had been exhilarating because it was downhill. This run was like that – she knew she was going fast, but it felt like the only barrier to her speed was how fast she could move her legs.

Of course, cobblestone streets and fancy clothes are not ideal for running. After half a mile, she tied the loose shirt to one side so it would stop flapping on her thighs. Her feet ached from the hard, slightly convex stones, and she had to watch the ground carefully for upended stones that might trip her at that pace.

One vendor whistled at her and said something vulgar as she dashed past. Another man jumped out of her way when he did not hear her coming. As the morning brightened more toward working hours, she had to slow and jump around various new obstacles, such as an old woman pushing a cart full of garments. The going was faster in the main part of the street, but horses did not make way for her.

Even with the assistance of the ring, however, Rianas felt the fatigue build. She ran as fast and as long as she could, but after about two miles her pace slowed. She had beaten her own personal record – of that she was sure – but her legs screamed and her feet were beginning to blister.

A grey and white mottled horse came onto the road from a side alleyway ahead, followed by a second. The two riders were unmistakable in their black cloaks. There was no avoiding them at her pace, though. As soon as the first cleared the alley, he pointed toward her.

Rianas dove off the main road into a row of flower and food stalls. An old woman started offering "pretty flowers for the beautiful young maiden" before Rianas jumped past two other patrons onto the busy sidewalk.

The closer rider had turned his horse into her path. The other rider was cantering off to Rianas' left. With nowhere else to go, Rianas yelled, "Help! Those men have been chasing me!"

The first rider growled something unintelligible at her. He was perhaps forty feet away, but Rianas clearly felt the ill intent telepathically.

The second rider was jumping off his horse. Rianas could see his face now. There were two long scars along his cheeks. His skin was dark and grey. She had never seen a Southerner from this close before, but he matched the description eerily.

An older man with spectacles and a cane stopped near Rianas, looking at the two black-clad spies. "May I help you, young men?" he asked. Two food vendors stepped around their stalls to block 'Scar'.

The second horseman jumped to the ground. This one's face seemed curled into a perpetual snarl. In heavily accented Northern, he said, "You come with us, girl. I've had enough of this chasing today."

Scar made a weak excuse to the people around him about collecting "this one" for the debts she owed. Rianas, despite the gravity of the situation, wondered if *anyone* would believe that lie. It served to catch a few people off guard as he politely made his way toward her, though.

'Snarl,' however, shouldered a young man out of the way while drawing a longsword from his waist. The young man seemed to skid across the ground.

The old florist screamed when Snarl drew his sword. The two other vendors put up their hands and backed away, no longer feeling as brave as before.

Rianas could see her situation deteriorating fast. She nervously flipped the leather thong out of the way on the dagger Arthur had given her. If she ran, she had no doubt that Snarl would either grab or stab at her from this close. If she stayed, she might get a lucky stab in before the first Southerner could grab her, but it was not likely she could stop both of them.

Her attunement to the situation seemed to magnify her telepathic powers. She could feel Snarl's hatred. He was definitely the one whose horse had bucked before.

The horses!

Rianas called to Snarl's horse, *"Please, help me. Kick him or something. I'll make sure he doesn't whip you again."*

The grey horse whinnied in assent. It pranced forward toward the snarling Southerner from behind. His focus was solely on her, now. He did not have a chance to defend himself when the horse reared up from behind. Just before impact, the noisy clatter of hooves and the horse's neigh got his attention. Swinging back with his sword, he saw the huge horse's front hooves barreling toward his head too late to react.

In an instant, he was on the ground. The horse fell forward. The spy's sword slid noisily across the cobblestone street and under a cart full of Gawdichian fruits.

The florist kept screaming hysterically.

Scar was just a few paces away. Rianas drew her long dagger and leapt rather gracelessly backward over a cart full of leather buckles and satchels. The merchant's goods spilled all over the ground.

People scattered in every direction. The grey horse was trying to get up, but the man beneath it was hardly moving.

The old man with the glasses swept his cane forward just in time to trip the Southerner, sending him into the pile of buckles.

Rianas took her chance to swing around from behind. She skidded across a box of flowers that had fallen to the ground. The bottom of her long shirt came undone, trailing behind her like a cape. With a swing of her arm, she stabbed toward the Southerner.

Scar was too fast. He spun around, whipping a handful of belts with his left hand and striking Rianas' dagger. A few of the belts wrapped around the dagger and he immediately saw his chance to pull her toward him.

Rianas used the momentum from her lunge around the cart to pull the two of them further toward the flower cart. The old man was still nearby. He poked at the Southerner with his cane ineffectually. The florist was now running across the street. Rianas let go of her dagger and stood up at the flower cart, looking for something she could use to defend herself.

The Southerner pulled Rianas' dagger from the tangle of belts deftly and jumped up in one fluid motion. Suddenly, the two were face-to-face.

The grey-skinned man grabbed her left arm with his gloved hand so tight she feared bones would break. Rianas used her free hand to fling an earthenware pot into his face as hard as she could. He tried to deflect it with her dagger, but the old man managed to strike him from behind and push his arm off balance. The pot smashed into wet pieces across the right side of the Southerner's cowl, sending a beautiful floral arrangement into his eyes, down his shirt and onto the street.

His hand did not release her. Instead, he pulled her into a bear hug while he swung the dagger around toward the old man so he had to step back. She could smell his oddly minty breath. Rianas' arms were pinned to her side. She kicked with all her might, but he lifted her into the air facing away from him. The wind left her lungs as she struggled against the man's iron embrace.

The first Southerner was slowly getting up. Now, there was no one left attempting to help her. Rianas struggled against his arms as he hefted her onto the second horse like a wet rag.

She could not think.

Scar reached his gloved hand around her throat. Leaning in, he rasped, "I can't wait to get you back to the master. He will be very pleased."

Rianas knew what to do! Her left hand wriggled free long enough to reach toward her captor's face. She made skin-to-skin contact just long enough to establish a mental link.

The now-familiar leap into the Southerner's mind brought her to a room full of warriors. They were all standing in a semicircle while facing an instructor wearing a war mask like the one Berryl had left with Lord Cerric.

Rianas knew she had little time. She tried to project as many difficult questions as she could into his mind. *"How far is home from here? How much are you being paid? Who is your boss? How did you jump up so fast before? What will —"*

That was all she could do. His other hand struck hers. The hilt of his dagger caught her wrist, yanking her arm above her head and sending shooting pain through her hand.

Was it enough? Rianas kicked with her legs in an attempt to pull herself upright, but the arm at her throat had her.

"Go!" she projected toward the horse below her.

The huge horse lurched forward into the street. It dragged Rianas and Scar with her. With his arm still holding the dagger above his head, he lost his balance, pulling the two of them to the ground.

It was all Rianas needed. His surprise and the impact on the cobblestone was enough to weaken his grasp on her neck. She twisted, bringing her right leg up into the Southerner's stomach with enough force to extract herself. Rianas rolled to the side, avoiding his arm and rolling into the middle of the street.

The Axarean warrior's new knowledge was marvelous. It seemed like she had trained alongside this grey-skinned man for months. Fast rolls and kicks were second nature to her. The man's training raced through her mind, and she tried to hold onto something useful long enough to give her an advantage.

Now both of the Southerners were getting up.

The first one, with a huge bloody gash running down the side of his scalp from the horse's kick, drew a throwing dagger. He was still snarling at her.

The second Southerner was slower to get up this time. Rianas backed away. Blood was trickling down her left wrist where her dagger's hilt had hit her. She could hear people shouting all around. The old man was gesturing toward her and yelling something she could not hear. The Axareans' horses were both trotting away down the street.

Two Sko'Port guards were racing up from the direction she had been going. With short swords drawn, they were yelling for everyone to drop their weapons. Rianas stood up, rubbing her wrist and checking for other wounds. The two Southerners begrudgingly dropped their weapons to the street. Scar was already pointing to Rianas and making up another lie.

Very quickly, a huge crowd had drawn together. The guards used metal chains to tie up both of the men. They did not even bother listening to the Axareans' pleas.

The first guard, a dark-skinned man of Kabaran origins, patted through Snarl's clothes. He found three other small throwing daggers and a small vial.

"It is illegal to carry poisoned knives in Sko'Port," the Kabaran guard said. He put the contraband into a thick leather pouch at his side.

Scar was shouting, "We are Axarean emissaries, you fool. Ambassador Ronag sent us to bring the Riverrunner back for questioning. If you detain us, I can guarantee you will –"

The second guard punched the Southerner in the stomach with his meaty hand. Then he proceeded to remove the black-clad man's other weapons. The guard found two other daggers in his leg pockets.

"We'll just be interviewing you two for a couple days," the second guard said sarcastically. "I'm sure this was all some misunderstanding. Eventually, the Ambassador will be told of your whereabouts, I'm sure."

With both of the Southerners finally tied up, the Kabaran guard started leading the two spies down the street. The second guard approached a few of the injured people on the street to make sure no one needed healing. His thick black beard hid any emotions he felt as he spoke.

When he turned toward where Rianas had been standing, she was gone. After picking up her dagger from under a few spilled belts, she trotted down the street and hopped on one of the grey horses. She heard the guard yelling after her as she rode off.

13. CAPTAIN MADDOX OREN

A few moments later, Rianas galloped around the corner to the main Upper Ward Guard headquarters. It was amazing those Axarean spies had been willing to attack her so close to this place. The situation in Sko'Port might be even worse than either Lord Cerric or Atrick believed.

Dismounting, she adjusted her shirt and retied her hair. Rianas was breathing heavily. An old man selling fine cloth pouches asked her if she was okay. She gasped out that she just needed to catch her breath.

The headquarters pressed up against the mountain. Utilitarian balconies of oak with iron handrails lined the building for four floors. A huge Sko'Port flag flew from a pole in front on the short lawn. A dozen men in black, buttoned-front uniforms were training on a sidewall against wooden scarecrows under the watchful eye of a broad-chested sergeant who was over six feet tall. The main entrance had a single guard. A line of perhaps twenty people waited to enter.

Rianas walked up to the line. More people were coming up to the building to make their cases to the court or do business with the guards. In one place, a couple was arguing. In another, a man clutched his arm where he had attained some sort of injury. Two young women held each other silently. Most of the rest of the group seemed quietly ready to discuss their problems in private. It took the guard a few seconds to determine where each person should go, and the line moved along quickly.

The guard looked Rianas up and down as she got to the front, as if he could decide where she needed to go purely based on her appearance. One look at the sealed writ from Lord Cerric she produced, and his eyes shot up to hers.

"I need to see Captain Maddox Oren right away," Rianas said as quietly and confidently as she could. "It is a matter of life and death." The guard nodded and pointed toward an important looking sergeant inside the main waiting room who was watching the various people as they entered the room. "Sergeant Winston can take you to see the captain. Show him your writ."

Sergeant Winston's eyes were hard, but he was quite kind as he led Rianas back into the building. "Do you need something to drink, milady? You look like you ran two miles to get here."

"I ran about four, I think." Rianas smiled back at the friendly guard when his eyes shot up. "Listen, I really need to see the captain as soon as possible. If you see my friends out front, could you have them sent along, as well?"

The sergeant said he would try. "Your accent is familiar. You must be a Riverrunner, too, eh? I left a couple years ago to work in the guards here, but I find I miss the homeland."

Rianas spoke idly about Ards and the local goings-on in Riverrun for a few moments while they continued down the sparsely decorated halls. Unlike the wide halls of the lord's palace, these were narrow, and the sergeant had to turn to the side for others to pass in the busy corridors. The floors were made of lighter colored granite, and the walls were mostly brick.

After about five minutes of walking, they came to a wider hall marked "Captain's Headquarters" by a huge wooden sign above. This hall was rectangular and had a collection of double doors leading off into what looked like the mountain itself. Sergeant Winston led Rianas to one of the doors on the left that had a stone marker shaped like the number one. Two quick knocks and a short man with a long mustache and carrying a hand bow opened the door.

Sergeant Winston spoke quietly with the other guard, who turned and said something to someone inside the door.

"Just let the damn girl inside, lieutenant," a voice boomed from inside.

There was a commotion. A man who looked somewhat like a hairy grizzly flung the door open the rest of the way. His long reddish hair going to gray and thick, neatly trimmed mustache masked most of his face. Huge round spectacles concealed the rest of it. The man was tall, barrel-chested, and not in the mood to wait for his lieutenant to open the door.

"What's your name, girl?" the man said, perhaps a touch too loud. He thanked Sergeant Winston in a dismissive yet polite gesture. The sergeant nodded and turned around to return to his post. The lieutenant, meanwhile, smirked and got out of the larger man's way.

"I am Rianas of Riverrun. I have this writ from Lord Cerric. Could we speak someplace safe?" Rianas looked around at the dozen or so other officers and civilians quietly doing business in the hall. Some of them clearly looked upset she was usurping their positions in line to speak with the captain.

"This is my guardhouse, girl. If there is a place in all of Sko'Port that is safer, I challenge you to find it," Captain Oren said. Then he broke into a huge smile and laughed. "Lord Cerric should spend more of his vacation time down here!"

Nevertheless, as he spoke, he relented and stepped aside to motion Rianas into his office.

Rianas stepped inside and immediately noticed the other occupants of the room. Two Knights of Sullaria were there. There was no mistaking them. Each had the Sullarian emblem of a golden dragon emblazoned on their armor. Even somewhat at ease, they wore full plate. Their helmets sat on a small table nearby. The closer one – a woman, somewhat shorter and skinnier – wore a green skirt, while the other wore a burgundy-red pair of shiny leather leggings that curved around his muscular legs.

Rianas' gaze lingered on the two. She had read books about Sullarian Knights, but only a handful of Green Knights had ever passed through Riverrun. They universally excelled in combat and horsemanship. Green Knights sought out impossible tasks in order to highlight their superior skills to the world. They sought adventure in far-off lands or worked with local nations to address problems.

Captain Oren looked up from the writ he had taken from Rianas and saw her looking at the two knights. He bellowed in his deep baritone as he pulled the door behind him, "These two are Knight

Ogerena Yelenar and Knight Ryalsgar Ogenson. Ogerena was actually just asking me about the status of the High Mine. She said she was curious how the wizard Atrick had fared."

All eyes on Rianas, Captain Oren motioned her to a stone bench cut out of the wall. Rianas took a seat and began explaining the battle in the mushroom forest, and their decision to push through to the end of the cave.

Green Knight Yelenar nodded her head before Rianas could say any more. "Wizard Atrick is a wise man. I regret being away when he went into the mine."

Captain Oren sat back in his huge chair. "So, Atrick thinks to expand the mine by a few miles. I'm sure the merchants of the city will be thrilled to learn that."

The other knight, Ryalsgar Ogenson, raised a gloved finger from his lap. "That mask Berryl brought is a bad omen, Maddox. It looks very similar to one I saw in Assyria about ten years ago. There had been a small army of bandits in the mountains, burning villages and killing travelers. A group of Assyrian nobles drafted militia from the northern cities and got help from the Southern Runlarian army to hunt them down. There were over four thousand casualties in that war. Normal bandits would have dispersed at the sight of such an army, but these men fought viciously. They had heavy swords and armor they shouldn't have had, and their organization was too regimented on the battlefield to be simple bandits.

"When their leader was finally forced to fight us – because the Runlarian army had taken out their last stronghold – he wore a mask like this. The man fought with the strength of ten men. He flung soldiers off their horses and was so fast they couldn't take him in single combat. Dozens fell trying to slow him down. He nearly cut a retreat through our lines, with his other men behind him. Those others seemed crazed in their zeal to follow him. The killing blow came from a White Knight working to guard the Runlarian General Ombendow. General Ombendow put his royal guards in the path of danger to stop their escape.

"Ombendow was thrown from his horse, and the knight used his Shock Lance to catch the masked leader off guard. The other bandits pounced at him. They ignored the blades of their attackers. The knight used his sword to attack the masked bandit. In the struggle, the knight knocked the mask off the bandit's face. Soon after, the other bandits overwhelmed the knight. I was young then, a Green Knight. I tried with my other companions to save our brother in arms, but by the time we finished the bandits, the knight had been mortally wounded."

Ryalsgar shook his head and lowered his finger. "Those masks all bear the same face. They provide the wearer great skill and strength. The Wizards' Council in Sullaria warns its knights that the cost of that power is unknown. I understand only about a dozen have ever been captured, and most have been lost again soon after."

Maddox shrugged his bear-like shoulders and put his hands in the air. "Ryalsgar, what would you have me do? Lord Cerric writes here that I should send half a legion of men into the caves to help Atrick. If we captured one of these masks, where did it come from? Is it possible some psychotic wizard is trying to send madmen across Arthos?"

"Psychosis," Ogerena nodded humorlessly. "That would be one possible reason. May I request a chance to join your expedition, Captain?"

Captain Oren flung his right arm in the air, gesturing toward Ogerena. "Of course. It sounds like I'll be sending half the guards into the mountain. Why wouldn't I allow a Sullarian Knight to go?"

"Not just into the mountains, captain," Rianas spoke up. "You see, we took the Nog forward camp just outside the cave. There was a small army camped at the foot of the mountain that would need to be defended against. Atrick intends to make a base of operations there. Old Andaria is on the other side of the mountain."

Rianas looked over to the two Sullarian Knights. "Also," she said, "Atrick thinks the masks are Axarean war masks." Captain Oren seemed dubious about sending soldiers into the mine, so she continued. "And my father is on the council in Ards. When Atrick came to recruit me for this endeavor, he convinced the Ards council to send a boatload of weapons your way. The shipment is already in Sko'Port. It will be here in a couple of hours. On top of that, they have agreed to produce more crossbows and ammunition to be directly sent to the Upper Ward Guard."

Ogerena smiled and spoke over Captain Oren's inappropriate epithet. "Old Andaria." The silence drew out. Captain Oren was about to say something when she continued, "And you, Rianas of Andarian blood, must be s*he who brings the voice back to her people*." The knight's smile was thin and mischievous.

"What in the five Dwarven hells are you talking about?" Captain Oren boomed incredulously.

Red Knight Ogenson nodded his head solemnly, looking at Rianas carefully. "Young woman, tell us please. What do *you* think we should do next?"

Rianas could not believe the two knights had heard of the same obscure prophecy Atrick had shown her. Something inside told her she should take advantage of a chance to make her case, though. So she did. "I don't think it is in Sko'Port's interest, or the Northern Realms', to allow Andaria to remain in the hands of Axarea. From what I've seen and heard since coming to Sko'Port, the Empire is unfriendly at the least. If there is a chance to put men and women from the Northern Realms back onto the southern plains of the Black Mountains, it should be something we all want. A small fort with the full force of Sko'Port and the Northern Realms behind it would reduce some of the crossings of the mountain, and it would give us huge insight into the Empire's activities along the mountains.

"Lord Cerric asked that the guards be sent in under cover of dark. He plans to have word spread that he is going to close the mine. He thinks the ruse will give him a chance to take some of those plotting against him by surprise. I suspect it will also buy him a little time to hide the fact that so many of the Upper Ward guards are out of the city. The Axareans have spies even in your Upper Ward. Axarean pursuers forced us to abandon our carriage this morning. They followed us from the High Mine to Lord Cerric's palace. Two of them attacked me less than a mile from here. I only made it out because two of your Upper Ward guards came to my rescue. That is why I ran the rest of the way here.

"There is extreme urgency to this matter. Judging by the size of the encampment at the foot of the mountain, Atrick will not be able to defend that ledge for long against such a substantial force.

"I personally want to see Old Andaria," Rianas went on. "I don't intend to stop at the exit of that cave. If there is any chance of going down that mountain and entering my ancestral home, I plan to take it. Something on that side of the mountain calls to me. I can't explain it. It is like my fate feels somehow drawn by that river that flows into the Old World."

Captain Oren's gaze appraised Rianas again. He sat silently for nearly two minutes.

The Green Knight Yelenar spoke into the silence. "She who fights the mountain will need help from many lands. I will follow you on your journey, Rianas of Riverrun."

Knight Ogenson quietly said he would be joining Ogerena on their newest crusade. Rianas did not dare look away from Captain Oren, but she said thank you nonetheless.

At last, the huge man nodded. "Atrick has helped me more times than I deserve," he said. "Lord Cerric is right, though. We put the city at risk by sending so many men into the mines at once. I'm not sure if I can gather that many men without spies finding out."

Ryalsgar raised his finger again. "There are warehouses all around the High Mine, captain. Perhaps you can stage from one of them. Commandeer a warehouse and post guards. Then, send your guards to the warehouse as they go off duty. You should be able to get your men to one of the warehouses without undue suspicion. You can transfer the men from there into the mine under cover of night. The streets won't miss your men for a couple of days. I suspect you will be able to throw your remaining force into overtime for a week or two."

Captain Oren agreed. "The coal warehouse is large enough."

Rianas thought about how they had returned from the far cavern. "We rode a half-full mining car most of the way back. Apparently, some of them are enchanted so that they roll under their own power. Perhaps you could send a few hundred men at a time through that way once you shut the mine down for the night. You could probably get the entire army in by tomorrow morning if you used the cars. It would keep them fresh, and let them carry more supplies."

Captain Oren smiled. "Well, girl, you are full of boundless good ideas. It looks like I have an army to move!" Captain Oren summoned the lieutenant back into the room and demanded lists of personnel.

Ryalsgar and Ogerena both got up when Rianas rose to excuse herself. Captain Maddox Oren told them to get to the High Mine coal warehouse before nightfall. The hairy man sat down at a long table to begin organizing units.

As Rianas walked into the hall, the consequences of the writ Lord Cerric had sent with her were already becoming apparent. Oren's booming voice called out to his sergeants and corporals. Two young runners dashed in opposite directions with lists of instructions before Rianas had even left the next chamber.

Ogerena Yelenar stepped next to Rianas and touched her shoulder. "You will see your homeland, Rianas. Knight Ogenson and I will do what we can to help."

The green sleeve of her tunic fell away, revealing more steel armor over the knight's arm and hands. Rianas wondered how the knight managed to look so comfortable in so much steel.

As they made their way toward the entrance of the building, the two knights genuinely seemed interested in Rianas' last few days. They asked dozens of questions, wondering aloud about the Nog attackers and requesting Rianas' opinions on some of Atrick's decisions. By the time they reached the entrance to the headquarters, Rianas had told the two knights everything about the last few days.

However, she left out as much as she could about her ability to read minds or use magic.

Still, Ogerena asked why Atrick had wanted her to interrogate the nogs. "Surely he knew that nogs have a rudimentary language at best?" she asked. "He could have hired any number of dozens of people in Sko'Port who could speak with the creatures."

Rianas shook her head. "I don't know. Atrick thinks I am special, but my ability is limited." Atrick's words of caution about letting people know what she could do rang in her head. Already, she had shown Lord Cerric. It seemed almost impossible to heed his advice.

Ogerena stopped as they entered the huge waiting room and crossed her arms. Her pale blue eyes pierced Rianas' as she said, "You are entitled to your privacy, Rianas. Tell us what is on your mind when you are ready."

Rianas opened her mouth. Shut it. Lying was not something she did well. She considered telling the two knights everything she was experiencing. She 'heard' whispers from at least four other people – others in the room whose thoughts she could have read by simply focusing her attention. It would be nice to share her growing fear that she might touch someone during a conversation and inadvertently end up in his or her mind.

Before she could say anything, however, Arthur ran through the entryway. "Rianas," he panted, "I'm glad you made it!" Sweat coated his brow. He had obviously been running for quite some time.

Berryl and Lazron were still outside in the yard of the headquarters.

There were a few brief introductions as the three went back outside with Arthur. Rianas explained quietly to the others what had happened inside, and Ryalsgar suggested they get some supplies and head directly to the staging area.

Rianas gestured toward the grey horse still tied to a hitching post. "I don't know what happened to Ronald, but the Axareans caught up with me. They almost had me, too, if it hadn't been for the help of those two guards."

The two guards were standing next to the two horses. Apparently, they had gathered the second horse on their way to bring in the Southerners for questioning. The Kabaran guard pointed to her and made his way over, hand on sword.

"Fleeing a crime scene is illegal in Sko'Port, milady!" the man said.

Rianas apologized. The Sullarians said she was with them, which seemed to mollify the man. After thinking a moment, she added, "They were both Axarean spies sent by the Ambassador from Axarea, Ladji Ronag. The one with the scars on his face has extensive combat training. I would wager the other did, too."

Rianas started to leave, but then she remembered the two horses. "Could you see those two horses to a good home? They have both been traumatized by their treatment at the Southerners' hands." She walked over to the first one and patted its nose, rubbing her other hand along the side of its long face.

Arthur asked the other guard to look into the status of Ronald, their driver. "He may have already returned to the High Mine where he is stationed. But since he led those two Axareans off, it would be awful if something bad happened to him."

"I will look." The guard was petting the other horse. "These riding horses will be confiscated by the guard. I can't guarantee a judge won't decide they must be returned to the consulate, but I will speak up for them myself. In the meanwhile, perhaps Jerrus and I can use their help to check up on your driver." He smiled at Rianas, gesturing to his partner.

Lazron no longer needed convincing to let Rianas go through the mine again. He smiled and hugged her. "Rianas, Arthur and Berryl have had many good things to say about your actions since you left Riverrun. I'm proud of you. I am only sorry you did not speak with me before you decided to go on this trip."

Rianas shook her head. They stopped at a small supply warehouse that doubled as living quarters for Ryalsgar and Ogerena. The two knights were in a corner changing into travel gear and full armor. Arthur, Rianas, Lazron and Berryl loaded travel gear into rucksacks at Ryalsgar's invitation. There were cooking pots, dried fruits, vegetables and meats, hard cakes, some sort of wrapped cheeses, and salted pork.

Rianas stared at Ogerena as she easily removed her armor to change into leather travel gear. The steel plates seemed so light. Rianas said as much.

"Yes", Ogerena nodded, placing the breastplate down onto the pile from her changing booth while she put on travel clothes. "Ryalsgar and I both have special Elven plate. It has been enchanted to weigh about a third as much as normal steel. When we finish our training to become Green, a Sullarian armorer refurbishes a retired set of armor for us. There are perhaps five thousand full sets in existence. New suits take years to fashion, and dozens of master artisans are employed just to replace the armor lost or destroyed in the last hundred years.

"This suit is something I only borrow from the knights. It identifies me as an ambassador of Sullaria." She finished sliding into her garments and then stepped out. Her muscular legs and arms were apparent in the tighter-fitting leather.

Ogerena picked up the breastplate and offered it to Rianas. She hefted it in her hands, marveling at its light weight. The material bent slightly around the edges to her touch, too, allowing it to mold more closely to its occupant.

"It's amazing!" Rianas said, feeling the corners. "The hinges on the sides must cost a fortune to make." An inscription inside the breastplate was in bright gold, glowing Elven lettering. It read *Levias Fortis'* in Elven. Reading the inscription sent a shiver down her spine, as if invisible fingers had trailed up her back and along her neck. The odd sensation passed almost as soon as it started, but she looked up at Ogerena and gave the breastplate back.

Ogerena began pulling her plate armor back in place over her travel clothes. Rianas returned to the pile of supplies Arthur was pulling down and packing as compactly as he could. Lazron had already packed enough food for a week with some cotton sleeping blankets, and Berryl was looking over Ryalsgar's rack of weapons admiringly. Ryalsgar offered longswords to the other men. Lazron and Arthur graciously accepted, but Berryl politely said he would use his own weapons. Ryalsgar and Berryl laid out their equipment to compare.

Ryalsgar's pride was wrapped in a black onyx sheath. Rianas and the others admired the red rubies embedded in the hilt of the longsword as he withdrew it. A streak of what looked like red metal ran along the thickest portion of the sword. The hilt had etched lettering declaring 'Ogen's Touch' on one side. The ornate guard looked like a flame. The sword itself seemed to Rianas to radiate magic. It was a work of art.

"This is Ogen's Touch. It has been in our family for four generations of Sullarian knights. My uncle gave it to me when I became a Red Knight. He always had a knack for the dramatic. He thought it was only right the sword went to a Red Knight. It is a

Flame sword." With that, he made a broad sweep through the air. The sword left a streak of red flame in its wake.

Rianas sensed the magical weave around the sword. The word *Ignis* was etched along the full length of the blade, cleverly included in the flame emboss. The sword's natural state had been preserved just after tempering somehow, such that its heat was that of a furnace. The sheath had a neutralizing effect on the magic, and the two parts completed the weave. Such a magical masterpiece would have taken hundreds or even thousands of hours to complete. Rianas marveled at the enchantment.

Ogerena had her own wonders. She packed a small healing potion for herself and offered small jars to each of her new companions. There was enough of the magical healing liquid in each jar to stabilize even a mortal wound. Rianas, Arthur and Lazron appreciatively packed the small wax-sealed jars safely in their own bags.

Her crossbow was a beautiful collection of Elven steel and wood. Despite being large enough to require two arms to lift, it was light enough for Rianas to lift with just one. Ogerena showed Rianas how to crank the piston into place. When she muttered "*Sa'ag*" and made a gesture with her hand, a blue light in the shape of a crossbow bolt solidified where the bolt would have been.

"You are a mage?" Rianas asked.

"Hardly," Knight Yelenar said. "More like an apprentice. I have learned a few spells. I apprenticed in Sullaria for three years, and I have spent most of my time in Sko'Port working with the Sko'Port mages. Their skills are specialized to manipulation of stone, but I adapted some of what I learned to create this spell. I have worked this particular weave so many times that it comes quickly to me. The bolt will not last terribly long, but its shape lets it fly fast and far."

Ryalsgar scoffed. "It makes her one of the best archers in Sko'Port. She can fire twenty rounds in a minute, too, which is far better than any other bowman I have ever seen."

The bolt slowly faded away. Rianas was stunned. With all the magic around, she could not understand why she had never seen more than a few small tricks growing up.

Lazron had finished packing his bag full of the knight's things. He hefted it with a grunt onto his back. "Rianas and Arthur have seen very little magic. In Riverrun, magic is not common. There are no mages, nor are there any apprentices. We have learned to make do without the convenience of magic for the last fifty years."

Ogerena nodded. "In Sullaria, the Elven mages have helped create items like this for hundreds of years. While the Elven Empire does not share its magic freely, Sullaria long ago became the center for magic in Arthos. Everyone in Sullaria is exposed to magic at birth, and the Sullarian Wizards' Council is charged with researching new ways to use magic. Elves who leave the Elven Empire often go to Sullaria to share their skills, or even to study."

Rianas had many questions she wanted to ask. The others were finished packing what they could easily carry, however, and Ryalsgar suggested they get moving. The trip would take about two hours on foot.

Arthur fell in beside Rianas as they walked behind the others. With her father on her right, she finally had some time to tell him what had happened over the last few days. He cut her off several times to ask for more details, and he hugged her a few more times. His eyes shot up at the thought of his daughter casting spells, but he said it did not surprise him that she had such natural talent.

"You have always surprised me, Rianas. I often wonder if you got your talents from your mother. You know, she was an excellent equestrian. That is why we had the farm, after all. She trained dozens of horses for the Runlarians before you were born." Lazron's eyes looked distant for a moment, as they usually did when Rianas' father spoke of his beloved wife.

Rianas asked if any of their other relatives had magical talent. Lazron shook his head no. Ogerena, apparently eavesdropping from ahead, turned around as they marched through a side street.

"Innate magic is very rare in humans, and it tends to skips a generation or two. Humans can often learn to use the weave even if not born with an innate talent. Actually, that is how the majority of us humans gain our abilities. All Elves seem to be born with innate magical ability."

Lazron and Arthur took turns testing Rianas' mind-reading ability.

Lazron smiled each time Rianas 'found' a word in his head. Arthur tested her more vigorously, giving her long sentences to recite. Ogerena and Ryalsgar both marveled at her talent.

Rianas felt at home with these five companions. Berryl made occasional jokes. Arthur warmly encouraged her. The two Sullarians treating her as their new charge made the entire situation somehow feel natural. Her father smiled and even clapped a few times. It was almost to Rianas as if they were at home entertaining old family and friends.

It was while doing this that they finally came to the High Mine coal warehouse Captain Maddox Oren had decided to take over.

A few guards in black button-up outfits carrying new Riverrun crossbows waved the party in. The side street was cordoned off with large crates to prevent unwanted eyes from seeing the line of men and women queuing up outside. Equipment on handcarts arrived a few at a time. Small squads of four to ten men walked up to the small road from different directions. The entire operation was being kept as quiet as possible.

After walking through the entrance and receiving orders from a short warehouse technician on where to set up to rest for the afternoon, the six companions went to help move equipment out of the way. Already, many guards had spilled in at the end of their shifts. The warehouse was full of weapons, food and gear. Guards and High Mine workers were loading the items into enchanted mine cars. Scores of conscripted mine attendants worked diligently to remove stones from the mine cars while the guards filled each up with gear.

Car twenty-three was assigned to the six companions and four other guards. It was a tight fit, with only enough space for their packs between their feet. The group got in and out a few times to find the most comfortable positions before going back to rest for the next couple of hours.

Lazron projected toward Rianas as they sat, "*Rianas, are you sure you want to do this? Based on what you said, there are probably thousands of Axarean soldiers getting ready to attack Atrick's little encampment. These men are trained fighters, but they may not be able to turn back such a large force.*"

"I am going back, Dad. Atrick needs help. I need to see Andaria again. If one extra set of hands makes a difference, I want them to be mine."

"I am afraid my training with a sword was a long time ago," Lazron thought. *"I am no mercenary or guard."*

Rianas nodded and reached out to touch her father's arm. He calmed visibly at her touch and smiled.

The sunset over Sko'Port shone into the large warehouse. With so many guards – all under orders to maintain low voices – the cavernous building sounded like a hive of bees. Whispering echoed all around. Many of these men would follow orders because that was how they were trained. However, there were also some men upset they would be away from their families for days. The promise of wartime pay seemed to have calmed most of the negative whispers. Still, to Rianas the feelings were palpable.

The four guards who squeezed into the enchanted mine car with Rianas and her companions were polite. They asked questions about what to expect. Rianas told them they would be making history, and it seemed to go over well with the others. Ryalsgar even smiled slightly.

The foreman shut down the mine a little after lunchtime. Instead of sending essential staff home, he diverted them to the warehouse. Within an hour, hundreds of mineworkers were managing the enchanted mine cars. Dozens of guards made a show of blocking off the roads into the mine and setting up a huge wooden stockade at the employee entrance. Citizens watched in awe and fear. Late coming soldiers said town criers were announcing the mine's closure across the city.

Men and gear filled nearly three hundred of the enchanted mine cars. As the last rays of the sun ducked below the western edges of the city, the caravan began moving quietly out of the warehouse and into the cave. Some drafted miners drove a few of the carts, while others cleared the path through to the huge entrance. The token guards saluted as the train of magical rail cars rolled up and into the mine, defying gravity.

The way in became loud as the cars rolled quickly down into the mountain. Guards shouted at each other in conversation as they went. Some seemed fidgety and nervous. Others nonchalantly munched on dried rations or drank from flasks.

There were a few dozen mages, too. Knight Yelenar surmised that nearly half of all the mine mages in Sko'Port were in this caravan. They were easy to spot. Their cars contained large cases of healing potions. Rianas wondered how Captain Oren had managed to recruit so many of the mages without exciting suspicion among the Axarean spies.

"The Sko'Port Wizard's Guild has three colleges," Ryalsgar stated. "There are Metallurgical, Air, and Biological Colleges. The head of the Biological College, wizard Dogar Lidri is an old friend of Captain Oren's. I suspect he used his contact to collect some mages and apprentices with healing expertise. Dogar may have collected some others, as well. He is quite a resourceful wizard."

Ogerena looked over toward the mages' cars. "Their help will be priceless if there is battle at night. A few light spells could blind nogs or rannogs."

Ryalsgar agreed, although he was more impressed by the new crossbows and Riverrun ammunition that had been given to many of the guards. "Those are fine weapons. If we are able to claim the high ground, we should be able to break the ranks of a charge easily with so many crossbows."

The carts ran down the mountain fast. Within an hour, they were flying through the now-quiet first mushroom cavern. Rianas shifted her weight to remain comfortable and ate some of the dried biscuits Arthur had packed. Her father closed his eyes and meditated, as did Ogerena and Berryl. Ryalsgar, however, remained attentive at the front of the cart, his fingers trailing across the hilt of Ogen's Touch.

Within the hour, the carts began slowing down. The huge cavern at the end of the rail line loomed before them. Nearly a thousand mineworkers were laying rails into the cavern already as the army disembarked. The cavern had taken on the look of a forest fortress. A stockade built from the great mushroom 'trees' lined the cavern. The largest of these trees supported short palisades on top, where Sergeant Thorgeir's men oversaw the lower reaches of the cavern.

Thousands of men unloaded. Maddox Oren himself marched to

the front of the army, directing his lieutenants. He waited until the group was mostly unloaded and facing him at the entrance to the huge cavern before he spoke.

"I will not be going any further." Maddox rested a huge hairy arm against a barrel full of foodstuffs as he spoke to the army. "It rests on you, the best the Sko'Port guards have to offer, to take control of this mine. From here, you have a march on foot. Do not delay. Wizard Atrick's mercenary army is fighting a battle a few miles away. Wizard Atrick will be your commander for the next week. Lieutenants Nigel, Adams, and Harold will be your direct superiors, but you shall all report to wizard Atrick. We will take this entire mountain for Sko'Port!"

At that, Maddox raised his fist in the air and let out a low, bellowing shout. His army of guards joined the low bellow, beating their fists against their leather and chainmail armored chests. Rianas could not help feeling excited. These men respected Captain Oren. They would follow his orders the best they could.

Shortly, the entire army was moving – this time on foot. Sergeant Thorgeir – much to his dislike – found himself gathering the sentries he had posted to join the army as well. Rianas felt the venom in his stare as she marched past.

Arthur projected, "*I wouldn't be too worried, Rianas. I think he is just upset at being overruled on where to set up his sentries.*"

Rianas was not so sure. As they marched into the lower sections of the mushroom forest, she excused herself from her companions to go speak with Sergeant Thorgeir.

Sergeant Thorgeir's archers were lighter on their feet than many of the other guards. Armor and supplies weighed down the Upper Ward men. The man looked at her as she approached through the throng of soldiers. "Come to gloat over who was right, young woman?"

"No. I came to apologize. You are obviously a veteran soldier, and you had positioned your men to protect the cavern against a much larger force. I just wanted to say that even though I am not a warrior, I am glad you will be fighting with us."

"I don't shy from battle. I just don't want to see men die for nothing." Thorgeir kept his pace in front of his men. He looked over to Rianas as he stomped over a small toadstool. His hard face cracked into a bit of a smile. "I suppose I should have expected you and the boy would manage to gather an army and get all the way back here in less than twenty four hours, though."

It was Rianas' turn to smile. Her legs seemed to be moving without her thinking, and she knew she should be tired from marching nearly three days straight. "Sergeant, I wonder if I could ask another favor? My father is the one who brought the Riverrun weapons you see so many men carrying. He is no good with a weapon, but he is a career councilman in Riverrun. He is quite organized; perhaps you could find something he can help your men with?"

The sergeant nodded. He turned to one of his corporals and told him to have Lazron work with the miners who had volunteered to join the Upper Ward guards in their expedition to the lower High Mine exit. There were nearly five hundred of them. They were not well armed, but they would be instrumental in building fortifications – assuming there was time.

Rianas ran back to her companions and spoke with her father. He was happy to help wherever he could, but asked Rianas again not to put herself in harm's way. Rianas guiltily said she would not.

It hurt to lie to her father.

Arthur shook his head as Lazron joined the miners. *Your father deserves the truth, Rianas. I would bet he knew you were lying.*

Rianas was in no mood to argue. It was not just her going into battle; it was the entire army. There was no way she would let her father get hurt just because she had this urge. The entire situation made her think again about the strange desire she had to see Old Andaria.

Why did she now have this desire to bring war on Axarea? Of course, the Axarean Empire seemed to embody everything evil to her. Should that drive her to attack them physically? She had never felt the need to attack people growing up.

Now, though, her arms trembled as she marched through the lower cavern. Some soldiers took turns wiping down the more slippery stones to make a wider safe path as others marched past. Rianas felt as if she should run though the exit a half mile away.

Something else boiled inside of her, too. The memories she had wrenched from the Southerner in Sko'Port earlier that day were sporadic, but he had obviously fought and killed before. His training had helped her a little. Skills like that could not merely be absorbed. However, Rianas felt his memories. She wondered what would come of this new feeling.

Arthur looked over and set his hand reassuringly on Rianas' arm. She was sure he felt her shaking, but he said nothing. He smiled warmly and made a joke about her outfit being a little too fancy for fighting.

"Oh, no! I can't believe I forgot to give the outfit back. Wait, you are still wearing your huge shirt, too. Better not get that thing all cut up, Arthur!"

The two laughed for a few seconds.

Then the light of a moonlit night started to bathe the end of the cave. They could see the exit. Briefly, the entire army started marching through into the night. When Rianas and Arthur came through the exit, it was apparent they had made it to the other end of the cave just in time.

Down the mountain about a mile, a line of torches and fires dotted the edges of the river. Atrick's mercenary army had built a small wall from the rubble across a portion of the ledge where the nogs had made their small base. It was obvious fighting had occurred already in the past couple hours. Hundreds more Nog dead littered the path to the ledge. Atrick himself was nowhere to be seen at first. As the army marched as quietly as it could into the clearing, Teran and Jalek ran through an opening in the stone wall. They stopped the lieutenants from marching their reinforcements straight up the hill.

Teran spoke with the lieutenants, and slowly a few dozen men at a time were sent up the hill, running from one stone outcropping to another.

Rianas followed Arthur and Berryl to say hello to Teran.

"Why send a few men at a time?" Berryl asked, after shaking the Assyrian's hand heartily. "Do you really think we haven't been spotted by sentries already?"

Teran shook his head. "Nothing is sure, but we easily fended off the preliminary attack at nightfall. They truly did not expect much resistance. It is good, too, because there are many injured men. Jalek's men managed to set up a few sentries of their own on the highest parts of the ledge. They believe that the force marching up the hill is moving as one huge unit. I don't know why."

It took nearly two hours for the army to make its way to the top of the hill. Men spread out onto the entire ledge. The miners who had volunteered set to work pulling stones into piles, and nearly half the guards helped. Rianas and Arthur moved stones for about two hours, helping to widen the short four-foot wall.

Atrick found them as the first hints of sunrise were peeking over the eastern edges of the Black Mountains. "Rianas, I see you have delivered more than I could have asked."

Rianas took the ring off her finger and gave it back to the wizard. "I never thought I would have met Lord Cerric, the captain of the guards, and two Sullarian knights all in one day!"

Atrick laughed. His face was haggard, and he was obviously very tired. "You have only begun to see your potential, Rianas. I see your father joined us. I just spoke with him. He has been very helpful with the wall. He was showing some volunteers how to stack the stones so the top of the wall would be safe to walk on. In coordination with the mages that came along, the fortifications are already taking shape."

Rianas told Atrick briefly about their adventures in Sko'Port over the last twenty-four hours. His face was serious when she described Lord Cerric's fear of spies, and more serious when she talked about the Axareans who they had misled.

"I wish Captain Oren had been able to come through himself. He is well liked by these men," Atrick sighed.

Atrick turned and gave quick orders to two mages, then turned back to Rianas. "Get some rest as the sun is coming up. I suspect that army down the river will attack us at nightfall."

14. RETURN TO OLD ANDARIA

For the exhausted, sleep comes easily.

As the sun came up over the Black Mountains, thousands of men and women rested. Many fell asleep, and others meditated. A few fires dotted the cramped camp, but the impending battle was hours away. It was much easier to keep so many men quiet after five or six hours slinging stones and building fortifications.

Midmorning brought the first signs of life back to the camp. The scouts, reinforced by Raskin Jorgen's brave and tireless miners, managed to outmaneuver a Nog unit as it scaled a nearby cliff. The fighting ended quickly. About seventy dead nogs were all that remained after half an hour of combat.

By noon, Lazron was helping volunteers haul some large boulders into a line along an upper section of the ledge. It was apparent in the light of day that a second path led up to that side of the ledge from the lower parts of the river. The mages and other volunteers easily pushed the loose rubble into stubby walls.

Rianas awoke shortly after noon. The lieutenants and veterans were reminding the army of the need for quiet. Arthur pointed to where her dad was working, and the two of them made their way up to the upper wall.

"That army is only an hour away." Arthur pointed as they scaled a rock and looked downhill along the stream. The Nog camp – that must have been what it was, because it looked so similar to the camp the mercenaries had taken two days before – was only a mile away at best. A few tents were set up closer, almost within bowshot. Nogs and larger creatures milled about at the water's edge.

From their vantage point, Arthur quietly pointed back to the main entrance to the ledge. If the Nog army wanted to take the cave entrance, they would have no choice but to take back this ledge. The higher side of the mountain was craggy on its downward slope. "If they are smart, they will send their main force straight up the same path Atrick used to get up here. They will probably send a smaller group up this way to try to break through here, but these huge boulders will force them to split their force. A few archers on top of each of these big rocks would make it tough to get through here."

Knight Ogenson stepped onto the rock behind them. His red shirt and red leather pants seemed almost to drink in the sun, and his right arm rested easily on the scabbard of *Ogen's Touch*. "Perhaps you are right, Arthur, but I think the Axareans will make a strong push here. They expect us to be greatly outnumbered, and these rocks give them a chance to split up our force, too. If they can get through here, we will have two bad choices— either defend our flank and risk being surrounded or retreat back into the cave by going through their army."

Arthur considered and agreed.

Rianas asked why they should be so concerned now that they had the Sko'Port guards helping them. "Shouldn't we be able to easily cover this section of the mountain with so many men down below?"

Ryalsgar's steely gaze settled on the Nog tents. "Yes," he said, "but last night I spoke at length with Jalek's sentries. I even did a little reconnaissance myself with the help of a Cidvagian hunter I found. That army is perhaps five thousand strong. But they have not sent a single runner back south down the mountain that we know of."

"So what does that mean?" Rianas found herself staring at the short tents, wondering if Rannog warlords were truly seven feet tall and as strong as oxen. She had seen artwork in school depicting the monsters as half-bull, half-lizard, with stubby tails for better balance.

"One of two things, I think." Ryalsgar had taken a seat on the huge boulder and was laying out his daggers, a small crossbow, and *Ogen's Touch* as if setting up camp.

"First, the Axareans may have signal flares or some magical means to communicate with each other. Large armies spread over plains like those below the mountain could communicate for miles in that way. It only requires a few dedicated personnel. I don't think this is the case, however. Nog armies are notoriously poorly organized. Nogs are not smart enough to learn another language easily. They would need help from humans or rannogs or some other creatures.

"Second – and I think more likely – they *must* take the mine. I assume the Axarean Empire expected these nogs to succeed in breaking through to Sko'Port. I don't think they expected to face a force this size on the southern edges of the Black Mountains, though. They don't just want to defeat us. They want to defeat us without someone else finding out their exploratory party failed."

"Perhaps." The three swung around to look at Atrick as he easily stepped onto the boulder with them. This rock was getting crowded.

Atrick looked much better rested after taking some time that morning to meditate and sleep.

Galen was behind Atrick, and there were three other mages whom Rianas had never seen before. "I think that when Mr. Jorgen captured that mask, the nogs were thrown into disarray. It isn't simple fear that drives them. They are driven by a *need* to recapture that mask."

Atrick pointed at the scores of soldiers stacking stones along the growing section of wall between the boulders, like webbing on a frog's toes. "The first outcropping overlooks the lower path to this ledge. We will place as many archers as we can there. Extra guards will reinforce these first two entry points. The bulk of our mages will be on the lower ledge, but two will be on this boulder, and one on each of the other five."

Atrick gestured as he instructed Galen and the other mages where to set up. After he was done, he asked Rianas to come with him. Atrick needed her translation skills with the Kabarans. The westerners would be in charge of holding one of the five walls.

For an hour, Rianas followed Atrick around and helped him communicate with the thirty or so men and women who did not speak Common well.

She ate a sparse meal with him. Atrick tried to convince Rianas to take the scroll back, but she refused. "Surely there is someone more capable of wielding magic in battle, Atrick? That raw power might be helpful in my hands, but someone with better control — like you or any of the mages that came with the guards — could do much more to help this army than I could, I think."

Atrick said he would give the scroll to Galen. Rianas felt relieved to have some of the pressure on her to control her errant magic reduced. Even so, Atrick shook his head imperceptibly at her as Galen took the scroll. *"Rianas, your power will outstrip that of these other mages soon enough."*

Guard lieutenants, sergeants and other leaders continued approaching Atrick with small problems or demands for his time. When it was apparent he was too distracted to use her services further, she excused herself.

Soldiers manned every makeshift barrier. They crouched, leaned, sat, or even lay to the inside of the short wall. In most places, it was only two or three feet tall, just enough to slow down the Nog advance. Fully half of the guards had crossbows, and they occupied all the high points across the length of the ledge.

In some places, larger boulders had been maneuvered into place to make the wall six feet tall or more. It would not hold up for long, but as the mages cast their *binding* magic upon the stones to prevent them from slipping, the entire army's spirits seemed to rise.

When the sun approached the western edge of the sky, however, a drum started beating from the Nog encampment. It started slowly, a low 'thrump thrump thrump', but soon the Nog army was moving. Tents disappeared and the army massed behind a giant rannog carrying a drum the size of a man.

The drumbeat was soon joined by others, until five separate drums were beating their sad 'thrump thrump thrump' in time. The front of the army began to march forward, led by a hundred or more giant rannogs. Many of them wore chainmail armor and carried massive shields. A few swung spiked chains over their heads as the army approached. Nogs raced in front. The smaller creatures carried black banners with what looked like blood stains streaked across them, running back and forth.

Atrick started toward the main pathway with Galen and two other mages at his side. He shouted toward men as he went. "Don't show yourselves until they are within range of your weapons."

Rianas stole a glance at her father, who would work with some of the miners to deliver ammunition when the battle began. He smiled and nodded, "*Stay safe, Rianas. Don't worry about me.*"

Arthur pointed toward the highest section where they had been earlier. Over the drumbeat, he shouted, "Ryalsgar is up there. He told us to stay in reserve, but I say we join him on that wall. There are only a few dozen men in that section."

Rianas saw where Arthur was pointing. For some reason, Jalek's men had moved back along the ledge and started climbing the steep cliff. There were fifty feet of wall with very few people upon it. It was so far from the reinforcement pool it would be impossible for them to get there in time to help. She nodded at Arthur and started following him in that direction.

"*Thrump thrump thrump.*" The sound grew louder now. The Nog army could not be more than half a mile away. The rannogs and nogs yelled battle cries as they climbed toward Atrick's small army.

The sun was close to the horizon. Rianas felt the anticipation of the battle ahead. She fingered the clasp on the dagger Arthur had given her. "Wait, Arthur. There's John; grab him too."

John was in another group of reserve soldiers. He looked like he needed a place to be. When Arthur waved for him to come along, the farmer from Riverrun joined the other two on their short climb to the small embankment where Ryalsgar and two dozen other soldiers knelt behind the makeshift wall.

Ryalsgar saw Rianas approaching and nodded before peeking back over the short wall. A few archers on either side waved at them, and Rianas even saw Sal to their right, smiling down.

"*Thrump thrump thrump.*" There was a loud roar from the army as they raced up the mountain. It was close now, winding through the scree and rubble perhaps a quarter mile away. Soldiers peeked over the short wall. Those who had not yet drawn their weapons did so now.

A chorus of guards and lookouts shouted up and down the long line of defenders, "Now! Take your places!"

Sal and the other archers jumped atop the boulder to their right. Rianas released a second dagger from its holster and wondered why she had not traded it for something longer. It was too late now.

Ascending the short wall shoulder-to-shoulder with Arthur and John, Rianas observed how Ryalsgar stood out amongst the other warriors. His stance was half-crouched. *Ogen's Touch* rested easily against the steel plate of his armor, and a small buckler hung lightly from his left arm. The Red Knight lowered his helm into place, and Rianas wondered at the fine steel mesh that covered his face completely.

The Nog army had split and was approaching the Sko'Port army like a mob. The short lizard-like humanoids spilled through every easy pathway. A massive rannog, perhaps the largest one, with a shield as wide as an ox cart and a red-painted longsword, dashed easily up the side of the mountain in front of a throng of hundreds of nogs peppered with other rannogs.

The lead rannog turned right again and again as he ascended, until his path was clearly going to take him straight for the section of wall Rianas was standing on.

"Fire!" The command went down the line of archers. Crossbows let loose across the front ranks of nogs and rannogs. A few of the rannogs slowed and even fell. Entire rows of nogs simply disappeared under the churning charge behind them. A second and third volley raked across the charging army as they closed the gap to the wall.

Rianas saw the nogs as they approached like a seething mass beneath the huge rannogs. Some wore leather armor across their chests. A few carried poorly built shields. Most of them carried swords that were about two feet long. Some carried spears only a little longer.

Then there was no more time to ruminate, because the army had arrived.

Ryalsgar's sword swung in a wide arc across the first nogs to approach the wall. Rianas stepped on swords and spears as the nogs tried to scale the wall unsuccessfully. Dozens of nogs died in the first few seconds. The creatures were unable to defend themselves against the longer weapons of the humans as they stabbed downward. The wall seemed to swallow the first and then a second wave of nogs.

A group of nogs charged at the wall, knocking some of the stones loose with their short spears. The Rannog warlord pointed and shouted what Rianas immediately recognized as *"Take down the wall. Make them fight us from the ground and we will crush them!"*

Rianas tried to grab at one of the spears, but could not without putting herself in reach of one of the others. She projected toward Ryalsgar and Arthur, *"The warlord is commanding the nogs to attack the wall!"*

John stabbed downward again and nearly lost his footing as a few of the stones pulled away. He scrambled back and Rianas stabbed a nog as it tried to jump up and overtake him.

Arthur swung his new longsword out and sliced another nog. Ryalsgar's flame sword leapt into a stream of fire as it swept across three spears at once.

One of the rannogs got to the wall perhaps a few paces to Arthur's right. The creature was easily seven feet tall. Instead of a sword, it carried a huge studded axe. With one swing, it knocked the guard holding that section of the wall onto his back. The guard did not move.

Rianas saw two crossbow bolts bounce off the huge monster's chainmail armor. She took a stone from the wall and lobbed it at the nog below her, knocking it out. When she looked over again, Ryalsgar was engaging the great beast.

Ryalsgar swung *Ogen's Touch* in a great downward arc toward the beast's head, but it shoved its axe upward to parry the blow. The Red Knight was faster, and he swung his weapon around into the beast's side, slicing into its thick armor.

The rannog was huge, though. Like a charging bull, its axe rose and fell, breaking the wall into pieces. Ryalsgar's blow only enraged the rannog more.

Ryalsgar slid in front of the wall, only feet away from Arthur and Rianas.

Rianas covered Arthur against the reaching arms of another nog by grabbing its outreached arm and projecting another blast of questions into the monster to knock it out. Now she knew how she could fight the nogs, but there were short swords and spears she had to avoid. She could not use her ability unless she was within hand-striking distance.

Ryalsgar staggered under a blow from the rannog. He stabbed his sword up into the side of the creature, right underneath its chain armor. The bull-sized beast lurched. It made one final swoop with its axe, and fell over.

There was a hole in the wall five feet wide, and it was crumbling under the assault of the other nogs. Archers were still shooting down, but nothing seemed to be slowing the larger rannogs. The warlord was now only a few dozen yards away. The huge rannog lifted its massive shield to swat away arrows as if they were gnats.

Ryalsgar was up again – but now he was on the wrong side of the wall. The warlord pointed at him, and dozens of nogs in white face paint and carrying short swords seemed to materialize from around the great beast to jump at the Red Knight. His sword once more caught flame as he sliced through the throng, pushing them away valiantly from the hole in the wall.

Rianas and Arthur looked at each other. Arthur smiled reassuringly before they jumped side-by-side into the hole where the dead rannog had fallen. From there, they tried to defend Ryalsgar's rear from nogs as they tried to surround him.

"*Thrump thrump thrump.*"

The sound echoed loudly in Rianas' ears. More rannogs had gotten to the wall around them. There were no other reinforcements coming. Fallen or badly injured guards lay to their left and right. John stabbed one rannog when it lurched forward with a crossbow bolt through its neck. He narrowly avoided its lumbering axe swing. A guard to their right bravely slew another rannog. The creature's spiked club tore the guard's black uniform to tatters. It seemed as if the giant creatures would bring down this entire section of wall in a matter of minutes.

Rianas and Arthur had no choice but to back up. The nogs helping the warlord were better armed than the others they had fought thus far. Their short swords had enough reach that Rianas could barely defend herself with her long dagger. She jumped to the side and scrambled backward up the fallen stone, stumbling while she frantically avoided blows from the crazed creature.

Arthur's longsword was longer, but he was soon backpedaling as well. Ryalsgar, still swinging his sword, was too far out in the midst of the attackers for Arthur to help him.

The sky had darkened. Rianas jumped up onto the crumbling wall and away from the reach of the nogs for a moment. She swung her light out onto her helmet.

Fireballs brightened the sky further down the ledge where the other fighting was going on. The glint of magical flames on armor shone throughout the battlefield.

"Thrump thrump thrump."

"We need reinforcements!" Arthur was thinking. He stabbed at one of the sword-wielding nogs, knocking it back from where it had been scaling the wall. *"There are so many of them here. If we are overrun, they will split the army into pieces. They will be attacked from behind."*

That is when Jalek's men began their assault from the left. From hidden perches higher up in the mountain, the Cidvagian mercenary and his followers jumped eight to ten feet off the higher stone walls they had scaled.

Jalek's attack was a huge success. The mercenaries speared nogs and rannogs alike with their surprise attack. Within seconds, the shape of the battle changed. Despite the huge force charging up this narrow path, some of the nogs were scared into retreat. The Rannog leaders temporarily lost their organized assault on the wall. The archers took advantage of the chaos from the boulder on the right, shooting into the unguarded rears of their enemies when they turned to fight Jalek's men.

Rianas reached for another nog when it became distracted. She grabbed its arm and easily invaded the nog's mind.

The familiar plains once again appeared. This time, however, the face-painted nog was standing next to her. *"How you get here?"* it asked, snarling.

Rianas nearly recoiled at the monster's words. However, she maintained her focus and tried to extract everything she could about the nog's knowledge of Sko'Port, just as she had before.

This time, information actually came flooding into her mind. Unintelligible documents, maps of these mountains, and terrifying commands from Rannog warlords all came streaming into her mind, too fast for her to process.

There was more, too. This nog had travelled countless miles from the west to be here. It had received orders over two years ago to follow Niz'Rul, the Rannog warlord, into the Black Mountains and find the exit point of this river. They were to send in a crew to see if it connected with a Sko'Port mine. Then the entire army was to enter the cave.

From within the nog's mind, Rianas saw the mask miner Raskin had captured, as well. It was on the Rannog warlord, not a nog.

She wondered how it had changed hands.

Rianas was no longer in the nog's mind. It fell away, limp but still conscious. Rianas jumped back into action, swinging her too-short dagger at another nog.

The Rannog warlord – that must be Niz'Rul – had reached the wall about twenty feet to their right. With a mighty swing of its longsword, it struck the guard who Rianas had seen slay the other rannog. The man flew back off the wall with the force of the blow.

Niz'Rul jumped easily onto the short section of wall. "To me," it bellowed in his guttural language. "Take the archers off the boulder!"

The nogs rallying behind him began jumping onto the cleared section of the wall around him.

Samuel and some of the other archers tried to take out the throng gathering on the wall. Some of the nogs fell, but the attack angle was poor. Niz'Rul's huge shield blocked arrows easily. That left the rannog a free arm to swing his longsword at any who approached him.

To Rianas' surprise, men with pickaxes and shovels were on the other side of the wall. Lazron swung his longsword to sweep the legs out from two nogs. The miners that had been supplying ammunition to the archers had taken up whatever weapons they could to defend against the enemy breaking through the wall.

Niz'Rul continued to sweep his opponents aside with his spiked shield or his longsword. He was unstoppable. He walked to the side of the boulder where the archers were perched.

Arthur looked at Rianas. "*I'll stop him. Take my sword!*" He handed her his longsword.

Arthur was the nearest man to Niz'Rul from the wall. Samuel shot another nog off the wall, and Arthur reached into his leggings for his last two daggers. He jumped over a swinging spear and kicked another nog as it climbed up the falling rubble that had been the wall. Lazron and a miner swept the feet of two other nogs in Arthur's way as he approached the huge rannog from behind.

Niz'Rul grabbed an outcropping of stone with his shield arm and scrambled onto the boulder. Two guards with crossbows tumbled nearly twenty feet to the ground when Niz'Rul swept their legs with his free sword arm. Arthur climbed up behind Niz'Rul.

Rianas could barely swing the longsword, but she hefted it in two hands to stab another nog in the shoulder. Then she used her foot to help pry it free. Lazron and a dozen other miners jumped onto the wall to help her. The warriors here were outnumbered. There were holes in the wall everywhere. It was almost more dangerous to be atop the wall than down below. Each step or sword swing was an opportunity to lose one's footing.

Rianas tumbled backward. Her feet slipped from under her as a dozen large stones tumbled forward. The broken section of wall crushed an approaching nog as stones slid forward. Rianas shoved the longsword around again from her back, clumsily knocking a nog over.

Without archers to slow down the attackers, Jalek's men would not be able to drive back the endless Nog horde. Rianas hefted the longsword once more and painstakingly thrust it into the chest of another nog. Then she left the weapon in the creature's chest and took her dagger out again to defend herself against one with a spear. She easily parried the creature's stab and pulled the spear toward her to close the distance, slicing the monster in the gut.

From this angle, Rianas could see Arthur tangle briefly with Niz'Rul from behind, his two hands grabbing the massive rannog in what looked like a bear hug.

Niz'Rul flung around. Arthur was little more than a cape whipping behind the armored beast. As it took a step, Arthur let himself fall to the ground, stabbing the creature's right leg just behind the knee with both hands around his dagger.

Niz'Rul screamed and stabbed toward Arthur with his longsword. The weapon made contact. Rianas saw Arthur's right side forced into the boulder upon which he was fighting.

"No!" Rianas shouted. However, another nog approached her and she had to defend herself again. When she looked back up, Niz'Rul and Arthur were both tumbling down the huge boulder onto a group of nogs trying to climb the wall.

Rianas' world began to shrink. Dead or injured nogs, guards and miners were all around her. She grabbed the hilt of the longsword lodged in the dead nog and heaved against its body, pulling the weapon out of the creature's gut.

She swung tiredly at a passing enemy. The light of her helmet seemed to be the only light remaining. She could hear people shouting in Northern behind her and to her left. Arrows started to fly again. Nogs and rannogs alike fell to the onslaught of missiles.

Tears streamed down her face.

Lazron and a few miners came into her view from the right. Her father stayed close to the other men. He used the reach of his sword to knock down Nog spears so the others could stab them or kill them with their shovels.

Rianas could barely lift the sword any longer. It dragged along the stones when she was not swinging, until finally she let it fall and used her last dagger.

The minutes turned into an hour. Rianas kicked, stabbed, swung and charged. Her arms were sore and she had numerous small cuts across her legs and arms. One nog managed to slice along the side of her helm, drawing blood just below her left ear in a painful slice that forced her to drink the small healing potion Ogerena had given her.

Rianas surely would have died there had it not been for the small magical potion.

Slowly, however, the battle turned. The archers used thousands of crossbow bolts, and from such short range, it was difficult to miss.

Jalek's men fought valiantly. They cut off any retreat the nogs might have taken.

Finally, the *"thrump thrump thrump"* abruptly stopped.

A magical lightning storm crackled through the air past Rianas and into a rannog. The monster jounced around for a moment before falling to the ground. The lightning storm struck out at a few other nogs before dissipating. Only a huge ball of light remained in its wake.

Rianas turned to see Atrick standing atop the boulder with Galen and two other mages. In the new light, he saw Rianas and inclined his head with a smile. Then, drawing out the magical scroll from before, Rianas could feel him assembling another weave of magic.

Rianas could see further down the mountain path. Where once there had been a Nog army, there were thousands of bodies. A battle cry echoed up from the guards as they ascended behind the remaining line of nogs. They had nearly won the battle.

Two guards rushed past Rianas from behind, easily slaying the nog that had been sparring with her. Suddenly, there were dozens of guards all around, and the archers seemed to triple in number. The enemy army had been defeated.

15. DAYBREAK

The moon was high in the clear dark sky. Stars broke up the huge expanse of darkness one could see from the rocky plateau. There were no trees here. Only the lower hills obscured what would be a panoramic view for a dozen miles south, west and east. A brisk fall wind buffeted the naked rocks. From this side of the Black Mountains, fall would be a time of dry, mild weather.

Between the jagged boulders and along the fast-moving creek, the Sko'Port guard and Atrick's mercenary army were the only people for easily a dozen miles in any direction. They efficiently gathered their wounded and reinforced fallen barriers. The mages and miners who had stayed out of the fight rushed from group to group, healing those they could and sharing final words with the lost.

Rianas tripped over a dead rannog on her way to retrieve Arthur. She did not enjoy the brisk evening breeze the way she would have in Riverrun. There was no beauty to the cold, moonlit sky with so many corpses surrounding her.

The dead rannog had an expression of disbelief on its face. These creatures were not as soulless as the nogs seemed to be. How could they bear so much hatred toward a people they had never met? Why did Axarea send them to assault Sko'Port?

Rianas lost whatever remained of her dinner on the creature's bloody arm.

Lazron called out to Rianas from somewhere behind her. She ignored her father and lurched tiredly to her feet. Soon, she was at a pile of Nog bodies, all full of arrows from above. Dozens of the monsters had scrambled over each other in an attempt to scale the remnants of the shattered wall. The archers had held them back.

Niz'Rul's red-stained longsword protruded from near the boulder's face. Rianas crawled over two dead nogs. Moving a third one out of the way took all her remaining strength.

"Rianas!" her father shouted. He was closer behind her now.

Rianas recoiled at the sight of Niz'Rul's eyes. Like a lizard, they moved independently. The one on the left rolled back, trying to focus on her. This rannog was still alive!

Killing on the battlefield was one thing, but killing an enemy because it had the audacity to survive? Rianas, dagger in hand, paused and watched the bull of a creature breathe laboriously. That was when she saw the human arm draped across its armored torso.

"Rianas, can't you hear me? Are you okay?" Lazron had caught up to her and placed his hand on her shoulder.

Rianas' eyes followed the arm to another nog. She shoved it off the pile. There, his body contorted from the fall, his other hand still gripping the hilt of one of his daggers from underneath the rannog's torso, was Arthur.

Lazron saw why Rianas had ignored him. Although he did not speak, she knew his thoughts. Through his hand, she could feel her father's compassion. This man had raised her. He knew what she felt. He also knew there was little another could do to assuage the feelings she had now. He stood silent.

Rianas spared another look at the dying rannog before reaching for its arm, which was pinning Arthur to the ground like a rag doll. Her father helped her lift it – the armored arm alone probably weighed fifty pounds – and sling it back over the creature's torso.

Lazron moved around toward Arthur's lower torso to slide another nog away. As he did so, Rianas was examining the huge rip in the right side of his shirt. The skin beneath the hole seemed intact!

"Can you...get me some water?"

Rianas stared, uncomprehending, at the tall man's face. Dirt from the fall crusted his eyes, but she clearly saw his chest rise laboriously. Rianas grabbed her leather canteen. "Uncover him the rest of the way, Dad!"

Lazron did not realize what was going on at first, but when Rianas pried open Arthur's mouth and shoved the water skin into his mouth, he coughed weakly.

Rianas' tears started anew.

Sunrise over the southeastern edge of the Black Mountains was full of joy for Rianas.

Arthur had suspected he was no match for the rannog. Just before climbing the boulder, he had popped off the wax seal on the small potion Ogerena had given them the day before and held it loosely in his mouth. When Niz'Rul stabbed him, he swallowed the potion almost accidentally. It was all he could do to stay conscious long enough to heave at the warlord's leg and push him off balance.

The fall had been fortuitous. Arthur had taken the last dagger from inside Niz'Rul's leg with his left hand to defend himself. As Niz'Rul fell on top of his arm, however, the warlord's own weight had forced Arthur's dagger through two scales in the beast's armor.

A few of his ribs seemed broken, but the young stable hand was sitting comfortably now. Arthur told Rianas as much after Ogerena had used her own remaining healing potion on him.

She had found them on her way from visiting Ryalsgar. The Red Knight's plate armor had protected him, and Ogen's Touch had claimed the lives of nearly two dozen nogs. Knight Yelenar's relentless crossbow assault on his attackers had saved his life. The veteran soldier was severely hurt, but alive.

Ogerena's hands were blistered and bloodied from firing so many times, but still she had managed to give Arthur the dose of healing potion.

"You were a hero last night, Arthur," Ogerena said. Her hand rested lightly on his chest. "If you had not attacked that creature, it would have hit me off that boulder next. Ryalsgar and I were sure to have died. We both owe you our lives."

Arthur beamed. His humor had returned even faster than his health. "Well, how else was I supposed to get a break from all that fighting? That longsword was *heavy!*"

Rianas laughed. Ogerena did not.

Ryalsgar was sheathing his sword after cleaning it. "Arthur, you do not understand what the Green Knight is telling you."

Rianas stopped laughing. She understood.

Arthur, however, did not accept the pending blood oath. "In Riverrun, where Rianas and I come from, we are taught that you help when and where you can. Besides, you saved all our lives with your healing potions, Knight Yelenar."

The Green Knight did smile at that. The expression looked odd on the iron woman's face. "Hmm, the two of you fight like you were trained in Cidvag or one of the Runlars. Rianas killed easily over a dozen nogs. And you, Arthur, managed to disable a Rannog war chieftain."

There were only a few dozen survivors amongst the Nog army. Niz'Rul had been bandaged up along with some other Rannog and Nog survivors. Rianas simultaneously dreaded and looked forward to her pending interrogations. Lazron and five other miners had hauled the beast of a creature away on a sling after they had bandaged him and bound his arms and legs.

"Niz'Rul's sword is enchanted," Rianas said, looking at the Elven writing along its blade. Under the rusty red paint, there was a fine etching of vines twining around the rune '*Auxilimanu*s'. The word was fine, but the Elven lettering seemed to pulse at her as she looked at the blade.

Ogerena looked over the blade, sliding her long slender fingers across the lettering. "I have seen blades like this before. They accent the user's ability. Essentially, the weapon will seek its path almost without the wielder's physical effort. It is the most common enchantment for a sword, because even a novice swordsman can use it. Moreover, in the hands of an expert it can make them even better. Some Elves have even been known to use the enchantment on arrows and other ranged weapons."

"The translation means *another hand*," Rianas muttered. It felt light in her arms, as if she could lift it easily with two hands around the hilt. She took a practice swing, marveling at the way the sword whistled through the air.

"You should keep it," Arthur said. Then he smiled again. "Unless giving it to Knight Yelenar would keep her from tightening these bandages around my poor ribs!"

Ogerena grunted and gave the bandages she had made for Arthur a final tug. Rianas tried not to notice the way the beautiful knight ran her hands along Arthur's exposed ribs.

"No," Rianas said. "I think you should take it, Arthur. You are better with a sword. Plus, you can lift it with one arm and it takes me two. I'd be forever tripping over the thing."

Arthur agreed. "You are a bit short to use a sword that long." He thought for a moment. "It will be fun to have a magical item! The people back home would be really impressed."

The sun rose into the middle of the sky. Carrion birds were circling above the growing piles of dead.

Rianas excused herself from Arthur's side to bring some warm soup from the food line her father had put together next to the river. There, far away from the piles of bodies, water babbled across loose stones and around larger boulders. The pathway was already cleared of evidence of last night's battle. Now, miners, mercenaries and guards lined up with their personal bowls and spoons to get something hot.

"You must have thought we had abandoned you last night."

Jalek's black armor stepped in line behind her. His armor bore so many new dents and scrapes that it no longer held its onyx luster.

"I think your move up the mountain drew the bulk of the army to that opening. They probably thought it was too poorly guarded." Rianas returned the cold stare of the huge man.

"Your bodyguard probably saved a hundred lives last night by attacking that rannog who jumped up with the archers."

"The wall gave us enough of a height advantage. If your men had stayed to reinforce it, Niz'Rul would never have gotten through." Rianas felt her temper getting out of hand, but she shook her head. "I'm sorry, Jalek. Your men probably stopped any of the nogs from retreating. In the coming days, that will be more important than anything else."

Jalek was silent a moment. His face was expressionless as he studied her. When he spoke, it was in a whisper. He leaned down so others could not hear him. "Many of the men that followed me here are looting corpses as we speak. It is a dirty job, but they will find enough gold and trinkets to make this battle worth it for them. It was all I could do to keep them from leaving after we cleared the cavern."

Rianas wondered why he was confiding in her. Atrick may have been right about the man's intentions. "And you? Have you found what you wanted here?" Rianas paused. She took a few steps forward in the long line before turning back again a little haughtily. "I won't simply run away, you know. Old Andaria is at the foot of this mountain, and I plan to find my people and fight for them however I can."

Jalek's bushy black eyebrows raised in a rare show of emotion. He straightened.

For another moment, the two quietly shuffled forward in line. Lazron served them both. Her father seemed so at home organizing a food line or helping to instruct men how to build a wall. Rianas wished she had that confidence. He traded a few words with Rianas. She told her father she would find him in a couple of hours and left the line.

Jalek stepped in place beside her again. "Rianas, I don't know if I can convince those men to stay here much longer. Those mercenaries are here for the gold and because they like the idea of being heroes, but they are not inspired to act."

Without waiting for a reply, the giant mercenary started up the path toward where his men were carrying bodies into burn piles.

Rianas brought the soup bowls back to Arthur. He laughed when she told him Jalek had called him her bodyguard.

John and Samuel came over to see how Arthur was progressing. The mages moving around the camp had stabilized most of the wounded. John's multiple stab wounds in his legs had healed almost completely already.

Samuel spoke highly of Knight Yelenar. He could not believe the speed with which she had shot her crossbow.

For an hour or so, the four talked about the battle and the events of the last few days. When Atrick marched by with Elias and Harold Fazian, Rianas excused herself to speak with the wizard.

"Ah, Rianas, I have been looking for you this morning. I would like to interrogate Niz'Rul when you are ready." Atrick gestured toward a set of newly erected lean-to style tents on the plateau where the new base was beginning to take shape. Captain Oren's men had bound the captured nogs and rannogs. Now, the surviving creatures sat on the ground in front of the new structures. Mages were tending some of their wounds.

Rianas was nervous. She walked beside Atrick toward the prisoners.

"Captain Oren sent everything we could have hoped for," Atrick said. He gestured toward the mages. "The battle went well last night. With so many healers, we only lost one hundred thirty seven men and women. The ammunition and weapons from Riverrun gave us a distinct advantage, too."

Elias had removed his armor. He was walking the camp with a loose shirt and pants. He looked much smaller. His sword still hung belted from his waist, but he clearly did not expect any combat today. Rianas wondered how long it would be before this place was attacked by an even larger force of Axareans.

"If what I have seen so far is any indication," Harold Fazian remarked, "we won't be replenishing our supplies of ammunition from this side of the mountain range. The only trees I've seen are only five or ten feet tall and wedged between boulders. It is as if someone stripped all the life from these rocks."

"It is odd," Atrick agreed, pointing toward the mountain peaks above. "There is considerable snow pack already on the northern peaks. Even here, there is enough that by spring we would expect plenty of runoff. These foothills are extremely stony, though. Perhaps we will find more fertile ground over the next hill."

Rianas wondered how many nogs and rannogs had lost their lives. The piles of dead were taller than a draft horse and they stretched a hundred yards.

Atrick saw her brooding expression. *"Rianas, our battle last night was one of self-defense. What befell these creatures was their own doing. Do not let their deaths weigh too heavily on your soul."*

"I know." Rianas still had to convince herself.

Harold filled his perceived gap in conversation. "The Kabarans and Jalek's mercenaries have expressed interest in scouting down to the edge of the foothills. I think it would be wise to send scouts to see what lies over the next ridge. Perhaps they can find wood to help us fortify this base, as well."

"Jalek?" Rianas wondered aloud. After her conversation with him earlier, the mercenary had left her thinking he would just as soon return to Cidvag.

Harold's gaunt, balding head reminded Rianas of a bird. He scanned quickly left to right while they walked. Finally, he settled his gaze on her. "Yes, he said some of his group was ready to see Old Andaria. He volunteered to lead a scouting party himself a few moments before I found Atrick."

Rianas blinked. She had used those same words with Jalek. Why had he changed his mind so quickly?

Atrick smiled knowingly at Rianas. "Prophecy is difficult to avoid, Rianas. Harbinas wrote…"

Rianas waved her hand impatiently. "I don't want to hear about your Prophet, Atrick. Jalek doesn't seem to care what happens here. The men that he is leading were looting bodies earlier. Why would they volunteer to go deeper into Axarean territory than we are already?"

Harold shook his head. "Jalek was adamant that he wanted to go further. He actually said *you* were the one who asked his men to volunteer."

Atrick chuckled softly. "No doubt his ego requires it of him. What did you say to the man?"

Rianas briefly recounted her encounter with Jalek. Harold and Atrick both chuckled. Before either could discuss it with her, however, they arrived at the prisoners.

Niz'Rul was behind the other captives. His armor was gone, and the warlord's huge, blackish-green torso and arms were bare in the brisk morning breeze. Numerous cuts and bruises covered his upper arms. There was a bandage on his leg, and the wound on his back where he had fallen on Arthur's arm during the fall was slowly oozing through a bloody rag.

There were scars all over the creature's body. As they came up to him from behind, Rianas saw dozens of long white marks across his back. They were old whip marks from years ago. Many of the scars overlapped. This creature had suffered mightily at someone's hands.

The Sko'Port guard had bound Niz'Rul's hands and legs together. He stretched against his bindings to rotate his head slightly toward Rianas when they approached.

Rianas had not had time to examine the rannogs during the battle. Unlike their more monstrous Nog underlings, the rannogs were more humanoid. Niz'Rul had a small, well-kept patch of hair above each huge, spiky ear. His neck was larger than his head.

"Come to finally kill me?" Niz'Rul asked. Rianas thought the language might be a Rannog dialect of Axarean. His lizard-like snout quivered when he spoke

"No, Niz'Rul. I want to know more about you," Rianas answered in the rasping language.

She no longer wondered how the words of foreign languages came so easily to her. Harold and Atrick's eyes shot up at her quick retort to the warlord, however. To them, her words sounded like thick Axarean mixed with a lot of spitting.

Niz'Rul was amazed, too. "You Northerners never bother to learn the God's tongue. Are you an Axarean?"

Rianas thought a moment before answering. "No. I am Andarian."

"Oh," Niz'Rul's tongue clicked the roof of his mouth with the Axarean word, which sounded more like a snarled 'Nuhh'. The warlord looked forward again. "The shaman told me I would be captured by the 'homeless descendants of the war of the plains'."

His matter-of-fact tone took her aback. Were there prophets everywhere outside of Riverrun?

"Can you understand it?" Harold asked. "How do you know Rannog?"

Atrick touched Harold patiently before Rianas was forced to explain. "I told you her ability was remarkable. She has an innate magical ability I have never seen before."

Rianas turned back to Niz'Rul. She walked around and crouched in front of him, forcing the giant humanoid to look into her eyes. She hoped he did not see the fear on her face. Niz'Rul weighed easily thrice as much as her. "A shaman told you we would capture you?"

Niz'Rul kept his mouth shut now. A smile seemed to stretch across the rannog's mole-covered face. He had said all he wanted to.

Rianas reached her hand toward the warlord's face. He bravely stared at her with his bluish eyes.

She was in his mind. Niz'Rul was beside her in a thatch hut large enough to host ten men. Three enormous female rannogs were there. One was cooking over a huge pot while the other two were winding leather into armor on a huge wooden table. At least one of the females looked pregnant.

Rianas knew these were his wives. She sensed a great pride from Niz'Rul that he had attained such a place in Rannog society.

"A mind reader? I have nothing to hide." Niz'Rul's words were in her mind. She could feel his presence next to her as he witnessed everything she did. *"The Emperor will protect me."*

"Why did he send you?" Rianas asked.

"I was selected to lead the expedition because these nogs lost a battle in Borsilk two years ago. Ten legions of nogs were sent on exploratory missions all over Arthos. These two legions were assigned to me." Niz'Rul did not seem to care what he told her.

The scene changed. Tens of thousands of nogs marched across an arid desert, and she floated in front of the line.

Rianas gazed at the Nog army. Only a fraction had come this way. *"Where is the rest of the army now?"*

"I did not lead it. The rest continued east from Borsilk. I presume the war on the coast is entering a new phase."

"Did you send for reinforcements when you saw us breach the cavern?"

The scene changed dramatically. Faces of nogs flashed before Rianas. Niz'Rul's arm struck out and grabbed one by the head, shaking it before he threw its lifeless corpse to the side.

There was a sense of fear and loss. There was also something else. Relief?

"No."

"Why not?" Rianas could not understand how an army this size could simply march around without getting continuous orders from someone else.

Another scene appeared. An unusually large nog was receiving instructions to enter the cavern as soon as they broke through to do reconnaissance. Niz'Rul was staring at himself in a mirror after giving the command, the Axarean war mask Rianas had seen in the caves on his face. He took it off and put it on a small travel table. The next morning, it was gone. A flash of scenes ensued, questioning other nogs and rannogs until it became clear the unit he had sent into the cavern had been responsible for the theft.

"I trusted those foolish nogs too much. I will be killed and my entire clan destroyed when the Supreme Commander discovers I lost the mask."

Of course! Atrick had guessed right. This warlord was the rightful recipient of the war mask. Somehow, the nogs that originally broke into High Mine had stolen it.

Something else lingered in the back of Niz'Rul's mind, though. A feeling of relief had accompanied the loss. Rianas wondered why.

"The mask holds great power," Niz'Rul said. *"It magnified my strength, my stamina, and my skill. However, the more I wore it, the more I realized it robbed me of my own mind. It was as if some other person was giving me instructions. I spoke and acted differently. This did not happen often, but the feeling was both empowering and terrifying.*

"I was instructed by the Supreme Commander to wear it all the time, but I could not. The strap that held it to my head did not fit me well. So I took it off when I was alone or with my close advisers. That is where I made the first mistake."

Rianas released Niz'Rul's mind. Unlike the nogs that she had knocked unconscious with her probing, the rannog continued staring at her. He breathed harder. Otherwise, however, he seemed okay.

Niz'Rul was no thoughtless brute. Fear had led him to make bad decisions. Rianas stared at the rannog for a moment in thought.

She stepped back. Atrick and Harold were asking her questions, but she did not hear them. The memories of Niz'Rul flooded past her vision even now. It took a moment for her to compose herself.

"I'm fine," she said when Atrick reached out to steady her as she stood. "Niz'Rul will tell us anything he can. He was the original owner of the war mask, but the nogs who entered the mine first stole it from him. He was so afraid of the consequences that he did not request reinforcements."

"Well…" Atrick stood straighter. Niz'Rul's gaze slid over to him. "I guess the battle for the High Mine has been won."

Harold and Rianas looked at Atrick. The statement seemed a little premature to Rianas.

"How about Andaria?" Rianas asked. "The local towns would have to know there is an army in these hills. There must be a town or city supplying this army. When they find out there are Sko'Port soldiers in the mountains, they are sure to react."

Harold nodded. "Based on the relatively sparse supplies that army was carrying, I'd say they were getting a wagon train full of food stuffs sent to them at least once a week."

Atrick shook his head as they walked out of the line of seated prisoners. "It won't matter. With the Sko'Port guard here, we can put a few hundred scouts in the lower foothills. If we capture the supply train, we will get horses, food and other supplies. We have enough picks and shovels to start building a fort. Within three weeks, this entrance to the mine will be capable of withstanding an attack from a small army."

Harold gestured toward the cliffs on the upper face of the plateau above the main camp. "If we had a watchtower built on that high ledge, we could see all the way to the plains from here. In the meanwhile, however, I'll look for volunteers to scout the foothills with Jalek's men."

Atrick smiled as Harold walked off.

Rianas stood awkwardly for a moment. Atrick seemed about to head toward a group of sergeants organizing the camp. "Wait, Atrick. What will you do with the captives?"

He turned toward her and his face became more serious. "The captives will be sent to Sko'Port in a week or so for trial. Most likely Sko'Port will find the entire lot guilty of waging war on Sko'Port. The sentence is five years hard labor in the lower mines. That is where most of the criminals in Sko'Port are sent."

"What happens to them when their time is served?"

"They are sent free. The Judges would likely banish most nogs or rannogs from Sko'Port. There are only rare exceptions for those who prove their reform. Rannogs might get along okay in the city. I doubt an Axarean would want to stay, though. The Axareans may be interested in paying ransoms for these captives when their time has been served."

Atrick started toward the tent city, but then he stopped and turned back to Rianas. "I will be required in Sko'Port again, soon. Lord Cerric will need men he can trust by his side. You have helped this expedition tremendously. I hate to ask for your help again, but there is something else I need."

Rianas was silent. In her head, she was visualizing a map of Old Andaria from school. It had been a parchment map hung from the wall of her history professor.

"I need you to think about *The Andarian Prophecy*. Tell me you truly think it is meant for someone else, and I will leave you to your own devices. But if you think I may be right," Atrick pointed down at the flowing water, "your destiny lies down that river."

Rianas smiled and shook her head. "Atrick, you have been an inspiration this entire voyage. I feel like it is time for me to make my own decisions. I hope that my father will understand. You know how I feel about prophecies."

Atrick looked about to argue. Rianas raised her hand. "I intend to see Old Andaria. If Jalek's men are going to scout the foothills, I will join them. Maybe I can convince some of my Riverrun companions to join me. I can't promise I will stop there, though."

"Ha!" Atrick threw his arms in the air jubilantly.

"We will come with you, Rianas of Riverrun." Ryalsgar tramped up the hill from behind her. The knight looked curiously at Niz'Rul as he passed the Rannog warlord. The Green Knight and Red Knight were side by side.

Rianas barely contained her smile.

"You should bring this with you," Atrick said. He produced the magical scroll Rianas had used before. He gave her the scroll despite her protests. "When I return from Sko'Port, we will meditate together for a few weeks. I have no doubt your magical skill will blossom with a little more training."

Somehow, Rianas did not think those days would come.

Regardless, she smiled and thanked the wizard. She promised she would use the magic wisely.

A few moments of goodbyes, and Rianas was walking back toward Arthur beside Ryalsgar and Ogerena. "I appreciate you coming with me. I hope I can convince a few others to join us."

"I am sure you will, Rianas of Riverrun," said Knight Yelenar. "The Prophecy believes in you, even if you do not believe in it."

Ogerena's blonde hair almost twinkled in the light of day. Rianas stared at the hair flowing out of the knight's helm as she spoke. She wondered what her own hair looked like. After sitting beneath a helmet for days, probably more like the curly locks of a dirty mop.

"Did your interrogation go well?" Knight Yelenar asked.

Rianas summarized what she had seen to the two knights. "The infighting over that war mask is probably the only thing that kept Niz'Rul from acting sooner. It is almost as if he wanted to march his army to its death. I don't understand. I am not sure he understood his actions, either."

Ryalsgar looked over to Rianas. His piercing blue eyes seemed to search into her soul. Without thinking, Rianas found herself pulling pieces of his thoughts together in her mind, "...*perceptive girl.*"

"If we had more time, I would want to bring that mask back to Sullaria." Ryalsgar's voice was even, measured. This man had spent years fighting Axareans across Arthos. His thoughts were succinct. Rianas could feel a gnawing worry in the back of his mind.

Ogerena turned back toward the captives. "Why not question him some more? Perhaps he knows the resupply schedule, or some other details that could help us."

Rianas sighed. She should have asked that question while she was in Niz'Rul's mind earlier. "I will need to speak with Niz'Rul again."

"First, let's talk to Jalek," Ryalsgar said, "and tell him how many people will be joining his expedition."

They found Jalek standing on one of the stones protruding from the camp's edge. He was looking out over the lower sections of the river and discussing something with hawk-faced Harold rather heatedly. When Jalek saw Rianas, his jaw set and he stopped talking.

Harold looked over his shoulder at Rianas and the two knights.

Seeing that Jalek was distracted, he pressed his case. "Jalek, I don't know if Atrick will allow the mages to go out there when there is so much work to do here. This position must be heavily fortified if we are going to avoid another attack."

"I'll be going with them," Rianas said. "I think we can convince Atrick to request volunteers from some other mages, too. If Jalek's men are willing to take us down to the bottom of those foothills, it is worth sending a well-armed party with them, don't you think?"

Jalek nodded. The man seemed to look perpetually unhappy. "Harold, we are volunteering to keep your Sko'Port guards safe. If I am successful, we will capture enough horses, carts and food to feed this outpost for weeks. Moreover, the longer this outpost is able to exist without the Empire finding out, the safer its occupants will be."

"Fine," Harold said. "I'll speak with Galen and ask for a few volunteers. My understanding is there are a few dozen doses of healing potions left, as well. I'll have them sent over to Knights Ryalsgar and Ogerena for safe keeping, but they should go with you."

Jalek's mouth curled upward. Rianas would not call it a smile on the serious man's face, but he nodded again. "Two Sullarian Knights are worth their weight in Gold Eagles, I'd say."

Harold walked off, clearly glad to be leaving Jalek. Rianas stepped onto the flat part of the stone beside the giant of a man.

"Thank you," she said. "It must have been difficult convincing the other mercenaries to keep fighting."

"Not as difficult as you might think." Jalek turned back toward the winding river below them. Rianas thought he was done talking. A few seconds of silence passed.

"I think we will leave tomorrow morning. I already sent a dozen scouts to where the river winds around that last hill. From there, they should be able to see out onto the Andarian plains." Jalek pointed to a hill about two miles away that obstructed their view of the Andarian plains. There were few trees and mostly rocks visible. The landscape would be difficult to hide in for long. From atop that hill, the view of the flat lands beyond probably extended for a dozen miles to the south, east and west.

Jalek adjusted the sword at his waist. "I promised those men each three hundred Gold Eagles for 'volunteering' with me. They can have the pick of the weapons they liberate. Their duty is to help me protect you on your quest, Rianas."

Ryalsgar grunted, "That is probably two years' salary for a mercenary!"

Jalek's dark eyes drifted over to Ryalsgar before he agreed. "Yes. I have promised something I cannot give. It falls on your shoulders to find payment for them, Rianas. For the short term, however, I should be able to keep those men loyal to whatever cause you see fit to pursue in Old Andaria. Many of those mercenaries," he explained, "have fought with me before. The money they can get as hired hands is what drives them, nothing else."

"I can't believe you," Rianas said. "That is more money than I have ever seen. There is no way I will be able to make good on your promise."

Knight Yelenar stepped in. "Perhaps, Rianas, their loyalty will prove its worth. We will capture some coin with that supply train. It won't be a huge amount, but it will be enough to convince those mercenaries you will eventually pay them. If you go forth into Old Andaria, these men might be just what you need to take a village. They are experienced bodyguards."

It seemed to Rianas as if everyone around her was going mad. War? Bodyguards? Three hundred Gold Eagles a piece for nearly a hundred mercenaries? Rianas threw her arms up.

Ryalsgar put up his hand to stop Rianas from talking. *"Rianas, if you want to see Old Andaria, you must commit your whole self. Jalek has just pledged his loyalty to you by recruiting these men. Think carefully before you accept his hand. However, I believe you must do this. If these mercenaries are as capable as Jalek seems to think, you can use them to scout far into Old Andaria. Without them, you will have to convince the Sko'Port guards."*

While Ryalsgar projected his thoughts to Rianas, Jalek had been agreeing with Ogerena about the supply train. "The horses will be more valuable, though. I don't think Sko'Port will manage to supply horses through the mine. The miners need to clear out the lower section before animals traverse that path. Even work horses would extend our range by ten miles."

Rianas thought about Ryalsgar's points. The pull of that river down below was still there. She knew even before agreeing to Jalek's help that she would agree to his help. With a hundred mercenaries and the support of Atrick's mages, she could venture into Old Andaria and see what had become of her ancestors. Perhaps they could even find a way to save a few – if there were any out there who wanted saving.

"Tomorrow morning we will head out, then." Rianas tried to put a brave smile on. "If we can capture a supply train without too many casualties amongst their drivers, we might be able to use the wagons to get us into the nearest village."

Ryalsgar smiled.

Jalek took his leave to coordinate with a few of the men down below. Knight Yelenar declared she would go recruit as many mages as she could for the cause. Ryalsgar went with her. Rianas was alone on the boulder.

A few crows had found the piles of dead nogs and rannogs. The sky, however, was clear and blue to the south. Rianas thought about the imagery of the storm the nogs seemed to have imprinted upon them. Why would the storm be *behind* them? Was Niz'Rul responsible for their brainwashing? If not, then who? There were so many questions surrounding the Axareans.

A cool breeze blew up the hill. Rianas put her hands in her pockets. The empty healing potion flask was in there. She took it out and looked at the tiny flask. In Riverrun, magic was distant. Her teachers almost never discussed it. How many people had died of disease or injuries in Riverrun for want of this miraculous magic?

There were other questions, too. If healing magic could heal physical ailments, what would stop humans with access to such magic from living hundreds of years? Could magic slow or even reverse aging itself? The Riverrun textbooks glossed over magic in general. Healing potions were described as rare items to be used sparingly.

However, since Rianas had left Riverrun, magic seemed to be everywhere around her. She had bought an enchanted light, cast magic from a scroll, worn a magical ring, watched a sword and dagger catch fire, and ridden in a magically powered mine car twice! Her own ability had blossomed into actual mind reading. The magic in the world seemed much more pervasive than the teachers in Riverrun had told them.

It was possible the loss of magic from Riverrun had been accidental, but Rianas thought about it. The adults and professors at the college were well travelled. Even those who were lifelong residents of Riverrun met Runlarians and students from other magical nations each semester. Had Riverrun made a conscious effort to avoid magic?

These thoughts danced through Rianas' head as she climbed down from the stone and made her way through the camp. She did not really know where she was going. Her legs carried her as she reviewed in her mind all the times magic had been discussed in school.

Her feet eventually brought her to where her father was working with a group of miners. They were making a flat piece of ground where boulders had been before on the upper ledge. The miners were carrying broken pieces of boulder toward one of the walls.

"Dad," she said as she gave him a hug, "I will be leaving in the morning."

Lazron smiled sorrowfully. "I know, Rianas. After seeing you fighting in front of that wall last night, I knew you would be leaving again soon."

"Will you come with us?"

"No," he said. "They need me here. Perhaps in a few days I can make my way out to the plains. I would love to see them. Your grandfather always spoke fondly of the golden fields of the Andarian Plains. He loved running his hands through the grass while he was hiking. He always said he felt claustrophobic in Riverrun."

Rianas was silent. *"I don't know how long I will be gone. I may never return. I want to find some of those who were left behind during the Andarian War."*

Lazron's eyes laughed and he beamed with pride at his daughter's telepathic ability. She could feel his joy.

"You will have good people to keep you safe. Arthur will watch over you. All of Riverrun will be with you."

Rianas sat down on a stone that did not look like it was going anywhere. "Can I ask you a question about Riverrun?"

"Sure."

"Why did our professors teach us so little about magic? I've been surprised and amazed ever since Sko'Port. It seems like the people of Riverrun would have been better off if we had traded some of our wealth for magic instead of focusing so single-mindedly on engineering."

Lazron looked at Rianas. The smile was still on his face, but his mind was racing. She could feel his mind as he thought to himself that he had always known this conversation would come.

"Exclusion," her father began, "was introduced in the early days of our founding." He sat beside her and considered his wording carefully. "The Axareans killed or captured Andarian mages first when they invaded. I don't know how, and your grandparents often discussed their own theories when I was small. I guess why doesn't really matter, only that it happened.

"When the Andarian refugees settled Riverrun, there were almost no mages amongst them. Those mages who did escape mostly took work in Western Runlar, Cidvag and Sko'Port. It was part of the unspoken contract with Cidvag. They demanded payment for the lives lost on their side of the war.

"A few stayed behind," he continued, "but when the Borsilkians offered their help, they conditioned it on the principle that exclusion from magic would breed a new kind of thinking. Their engineers and chemists had been dreaming up new ways to live with the lack of magic for centuries. They thought humans might be successful as well, and here was their opportunity.

"Riverrun needed money to build new homes for the refugees, and Borsilk was willing to provide it. Their engineers and chemists helped us design the *Riverrunner* boats. They gave us the plans for the telegraph system we run. The condition was that we teach curriculum solely based on the sciences."

"Even when there was a clear benefit to magic?" Rianas asked. "How about healing potions and magical light enchantments?"

"There are many places where magic seems better." Lazron sighed.

He fingered the wedding ring he still wore on his hand. "The Borsilkians gave us the resources to build our homes, though. They also showed us how to enrich the lives of all our residents. You see, Rianas, magic is only useful to those who can access it. All the people in Riverrun, though, can use our science and technology.

"Once we learned how to access the power of the Anasko River, the entire nation was able to benefit from its energy. Anyone with training can operate the Riverrun paddle ships. The telegraph lines we began experimenting with a few years ago connected the council, the docks, the college and hundreds of other people. These things take effort and time, but it is effort and time that any of the Riverrun citizens can provide."

Lazron had bought into the magical exclusion principle for the most part. Nevertheless, even he had made exceptions. Rianas was one of those exceptions.

"Then how did you justify my ability to speak with animals?" she asked a little angrily. "Why not use magic where it *was* faster and better?"

Lazron bowed his head, still fingering his ring. "Many of us did. Most of the council members had enchanted items of some sort they used when they needed to. A few bought healing potions from Runlarian merchants. We have an enchanted stone in the food cellar that stays as cold as ice year round, if you recall.

"When you first started showing your abilities, I couldn't believe they were true. As it became apparent you had magic in your blood, I was elated. I suppose next year or the year after I would have had to send you away to a school for mages. The truth is, Rianas, Riverrun will eventually lose its bet against magic."

"What will happen when people turn to magic again?"

"It will continue to slowly creep into the nation. Magic is all around us. We cannot ignore it. Even the Borsilkians are exposed to it all the time. They have purchased enchanted items from mages to help them solve problems. The same magical herbs and trees grow in their lands as in others. The Borsilkians themselves are different, though. They are unable to cast magic or be a direct recipient of its gifts.

"I think the gifts of the 'sciences' have helped Riverrun grow and be successful beyond what it otherwise would have been. Many of the other council members have felt the same way. I suspect it will continue to be that way for many more years. Once we learn how to do something with coal, or how to make a new chemical or metal, we can pass that knowledge on. The college will probably draw more people to it in the coming decade. The Borsilkians think magic stifles achievement. They want to stoke great advancements by reducing the easy answers magic sometimes offers us. I tend to agree."

Rianas thought about all the lectures she had heard. Steam power and hydraulic power were new sciences, and she only knew what little she had read, but it did seem to hold great promise.

"Mom would still be alive if you had readily been able to buy a healing potion to use on her, wouldn't she?" Rianas regretted the accusatory tone as soon as she asked the question. Her hand shot out to her father's to take away the sting from her words.

Lazron looked up from his ring. His face was solemn when he nodded. "The world is not black and white, Rianas. That lesson takes some people their whole lives to learn." He shut his eyes, and Rianas could feel the sorrow as much as see it.

"I will try to find a middle path, Father," Rianas projected.

Rianas stayed a while to talk about home with her father. It felt funny even calling it home, now. In only about a week, Rianas' whole outlook on the world had changed. A month ago, she had wanted to travel around the world and see its wonders. Now, she wanted to see Old Andaria, and wrest its control from Axarea.

Her father was still supportive. He told her how the main Riverrun council had thrown its full support behind Atrick's gamble that he could get through the Black Mountains. Even Mr. Locks had been happy to help when he had seen Lazron the following day.

Every forge operator and helper he had working for him was in the shop when Lazron had arrived, and Mr. Locks had said, "War wit' Axarea'd gimme greet ple'sure!"

Rianas laughed at her father's take on the forge operator's accent.

The council had also discussed raising a militia of volunteers. Riverrun was a small nation – the whole Anasko River held less than a quarter the population of Sko'Port – but some of the council members thought it was time for them to start training an army in case war really did come to Sko'Port. Riverrun would not be taken by surprise if war did come to the Sko' Sea.

When Rianas finally left her father, he bade her farewell with a long hug and a kiss on the cheek. "Take care, Rianas. You make me proud."

"Dammit, of course I'm coming with you!" Sal yelled.

Rianas had seen her hobbling around on a spear, using it for a crutch. Her wounds were healing slowly because they were not life threatening and the mages had saved their remaining healing potions for the mortally wounded. Rianas considered that perhaps she should not have mentioned what she was doing to the miner's widow.

Sal only had one desire now – kill Axareans. She had started bouncing up and down when Rianas told her what she was planning. When Rianas said that perhaps Sal would like to catch up with them when she was fully healed, the bigger woman spat on the ground and threw the crutch away.

"Please Sal, calm down. You need a little more time to heal before you go hiking across this mountain."

Sal was beside herself. She wanted to come with Rianas. She *did* lower her voice, though. A little. "If you try to leave without me, I will just follow the river and meet you there anyway. I'm capable of taking care of myself. Just let me come with."

"The people we are going with are used to scouting, Sal. We would need to keep up with them. It will be dangerous, even for people who don't have slow-healing stab wounds," Rianas retorted. "I want you to come, but don't you think you should take it easy for a week or two?"

Sal's anger subsided, and her wide shoulders heaved. A short, suppressed sob came out. "I just...I have to do something. Merrin is gone."

Rianas reached for the woman. She put her arms around her neck. She could say little to console Sal. Rianas just stood there holding her. A few minutes passed. Sal wept quietly into Rianas' knotted hair. Finally, she looked up with her red eyes and smiled wanly.

"Keep a place for me, will you? If I can convince someone to heal me more, I will join you tomorrow. If not, I will find a way to join you later."

"I will, Sal. We would be privileged to have your help." Rianas smiled. Then she thought of something. "Go see Knight Yelenar. Tell her I asked that you be capable of keeping up. She may be able to do something for you."

Sal nodded. "I will. Right now. Thank you, Rianas!" With that, she grabbed her crutch and hobbled off at a brisk skipping walk.

Rianas hoped she had not made a bad choice. Sal needed time to work through her grief. Her anger made her a fierce combatant, but her skill was in mining, not war. Still, Rianas was happy to know another familiar face would be with her in the coming days.

It was funny how quickly she had become accustomed to some of her companions. Sal, Samuel, John, Elias, Atrick, Teran, and Berryl – all of them seemed like long-time friends now.

Then there was Arthur. Rianas saw him waving at her up above. His goofy long-armed wave brought a grin to her face. *He* had gotten enough healing to be up and walking again.

"You seem like you are getting around fine. Are you ready to do some climbing?" Rianas asked Arthur.

"I have a magical sword." He smiled like an idiot. That was all the response Rianas was going to get.

Rianas laughed.

16. ANDARIA

Just after reaching the top of the last foothill, the scouting party got its first unobstructed view of the Andarian Plains. As far as the eye could see south of the foothills of the Black Mountains, there was grassland. Only three things broke them up.

The first was the river. The creek that flowed out of the mountain here joined with a larger river flowing west. Occasional trees or low-lying swampy bushes dotted the edges of the river. It cut a relentless westerly path through the plains.

The second was a small village about eight miles to the west. Short buildings huddled close together along the river. Four or five tiny boats idly fished in the slow moving river, but it did not appear deep enough for shipping. A road ran through the town and could be seen extending further west. It ran past the foothills near them before splitting off into small dirt paths through the prairie heading south.

The last objects to break up the plains were the massive farms that ran along the river for miles to either side of the town. These garnered the most attention. Stone walls perhaps eight feet tall surrounded thousands of acres. Men pulled strange wooden towers along well-travelled tracks in the farms.

Jalek had sent his best scout, Basan, along the river to see what was going on. Yesterday, he had returned with grim news. Each of those two- or three-story towers was a small siege engine. Southerners occupied the towers with pedestal-mounted crossbows as big as horses.

The worst parts of the towers were their targets.

Hundreds of men and women were working the fields. Men worked while chained together in places, and in others, they worked free. However, all of them did so under the watchful eyes of the slavers. The town operated like a massive work camp. At the end of the day, the workers shuffled back to warehouses. Slavers fed them and allowed them to take care of their personal needs for the evening. The process repeated itself day after day.

"We have to find a way to free those people!" Rianas had almost shouted.

Jalek reacted more calmly. He and the knights, as well as Arthur, Elias and Galen had gathered in one of the commandeered Rannog tents to discuss Basan's findings. Rianas followed the others and found herself in the tent.

"What we need to do," Jalek said, "is capture that caravan without the town being alerted. If the slavers discover us, a force our size will never make it within two hundred yards of those weapons. Hell, they could even haul them out here and assault Atrick's fortifications before they have truly begun."

Ogerena agreed with Jalek. "Judging by their height and size, those are torsion spring ballistae. They would be capable of shooting multiple arrows at once. I wouldn't doubt they could fire over a quarter mile. I've seen such weapons in training exercises in Northern Runlar. Don't question their lethality. We cannot approach that town without heavily armored soldiers or some other way to neutralize those weapons."

Elias and Arthur worked with Basan to develop a map of approaches and locations of the mobile watchtowers.

Jalek, on the other hand, had been more interested in the status of the mile-long caravan of supply wagons Basan had seen loading supplies at silos outside of the town. "If they finish loading today or tomorrow, they should reach here by tomorrow evening. This pass here would be the perfect opportunity for an ambush."

Rianas and the two knights helped Jalek identify the best approaches for the caravan. With jagged rocks all over, there were hundreds of hiding places for the small force. They picked places with good vantage points. The attack would begin as soon as the last wagon passed the peak.

Knight Ogenson volunteered to rush back to the main camp and have Atrick's army set up Nog and Rannog tents about a quarter mile down from the cave entrance. They must be where they had been before the final attack. The ruse would not hold for long, but with a few strategically placed fires, Jalek and Ryalsgar thought they could lure the wagons over the first hill.

The next morning, the wagon train set out to resupply Niz'Rul's army. From behind a jagged piece of sandstone, Rianas and Arthur watched the wagons roll up the rough pebbly trail one at a time. The first few dozen wagons passed.

When the final wagon rolled past the crest of the hill, Knight Yelenar sounded a shrill whistle. All the archers in the group fired at once, taking out dozens of the drivers at the rear of the caravan and most of the armored guards.

Three lethal volleys of crossbow bolts rained onto the wagon train before any resistance was able to form. A large, well-appointed wagon in the middle of the line bustled with armored soldiers who took to horseback. Their leader, a young man in a fine yellow tunic and bright red pants, rode low to the ground as he charged back toward the town.

Jalek and half a dozen of his best-armored men jumped in the path to prevent escape. Rianas stood from her hiding place and yelled for the horses to stop. Two of the five horses actually bucked their riders, and the other three were confused enough that Jalek's men were able to knock the men off the huge horses.

A short battle ensued, with the heavily armed guards ferociously fighting to break through and protect the lord.

"One hundred eighty horses, forty five wagons, twenty crossbows, two hundred short swords, and enough food to keep Atrick's army fed for three weeks. There is wheat, corn, some type of dried pasta, jars of some type of sauce, and even a few hundred yards of threads and leathers."

Jalek was reading a list that Galen had compiled. They were inside the huge tent where Rianas, the knights, Arthur and Elias were gathered. They had captured it from a particularly well decorated wagon, along with its owner.

They had captured nearly forty Axarean Southerners and a dozen nogs. Rianas could not believe how successful the battle had been.

Jalek continued reading through some other items he found of interest. Approximately four thousand Gold Eagles' worth of Axarean currency had been seized. Ryalsgar was stowing that into a huge oaken lockbox as Jalek finished his summary.

Elias was shaking his head. "Do you really think we captured them all?"

"Yes." Jalek's succinct voice said he had complete confidence in his men. "The ones we didn't kill, at least."

"I have an idea," Arthur spoke up. "Why not bring the wagons with us and use them to get closer to that town? We could take the Axareans by surprise. We could be inside the town before we were discovered."

Ryalsgar agreed. "That would be an excellent way to get close enough to take out those ballistae."

Jalek's men had tied up the Axareans in the backs of half a dozen emptied wagons. Rianas knew exactly what to do. "I'll see what I can find out from that captured lord."

Knight Yelenar and Galen joined Rianas. They walked out of the huge canvas pavilion and down the line of wagons. A few of the mercenaries stood guard at the three wagons full of prisoners, but mostly the rest of the men were tending horses and checking the various wagons for maintenance issues.

There was a mood of excitement around the mercenary party. A few men waved at Rianas as she walked by. Some smiled politely. She recognized one of the men. He had been in the path of one of the horses she calmed down and stopped from plowing through him. Without her help, he probably would have been cut down by the Southerner's battle-axe as he rode by. All along the path, mercenaries were talking about Rianas' ability with horses.

Galen pointed to the third wagon. "In here."

Pulling back the flap, Rianas saw the lord sitting on the bench seat, tied legs to hands with the other dozen or so men. His doublet had been torn across his arm in the battle and he bore bruises across the side of his face where he had been knocked from his horse.

As soon as Galen pulled back the fabric, the lord pulled at his restraints.

"Let me go!" the lord shouted. "I am Lord Caldus' brother. If he finds out you have kidnapped me, he will bring Marquis Briley's entire Garrison from Gavala. You will be killed slowly for abducting a member of Axarean royal blood."

"Gavala." Rianas let the name roll around in her mouth. The lordling's Southern was somewhat less offensive to the ears than the rannog's Southern. She helped Galen pull the man up and out into the road. They both grunted as she maneuvered around the other sweaty occupants of the wagon. "That is an old Andarian city a couple hundred miles to the west, is it not?"

Lord Caldus was still swearing at his handling. When Knight Yelenar pulled the ropes around his legs to set him onto the ground, he quieted down. The Sullarian's armor spoke volumes of her origin. The lordling no longer thought the mercenaries were bandits.

"How did you get here?" he asked, eyeing the Green Knight. Rianas sensed a slight hint of fear in his mind.

"I think it is time for you to answer some questions for us, Lord Caldus," Rianas said politely.

Lord Caldus' brother was a young man, perhaps in his early twenties. His short sword was immaculately designed, and his outfit was made of a silk softer than any Rianas had seen before. The man was handsome, too. His brown hair was long and straight, his nose perfectly shaped. Despite the cuts and bruises from his capture, his low-cut doublet accented his muscular chest. However, the haughty way he addressed his captors grated on Rianas.

"When are you scheduled to return to the town?" Rianas asked in Southern.

The lordling ran a finger under the tight rope around his wrist. "Three days." He did not even look up.

Rianas nodded. That would work perfectly for Arthur's plan. "Where is the leader of the town? What do you call him?"

"Lord Caldus, you imbecile!" he spat.

Rianas stood back. She quietly told the other two what she had learned. "Do you think we could use him to get closer to the town?" she asked in Northern.

"Perhaps," whispered Knight Ogerena. "This wagon train will be nearly a mile long. If we arrive at night with a few dozen wagons, we might be able to get enough men in the backs of them to work our way into the town."

Rianas removed her leather gloves. "What is your name?" she asked the lordling.

"I am Antone." The lordling was trying to get control of the situation again. It was apparent he was not going to be summarily killed. "What is your name, milady?"

His flirtatious gaze was almost laughable to Rianas, but she maintained a neutral face. "Antone, we plan to go into town. I would hate for a lot of people to get hurt. Can you help us?"

As she finished her sentence, Rianas let her bare hand touch Antone's cheek. She wanted to use finesse this time. Instead of barreling through the lordling's subconscious, Rianas willed herself slowly into his mind.

"Perhaps we can come to some sort of agreement?" Antone asked as Rianas stroked the side of his head. He smiled, showing off his perfect teeth. "Lord Caldus would be glad to have me back. If you brought a few of your men with you, I could get them in to see my brother."

Rianas was inside Antone's mind. Gently, she teased at his thoughts. *"How?"* With some effort, she slipped back into her reality. "How?"

"I don't understand the question. I would go back to town. Let me ride in front of my carriage. Lieutenant Azran will probably wonder why the rest of the wagon train is not behind me, but I can tell him I got bored and decided to return early."

Antone did not seem to notice how loose his tongue had become. Rianas, her hand still softly touching Antone's cheek, decided to see how much information she could get without the lordling noticing. *"Would he be happy to see the entire wagon train?"*

"Yes. I mean, well…I guess so," Antone stumbled. His eyes rolled around a bit as if he was trying to focus. "You don't need to bring the entire wagon train into town, though. Just one wagon would be fine. I'm sure my brother will help you rid yourselves of me." He tried being coy again. "Perhaps you would like to stay a few days after we get this unpleasantness worked out. I could show you the lord's mansion. Bonshus is a very beautiful village."

Rianas could not believe this man's gall. Instead of shaking her head or rolling her eyes, though, she smiled. Sexily? Who knew, but she hoped it would work on this buffoon.

"How would we know it was safe to travel past those ballistae?" Rianas asked. It took all her concentration to stay out of the man's mind while still compelling an answer. Her voice almost shook, and her head was starting to pound. It was as if she were trying to extract information by using a rope attached to the front of her head.

Antone, however, did not seem to notice. The man's glazed eyes looked at Rianas. "You wouldn't have to worry. Lieutenant Azran does not have men in the towers unless the slaves are working the fields. After sunset, most of the town guards would be in the manor or watching over the slave-holds."

Antone had told Rianas just what she needed. "Maybe we will bring a few wagons with us into town. Can you help us talk to Lieutenant Azran?"

"Sure. As long as he sees I'm safe, you should be fine." Antone was clearly misunderstanding the intentions Rianas actually had for Bonshus.

Did he actually think Rianas would simply return him to the town? Rianas wondered as she released Antone's mind and slipped her hand from his cheek. The color seemed to return slowly to his face. Speaking in Northern, Rianas asked the mercenary guarding this prisoner wagon to help the man back in with the others and make sure he was kept unharmed.

"I think I know how we can get into the town," she told Galen and Ogerena. "Those archer towers are unmanned at night. We can pull in with enough wagons to carry our entire group a little after sunset. We could send men out into the fields around the town as we get close enough, then bring a few dozen in to take out the guards at this manor he speaks of."

They were walking back toward the large pavilion as they spoke. Galen shook his head. "This man may be able to get us close to the captain of the guard-"

"Lieutenant Azran, he called him," Rianas interjected.

"Lieutenant Azran, fine. But what makes you think he will sit quietly once you see him?"

Up front, Knight Yelenar swayed her head graciously back toward the other two. "Rianas is right, Galen. It will not matter what the lord thinks will happen. If we bring the entire force into the town, we should be able to overrun their defenses. The most difficult part will be subduing that lieutenant before he sounds an alarm."

She said this as she pulled back the flap to the pavilion tent. The warm air inside reminded Rianas how cold it was getting at night even on this side of the mountains.

Jalek and Ryalsgar looked up from a huge piece of bleached tent material they had been using to generate a map of the town. Stones and coal marks were all over the material. Basan was marking an approximate location of another tower with a piece of charcoal.

Rianas told the others what she had learned.

Jalek smiled thinly at the idea of just riding into the town. "You realize you are talking about open warfare with Axarea, right, girl?" The idea actually seemed to make the humorless man want to laugh.

Rianas could not help smiling. "I do. What's more, I think Antone will give us the leader of the local militia if we can sneak enough men on that first wagon."

Arthur was incredulous. "There are probably a couple hundred soldiers in that little town. Think about it, Rianas. If there are three thousand residents, the slavers among them would all be heavily armed."

Jalek's smile was still there. "Normally I would agree it was a bad idea. But we still have the element of surprise. If we could drop about half the men off in the fields on our way in, the other half could help secure the main road and capture whoever rides out to meet the wagons."

Ryalsgar nodded emphatically. "That's right," he said. "We bring picks and hammers for the men who we send into the fields. They can break into those ballistae towers closest to the town. There are probably five or six of them within close range of the buildings. It would give us a huge advantage. By the time fighting starts, we should be able to get those things aimed at any large forces they are able to muster."

The pavilion was filled with chatter as everyone gathered around Basan's map of the town. Knight Yelenar offered some suggestions on how the ballistae worked. Arthur volunteered to find tools for the men who would take the ballistae. Galen volunteered to ride with Rianas in the front wagon.

For nearly two hours, the group strategized their attack.

Galen and Rianas broke away as Jalek and Ryalsgar started naming men for each of the wagons.

"They may have their own mages in the town, Rianas," Galen said. "Are you prepared to use magic when this lieutenant approaches?"

Rianas had not really considered the Axareans having mages. A few strong spells from the other side could wipe out their attack. She fingered the scroll in her pocket. "I have the scroll Atrick gave me. I could cast something dangerous, but I wouldn't know how to tell a mage from someone who doesn't know magic."

"A trained mage can spot another within a few hundred feet if he has learned how to 'see' the weave being manipulated. I could probably spot one readying magic within a few dozen yards."

"What would we do if we saw one?"

"The easiest thing would be to have an archer kill him," Galen said quietly. "We should take Knight Yelenar with us in the first wagon. Her magical crossbow would be fast enough to take out any targets we gave her."

Jalek thought the Green Knight would be better suited for the reconnaissance around the town. Her previous training with ballistae would make her invaluable to the men as they captured the great siege weapons. Galen grudgingly agreed they would do what they could to neutralize the lieutenant's men when they approached.

"I'll ride in the back of the lord's wagon, too," Arthur volunteered. "With my magical longsword, I should be able to help."

Rianas smiled at Arthur. He had been waving that thing around with his uninjured arm for two days now. He said he felt like an expert swordsman when he was holding the weapon, and he had successfully disarmed two of the wagon guards during the sneak attack a few hours ago. Perhaps the magic in that sword was more powerful than she had thought.

Jalek named three other men for the first wagon – Basan, Rum'Osk, and Uld. "Basan has worked with those two before. I'll drive the second wagon with Ryalsgar and five other volunteers. We will disembark as soon as this lieutenant discovers who we are."

"Rianas, it will be up to you to determine how this battle goes. I hope that the initial fighting does not alert a huge contingent of the city guard. A full company of guards would overrun us. If there is a lot of foot traffic on the streets, we may be forced to fight building to building. Your magic will give us the advantage over their men."

17. WHERE THE STONE LANDS

Lord Antone sat nervously on the front seat. Arthur had tied the Axarean's feet to the floor and one arm to the armrest. He had pulled the sleeves of Antone's doublet down to cover the rope around his arm. It looked like the haughty man was lounging on the passenger side of the wagon while Rianas drove the horses.

Galen had suggested Rianas drive the horses. With her natural affinity for the animals, they barely required the reins. A few soft words now and then had kept them moving with few complaints since they had started a couple hours earlier.

Rianas' hair was blowing loosely in the cool early-evening air as they steadily led the other fifteen wagons into the town. She had pulled the long white shirt she had borrowed around her waist, and she had patched her ripped leather leggings. A few minutes at the creek washing up had left her feeling cleaner than she had since Sko'Port.

Being clean did not change her sense of exposure, though. It was as if a hundred pairs of eyes were watching her from up ahead, where a loose collection of a few dozen warehouses and small buildings came together into Bonshus.

They had ridden between the first two stone walls a few moments before. No one was out on the road just after sunset, as Antone had told her. A few barn houses had lights on in the distance, but the cornstalks on either side of the road here blocked their light. Brown cornfields to the right stood the height of a man. To the left, younger corn crops looked like they were mostly picked already.

Either way, this would probably be the last harvest for the season.

The road was wide enough for two wagons to pass comfortably.

Every few hundred yards a dirt path led into the fields. Rianas did not look behind her, but she knew men were jumping stealthily out of the wagons and running into the fields as they passed.

The first building of the town was three hundred yards away. Lord Antone pointed with his free left hand at a couple dozen men wearing brown uniforms and carrying lanterns hooked to poles at the fronts of their horses. Each was wearing chainmail. They carried a sword on one side and a hand crossbow on the other.

As they got closer, Rianas counted fifteen of the soldiers breaking away and heading toward them. The others continued riding down side streets. Rianas put a hand on Antone's leg. "Send them a friendly wave."

Antone tensed. The riders were no more than fifty yards away when he raised his hand. "Good evening, lieutenant." It was friendly.

Lieutenant Azran must have been the man at the head of the group. He was obviously a Southerner. His greyish skin seemed almost black in the lantern light. The man's dark eyes and short beard were obsidian in the twilight. The tight fitting helm on his head did little to contain the long black braids that ran down the man's back and shoulders.

The lieutenant reigned in his horse. He put a hand up to stop the rest of his men. The others were a mix of pale skin and grey-skinned soldiers. They looked on seriously. A few let their hands naturally fall to the crossbows at their waists. Their leader squinted to see Antone in the darkness.

"Lord Antone," the lieutenant said.

Rianas maintained a straight face while the lieutenant broke away from his horsemen. He trotted toward the line of stopped wagons. His guards were just within bow range. "Where is the rest of the supply train?" he asked.

As he got within sight, Lieutenant Azran did a double take at the sight of Rianas. "Where are your guards? Who is this girl?" His surprise was evident. His hand shot down to the sword at his waist, half-drawing it even as he asked the questions. His horse carried him closer still, and Rianas worried the ruse would not hold.

Antone had rehearsed lines with Rianas dozens of times. With her hand placed on his naked hand, arm or neck, she had guided him until he had it right.

"You won't believe what happened, lieutenant," Antone said. The lordling smiled his perfect smile and waved his free arm expansively to include Rianas somewhat provocatively. "On our way out there we found a small caravan of travelers from out east whose land ships had broken down. This beautiful young lady here has business in Gavala. She asked us to help her get there. Of course, I said yes. I'm hoping she will stay in Lord Caldus' manor tonight with us."

Rianas had her hand pressed up against Antone's leg. She smiled at the lieutenant, wondering if he could see how nervous she actually was. Arthur shifted almost imperceptibly in the back of the wagon. In perfect Axarean, she spoke. "This wonderful man here has helped me tremendously today. Would you mind escorting us to the lord's manor, so I may thank his brother for this wonderful hospitality, as well?"

Lieutenant Azran looked Rianas up and down. It was not the first time since this trip she had felt like livestock being examined. Whatever he saw apparently put the grey-skinned man at ease. He turned around in his saddle and shouted to the other soldiers, "Arday, Jontur, escort Lord Antone to Caldus' estate. Harrian, let the stables know these other wagons are pulling in." He turned back to Rianas and flicked his wrist dismissively toward two of his men. "Follow those two."

Rianas smiled the biggest smile she could muster. It felt faked. Lieutenant Azran, however, nodded and turned away. The rest of the horsemen followed him down a side lane.

Arday and Jontur rode a few yards ahead to the left and right side of the wagon. Rianas did not relax at all as the four horses started trotting down the lamp lit street toward a large building at the center of town.

Antone looked nervously at her. "I've helped as much as I can. Why don't you just let me go?"

Rianas left her hand pressed into Antone's leg. "Thank you for your help so far. You have probably saved many lives already." She felt his body relax a little at her soothing words. With her other hand, she flipped a small hourglass over and waved nonchalantly at the wagons behind her.

The other wagons headed toward the stables behind Harrian. Rianas hoped everything went well for them. Galen was whispering to the other men in the back, and she heard swords sliding from their scabbards.

Cobblestones paved the way to Lord Caldus' manor from here. For a couple hundred yards, utilitarian shop fronts with small patches of grass or shrubs in front lined the street. Street lamps flickered dully above. The shops were closed, and no one wandered about.

The manor itself had a short wall around it. Two soldiers with pikes stood guard. Arday or Jontur (Rianas really had no idea which was which in the pale light) exchanged a few words with one of the guards. Lord Antone's wagon was allowed to ride straight through the entrance into a grassy garden sparsely populated with a few plum trees.

Rianas thumbed the scroll in her pocket as they approached the large building. A pale-skinned butler with grey hair and a limp stepped onto the porch as the wagon pulled up. Arday and Jontur turned long enough to salute Antone briefly before they rode back through the gates.

Tall columns supported a covered loading zone in front. The brick two-story building was well lit inside. It sounded like there was some sort of small party. Antone had told Rianas lords, ladies and military officers from other towns were constantly visiting the manor.

The stables were just ahead, and there was a large circle for wagons to turn around. Two light-skinned men wearing shackles around their necks were cleaning out the stables. They glanced over as Rianas pulled the horses to a stop, but bent back to their rakes almost immediately.

Rianas' blood began to boil. The stable hands only wore pants despite the cool evening air.

As the butler walked up, Rianas could see a decorative shackle around his neck, as well. Keeping her anger in check, she eased a dagger from her waist. "Stay here, Antone." She stood up.

The butler saw the dagger in Rianas' hands and his eyes shot up to hers. "Miss, shall I introduce you to Lord Caldus?" The fear in his eyes did not travel to his voice.

Rianas stepped down from the wagon. The butler was so tall that the "necklace" sat at her eye level. There was a large hole for a hook in the front. Leather lined the rest of the shackle to prevent chafing, but its use was clear.

"I've come to free the people of Bonshus. Andaria's chains will be broken today." The whispered words came almost without thinking. She spoke them in Axarean, which was the same language the butler had used to address her. "How many people are in the manor?"

The butler's eyes were wide. He hesitated. When Rianas grabbed his arm and stared into his eyes, the words came out quickly. "Uh, well, there are Lord Caldus, Lady Caldus and ten officers, plus Baron Degrant's treasurer and mage Therzon."

Rianas projected toward Arthur, *There are thirteen people in the manor, plus a mage.* There were too many for them to take on their own.

By now, the rest of the wagons should be at the town's main stables. Rianas hoped they were okay. She glanced back at the hourglass hanging from the side of the wagon. The others would begin their assault in about thirty minutes. In the meanwhile, Jalek's mercenaries in the stables would try to capture as many horses as they could.

The butler stood frozen in front of her, clearly weighing whether to stay or flee.

Rianas looked over to Antone. He was staring at one of the windows as if willing someone to come and save him. She turned back to the butler.

"Is there an armory inside?" she asked.

"Yes. It's through the kitchen. There are a few dozen weapons and some armor in there. But only Lord Caldus and Lieutenant Azran have keys." The butler was twisting his arms with his hands nervously. "What are you going to do? There are soldiers all over this town."

Galen peered out behind her and whispered in Northern, "Rianas, the guards at the gate will come as soon as we start our attack. They may even call for help. We should just wait out here until the attack begins. We can take the soldiers by surprise as they come out. Your scroll should give us the advantage over those soldiers. But we need to neutralize that mage."

Galen was right. Rianas wondered what they could do. The butler, whose arm she was still touching lightly, thought, "*Mage Therzon likes to smoke his pipe in the rear yard. A few of the others may be there, but that might make it easier to take him.*"

Rianas released the old man and smiled. "Thank you. Now, go inside and stay safe when the fighting starts."

The butler, his eyes glazed from the invasion of his mind, focused on Rianas again. This time, his gaze was less nervous. "No," he said. "If you will be fighting the Axareans, I will do what I can to help. Let me go speak with the other servants. Perhaps we can do something to help when your attack begins."

With that, the butler hobbled quickly over to the stables. Rianas watched the old man go. She relayed the situation to the men in the wagon. "I think two of us should stay up front. Galen, see what you can do to stop that mage. Arthur and I will stay here. I can cast a spell when the fighting begins."

Galen crawled up front past Antone. Basan, Rum'Osk, and Uld joined him. They ran over to a large shrub to remain out of sight. Arthur joined Rianas near the door to the building. His longsword was out, and Rianas could see he had scraped off most of the red paint. The weapon's edge glittered in the light of the lamps.

Rianas took the scroll from her pocket. The magic within called to her. She examined the double entry doors and drawn curtains of the windows, trying to think of what she could cast when the battle started.

"Those guards will be at our backs," Arthur said quietly. "Antone won't stay tied up long, either. Once he sees we are distracted, he will probably free himself within a couple minutes."

"Maybe they can capture the mage without anyone finding out."

"I don't think we should plan on a maybe. Let's bring Antone into those stables. From in there we can ambush whoever comes out the front of the manor. It gives us a little more cover, and puts the guards in front of us, too."

Rianas glanced at Antone, then over to the stables. "Okay."

A few moments of struggle ensued with Antone. He tried to pull away. He even got out a muffled shout before Arthur stuffed his face with a leather bit. He quieted a little after that, but Arthur had to crab-walk him into the stables. The lordling pulled against the rope tying his arms together and managed a muffled "mpghhh" when Arthur shoved him into an empty stall. Amazingly, the two guards at the gate did not even turn around to investigate the commotion.

"That ought to hold him for a little while," Arthur said. He smiled and drew his longsword again. Despite the gravity of the moment, he managed to strike a pose holding the enchanted weapon. That goofy grin was back on his face just for Rianas. She chuckled softly and shook her head.

Atrick had used a small trickle of magic to dry a spot on that boulder. If she could do something equally innovative, perhaps she could keep her spell alive longer. Rianas looked up at the pillars over the porch. The horses were staring back at her where they stood in front of the door.

The stables were full of hay.

"Hay," Rianas whispered.

Rianas opened the scroll and walked over to a few of the bails. She cut the twine around as many as she could reach with Arthur's dagger. Antone and Arthur were both staring at her as if she had gone mad. She climbed on top of a wooden chair at the back of the middle stall. The smell of horses almost gagged her here, but it would be perfect. She had a good view of the street to her right, the guardhouse, and the main manor entrance ahead. Best of all, she was mostly concealed by the huge pile of unfettered hay bales.

The last few grains of sand drained out of the hourglass that Arthur had brought over from the wagon. Rianas listened for an indication the attack had begun.

It seemed like only seconds passed before a horn blew from toward the west edge of town. Arthur tensed and crouched down, his sword in hand. Antone started struggling madly against his bonds in the locked stall. The horn blew two more times and abruptly went silent.

Rianas silently wished luck to Jalek and Ryalsgar. There was yelling coming from the north side of town near the river. The two guards at the front of the manor grabbed shields and lowered helms on their heads. One pointed up the road toward the river and said something to the other.

The party inside the manor went silent.

The ground shook and the manor seemed to shutter back and forth. Galen must have pulled some of the stones down in the back with his magic. Rianas looked down at the scroll and started her weave.

"Caelia, Ignia." The weave followed her commands.

Rianas became thousands of strands of hay, a few small bunches rising into the air, and then entire bails' worth. A steady stream became a river of small straws. Each was like a tiny finger to her, awaiting her commands.

Up the steps and around the front doors they crept like tens of thousands of caterpillars. They drifted on a light breeze barely a foot above the ground.

Rianas could feel the approaching soldiers on the street to the west. Their horses galloped toward the east side of the city, and it sounded like they would pass the manor in two or three minutes. There were people inside, as well. The initial surprise of whatever happened in the back of the building had subsided, and the manor was becoming a hive of activity.

Just as the first straw was coming down the other side of the front entrance and approaching the gate, the manor's doors flew open. Rianas saw Lord Caldus —easy to tell apart from the others because his face was shaped so similarly to Antone's — as he charged out of the house and right into *her*.

Lord Caldus put his arms into the air. His sword was in his hand, but it did little to stop the onslaught of tiny straws. Rianas was there, everywhere, surrounding each of the soldiers, Lady Caldus, and everyone else who exited into the night. They waved their arms at *her*, protecting their eyes. Two men tried to shout warnings, but dozens of *her* 'fingers' raced into their open mouths.

Lord Caldus and the first two soldiers to clear the door slipped on the levitating straws, sending them sprawling across the brick porch.

Rianas traced each person with her tiny 'fingers'. With so much of *her*, it was impossible to move fast. Instead, she simply coalesced as much of *her* as she could around each person. They swatted at their eyes and faces and tried to fend the faster-moving straws from slicing them. However, Rianas was not wasting effort trying to injure them directly with the hay.

In a flash, thousands of individual pieces of hay were alight. Rianas herself felt like a raging inferno made of tiny cells. Hundreds of *her* 'fingers' were pressed against each soldier. Their armor, clothes and hair caught fire, and a chaotic dance began on the front porch.

Lady Caldus' cotton dress caught fire in seconds. She dove back inside to douse herself with water from the kitchen. Some of the soldiers' gloves disintegrated, leaving burns on their hands. The two with hay in their mouths belched fire as they screamed.

A whirlwind of flame stole the oxygen from the air around the men and women. Just as Rianas had watched Mr. Locks quell his coal furnace by pulling the vent closed, Rianas pulled a tiny wall of flaming hay into a semi-circle around the soldiers at the manor's front entrance.

One by one, the Axarean nobles and their guards fell over. Four of the soldiers were on the ground, and Lord Caldus fell to his knees as he tried blindly to escape through the wall of flame. As the others moved, she moved with them.

An explosion rocked the back of the house. Rianas focused on the ball of fire that she had become. Part of her felt Arthur rushing away from her corporeal body to engage two soldiers as they exited a side door into the stables. A panicky voice inside her said she needed to return, but her focus needed to be absolute to maintain the flaming wall.

Another soldier fell to his knees. The guards from the gate were pointing at *her* now.

Then something must have given her corporeal presence away. One of the gate guards saw her inside the stables and nudged the other. Rianas sent another bale of straw 'fingers' in their direction to slow them down, but they were running.

Another soldier fell down. There were two more soldiers at the entrance. One was using his tunic to knock back the flaming hay as it approached him. The thick leather would not catch fire from the weak flames Rianas was producing. She drew on the weave and gathered a few thousand more straws into her being. Burnt straws floated to the earth, like breath escaping her cloud-like body as it stretched across the lawn.

Another shudder went through the mansion, and windows blew out on the second floor. The two guards were only a few dozen yards from Rianas' body. Arthur fought the two officers at the same time, his sword moving fluidly from one to the other. He could not protect her from the other two guards, with their shields and chainmail. They were almost to the stables.

Just as she was about to release the flaming hay wall, the two men who had been cleaning out the stables jumped out of the bushes beside the running guards. If not for the flaming straws distracting them, the two half-naked men would have been easy to see. With their visors down and their arms waving in front of them, however, they did not notice the two Andarians until a strategically placed rake tripped one of them. The other's head jerked violently back when he was lassoed with a leather pulley from the stables.

A fat man in thick robes suddenly flew out of one of the second floor windows. Glass sprinkled onto the lawn around him as he landed like a cat on his feet. Rianas felt her concentration on the flame wall weaken as the man looked at her cloud-like body.

"*Cease!*" the mage yelled in Elven. He lifted his arms toward the wall of flames and cloud Rianas felt her magical form being torn apart. The pain was distant but real in her mind.

Where was Galen? Rianas was panicking. She should have asked a few of the apprentices to accompany her into the town. Another mage would have made this much easier.

The two stable hands were wrestling with the guards on the lawn, but two soldiers were still fighting through her wall of fire, waving their tunics like giant nets in front of them.

Thousands of straws fell to the ground. Rianas strained to keep *herself* together. She pulled an entire bale of hay from the bottom of the stack she had been cutting and sailed it toward the mage in an effort to distract him. She could feel the weave starting to break up. Her physical body could not keep this magic up much longer.

There was fighting inside the manor, now. Perhaps other soldiers had come, or maybe there were other guards the butler had not thought to mention. It sounded like someone was tearing the building apart from within. The *fingers* closest to the building showed her burning curtains and rugs where she had gone inside. Lady Caldus was attacking one of Jalek's men – Uld, it looked like – with a coat rack. She had broken the end off and was using it like a spear. Uld had a huge gash on his sword arm. He was fending Lady Caldus off by dodging behind chairs in the dining room.

The bale of hay crashed into the mage from the side, knocking him to the ground. Rianas immediately felt her control over the burning straw return. She pulled, sending the entirety of the remaining hay into the air.

Now Rianas was a flaming leviathan with tentacles spreading across the entire front of the manor. The thin carpet of smoky fire obscured the yard and the street beyond.

The horses barreling down the avenue to investigate the warning horn bucked and turned at the sight of Rianas. Like a many-armed god rising from the earth, the straw coalesced to form a wall in front of the riders. Ten of the men lost control of their mounts. Another dozen or so maintained control and rode right for her, pushing through.

Rianas strained as the horses pierced her wall. It felt like she had been punched in the stomach, but as the riders approached she wove the straw into a great net just above the horses' heads.

Two of the riders' necks snapped, and seven or eight fell from their horses onto the paved road. Three others managed to make it through, and these men steered their horses toward the stables where she was.

Rianas opened her straw *hands*, letting the flame take all the straw at once now. The lawn, street, and porch glowed like the sun with the heat. The men coming at her caught fire on their horses' backs. Just as the animals cleared the gate, she coalesced into another wall of flame in front of them, searing their riders' bodies.

The yard was aflame. She had managed to avoid the animals and her allies, but the rest of it was an inferno. Flaming bushes and trees sent smoke thirty feet into the air. The front of the manor was awash in bluish-white fire. Lord Caldus and the two remaining soldiers pulled each other into the building to avoid the blaze.

The two slaves had either killed or knocked out the guards they had ambushed on the lawn. Each picked up one of the weapons and shields as they ran toward her corporeal body.

Rianas could not sustain the straw leviathan much longer. Thousands of her *fingers* were falling to the earth. Others simply floated away in the heat of the fires now burning on the manor grounds. The front of the manor had flames licking up towards the roof. The wooden gate was impassable. Rianas gathered what remained of *her* into a ball of smoldering ashes. She soared a few dozen feet into the air before diving onto the remaining soldiers that were in the road.

She was once again standing in an empty stall. Her fingers tingled and smoke was coming off the glove on her left hand. She shoved her hand into her armpit and used her arm to pull each glove off. Rianas looked at the blackened fingertips where the weave had rushed madly like a wildfire from her hands.

Rianas slowly became aware of the scream coming from her own mouth as she looked down at her burned fingers.

One of the stable hands got to her first. He gave her a bucket of water meant for the horses, which she dipped her fingers into gladly. The second stable hand yanked a sleeve off Rianas' shirt. He dunked it in the water, and immediately started binding her hands. Neither spoke as they worked.

Arthur was by her side. There was someone else's blood on the sword and across his chest and legs. He was not smiling now.

"We need to get someplace safe," Arthur said. "Those men on the street will be after us as soon they get their wits about them."

"Where are the others?" Rianas asked. There were bodies and injured Axarean soldiers across the lawn. There were more along the burning porch. The leaderless horses pulled the wagon Rianas had used to get here haphazardly down the street. The sounds of fighting within the building mixed with the loud crackling of fire, but she could not identify any of the voices.

The Axarean mage was rolling around on the burning grass, trying to extinguish his burning robes unsuccessfully. The entire scene was grizzly. Rianas wanted to vomit.

"I don't know," Arthur said. "If we stay here, though, I'm not sure I can protect you. Those soldiers all have crossbows."

What happened next would have been funny if not for the gravity of the situation.

Four crossbow bolts flew into the stalls. One landed in the shield of a silent stable hand. He jumped at the 'thunk', and then pointed to where five or six soldiers were aiming at them from behind the short wall that surrounded the burning property.

Arthur grabbed Rianas' upper arm and dragged her through the stalls into the back hallway of the stable. The stable hands ducked in behind her, using their shields to ward off a few more attacks.

"Through here," one of the slaves said, pointing to a rear door.

Rianas held her wrapped hands away from the walls and shouldered her way in a half-crouching run into the small side yard with the others. Arthur ran ahead toward the wall that surrounded the manor, his back lit up by the fire on the other side of the building. The other two men pointed toward a small fig tree as they helped her run across the yard.

When Arthur saw the tree, he knew what to do. He helped Rianas up into the branches, and then pushed her over by grabbing her feet and shoving her up. Then the other three climbed the small tree behind her, joining her on the opposite side of the wall.

The manor fire cast flickering shadows across the ground. Another explosion shook the ground behind them, and the crack of the wooden pillars in front of the mansion preceded the roof caving in on the front of the building.

From this side of the street they would have a moment before the archers could get to them. Rianas looked around for a place to hide while she started another spell. They could not run to the left because they would run into the soldiers. To the right, there were perhaps two dozen men in the road with swords out directing scores of shackled men and women to grab buckets from a well.

Arthur pointed at the slaves. Rianas nodded. "I know what to do." She looked at the two stable hands. They were still carrying their shields. In Axarean, she asked, "Can you keep those archers away from me for a couple minutes if we hide behind that wall?"

The first man nodded. "Make it count. Those slavers are good shots with a crossbow. You won't have long."

Arthur led the small group up against the wall of a building that gave them good partial cover. Rianas could still see the fire brigade from between the slats of the next building's stairs. "This will work," she said.

Rianas raised her burned hands and examined the scroll. "*Caelia, Glacia.*" She pulled the weave together, gesturing toward the full buckets as the slaves ran toward the burning manor.

The 'thunk' of an arrow hit one of the shields. Arthur and the other two men stood between her and the other side of the road. Rianas could not see the soldiers approaching, but she knew she did not have long.

The buckets jumped into the air, and the cold water swirled like two dozen cyclones into a huge ball a hundred yards away. Rianas' consciousness jumped into the ball of water. The heat steamed off the huge ball as it roiled closer to the ground under its own weight. Rianas splayed her fingers and let spikes of ice form as they shot to the ground. She was no longer concerned about conserving her energy. The only thing that mattered was taking out as many of the slavers as she could before they could react.

With the sound of hundreds of broken glasses at once, the foot-long ice shards came raining down on the slavers. Some ran or used their swords to stop the impact, but the glass-like shards killed most of them instantly.

Rianas was back in her body again. One of the stable hands bucked backward into her, an arrow in his upper shoulder. Arthur took a dagger out with his free hand and flung it.

Soldiers were running across the street toward them as they loaded their weapons. As they got within about twenty yards, however, a rain of arrows came from the rooftop of a building a few doors down. The missiles hit and killed two Axareans instantly, and the others dove for cover behind lampposts or benches wherever they could.

A few of Jalek's men were on the roof of the next building over. Perhaps four men were up there, firing down at the remaining soldiers. Arthur took advantage of their distraction to kick at the door behind them. He yanked it open when the handle fell apart and pushed the injured slave in first. Then he pulled on Rianas. She did not need much encouragement to dive into the darkened building.

Inside the warehouse was a small front office area with a small wood stove in a corner and some simple chairs around the stove. On the far side was a low table with chains and shackles hung above it.

Arthur leaned against the door and Rianas pulled the hand lantern from one of her pockets, illuminating the small office. A solid wood door with three large fastened locks led to the warehouse. "Can we get through that door?" he asked.

The uninjured stable hand saw Arthur wave his arm in the direction of the door and turned to Rianas. "There are more Andarians in the back warehouse. Most likely there are a couple guards, but usually they stay up front at night."

Rianas nodded as she eased the injured man onto the floor. "We need to get this man a healing potion. It looks like he will be okay if we do not move him much. Grab some of those rags from the corner and wrap up his shoulder. I'm going to – ahhgg!"

Rianas had forgotten about the burns on her hands. When she gripped the arrow, the pain shot through her fingers. She could not even hold the arrow except with her palms. Arthur flung a couple chairs up against the door, wedging them into some loose floorboards. They would not hold long, but the chairs would slow someone down…probably.

Arthur grabbed some dirty rags lying in a corner of the room. He shuffled through them and found a few that looked relatively clean.

"Here, let me do that," he said. "See if you can get that door open with this man's help." He gestured with his head toward the half-naked man who was sorting through a few tools on the table. "Maybe we can get away through that back door."

Arthur kept talking while he broke the arrow with the help of one of his daggers and pulled the separate pieces away from the man's shoulder. "This place is filled with soldiers. I hope Ryalsgar and Jalek are okay."

There was shouting outside. Something thumped into the front wall and Rianas could hear footsteps as people ran by. There were no open windows to look out, but she rushed over to the man in the leather-lined collar. "Do you think you can use these tools to open that door?"

"I'm looking for a pick – ah, here's one."

Rianas gingerly unfurled her scroll again, in case she needed it. There was charred paper where her fingers had held it before, but the words – and more importantly the magic within them – were intact.

"What's your name?" Rianas asked as the man set a pick under the first lock bolt and struck it loose with one heavy blow from the mallet he had grabbed.

"Duncan. That's Irving lying on the ground." He pried the broken iron out of the way and moved the pick down to the second lockbolt.

Outside, there were more footsteps, followed by someone shoving against the door. Arthur was still on the ground wrapping Irving's bloody shoulder with his back to the door. Rianas ran over and shoved her foot under the doorsill.

Duncan had to slam the hammer against the second bolt a dozen times to break it free. There was sweat running down his back as he lifted the mallet. Arthur glanced up at Rianas as he tied off the makeshift bandage. Blood was dripping all over the floor behind Irving's shoulder and he seemed close to passing out. "I'll hold them back for a few minutes. Go, Rianas."

"I'm not leaving you Arthur," she said. She nearly flew off the door as whoever was on the other side shoved it again. Arthur took her place, placing his sword within arm's reach against the wall.

"I'll be right behind you. You're the only one with a light. Go!"

Duncan used the pick like a pry bar to pop the last lock off, and the heavy oak door slowly swung into the warehouse. Rianas stuffed the magical scroll under her arm and gave another look at Arthur before using one arm to help Irving stand.

Rianas only took half a dozen steps before coming to a halt.

Inside the warehouse was a narrow hall, perhaps thirty feet wide and many times longer. There were cots shoved in neat rows from one end of the room to the other, with a small space in the middle for a small cooking stove. The walls and some of the cots had sacks or small, rough shelves above them, covered in dried foods and loose pieces of cloth.

The beds were mostly empty. The occupants, perhaps a hundred men wearing loose, simple shirts and pants, all had collars around their necks and chains between their feet. The Andarians scrambled against the far wall in fear. They had flipped over some of the cots.

Rianas felt time stop as she took in the sight.

These were Andarians. Their light-colored skin and wavy brown hair was quite different from the Southerners' grey skin and straight, black hair. Some of the men were older, but the light iron chains connecting their ankles hobbled them all. With those chains on their ankles, none of the men or women in this warehouse could run.

The door behind them shuddered again and Arthur grunted. Rianas eased Irving onto a cot. "Can someone help this man? He was shot by a crossbow."

She hoped there was time. She jumped over a few cots to get closer to the huddled mass of slaves. As she was running, she grabbed the scroll gingerly with her left hand. Two old men shuffled past her to help Irving.

"I can free you," she stated, holding her right hand up to calm a few people who flinched as she bounced onto the floor. "We need your help, though. There are Axarean soldiers all over town fighting our men, and I fear my companions are going to be outnumbered."

A man in front shuffled up to Rianas. He was holding a broken piece of wood from one of the shelves. "We will help. Are you the one who killed the slavers out there?" He gestured toward the wall. They must have been able to see her ice attack on the slavers through the openings in the slats.

"Yes."

"We will help however we can."

Rianas smoothed the scroll onto a shelf with her palm so she could read it. Her fingers made her want to scream, but she pushed the pain aside as best she could and concentrated on the words on the page. This weave would have to use as little magic as possible – she could barely think through the pain, and there were many people here.

"Duncan, bring your hammer." When he came up to her with the mallet, she pointed at the two rings closest to the shackles on the slaves' ankles. "These two rings will turn ice cold. When you see them change color, strike them with the hammer. If I'm right and this iron is unstrengthened, you should be able to break the links with one or two hits from the hammer. Be quick. We need as many free legs as we can get."

"*Glacia!*" Rianas was two tiny pockets of air, floating a foot or so in front of her. She *landed* on each of the rings just long enough to feel the icy below-zero temperatures, and then drifted slowly away just in time to avoid the hammer blow from Duncan.

It worked! Duncan smashed both rings with just two hits.

The next slave hobbled up without hesitation. Rianas took care to avoid the Andarians as her icy bubbles of air floated around the room.

Seconds turned to minutes. One after the other, men rushed up to have their shackles removed. Rianas' body could hear sounds behind her. She ignored them and worked as fast as she could. Duncan kept swinging the huge mallet for a few minutes. Finally, Rianas was dimly aware someone else took over.

The sounds of fighting behind her got louder, but the icy baubles continued their inexorable quest to free as many of these Andarians as she could. Maybe half the men were free now. The room was full of shouting behind her. Arthur came into view between all the feet. There was more blood on his leather vest and sword than before.

Maybe thirty minutes went by as Rianas manipulated the tiny pockets of icy air around the room. When she freed the last pair of legs, she released her magic and returned to her body.

She felt cold and exhausted. She had taken so much heat out of the room that she could see her breath in front of her. She turned around and saw a dozen of the men carrying tools as weapons. Four others had short swords and armor they had taken from Axarean soldiers.

"Rianas, are you okay?" Arthur put his hand on her shoulder. One of the older slaves placed a thin blanket around her.

"Yes," she said. "I think so. Just cold. We need to get back out there and help Ryalsgar and Jalek."

Arthur smiled at her reply. He gestured up front and said, "These men already saved us. If we go out that door, there are dozens of Axarean soldiers still fighting in the streets. Do you think you could cast another spell?"

Rianas did not know if she could. Her arms were shaking and she was shivering in the cold. Someone was stoking the coals in the cooking stove, but all the other movement in the room was making her head spin. Rianas was only barely aware of the clattering in the room. The men and women were disassembling cots. Some of them wrapped chains around boards pulled from the rafters or walls to make iron clubs.

"I'll try." She grabbed the scroll gingerly and walked/stumbled toward the front door.

The streets around the manor were full of shouting. Rianas could hear swords clanging and horses thundering about outside. When she opened the door, she immediately smelled the acrid, smoke-filled air and saw the raging fire where the manor used to be. Lieutenant Azran and perhaps thirty soldiers on horseback were riding slowly from building to building about two hundred yards away, heading towards them.

Rianas looked back at the Andarian slaves. To Arthur she said, "I can probably cast something that will take a few of those men out, but I don't think I will be able to keep it together long. If we are going to win this battle, you will need to take advantage of my magic right away."

Arthur raised his sword. "I'll do whatever it takes, Rianas."

Duncan had grabbed a sword from an Axarean they had stopped from trying to get in the warehouse. He saluted, as did three others slaves.

Rianas stepped onto the porch and into the street. Out of the corner of her eye, she could see Jalek's men still on the rooftop one building down. She hoped there were more, but it did not matter now. She lifted the scroll in front of her face and searched for the right words.

"*Ignia, Glacia, Caelia!*" She still did not know what would happen. The weave coalesced into a thick cloud of smoke from the fire. She sucked the heat from the flames a hundred feet away. The roiling smoke turned into a superheated black cloud, which blew like a tornado right toward Lieutenant Azran and his men.

Horses bucked as the fiery ball of smoke approached. Most of the soldiers tried to get out of the spell's path, but Rianas let it spread like a pancake over the road. *She* filled all the cavities.

The ball of smoke slammed into Azran first. The wall of force flung him off his horse along with a dozen of his men.

Men flung their superheated shields and swords away as they scrambled to escape the heat. There was mass confusion and coughing as the ball of smoke filled men's lungs.

Rianas could not keep the fire burning, though. Her mind was worn out from casting magic for so long. It took all her effort to pull the smoky cloud that was her temporary being together around the Axarean soldiers.

She felt more than saw dozens of Andarian slaves running out of the building towards the soldiers. They charged forward as fast as they could run, but the distance was too far. Rianas swirled the cloud around to block the soldiers' view as long as possible, but she could only hold it together for a few more seconds.

The Axarean soldiers were in disarray as the Andarian slaves descended upon them. Dozens of men carrying makeshift weapons used clubs, chains and a few swords to attack the heavily armed Axareans.

Arthur stabbed Lieutenant Azran. He pulled his sword free in time to parry the attack of another soldier. Rianas dropped to her knees and let the scroll fall to the road. She watched, tears in her eyes, as the Andarians disarmed or killed the remaining soldiers.

Jalek's men helped. At least twenty of them caught up from behind the Axareans, preventing retreat. They used their crossbows to cut down the remaining men on horseback. Ryalsgar himself was there, calmly swinging Ogen's Touch in a fantastic arc of flame.

A massive hand settled gently on Rianas' shoulder, easing her up. Jalek was on the other side of that massive hand, blood spattered across his armor. His sword was gone and his helm had been lost. A bloody gash dripped into his eyes. Even with blood slowly dripping down his brow, he managed to look as invincible as always. This time, however, his black eyes seemed to convey a fathomless understanding of Rianas' roiling emotions.

"The Green Knight did everything we could have asked of her," he said, destroying the moment. "There are maybe a hundred dead Axarean soldiers on the east side of town. The scouts we sent to take over those ballistae must have been firing for an hour. Lieutenant Azran lost dozens of men trying to get out of there."

"Galen was in the manor," Rianas mumbled. "I haven't seen him since before the battle began." She lifted herself up and started stumbling in that direction, fell, and pulled herself to her feet again.

"You are in no shape to search for him, Rianas," Jalek said. He brought her over to the stairs of a building and helped her sit. "Besides, I will need your help talking to these slaves. It seems they all speak Axarean, and Elias is the only other man among us who can communicate with them."

That is when Rianas saw the dozens of freed Andarian slaves behind Jalek. They must have been the men who the slavers originally tasked with fighting the fire, because some of them still carried buckets. Most still had shackles about their feet.

Rianas wearily stood again. "I need your help," she addressed a few of the Andarian slaves nearest her. "There are some of our men who went into the manor during the attack. Can you look for them?"

"We will do whatever we can to help, miss," said a middle-aged man carrying a club. "Thank you for what you did tonight."

Half a dozen men ran toward the smoldering ruins of the manor.

18. THE HAMMER OF ANDARIA

The list of dead made Rianas sick.

Twenty of Jalek's mercenaries were gone, including Rum'Osk and Uld. She had only briefly spoken with the two during their ride into town.

Dozens of Andarian slaves had lost their lives toward the end of the battle, as well. Many of them had charged doors or attacked slavers with little regard for their own safety once the meaning of the commotion outside their barracks had become apparent.

Elias and Knight Yelenar had been badly injured during the combat, but the knight had healed herself as well as those who had come with her to capture the ballistae.

The fight to capture the final ballistae had taken well into the morning hours. Slavers on the west side of the town had occupied two of the towers when they realized what was happening. One of the large bolts struck Elias while he was leading a team and a few dozen horses to pull four other ballistae within range of the last holdouts shortly after dawn.

Galen had barely survived being crushed when the attack began. Mage Therzon had sensed the men as they approached and hurled a stone statue at them. Despite his size, the Axarean mage was quite fast. Rianas and Arthur had looked for the mage's body with Galen after Andarians extinguished the fire, but it appeared the mage had escaped.

"Jalek's men helped me fight off the soldiers that were patrolling behind the building," Galen said. "That is why we couldn't get to the front in time."

Knight Yelenar captured Lord and Lady Caldus. The knight had raced to where the road exited toward the west to stop the Axareans from escaping. Rianas could barely believe she had so quickly captured so many of the ballistae and managed to block off the western road.

"They weren't there to protect against invaders. They were installed to keep slaves from escaping," the Green Knight explained. "At night, the guards mostly left to go home, just as you learned. Only six of the ballistae were even guarded, and two of the guards were actually sleeping when we found them." Knight Yelenar smiled her beautiful smile and shook her golden locks in disbelief.

Knight Ogenson was coordinating Andarians in the small square. Nearly two thousand men and women were gathering in the cold morning air. The news of their pending freedom had spread like wildfire among them; excited and worried faces were everywhere.

Jalek for his part had a thin smile on his face as he used a few sentences Rianas taught him to instruct the able-bodied slaves on how to break the chains around their companions' necks and ankles with the tools they had gathered in the square. Men free of their bindings were interspersed throughout the crowd.

Some of the unshackled Andarians were helping to loosen the bonds of the remaining men and women, but a couple hundred were milling around in front of the wall that had surrounded the now-destroyed manor.

Arthur walked over from washing his leather chest plate and sword. There was a huge smile on his face as he approached Rianas. It disappeared when he saw Rianas worriedly looking around.

"Where are the children?" she asked him as soon as he was close enough.

Arthur looked thoughtful. "Maybe there are some buildings we haven't checked yet?"

"No. Jalek said they had checked each building twice. He even sent riders out to the farm buildings, but there was nothing but grain, hay and corn in those buildings. The slavers even kept the horses in town. Duncan said most of the livestock and slaves were kept in town so the slavers could keep track of them easier."

Arthur's face grew serious. "We'll find them, Rianas."

"I know," she said. She started walking toward where Ryalsgar was showing a group of Andarians how to position a pick to loosen their iron collars without injuring themselves.

"Did you get some rest, Rianas?" Ryalsgar asked after repositioning a pick on a woman's neck for a young man who then nervously tapped a hammer against a rivet. When he stood, his spotless armor gleamed in the daylight.

"I slept a couple hours. Has anyone been able to tell you where the children are?"

"Some are in Gavala, the regional capital." Ryalsgar easily changed between Northern and Axarean. Jalek had not even realized the Red Knight was capable of speaking Southern. Now, however, he spoke Northern to Rianas. "Others have been brought to the larger towns west of here. These men and women aren't completely sure. I would wager most of these slaves never got to leave this village."

Ryalsgar's blonde locks of hair shook with his head. "These people were allowed to have some degree of autonomy when they were done working for the day, but women with child were sent off to the bigger towns and cities. The slavers brought them back here when they had their children, but the children stayed behind. There are huge schools where these people have been taught the importance of following their Axarean rulers without question."

"That's horrible," Arthur said. "The children never even get a chance to know their parents!"

"They do," Ryalsgar said. "The slavers send the children back to their families when they are old enough to work themselves. Some of the young men and women out here are only twelve or thirteen. These Andarians will need years to work through their tragic upbringings, though."

Ryalsgar turned a young man's hand around on the hammer and instructed him to strike harder as the woman's eyes grew large.

Nervously, the man swung the hammer harder this time, finally loosening the rivet on his companion's collar enough that he could start prying at it.

One of the men Rianas had freed last night spotted her. He walked over confidently, carrying a chain in one hand and a broken collar in his other like prizes.

"I am Dorian Mallen. On behalf of the men and women you saved last night, I wanted to express to you our eternal gratitude," Dorian said, bowing his head and shoulders slightly.

Rianas smiled. "The people who helped you last night all decided to work together to free Bonshus," she said. "I only did what I could to help."

"Ha!" Dorian said. "Not only did you take on mage Therzon and Lord Caldus, but you used your magic to free a hundred Andarians all by yourself." He gestured toward the group milling around near the wall. Some of them were pointing at her now, and dozens of them were starting to approach her.

"I am Andarian," Rianas said, "just like you. I came through the Black Mountains a couple days ago and saw an opportunity to help bring hope back to Old Andaria. Really, I couldn't have done much if not for the mercenaries who agreed to come with us."

Dorian just kept bowing and beaming proudly. He waved over to some of his companions. "This is her!" he said.

Within a few seconds, the crowd shouted a cacophony of "Savior!", "Thank the spirits!", "Thank you!", and "You saved us." A mob of freed Andarians surrounded her.

It took a moment of shouting and shuffling for Dorian and Arthur to shoulder the reaching arms out of the way so Rianas could move. Arthur pulled her toward the wall. *"You'd better address them. In their minds, their freedom is owed to you."*

Rianas put a foot on Arthur's knee and climbed up onto the wall. The early afternoon sun had managed to warm up the brick, but a brisk breeze carried the smell of burning debris from behind her. His hand lingered on her foot reassuringly and he smiled up at her. Rianas reflected how much older he seemed since they had left Riverrun as she flashed a smile back to him.

Now there were perhaps two hundred dirty faces looking up from the crowd. It seemed like all the Andarians in the square were stopping what they were doing and standing up.

A chant started by Dorian began rolling through the crowd, gaining volume. "Hail, Rianas! Hail the return of Andaria!"

Rianas nervously looked out at the crowd. She listened for a moment in wonder. A Runlarian proverb about the pebble rolling down a hill came to mind. Why were all these people cheering *her?*

"Hail, Rianas!"

Her eyes found Jalek in the crowd. His arms were crossed, but instead of his usual scowl, a slightly discomfiting grin was there again. She thought she *felt* more than saw him nod at her like a proud but serious professor.

Her gaze slid to the right until it rested on Ryalsgar. The Red Knight was studying the crowd curiously. Ogerena had joined him, and she aimed her out-of-place smile at Rianas. The two stood close together.

Arthur was still below her. He turned away from her gaze with a smirk, lifting his gangly arms to hold back the outstretched arms of men and women alike.

"...Andaria! Andaria! Andaria!" The crowd was feeding off its own energy now. Dorian was working those around him into a fervor, stomping his leather-soled feet on the ground in cadence with the chant. The entire plaza seemed to crackle with the human energy like nothing Rianas had felt before. Even the hair on her arms began to prickle.

She raised her hand to acknowledge the accolades she was receiving. Immediately, she regretted the gesture. Instead of the shy wave of thank you she intended, her arms came up too fast – and together. The excitement of the crowd crested into a massive, single voice shouting "Andaria!"

Then the "shush" and "quiet" went through the crowd from those up front. Again, Dorian seemed to be the instigator, like some loyal dog guiding its wayward sheep. In only a few seconds – before Rianas could reel her arms back down – the crowd was mostly quiet.

Hundreds – thousands – of eyes fixated on Rianas. Men and women that had not even been there a few moments ago were pouring into the street to see their 'savior'.

She thought maybe now would be a good time to run away.

Instead, she pointed right – toward the south –and spoke. The words came out as if they had always been there. She was merely saying what had been in her mind since the first day she had met Atrick. It seemed as if they had been there much longer, perhaps her entire life.

"Fifty years ago, the Axarean Empire attacked and enslaved the nation of Andaria. Without warning, they invaded our southern towns and cities, rode across our peaceful lands, and consumed everything south of the Black Mountains.

"But last night, Bonshus became the foundation of a new Andaria." The words came easily, and Rianas raised her voice over the hoots and hollers of agreement from the crowd. "Today, we take our war on Axarea to our own homeland. We will retake every last farm, hamlet, and city of Old Andaria. You are just the first. From here, we will march across the plains and free every Andarian! Your children will know freedom, our families will be reunited, and the Axarean Empire will know we will never bow or serve them again!"

Dorian took up a shout of "Andaria!" again.

However, Rianas knew she had to say more. Deep in her mind, she regretted asking help from these poor slaves. She could not stop, though. She was a pebble, collecting other pebbles as she rolled down the mountain. Her words were not entirely her own. They belonged to a deeper part of her soul, one that felt inextricably linked to Andaria.

Her arms came up again. Rianas was not as loud now, but it did not matter. The crowd grew so silent she could hear her heart beating like a team of racing horses against her chest.

"Now, though, I have to ask for volunteers. The men that helped free you have risked their lives for the dream of Andaria. But there are dreadfully few of them. When the Empire discovers what we have done, they will send an army to quell our rebellion. Our strength will come from within. The Axarean Empire can replace every soldier we kill. We must raise the cost of quelling our rebellion so high that the Empire has no choice but to empty its armies against us. They must know they can never make up the cost of holding Andaria.

"We need an army, and I could use every man or woman among you who is willing to fight to free the children of Andaria from the

Empire's hands."

Rianas had nothing else to say. Sweat inexplicably poured down her brow. Her knees were weak. Her heart felt like it might explode, and she was questioning why she had even opened her mouth at all. She could have simply thanked them and told them how to get back to Atrick's fort. She could have talked with Arthur – or really anyone else – about what they wanted to do before making a speech.

However, that was not what she had done.

An older woman a few yards away raised an appropriated blacksmith's hammer into the air. "I will fight until I die to bring Andaria back! I am freedom's hammer!"

The voices inside her mind had stopped babbling incoherently. In their place was a palpable sense of purpose.

A few yards away, the man who Ryalsgar had been helping and his young female companion both raised their removed collars above their heads. "We will fight!"

The voices inside her mind broke out again. A single, unified voice echoed through her skull.

Dozens of men began raising their arms. Many held chains in their hands. In the back of the crowd, men and women started raising their arms as well. Hundreds of arms were in the air, and the shouting began anew.

"We are the army! We are the hammers of Andaria!" Dorian was hopping up and down and pumping his arms in the air, getting men and women around him to raise their arms and do the same.

The voices inside her mind rose from a confused mob of voices into a single singing chorus of hope.

Arthur's hand squeezed Rianas' foot, bringing her back from the ethereal world. There were a few people watching with detachment. Some of Jalek's mercenaries looked on silently. The rest, however, seemed wildly excited. The people of Bonshus were inspired.

But who inspired them? Her? What reason did they have to raise their voices in unison?

When she glanced toward Arthur, his goofy smile was there. His lips did not move, but she could read his mind easily as he projected at her.

Brian Tenace

"I believe you have found your army."

ABOUT THE AUTHOR

Brian Tenace loves spending time with his family, where he hounds them about the world of Arthos incessantly. When he is not writing or dreaming about the characters of Arthos, he can generally be found touring the various natural parks in North Carolina.

PLEASE LEAVE A REVIEW

Do you like this book? The best way you can show your appreciation is by telling someone else. A review or a suggestion to a friend would be greatly appreciated.

Find an error, or just want to contact the author? Email feedback@arthos.world

Check the Arthos homepage at www.arthos.world for author insights, custom maps, and other offers and fan art.

Made in the USA
Columbia, SC
05 July 2021